Jesus
The Human Face of God

Jesus
The Human Face of God

SAMANVAYAM - Contextual Theology Series - 8

Editor
Cyril Kuttiyanikkal

THE INDIAN SOCIETY FOR PROMOTING CHRISTIAN KNOWLEDGE
1710 300 years 2010
of ISPCK in India
ISPCK
Supporting Communities since 1710

2019

Jesus the Human Face of God — published by the Rev. Dr. Ashish Amos of the Indian Society for Promoting Christian Knowledge (ISPCK), Post Box 1585, Kashmere Gate, Delhi-110006.

ISBN: 978-93-88945-27-1

Laser typeset by

ISPCK, Post Box 1585, 1654, Madarsa Road, Kashmere Gate, Delhi-110006
• Tel: 23866323

e-mail: ashish@ispck.org.in • ella@ispck.org.in
website: www.ispck.org.in

Contents

Part Three
Practical Theology

Part Four
Lived Models

Introduction

With a view to foster contextualized theological formation, adopting the method of direct exposure to the concrete life situations, CMI Congregation started the venture of Samanvaya 25 years ago. One of the three typical Indian contexts identified was the Inter-religious context of Rishikesh, (besides the rural and tribal contexts of Chhattisgarh and the urban and social contexts at Bangalore and Bhopal) where the students are given adequate opportunities to encounter the religiosity of Hinduism, Sikhism, Islam and Buddhism. The emphasis on the theological formation in the second year at Rishikesh is "Jesus Christ and the Human," where the effort is made to gain a deeper and clear understanding of the person of Jesus, who being the way, the truth and the life addresses the human dilemma and answers the human search for the divine.

At Rishikesh the students get a lived experience of Hindu ascetic life and ashram life, besides becoming familiar with the popular Hindu religiosity and practices. They enter into dialogue with the ascetics and monks and get ample occasion for becoming co-pilgrims in the spiritual journey. Their lives at Rishikesh become an occasion to face directly the challenges of witnessing to Christ in a pluralistic context and become aware of the sensitive issues involved in the inter-religious relationship. As a result of the inter-religious encounter, new questions are raised, new theological reflections are elicited and both the students and the staff are lead to deepen their commitment to Christ.

Cardinal Franz König said, "For the Christian church of the third millennium, there is nothing more harmful than ghettoization from the world and other religions." Several enlightened theologians and leaders, especially in the non-western world, have tried to enflesh the Gospel in non-western cultures. One of the common feature of these theologians is their commitment to both Christ and their culture. Their efforts tell us that we need to imagine Christian community as the leaven which has to be permeated into the fabric of the society and not as Noah's ark to which everyone must be carried into. The church has to be envisioned as salt which loses itself in order to preserve the community, in order to be at the service of the society and not an institution which has clear cut boundaries to keep some inside and others outside. However, one should also avoid the extreme, like the Mukyokai movement founded by Kanzo Uchimura, who took the utmost position of focussing only on the invisibility of Church. For him faith in Christ is what brings the Church into existence; therefore, the Church should be just as invisible as is faith.

What is required for the future is primarily to replace the existing mind-set, which looks for conquering people and snatching them out of their parent culture, with a new model, new paradigm and a new mind-set. The inter-religious context of Rishikesh gives the students and staff of Samanvaya a unique opportunity to enter deeply into the religious ethos of our Hindu brethren. Every encounter for them is an occasion to interpret and re-interpret both the Christian heritage and the present-day context. Several theologians have tried to re-interpret hermeneutically the Christian heritage, while others have used hermeneutics to re-interpret the cultural context of the people. J. L. Segundo speaks of theologizing as the hermeneutical circle which is the continuing change in our interpretation of the Scriptures demanded by the continuing changes in our present day reality, both individual and social.[1]

It is true that there is a greater awareness among the circle of scholars about the interplay between faith, religion and culture. They are aware of the influence of cultural baggage on the Christian heritage as well as the cultural underpinnings of the present-day life context. It is also true that they are taking the culture of the Biblical times and that of the present context seriously. Some would even define culture as what makes people and use cultural elements in their theologizing effort. However, not many have been able to produce a fully acceptable contextual theology. Therefore our life in Rishikesh where we have a face to face encounter of the faith expressions of religions provide us with a unique opportunity for triggering a contextualized theological thinking. The students and staff encounter the basic elements in both the Biblical and the Indian (Hindu) world views.

Many intellectuals, practitioners and theologians are part of our venture of a contextualized theological endeavour over the past 25 years. The completion of 25 years calls for fresh theological reflections and formulations. At this juncture we wanted to think together afresh and bring forth a volume about our lives in the inter-religious context of Rishikesh. The articles in the book are written by scholars who are/ were the teaching faculty (except one) both resident and non-resident at Samanvaya.

The overall plan and presentation of the book is envisaged in four parts. Part one looks at the concrete Indian situation especially the plurality of religions and the emerging religious circumstances and milieu. We are doing theology in this changing context. The first two articles are mostly on the methodology of doing theology today. T.K John in Chapter 1 tries to recharge theology with that fire-power known as contextualized theology. He wants to "re-connect two vital and most important poles, human experience of exploitation poverty and injustice in the Indian context and the Word of God available in the living tradition of the Church". He encourages the Indian theologians to think for themselves while benefiting from the thought of others. His article narrates the process of contextualising in the Indian context giving a detailed survey of both the context and the process of contextualisation.

In Chapter 2 Dr. Joseph Chittooparambil reflects on the contextual methodology needed in a pluralistic society for doing theology. According to him any theology to be culturally intelligible, pastorally meaningful and theologically relevant has to reflect the actual lived situations of the people, their history, philosophy, culture and tradition. Theologising in the Indian context has to take into account the communal, critical, constructive, contextual and liberational aspects. For him 'any countercultural and theological discourse in India has to be rooted in the socio-cultural and religio-cultural realities, determined by poverty, religion and caste and be in continuous dialogue with as they represent different aspects of the Indian reality as a whole.'

Davis Varayilaan in Chapter 3 looks back to the history of Samanvaya and takes stock of what has been achieved. He explains how from 'its inception, Samanvaya has contextualized its theological formation and education'. He further elaborates on its 'method of exposure-immersion, experience-reflection, and interpretation-action'. Samanvaya achieved the contextualization pedagogy by its concrete programmes of immersion, reflection and re-interpretation. He explains how 'the exposures to the context, pilgrimage to holy places, live-in experience of Indian Christian Ashram were there from the beginning and how the live-in experience of Hindu Ashram was included as part of the academic programme from 1999.'

Part II of this book is dedicated to the Biblical and Christological reflections. George Kaniarakath through his article in Chapter 4 articulates the universal vision of Luke presented in the Gospel. Kaniarakath deliberates on the attitude of Jesus towards the non-Jews, especially the Samaritans, people of other persuasions and women. He recalls that although Jesus was born a Jew, his mission was beyond the Jewish frontiers. This broader vision and mission of Jesus according to him is important for the students of Samanvaya. He says, "It is highly relevant in the Samanvayan way of reading, understanding, and interpreting the history of salvation in a wider and more realistic perspective, in a world of religious and cultural pluralism."

In a nation where there is religious intolerance, communal violence, caste division and other atrocities, a Christian vision of living in harmony is of prime importance. Such a vision has to be well supported and subordinated to the Scripture. Benny Thettayil in Chapter 5 takes up this subject and speaks about the importance of gaining a deeper knowledge of other faith traditions, which in turn will help one to understand one's own faith better. Glancing through various biblical approaches he speaks about the importance of a respectful exchange of spiritual experiences as a necessary skill to work in the cross-cultural and pluralistic world.

The great Indian monk Abhishiktananda holds that the meeting of religions happens within the cave of the heart. The sharing of the religious experience is the most basic element in the interreligious encounter. For that every Christian has to be faithful to his/her calling to become another Christ. From the Pauline perspective, Thomas Srampickal in Chapter 6 focuses on the importance of putting on Christ, which, according to him, involves adorning ourselves with the divine characteristics like compassion, kindness, lowliness, meekness, patience, love, etc. Quoting Paul he tells, "as we accept the Gospel through faith and live it, Christ is not outside us but inside us. The Gospel mirrors his image or somehow objectifies Christ for us, so that we may more and more perceive his glory. This beholding of the Lord and the transformation into him happens within us. The direction of the movement in the process of our transformation is not to the model of an external one, but to the image of Christ present within us, as we adore him in faith in our hearts."

Joy Kakkanatt in Chapter 7 furnishes the reader with the Indian understanding of secularism and the noble values, such as respect for pluralism, diversity and democratic values etc., associated with such a vision of a secular world. He reiterates that the God of the Bible is the one who is sympathetic to the world and the one who is involved in the human history with compassion. He calls the Christians to develop such a spirituality as to enable the practitioners to become imitators of this God whose compassionate face is revealed in Jesus.

Part III is devoted to the vision for the future. It reflects on the different dimensions of the emerging Christian life in this changing pluralistic ambience. "Wandering from place to place is the typical method of instruction employed by Jesus", states Sebastian Elavathingal in his article 'Wandering with Master' in Chapter 8. He compares the three years' experience of Samanvaya's students in three different centers to that of three year wandering of the disciples with Jesus. He points out that the disciples learned from direct experiences of life as well as from the timely instructions given by Jesus. Elavathingal goes one step further and speaks of this wandering not on the physical level but on the higher level of spiritual transformation.

Chapter 9 speaks about the importance of the incarnational method in the contextual theological endeavour. Dr. Naiju Kalambukattu says that theologizing in context becomes a serious imitation of the style of Jesus, the Word that became flesh and dwelt among us. He reiterates that the mission of Church in the present world is the continuation of the mission of Jesus. However, while carrying out this mission, we are to take into account the life situation and context of the people. For him "mission is the incarnation of Christian faith in other cultures."

In Chapter 10 Bishop Gratian, the first Bishop of Bijnor, who was closely associated with the evolution and development of Samanvaya at Rishikesh, portends 'Samanvaya as a new vision, a new project and a concrete realization of many who wanted a different formation needed for the future'. He further states that it dreams of creating an Indian Christology, Indian Theology and Indian Liturgy. After taking stock of the several missionary approaches vibrant in the diocese, like ashram movement, social and educational apostolates, health care and poverty eradication initiates, and the growing Christ-devotees movement, he envisions a Church "which is seriously engaged in the formation of a new society where every human beings can live in true fellowship with others, in deep communion among all, with justice practised and meted out to everyone, in true joy and happiness."

The focus of Chapters 11 and 12 are more of a futuristic vision of ecclesial engagement in the pluralistic context. Dr. John Chathanatt SJ takes up the challenge of doing theology in the Indian context of plurality and differences, and life-negating experiences. His article in Chapter 11 focuses on the sacramental significance of the critical engagement with the socio-economic, religio-cultural and political realities of India, as each of these issues have a moral/ethical dimension. So the starting point of theologising for him is the social questioning which he calls a faith-search for the fullness of life to find and attain the fullness of humanity. In this process he calls for the utilization of the resources and methods of social sciences as well as the use of philosophical method as tools, where the Word of God is made to interact with the human situation resulting in the reflection, action, transformation and conversion of heart to Christ.

Chapter 12 draws the contours for a contextualized Church in India. Dr. Cyril Kuttiyanickal shows how both Hinduism and Christianity have evolved and developed over centuries in different cultural contexts and contain within them gems for the future generations. He thinks that their mutuality and interaction might prove beneficial for both. Therefore he envisions a church in this context of plurality, a church which has an inclusive and interreligious vision based on the best of these spiritual insights, values and cultural traditions. However, he is also careful that the basic vision of the Church remains Christ-centred, where proclaiming faith in Jesus is ensured, while the best of Indian culture is preserved.

Part IV of this book is dedicated to the lives of those who have successfully achieved an integrated life in this pluralistic context and time. Yann Vagneux, in Chapter 13 surveys the life and priesthood of swami Abhiṣiktānanda, who believed that he was consecrated by God for a special ministry that extends beyond the then-existing ecclesial manifestations to a ministry at the service of the *mystery* and the revelation of the Mystery. Abhiṣiktānanda was lost in the mystery of God for which he had "forsaken his distant homeland, France, to settle on Indian shores where his priestly ministry was mainly lived in the midst of his Hindu brethren. For sure, Abhiṣiktānanda's priesthood and life are unique and cannot be transposed. Yet the unique glow of his priesthood has lost none of its power to inspire any soul who, like Henri le Saux, is moved by a deep desire to meet the real heart of India and transmit to it the newness of Christ."

Chapter 14 presents the life and ministry of Vanadana Mataji. Dr. Louis Malieckal through his article reveals the way Mataji transformed herself first into an authentically 'Indian face' of the 'Christian Faith', and finally the manner in which she proclaimed or communicated this image to others in India. He wants the future generations to gratefully look up to the model lived and personalized by Vandana Mataji for about seven decades. Malieckal presents her life and her legacy as an example of how we can make deeper discovery of our faith in Jesus Christ, in dialogue with other faith-holders and through increasing knowledge of their Scriptures, as well as through authentic inculturation of our life and prayer-forms.

Fittingly the last Chapter (15) presents the life of a person who has achieved *samanvayam*, an integration of life. John Chakkanatt draws the profile of the saintly life of Fr. Thomas Kochumuttam, the present guru or Acharya of Jeevandhara Ashram, Jaiharikhal. Chakkanatt shows how the presence of Fr. Thomas has given a spiritual ambience to Jeevandhara ashram. He says that 'the ashram reflects the depth and spirituality of the *Acharya*. Since the ashram and the guru reflect the Indian spirituality with its culture, art and architecture our Hindu brethren feel at home and easily elevate their hearts to Christian mysteries.'

Although the articles in the present volume expose the views of the individual writers, they carry the task of trotting out a contextual theology in the making. They are a ready reference for any contextual theological project. Given the issues and pressing problems of our times, these articles will lead to the emergence of serious contextual theological discussions. Indeed, such critical and creative conversations and discussions are the keys to fit together a coherent, practical, orthodox and relevant contextual theology.

Dr. Cyril Kuttiyanikkal

Endnotes
[1] J.L. Segundo, *The Liberation of Theology* (New York: Orbis Books, 1976), pp.8-9.

Part One

Methodology and the Inter-Religious Context

Contextualization as a Theological Method:
Challenges of Emerging Context
for Theologizing in India

T. K. John

The Problem

Twin issues call for attention and solution. One, to reflect over any issue to understand it there is the need for appropriate method. Second, when divergent issues are there to be attended to the demand on the comprehending mind increases and proper co-ordination of methods has to be evolved. Keeping this in mind the above theme is taken for reflection.

We listen to the whisper of the above theme? It tells us softly: cook your food by yourself, instead of prepared food from the local hotel. The self-cooked food can always be enjoyed with relish. Own labour to actualize own plan investing in own effort at assembling the materials, with close attention to the process that will tickle the taste, all crowned with satisfaction—all these contribute to awakening of inherent creativity. Investment of one's time, spending of personal money and developing one's skill will add to the mental satisfaction. The reasons are evident. One grows a little more as a woman, as a man. And, the God who fashioned us is thrilled. God's investment in the making of each one of us is worth the expectation.

In other words: think for yourself and then benefit by learning from the thoughts of others. That is honourable and worthy of man/woman. Many thoughts get fused by such a social event by enrichment.

This we apply to the method in contextual theologizing. The context belongs to different faiths and traditions. Some are poor some well to do. Some are old, some young, male female, healthy sick. We understand the local culture, the regional and the national as an assemblage of many such streams. This vast India is our contexts. It is in this situation we initiate Faith reflection. Contextual theologizing gradually evolves.

When applied to philosophy and theology the demand assures result commensurate with the investment. Think for yourself and you can always benefit from the thought of others—that can be the sound and humanizing method. This is what is now being considered as part of contextual theologizing.

Incarnation

Incarnation is the love and care of God for us in a capsule, contextualized. It is a divine gesture of graciousness. God values and appreciates what we have in our culture. That becomes the body, the blood, the bones and marrows, and the sinews of the Word incarnate. That unique event is Jesus Christ, God and Man.

God assumes the human nature because it is created by God and so it is endowed with inestimable values. Therefore the word Incarnate is precious. We see in Jesus the invisible God and God's gift of humanity. And we see ourselves reflected in the Incarnate God.

Through His hands and legs the goodness and transcendence of God is brought home to us. When we look on him it is God we look at. When we touch Him we are electrified by God's motherliness. His soothing words and healing hands almost touch and kindle our hearts. God becomes a consoling and ever-assuring presence when we are afflicted and broken. His melting heart and gripping eyes move us to comply with His commandments for our wholeness and wellness.

Through His words to the hundreds, through His works of feeding, through His presence at bedside of the sick, tomb of the dead, house of the sinners He was doing one thing: interpreting the Father's love for all humans all His children, the household of the Father in heaven now on earth in and through his Son. We see the divine method in action.

In that process Jesus used the mind and feelings of Moses and the prophets after him. He used profusely the peasant culture, the shepherds' commitment to the fold, the traders' skills and industriousness, the worth and preciousness of the poor widow's coin, the mercy of the good Samaritan, and the joy and forgiveness of the 'waiting father' for the squandering son. The images and parables He used, the life-style He embraced, the different feelings and emotions He expressed all constitute His approach to communicate Father's love for His people. Jesus said at the end: go on doing likewise, to generations to come.

The great divine experiment has to proceed through history according to the exigencies provided by divergent *contexts*. These are going to be many and diverse.

The first *context* for Jesus was the womb of Mary the Immaculate Mother. There was the mystery of the Word becoming flesh in her womb. Part of the same was the mange, the normalr habitation of cattle heads. The next was the small home in the small village culture of Nazareth. He was a regular temple-visitor. All Galilee, Tire and Sidon are the places Jesus traversed with His services of healing feeding and teaching. Thus "Jesus went about all the cities and villages, teaching in their synagogues, and proclaiming the good news of the kingdom" (Mt 9:35). Parables He used. Salt and light example He used to drive home the message to the community of disciples and others who listened. It was *contextual* communication: language, life-style, idiom, parables, illustrations all drawn by His experiences and observations of life and culture of the people. Through the peoples' mindset and life experiences Jesus communicated the message He had from the Father. The Jews, the Samaritans, the Greeks, the Romans all were His admiring listeners.

The Akash Ganga is flowing, the heavenly light is lit, the waves set in motion, will reach far and wide. Further down the river will swell, and the number of the beneficiaries will also swell. This is the pattern He handed down for the Church.

The Apostolic Churches received the waves that brought the Good News. Contexts were many and according to each the method of taking shape also varied. The regions east and west the News travelled. Antioch and other centres eastward and Macedonia Malta Alexandria etc in the West.

Through the seven Churches named in the Book of Revelation (Rev.2:1-29 –3:1-23) that grew in response to seven different cultures, Jesus, the risen Lord, continued this process. Through the cultures and languages the process of diversification continued. Incarnating the Church in diverse places and cultures is the new phase. The different Apostolic Churches contributed further to the universalisation of this process of God's salvation reaching His people. What was initiated in one place by one Man now got universalized and contextualization. Methods changed according to Contexts. Many believing communities grew up, each according to the local culture.

Context

The word refers to a particular historical place or situation and time: at a particular time, in a given place or through a trend or event. On the face of the earth contexts are millions. This is because of several factors at work: like the interplay of cosmic forces or planets, the elliptical rotation of the earth, their impact on earth which generate climatic diversities for the activities of the life-force (i.e. the *elan vital* as treated by Henry Bergson). Charles Darwin through his Origin of Species (1859) has reflected upon life-systems in different contexts.

Diverse cultural contexts necessitated evolving of flexible methods of nurturing the new Churches, their liturgies and different theologies. In trying to explain the great event by different cultures theologies and liturgies began to sprout. And the many ministries developed. The classical elaborations during medieval times climaxed the first phase of what is known as Scholastic Theology.

With the coming of Liberation Theology method begin to change: the metaphysical of the system builders had to give way to the experiential of the poor, of the exploited. Faced with problems of massive poverty, of injustice, of colonial atrocities, of violations of rights of indigenous peoples as well as problems of industrial workers Church's deeper involvement in the society began to demand new approaches. New contexts demanded new methods.

Similarly Christianity's reach to new societies worldwide necessitated new methods of sharing the Good News. Metaphysics in theology had to give way to social sciences. Methods in metaphysics began to be replaced by the methods of social sciences.

The patriarch of Liberation theology, Gustavo Gutierrez introduced a mutation for theological method: 'Critical reflection on Christian praxis'. By praxis one does not mean practice but the process of transformation of society seen as marked by unjust practices by a process of involvement ad experience by committed action for change for the better.

Method

Method is organized reflection on a theme in its formal and structural aspect intended to expose the bases and presuppositions. It is systematically undertaken and scientifically analyzed and presented in an orderly manner, with illustration or examples from the context.

Social sciences like economics, sociology, political science, anthropology and psychology have recognized methods to merit the name science. Philosophy as a discipline of organized reflection on ultimate meaning of all reality can also be helpful in theologizing. Jacques Maritain the French philosopher-theologian has the following four levels to human knowledge: empirical sciences, mathematical science and theological science, and the revealed (1). Intuition is at work as the final phase. Theology or any science is not a mere bundle or collection of thoughts however lofty and deep they are but organized reflection on knowledge systems, including revelation.

Scholastic theology through Greek metaphysics produced the definition of Anselm on theology as 'Faith disquisition by the human mind'. The impulse to move on came from the many fresh developments triggered by the Vatican II with its call to focus upon the local Church: its theology and teachings, its rites and liturgies, its spiritualties and the many movements. These were further stressed by the Church in India Seminar held in Bangalore (from 196...). Indian theology, Indian liturgy, Indian spirituality etc were further developments budding forth from that seminar. Focus on a theological Method for theologizing in India is an outcome of the same development.

Methods in Traditional and Emerging Theologies

Inherited theology begins with Revelation which has certitude and credibility as an established discipline. It has been largely structured with the assistance of Greek metaphysics, a service done by Aquinas using the metaphysics of Aristotle.

In the newly emerging theologies the human experience of liberative struggles of the oppressed is the starting point of theological reflection. It is the fresh and warm experience of the committed involvement for restoring the deprived freedom and rights of the oppressed and deprived as well as discriminated communities in India. The experience of struggling human reality in India is emerging as the starting point of theologizing.

Of course Revelation is the normative principle without which it will not be theology but mere sociology. Sociology contains truth about human society. But that is not enough. Besides, the role of Indian religions is another element to feed into the theologizing process.

Diversity of living beings is a necessary consequence of the activity of this life-force influenced by the planetary movements. Given-ness of the situation of the particular place as opposed to any general situation is therefore the mark of the context. *Papaya* fruit is essentially the same wherever it grows but the colour etc. may change to some extent depending upon geographic vagaries. Therefore contextualizing implies reflecting upon an event or situation or society in a *particular place* on a particular issue or situation. The word of God is ever in interaction with the people of the place.

For us it is the Indian context. In the light of the Bible with the help of the social sciences Indian human situation and whatever is happening currently, is reflected upon guided by the Faith.

Indian Contexts

Indian contexts are many and diverse, some repulsive some promising. Firstly, there is the racial context: six anthropological races living and interacting in India call for particular attention in articulation of the Faith. Each race has its language, its life-style and world view. Racial conflicts are endemic to the very identity. Of late some process of mitigation has been at work.

Secondly, there is the context of the indigenous peoples. The earliest inhabitants with their community spirit promoted by singing and dancing, and their affinity and closeness to nature, hard toil, they celebrate life. Now they are at the receiving end of the corporate who dominate the scene threatening their identity. The people of the 'seven sisters' or the hill States in the North East further add to the indigenous population of India.

Thirdly, there is the life-struggle context. The fast growing economy of the cyber-industrial magnates in contrast to the massive working class with their rights and organizational power diminished gives another picture. In general it is a land of contradictions and at the same time with good record of living peacefully in spite of occasional ruptures. To India's credit Marx's prophecy did not take place: as the likely country for revolution to take place, according to his analysis. On the contrary a revolution did take place: but peaceful and non-violent, via Satyagraha of Mahatma Gandhi.

Fourthly there is the vast subaltern context formed by the Tribal Dalit population of India. Just above them are the Other Backward Communities. The subaltern—OBC tie up constitutes the vast majority of the sub-continental population. The entry of mighty corporates with their multi-national linkage will pause powerful challenge to the above groups.

Fifthly there is the religious context. There are nine religions in India. Five are of Indic origin and four of Semitic origin. The Indic religions are the many tribal or indigenous religions, the Vedic-Brahmanic-Classical Hinduism, Jainism, Buddhism and Sikhism. The other four are of Semitic origin and centuries ago came to India and settled down and made India their home. These are Judaism, Christianity, Islam and Zoroastrianism also known as Parsee religion. Bahai sect also is there although it is regarded as a modern sprout from Islam. Monotheism is central to the Semitic religions whereas there are monotheistic concept in sectarian Hinduism known as Vaishnava and Saivaite sects. The Smarthas are less in number.

The two Semitic religions and the five Indic religions seem occasionally to be at logger-heads. Occasional irruptions have been affecting peace and order.

Sixthly though colonial rule gave way to the native, yet vestiges of the culture of the former still lingers, even internalized. The colonial rule vanished but colonial cultural elements can still be seen as sheltered by the nation at various levels. This requires critical analysis. Cfr. Ashish Nandi's book The Intimate Enemy (Oxford, 2009).

Seventhly there is the historical context. You can count on the historical context when traditions are discussed, listed and celebrated. But sometimes statements at gatherings show absence of signs of historical contexts. Memory of the past, pleasant and painful, has been a major source tension among communities in India. Some mindsets are past-oriented.

Eighthly there is the heritage background: great literature comprising of religious epics, romantic stories, dramas in their diversities, poems and aphorisms containing wisdom sayings and novels. Their growth in the regional cultures have been phenomenal. Along with this is the world of philosophies. Six distinct systems and three *acharyas* and their philosophies contribute immensely to the cultural heritage of India.

And, there are the contributions to the national heritage by artists and sculptures in abundance. Ajanta Ellora Kaneri caves have their own stories to tell to generations to come.

Finally there is the world of ascetics and mystics, mendicants and renounces. Visit the Kumbha Melas, coming in twelve years- six years cycles when millions assemble for their ritual bath from all over the world at Prayag the conjunction of two sacred rivers Ganga and Yamuna. Haridwar, Rishikesh, Varanasi, Kusinagar beyond Gorakhpur are important centres for them.

Method in Contextual Theology

The following elements are emerging as the constitutive of Method in Contextual Theologizing: Vision of the Kingdom of God, Commitment to the project, experience born of committed action for change, questions and Issues arising out of it, reflections guided by Social Sciences, and philosophical insights, leading to Theologizing, followed by pastoral action. Periodic reflection over the above dynamics will further deepen which could flower forth in fairly good result in apostolic service.

First, the ultimate criterion for theologizing has to be God's plan for the human family expressed by Jesus Christ who inaugurated the Reign of God. It was foreshadowed by Prophecy and the First Covenant whereby community consciousness was preserved and God-human relationship established by a sacred promise. The Cross and the self-giving sacrifice stand as a declaration to all generations. At great cost the community of God has to be shaped, nurtured and protected.

Second, the theologian has to be committed, verbally and actually, to this God's plan so that it becomes his passion for ministry. Elimination of poverty and illiteracy, of discriminatory social practices like caste and gender, taking steps in dialogue with estranged groups etc are such initiatives. 'Armchair theology' that confines to dominate classrooms, libraries, seminars, 'pure research' without field experience of the struggle for the Kingdom of God also is there. But that is not enough. Both the teachers and the students should be like the First Master who 'preached what He practiced'. It is not Indian theology if this is absent in both teacher and the taught.

Third, consequently, the commitment has to be verified by actual involvement in the Kingdom oriented service or fresh initiatives. Intellectual activities like writing, organizing seminars, or inter-religious or inter-caste gatherings, peace initiative etc are desirable activities that promote the Reign of God in our country. But validation will be minimal if the experience of the struggle to alleviate degradation of the people of God is absent.

Extremely important are steps aimed at elimination especially of poverty and caste practice. But here the validation and authentication has to come from experience of the field born of actual personal involvement. Dealing with words alone has no credibility. Field work is as important is as library.

Fourth, periodic reflection over the above is best done with the assistance of the social sciences: economics, sociology, political science, anthropology, psychology...Philosophy also should deepen the reflection. This exercise of periodic systematic reflection will benefit both pastoral ministry and the regulation interpretation of the word of God on Sundays and such days. Because religion should walk contemporaneously with development in the secular society.

A wonderful phrase that helps us in these ventures is 'creative fidelity'; With our eyes fixed on the future, and drawing resources from the past experiences when we plan to act we can become assured of the richness of the method which can be termed as 'creative fidelity'.

The core of the Vatican II document *"Gaudium et Spes'* (The Church Today) shows the anxiety, the eagerness and the hope that the Church has to be a growing community walking apace with world on the march and should inspire teachers of theology to be ever in touch with the struggling human community and not an outdated organization.

We derive substantial benefits from the past experiences to be ever creative in the ministries. In the light of these when planned action for the Kingdom is initiated one can be sure of being on the right track. That phrase possesses a high degree of infallibility, because truth and discernment will shield us from error. When 'creative fidelity' operates in our mind by providing a framework for planning and assessing regularly, one can be free from wrong steps. With these steps contextualization as a Method fit for theologizing in India will be productive, secure and fruitful. The universal is contextualized flawlessly. This is the task of the theme before us.

For context is where we are and what we are here and now as a believing community internalizing truths that belong to eternity and acting as a convinced and committed group in India right now.

Turbulent India in Search of Authentic Identity and New Direction
At least five visions are at work behind the wide-spread turbulence on the surface. India is a whirl pool set in motion by pursuers of different ideologies.

First of all there is the new identity claim by advocates of an exclusive claim: a Hindu Rashtra. They are moved by what is known as Hindu Nationalism. Nationalism was the goal in Germany, Italy etc decades ago. Though the cause advocated is an extinct one now, its advocates are increasing in number globally. The goal remained hidden during freedom struggle but now it is raising its head vocally and forcefully:

V. D. Savarkar's vision of a Hindu Rashtra. The voice is shrill and direction unidirectional.

Then there is the 'secular democratic India' of the current Preamble and the currently operative Constitution. It has survived almost decades of stresses and strains. The supreme merit of this secular identity is that it was shaped by two generations of men and women who struggled hard to secure India's freedom.

Thirdly there is the Marxist vision of India. Locked up in the forests in Chhattisgarh and other central Indian States one can hear occasional gunshots and see bloodshed. This is the extreme form of the Marxian India spearheaded by the ideology of Karl Marx. Communist Party (Marxist) and Communist Party of India are promoters of the ideology. And the Leninist group takes to steps including violent steps. Overthrow of the society that is unjustly structured and establishment of a classless society is the goal of the violent group.

Fourthly there is the Tribal-Dalit- OBC vision of India. It is the hitherto silent large group of Indians, dominated by the Upper-Caste weight for centuries. The net-work has been staking their claim to govern India in order to repair the damage caused for centuries by caste system and to be a true community of equals.. But unity is yet to achieve.

Finally there is the Judeo-Christian vision. Bible's understanding of the Kingdom to be the motivation for evolving a human and humane community is its base. Once exclusive now the vision has offered dialogue as a way of starting a conversation, with due respect to diversity in religion, cultures, races and other elements. Just as a bud slowly opens up with emerging petals moving in different directions to its final identity, the vision is becoming more and more open to other claims for dialogue.

Issues Responsible for Turbulence

India at present is experiencing turbulence in several sectors. Identifying elements responsible for it is necessary.

Indian freedom struggle was a protracted one. It stirred up in the minds of the participant's hope of a new India. The aspirations and hopes soared high. But full realization is the problem. Current turbulence is the outcome of these still-unfulfilled aspirations. This will affect every sector of the society: economic, social, cultural, religious.

Economic level: society is divided into two blocks: the ruling block and the ruled block. All power is virtually in the hands of the ruling block. With that accumulation of the resources takes place in the higher sector and deprivation at the lowest level. Unequal distribution of the sources of living has generated discontent among the deprived and marginalized. On the one hand, the wealth of the super-rich has multiplied, say, a hundred times. Deprivation of the ruled block has increased. The protest in varying forms rise up.

Social: society in India is structured hierarchically. Equality is assured in the Preamble which is a covenant. But equality is not realized in the society. For instance, look at caste system. It remains un-mitigated which is still a scandal to the educated everywhere and a shame for all of us. For outside the four recognized social groups, organized hierarchically, are the Scheduled Castes. In spite of the Preamble and the Directive Principles of State Policy which are there for implementation inequality in the society has not changed. Anger is building up. One day it can irrupt. Fragmented groups are getting organized. Consciousness of the abominable inequality practiced always is growing.

The youth among them are getting educated and see the inadequacy of the present situation. There have been attempts at assault on those who protest aloud. But such efforts at repression are met with condemnation from the wider society.

Political level: In India we have parliamentary form of democracy. Political parties enjoying majority after he election assumes responsibility for governance. Each party has its own ideology. But Indian hierarchical culture also influences these parties. Discontent is generated by non-fulfillment due to corrupt practices and accumulation and exercise of power by vested interest groups.

Cultural level: culture as an interpretation of beliefs values customs and traditions, a by-product of the ideology at work in the particular social grouping which is subject to periodic tremours. For example there is caste system in India. It is a cultural system but not a value. For example the Scheduled Castes are not allowed to mix with the society freely. They will pollute! Hence they have still to live in 'Cheri', the living place assigned to them in the village marked out for them at safe distance from the 'people'!

This writer was told by the Sisters who run an English medium school in one particular city that cool water kept in the examination hall by an attendant lady in May will not be drunk by thirsty students writing the examination. Reason: fear of contamination by pollution! It was suggested: take some from among the students to the school laboratory, boil water up to steaming. If some elements more than $H2+O$ is found in the steam evidence is there that the water brought and kept in the hall has polluting element!

Has pollution of a human being by being together at table, or work place or travel ever been proven by test in a laboratory? It been tested and established scientifically that one human person can pollute another human being just by presence or contact or sitting together or be common meal? That is the moot question.

At the Religions level. Religion is a system of beliefs, rituals, and celebrations pertaining to the realm of 'the 'sacred' or 'the super-natural'. It is a fundamental need of the people. It is expected to be the arbiter, teacher, provider of directions and meaning for the struggling humanity. It is expected to be the safe pointer or arrow mark for the beyond, especially after cessation of life. People need certitude about life-after death. Finally Yama yields to the earnest enquiry and offers his insight.

But due to frequent conflicts among them and inadequate mutual knowledge and respect for the faith and practice of another believer, the vocation of religions to play its providence-assigned role is yet to take place fairly well at the national and social levels.

Because of unethical transactions and dynamics at the economic social and cultural levels, religion can be appropriated by the ruling block, perverted by the illiterate and fundamentalists and rigidity of the dogmatists. It can be dismissed, as Marx did, by angrily condemning it as 'the opium of the people supplied to assuage the deprived as delusive and misleading substitute.

In order to have correct perception of the dynamics at work in the social, economic, political and cultural fields, theology these days has been trying to get assistance from the social sciences. Each of these has its own proper method of developing the knowledge system. For sciences will categorically ensure where what why and how truth in the empirical world lies with the test of absolute verifiability. It can detect and expose the unjust structures, associations and their network and denounce them in the open society. One cannot escape with nebulousness. Truth has to be highlighted for its promotion. What religion or philosophy sometimes mystifies by abstractions and abstruseness social sciences will demonstrate with convincing and shocking clarity and verifiability.

Contextualization for Evolving a Theological Method for India

In the following pages a brief presentation of the steps in the process of theological reflection that is emerging. Indian theological method is gradually under experimentation, for good. The method in theologizing in India starts from the particular context.

First requirement: Experiencing by the Theologians, both students and teachers.

Starving homes, torture chambers, night shelters, hospital beds and such situations raise questions for all. Some hear the questions and some do not. Beasts of burden like camels, buffaloes, asses do have questions within but are not expressed. Victims of unjust treatment or punishment do have questions in the form of yelling in anguish. Low-paid labourers, bonded labourers etc also have questions boiling in their minds sometimes poured out but mostly suppressed. Indian social structure had pushed out a group called panchama because they are 'polluting'.

Above we have a series of questions. These are the actual experience of the marginal or affected sections of the people of India. It is here that contextualization of Indian theologizing commences. It is here that the first step in the method in contextual theologizing begins.

We have the supreme example in Exodus: Yahweh's inner sensibility revolted when the anguished yells from the brick-kilns of Egypt resounded within (Ex 3:7). Exodus from the dungeons of human making: prisons, out-caste system, slums, night-shelters, brothels, 'cheris' etc take place when questions are raised: why this situation? Who created his structure and imposed on the undeserving.

Liberation theology was born when Gustav Gutierrez and fellow Christians in Latin America raised the questions: why most live in poverty? How can the rich gloat at luxurious tables? Why are some poor on this very rich earth?

Questions are held as Invitations for Mature and Responsible Reflection

There comes a time when individuals, cultures and nations halt and put question to them: for centuries others thought for us, decided and acted for us and we learned from their cogitations. Is it not time that we think for ourselves and decide for ourselves? Before the sprout of teeth infants are fed on soft food or even food chewed by the mother is inserted in the mouth. But all dependence is gone when self-management begins.

When the sun of consciousness rises on the horizon of individuals and cultures they assert their God-given identity and rights. They take to self-management.

The new Churches across the world have been involved in such a process of self-management, as truly local and universal. This is also the wish and will of the Church. Freedom to think for oneself and decide and act accordingly is constitutive of being a person. Not even God demands its diminution at any level. That faculty and its exercise cannot be dispensed with nor surrendered to any. The Bible is the norm-provider. We understand contextual theologizing as such a venture. Food prepared at home is always tastier than when ordered from the nearby restaurant. Theology born out of home experience is contextual theology.

And Indian context keeps changing quite rapidly. Today's questions cannot be met by past solutions, however rich. We can always draw benefits from them.

The task before the Christian community in India is for shaping an Indian theological method. A nation that is very ancient and has produced a rich heritage deserves to be honoured by own theology using its own resources to honour Revelation of God. God's offer is for all. Religions play one role in mediating God-access according to Indian experience in.

Human Challenges before Religions in India

The provocative challenge of Rabindranath Tagore to the temple priest is to come out of the traditional rituals and create new ones incorporating the hard labour of the path-maker and rock-cutter. Similarly the theologian in India is challenged to enter deep into human reality and experience the anguish and affliction of the people, especially of the deprived and the marginalized. It is out of the bitter truth of liberative struggles that religion has to establish its credibility. India is the land of religions. India is also known as the laboratory of spiritualities.

But three puzzles that India is faced with. One is the staggering poverty of millions, secondly how is it that poverty co-existed with religions. Thirdly how is it that caste as a social practice denigrating and diminishing the humanity grew and co-existed with religions over the centuries?

The percentage of the poor in India in relation to the total population is shockingly high. Therefore the question has been that the many religions seem not to have addressed effectively the problem of poverty of the people in India.

There is yet another problem that has been shocking: cast practice in India. Equality figures prominently In the Preamble of the Constitution of India. This is another contradiction or task for the nation: caste is central to the structure of Indian human community.

Role of Socio-Cultural Analysis in theologizing

In order to get clarity on these issues scholars versed in the Indian human and religious situations have suggested that a socio-cultural analysis is central to theologizing in India. Such an analysis is a process through which one gets a fair understanding of the human situation by exploring its historical and structural relationships. Also one gets both the objective and subjective dimensions of the human reality in India. Therefore it is important to understand both the religious and cultural dimensions of India. In a country where illiteracy is still phenomenal various explanations are expected as to why poverty is still there. Some attribute it to fate, others to backwardness in general etc.

But the historical and structural relationship of poverty needs to be understood. Also the economic the social the political and the cultural dimensions need to be explored. Since religion is the cultural dimension of a society our country with extreme poverty and plurality of religions co-exist. This also needs to be explored.

Both poverty and religiosity are marks of the Indian context. Contextual theologizing depends for its growth sufficient clarity about these existential realities.

One is the basic realities of living. The recent farmers' march in the country is a symbol of these problems. First there was the mammoth march of farmers in Maharashtra. Hundreds of kilometers travel on foot to reach the citadels of governance was a strong invitation for all Indians, to consider the plight of farmers. When industry, cyber and other technologies draw huge finances from the state, farmers are also drawing the attention of all. Agriculture sustains the people: those in industry, those in technology, and those in administration.

Second is focus upon the merits and demerits of the religious beliefs and practices, as well as the ethical-moral values that had been sustaining the human community over centuries. The plan and providence of an-all-benevolent God, Father and Mother of the human family should be diligently and respectfully brought under purview. God had meticulously designed the welfare of His children.

Thirdly creativity and innovativeness should mingle to absorb some of the festivals coinciding with change of seasons and give shape to celebrations in which both the Semitic and Indic sentiments fill the air. We are too much tradition-worshippers. If one generation in the distant past created something beautiful at that time it should not benumb another generation's privilege and responsibility to reshape them incorporating the new.

Fourthly, an honest appreciation of the heritage of the human communities living around is desirable. This could be best done with the assistance of the growing social sciences that are concerned with the study of the human person in the contemporary society. This is helpful to understand the current human issues in order to evoke proper response in the light of the Bible. Since Indian scriptures are regarded by the Hindu spiritual leaders as inspired, and rich in meaning, they too are interacted with. This requires consistent attention and planning in our theologates.

Fifthly, the question that should engage the attention of all is: seventy years after we began self-governance the nature of the poor in our country has not changed substantially. Recently a report drew attention of all: top one percent of the Indian population has over hundred billionaires and the bottom poor of the country still in poverty. And their number increased phenomenally. The old formula; rich become richer and poor become poorer, still a reality. This is a negative verdict upon so-called responsible self-governance.

Role of Social Sciences. Traditional theology has been formulated largely by philosophy. St Augustine and later Aquinas launched that method. Bernard Lonergan the Canadian Jesuit has treated extensively the journey of the human mind in this process, in his comprehensive book titled INSIGHT. Scholastic theology has greatly benefited from these methods.

Philosophy does come in. As a reflective science it can further contribute to the deepening of the probe into reality by the human mind...

One may recall the revolt in philosophy, especially launched by the Existentialist philosophers like Kierkegaard, J. P. Sartre etc. One factor was the birth and growth of Modern Philosophy. Another factor was the neglect of human experience in philosophy. In India we are familiar with Siddhartha and his thinking that has influenced Asia and beyond. He starts inviting the attention of all to the problem of human suffering. Suffering is an acute human experience. Buddhism is the final outcome of reflection on suffering.

The emerging theology, of which contextual theology is an example, is largely influenced by Gustavo Gutierrez known as the Father of Liberation Theology. For him the starting point is the experience or phenomenon of poverty. Theology today is radically challenged by his contribution.

Of late social sciences like economics, sociology, anthropology, psychology are increasingly used to reflect theologically on a given situation, as mentioned above, and respond. Transformation of the human situation is the goal.

Again, why and how social sciences to theologize? The assumption is that the human person has a body! For the body to be alive the first requirement is food. Its production, distribution, availability are dealt with in economics. Starvation deaths, ill-health, sickness etc are dependent on non-availability of food. Over-pricing will prevent the poor from securing it. Here Economics and ethics are at work.

The human person is not alone, but lives in a society. Inter-personal relationship, group behavior, individuals and the community, leadership service in the community, all these concerns are studied for the person to live in the society. Here Sociology comes in.

Society is organized to conduct its affairs. There are duties and responsibilities laws and their sanctions mutually agreed upon for smooth functioning of the society in a given lace and time. There can be various kinds of grouping of these communities. Here comes the problem of governance. Political Science assists theological reflection taking these and related requirements into consideration at the Faith level.

Tribes and races are born of various factors related to the above considerations on topography. Among the tribes community bond is important. Anthropology deals with the different races and inter-tribal and intra-tribal ethics and morality. Integrated functioning of the society depends much on healthy interpersonal relationship irrespective of whether one belongs to the governance group or governed group.

In the absence of good knowledge of these factors Proclamation of the Good News will be impossible. Mere spiritualism without attending to life issues like poverty, health, literacy, some land to build a house or to cultivate needed food, medical care, addressing of conflict issues etc will be like pouring water on the sand.

Finally there is the dimension of religions. History and sociology of religions do provide sufficient empirical data about faith-traditions other than the Judeo-Christian. The presence of world religions is seriously and respectfully dealt with in universities and seminaries. Besides today we have been witnessing the growth of a new discipline, known as Theology of Religions which is different from phenomenology of religions. Contextually this is of vital significance. For it is in this 'land of religions' that the Church in India is charged with the mission of serving the Reign of God.

Bible is God's word communicated to the human family. God's intervention is connected with divine project in human history. That project is a vision which is creation and shaping up of a human community called in the Bible as the Kingdom of God. It was prefigured in the Old Testament and inaugurated by Jesus Christ. In and through the person, life and teaching of Jesus Christ the Kingdom was inaugurated.

God's dream was creation of a human community reflecting the divine community. It is de facto now seen as fractured, disfigured, and hierarchically structured. Poor-rich, high - low, male-female, touchable-untouchable, healthy-sick divided society which needs to become a community. Christ was sent by the Father for the restoration of the divine plan.

In the Book of Genesis we learn of the divine plan and method for restoration. Moses has had the full experience of disfigured and oppressed human community in Egypt. It was from within this afflicted human community that he was called to help liberate the afflicted in Egypt. It is his experience of oppression that fired him with the energy to respond.

Here we have a major source in theologizing in India: experience of the affliction of the broken human community in India. This experience come from judicious espousal of the worthy cause promotive of the values of the Kingdom Jesus preached.

The Model for the Exercise: Jesus Himself. An excellent teacher that Jesus was, He told the disciples, 'listen, then, and learn what the parable of the sower means' (Mt 13:18). Jesus interprets the parable He had told the huge crowd that had come to Him to be healed and to listen to the great teacher of life-promoting wisdom. Here we have a beautiful case study in contextual theologizing. The crowd around Jesus seems to have been constituted mostly of peasants. So He reflects over one aspect of a peasant's life and derives its meaning and significance for them. Here we have a case in contextual theologizing. It is introduced by Jesus in His time. Through the varied performance of a tiny seed He is drawing attention to the proper disposition of the mind to listen to, ponder and respond to God's word. Good soil produces a hundred fold. Minds open to truth will in like manner respond whole heartedly. The outcome is predictable.

When one looks at the Indian tradition interpreting the *sruti* texts is there. Indian scholars like Sayana, Sankara, Ramanauja and others have developed the science of vyakhya and bhashya. Bhashya by Sayanacharya, on the Vedic Samhita, by Sankaracharya on the Brhma-sutras which are the Upanishads reduced to sutras (aphorism), are examples at hand. Some of the Upanishads contain very exalted vision of the human person. The *sutrakar* Badarayana put them in certain form which inspired Sankara to weave his *advaita* insight it is because he found in the *jivatman* certain nobility and worth: almost equal to the divine. Next step of course was to consider human as one with the divine.

But social reality was not within their perspective of interpreting or analyzing. Indian human situation is quite perplexing, even depressing. That also should be part of religions' responsibility.

Indian Community and its Structure. It is hierarchically structures. Caste is the criterion. The lower in the hierarchy the less of humanity one possesses.

Economically too the same structure is operative. For the Dalits are mostly landless and constitute the mass of agricultural labourers. Then just above them are the two communities that deal with wealth: its production and the mode of distribution, the *shudras* and the *vaisyas*.

On close analysis one will find that there is convergence of the caste hierarchy and economic hierarchy, especially in terms of economic power and resource holding. Here at the lowest rung of the social ladder will be the poor, then the marginal class with minimum resource to maintain life. And those above will be the well-to-do and above and top in the ladder are the rich. Sociologists have named this organization as the ruled class and the ruling class.

Past leaders like B. R. Ambedkar, Mahatma Phule and Savitribai Phule were among prominent social critics that have highlighted and protested against the non-egalitarian nature of the society due to caste-class divide that affects social cohesion.

When abject poverty invades a section of the society and another section is living in superabundance with financial social and political power all in and with them. Then the conclusion is that the society lives with a contradiction. The inequality cannot go on indefinitely. From among the deeply affected or from some other sector individuals or groups will begin alerting the wider society of the explosive nature of the human situation. The poor who are victims of the unjust and exploitative situation may not be aware of it as intensely and deeply as those who analyze the situation. That is because the centuries of oppression, exploitation and domination led to internalizing of the system and values.

In India this situation is further complicated because of gender discrimination.

The social contradiction arising out of these human issues gets accumulated. Revolution takes place when the accumulated grievances are not attended to on time. The French Revolution, Bolshevik Revolution, Cuban Revolution are there in history and forthcoming generations could derive lessons from such irruptions.

Freedom, autonomy, rights and responsibilities, welfare -- under God' – these are the criteria used to interpret the events mentioned above.

In the text highlighted above Jesus is explaining the parable. The parable is about the seed sown by the peasant. The seed is smallest parcel of vital potencies encapsulated by the tree. It has a future written on it. The word of God is compared to it. Once grown the tree shelters many living beings, nourishes many and becomes a symbol of economic activity. Gandhi has stated that for a hungry person God comes in the form of bread. The good that a tree bestows on birds, animals, the human beings is seen as God's benevolence reaching these beneficiaries.

Such fullness of the human person can be stated to be the very core of Christian heritage. It entails that we acknowledge our true identity, affirm it with deep conviction and commit ourselves to stand by it at all times. That implies that we are prepared to struggle in order to secure it for as many of our brothers and sisters. Of course demands and responsibilities are to be taken seriously. Endowed with the faculties of deliberation, decision and execution, appropriating from all that is placed around us, we shape our life, move towards our destiny. In and through creation-revelation package divine collaboration to the full is guaranteed. This is part of the vocation of the individual, of the community, of any culture/religion. The Church in India is invited to that creative phase of her existence as an authentic local Church. She is called upon to assume that responsibility and strike deep roots in the land that belong to God and His people. This non-negotiable principle is the solid foundation for the recent phrase theologizing in India.

Armed with these truths of fundamental values, we as members of the Church in India have to look around and locate the mass of our brothers and sisters that are deprived of these God-given endowments. With deep faith in God and love for our people we are invited to enter and pitch our tent in their midst. We have to walk with them work with them struggle with them in order to enable them to enjoy the God-given status as children of welfare-providing God. Having secured the faith love and acceptance of our people we identify ourselves with their life-struggle. That means we insert ourselves within the people and work with them. We expect resistance when we touch or turn our attention to those who oppress them. With patience and caution we organize resistance stemming from heavy-footed oppressors and join the fight. We take time to gather the experiences to analyze interpret and articulate them. We need to create public opinion towards this mega breach. That is also part of Indian theologizing.

To articulate without insertion and struggle is what Pope Francis stated: 'we cannot become starched Christians, too polite, who speak of theology calmly over tea'. Insertion in the struggling society, analyzing the forces at work, interpreting and planning appropriate response in collaboration with like-minded fellow-citizens is expected of everyone who 'preaches' or 'teaches'. We learn to think for ourselves we promote thinking by others. 'Teach what you practice' is the advice of the celebrant while conferring the diaconate ministry.

Kingdom of God is the project of God, of Christ, and of the Church. We are in its service. A simple word for that rather ethereal world is 'community'. Its authentic expression and one's adequacy at it has been a concern in recent times. From teaching/learning theology, the move was towards theologizing, an ongoing process. Traditional theology, a fully shaped product could not function in a bubbling social cauldron. It was shaped by forces of past times and climes. It had its specific context. It failed to interact with our context that was entirely different.

A Major Lacuna: absence of Inter-scriptural Interaction

Exegesis and hermeneutics precede theological reflection in the Christian tradition. In India *bhashya* has evolved after Yaska's *Nirukta*. Badarayana had in his *sutra* literature, which is codification or reduction into *sutra form* of the revealed *sabda* existing eternally in brahma, imparted to the sages. Shankaracharya and Sayanacharya have their own approaches to these sources through their bhashya. Reason and logic play a major role. But they have operated within religious boundary, especially subject to the authority of Sabda. The human struggle figured only when categories like *maya,* an unverifiable category, was excogitated and introduced to explain human living problems like poverty, pain suffering and death. Bhakti-impelled bhashya was the exegesis of Ramanuja.

Christian exegesis has not yet interacted with any of these. *Without inter-scriptural* exegesis, and hermeneutics no progress is possible in the line of the opening made by Nostra Aetate and Ad Gentes.

Dayananda Swaraswati has placed before us his *bhashya* of Gospel texts, especially of the Synoptics. That is in circulation among his adherents, in their cultural centres and educational institutions, with wide coverage. But what is missing there is the scientific approach that distinguishes Christian exegesis. *Satyartha Prakash* of Dayananda Sararaswati cuts a sorry figure while dealing with his exegesis of the Synoptics. I am not yet aware of any bible scholar tackling that issue.

The contribution of B. R. Ambedkar and a host of human rights activists and certain NGOs have contributed to the grassroots level penetration of God's word, and, in reverse, in highlighting burning human issues and struggle in the light of God's word. Indian theologizing has been paying heed to that warning. Dalit theology, a new branch of Indian theology, has profusely relied upon protesters like Ambedkar, Phule Savitri and Periyar. Ambedkar warned that economic development without social transformation is lopsided in its approach.

It is at this level that the sowing seeds of Theologizing in India are to be commenced. Both critical assistance of religions and analytical assistance of human struggles have to be inseparable parts of theological interpretation and corresponding action.

Just as it was 'peoples' reading of the Bible', with their experience of oppression, poverty and inequality, that gave birth to a new theology in Latin America, it was India's experience of colonialism, poverty, injustice, oppression and gender-caste-discrimination based on purity-pollution mania that provided impetus to think afresh by reformers. Of course Liberation Theology was an inspiring model. This has assisted the experiment with what is known in India as contextual theology or theologizing in India.

We know that lightning and thunder accompanied the first major intervention of God in human affairs, via Mosaic experiences. If so theology, organized reflection on the word and actions of God in pursuit of God's dream for the human family, should embody the fire-power of the Bible and the anguish the anger, the humiliation and anxiety of the poor and the Dalits of India.

That fire-power was missing in inherited theology. The Egyptian experience of subjugation that marked the Exodus narrative, was absent in the theology though born of the same Biblical narrative. The agony and anguish of struggling humanity should inflame the will and stir up the hearts, and supply kinetic energy and mobility to our legs to walk into the place where struggle is afoot or fire is to be ignited.

Assisted in its formation by Aristotle's metaphysics scholastic theology became 'the queen of sciences'. But when developments like industrial revolution, loss of the working class, birth of modern philosophy, Existentialism, Personalism, and above all Marxism appeared on the scene with their loud and attractive claims the 'queen' was found to be ineffective. A return to traditional theology in the form of Neo-Scholasticism, was the last bid to revive. But the times and trends ignored it.

A theology lacking in that fire power greatly failed us in India. It could not question caste in India, even in the Church. It could not question colonial occupation. It could not disdain collaboration with colonial masters. That theology could not stir up Indian Christian youth to join the freedom struggle. Neither did it question gender discrimination.

To recharge theology with that fire-power is the goal of 'Indian theologizing', known as contextualized theology. Indian theologizing is engaged in that task. Indian Theological Association is a platform to share and exchange the findings in that effort at the many centres in India. Most of the themes taken for treatment over the decades, and especially the statements, reflect this concern.

Conclusion

What then is new in Indian theologizing?

Answer: Firstly, It tries to re-connect two vital and most important poles, human experience of exploitation poverty and injustice in the Indian context and the word of God available in the living tradition of the Church. Creative interaction between these two poles results in a transforming theology. Mathew 9 35-38 presents the picture of Jesus entering into the midst of struggling human community which stirs up in him compassion for the human situation. And he responds creatively.

Secondly, human experience is the starting point of the entire process. Experience implies involvement in view of a goal. That goal is a better society. Existing society is quiet unjust and exploitative. Change of that implies a stand has to be taken in view of change, organized action to remove the negative. That meets with resistance. The entire process and the situation are analyzed with the criteria of the Kingdom of God. The entire process is now rigorously analyzed and interpreted. This entire process is keeping in mind the criterion of God's plan for the Reign of God.

Thirdly social science methods come handy for the interpretation. The process is interpreted systematically with the active assistance of the human sciences (economics, sociology, political philosophy, psychology, anthropology, *etc.* Interaction with Indian religions too is part of the process of reflection. Because psychology, economic transactions, political processes, all these so-called social/human sciences are also shaped by the religiosity of the people of 'this land of religions'. This is central to Indian theology.

Gandhi on his return to India after studies in England went round greater part of rural India to learn Indian rural life. This he analyzed and placed before the people the lacunae in it. He called for followers to enter and respond.

Fourthly, engaging in these activities in the light of Scripture, including Indian scriptures, and Tradition is the most essential step.

Experience of liberative struggles (especially of the Dalits, tribals, women, the poor, the unclaimed migrants, the bonded labourers) makes it the voice of truth. Committed and continued action to bring about change is a necessary sign of theologizing as a living process.

Fifthly, good familiarity with classical theology, especially the Patristics, is beneficial for deriving pedagogical and methodological insights.

Sixthly, articulation of the insights gained can be in many forms: systematic writing, presentation through drama, poetry, story-telling etc to make it living and vibrant.

This is possible only if the theologian in India is part and parcel of the struggling and the deprived at many levels, and not a mere purveyor of highly developed theology from the Western theological markets. In Indian theology one should discover the voice of the Indian Christian sharing the Good News along with the struggles of the poor.

II.   Challenges India has to face and Christian Community has to collaborate

The major challenges

1. The California fire is often a subject globally reported and discussed, year after year. The social media like Television captures and disseminate worldwide and people stare aghast at the catastrophic wild fire on its way. Will such a flame, a human-social fire engulf our nascent republic? Fundamentalism in religion, intolerance towards the other, advocacy of mono-religious or mono-cultural identity as a major challenge and threat to the programme mentioned above.

2. The liberator of Israel from their oppressive situation in Egypt, Moses, could boldly demand freedom because he had experienced oppression and enslavement in the brick-kilns of Egypt. Experience provides credibility for the liberator. But the number of such Christians is limited in number.

3. India is faced with such an ideological *tsunami*. The Indian context has changed suddenly, radically. The four pillars of the Indian Constitution, namely, sovereign, socialist, secular democratic India, are under threat by forces of an alternate ideology that was developed by dissenters of the approach of the founding Mothers/Fathers. This needs urgent collective and community level attention. This is the major challenge India is suddenly faced with.

4. The dictatorship of the Global economy is operating with vigour like *tsunami* releasing immense tidal waves. The weaker sections of India are in peril. While the Constituent Assembly was finalizing the draft its architect Dr. B. R. Ambedkar had warned that political democracy for India will not survive as long as social democracy is not actualized. He has been right when we look back at our pace of self-handling of our affairs. What we have in our country is social dictatorship in the form of hierarchical structuring of the society, aligned with the national capitalists. Will we be able to withstand it? Doubtful because social structure and economic structure always feed each other.

5. The major complaints against the Semitic communities in India, Christianity and Islam, had been that their sacred places, scriptural, liturgical, cultural resources are outside India. Their holy places are also outside India. Their supreme authorities are also outside India. This is chief among the reasons for the founders of the ruling ideology to culturally dis-own these two communities. This is unacceptable to any citizen of India, especially to the Muslim and Christian communities. But is there truth in what they accuse us of?

It is important that the Christian community grows with deeper knowledge of Indian realities. This is important for the leadership: Priests, Sisters, ecclesiastical leaders. It is worth checking our libraries to notice the quantity and quality of books there, its usage, and especially those in the regional languages. Next to be re-checked is the syllabus in formation houses, both of the religious and of diocesan training centres. We have to merit and earn our citizenship.

Books consulted

Jerald James Larson, *India's Agony over Religion*, State University of New York Press, 1995 Pp 392.

John T.K.SJ et al (ed), Amaldoss, Michael (ed) SJ, Gispert Sauch, George SJ (ed), *Theologizing in India, Selection of Papers presented at the Seminar held in Poona*, October 26-30, 1978, Bangalore: TPI, 1981, 446.

James Massey| TK John SJ, *Retinking Theology in India, Christianity in the Twenty-first Century,* Manohar| Centre for Dalit/Subaltern Studies, 2013, 472.

Profs. George Keerankeri, S.J. & V.P. Srivastava, Editos, *Taking Text to Context, a Festschrift in Honour of Fr.T. K. John S.J., on the Occasion of his 75th Birth Anniversary,* ISPCK-Vidyajyoti College of Theology, 2011.

Centrality of Dialogue in Doing Theology in the Pluralistic Context of India

Joseph Chittooparambil

Pluralism as a political philosophy can be understood as the recognition and affirmation of diversity within a political body, which permits the peaceful coexistence of different interests, convictions and lifestyles. Pluralism thus tries to encourage members of society to accommodate their differences by avoiding extremism and engages in good faith dialogue. India is also a political concept, independent nation above sixty years old with a past history of around two centuries under the British rule. To understand India as a civilizational unit or as a political entity it is very important to get into the immense diversity that it characterizes. In India we have people of many races and ethnic stocks – the Dravidian, the Arian, Negroids, Paleo-Meditarenian, Proto-Australoids, Mongoloids and so on. It is also one civilization with many cultures and languages and a country politically with many states reflecting to some extent its linguistic and cultural diversity. Suffice it to recall here that there are 18 official languages in India and as many as 1652 languages spoken as mother-tongues.[1]

The picture of India we have is that of a country in sharp conflict: ethnic, cultural, ideological, etc. Some groups and political parties ideologically and politically favour liberal capitalism, some others represent more egalitarian ideologies and still others follow the legacy of Gandhi as the ideology more suited to India. They are all in conflict with each other. The fiercest conflict, however, is between Brahminic caste-ideology and the challenge represented by marginal groups like the Dalits and the tribals.[2] In the light of these conflicts and the pluralities of cultures and traditions a theology that makes sense in India has to safeguard a dialogical character that takes note of the different perceptions the different cultures uphold. Felix Wilfred asserts:

> Theology would make sense in India as service to life and it needs to be fostered through continuous dialogue.... Moreover, we are in the midst of a serious conflict between the forces of life and the death-dealing powers of darkness. The dialogue indeed here is not something referring simply to intellectual discussion, rather relating to the realm of praxis.[3]

Every generation is rooted in and nourished by its religious tradition, which is the bearers of the culture and spirit of the people. Today social and religious structures have become the arena of the conflict between the traditional value system and the challenges of modernity. There are also the conflicts between the macro and the micro, the dominant and the subaltern, etc. - the big and the powerful against the small and the weak, the former trying to control the later and the later refusing to be dominated by the former. We see a tension between the opposites: tradition and modernity, globalisation and contextualisation, fundamentalism and pluralism, old and new. To make it culturally intelligible and pastorally meaningful the theologians need to begin from scratch and engage in a theological praxis and articulation of the thoughts that reflects the actual lived situations of the people, their history, philosophy, culture and tradition.

Theology is part and parcel of the process of study and reflection on the problems and questions facing the people and as a search for ways and means to meet the challenges of life. Theology conceived and practiced in many quarters has been criticised, as is divorced from the actual realities of life, making it irrelevant and meaningless; and so it is in crisis. Theology needs to grow constantly through its service and not cultivate itself for its own sake. We cannot take it for granted the traditional way of imparting theological education in abstract concepts, borrowed from a particular philosophical system, emerging from a western cultural context and distanced from the life and reality of our people and country.

The Change in theological methodology

Method in a science is like the heart of the human body and the crisis in theology can be located in the methodological crisis. The reason for it is due to the rapid advancement in the fields such as sociology of knowledge, the epistemological, methodological and hermeneutical sciences, historical methods, linguistics and critical theory. As it is understood a theology is written first, and a reflection on the operative theological methodology comes later. A theological methodology therefore can sometimes be called a 'second act' abstracted from the cognitive work in which theologians engage themselves. Faith, which is theology's object, has one dimension that is universal and perennial, and another that is particular and historical. Accordingly, theological method also must encompass these two dimensions.[4] Today most theologians have reached a consensus that theology and interpretation have to be contextual, and that the methodology for the same should undergo a change from the traditional, dogmatic approach to contextual one.

In today's technological and pluralistic world there are divisions and conflicts in human family that eat away the vitality like cancer leading to despair and negativism. Added to this we scare at the ill effects of globalisation, religious fundamentalism, communalism and discrimination based on caste caste, creed, language and gender etc. Many of the pastors and theologians in India are convinced of the fact that the traditional method of theologising uncritically followed was irrelevant to the lives of the people as it was often seen as an academic requirement for entering into the official ministries of the Church. George Soares-Prabhu states, "Poverty-Religiosity-Caste constitute India's *samsara*, its cycle of bondage".[5] These three factors – economic-political, cultural-religious, personal-social – are dialectically interrelated and influence mutually. If we the Indians are to make any positive contribution to theology it is essential that we begin with a serious reflection on our theological task and the problem of theological method in the three-fold context of (1) the meeting of religions, (2) the poverty of the masses and (3) the confrontation or rather reconciliation between the religious and the secular attitudes to life.[6]

Hermeneutics has demonstrated that the pre-option, pre-understanding, and pre-judice present in the human understanding and interpretation falsify the claims of objectivity, neutrality and value free knowledge. In the west if a theology centred on meanings has not been able to come to terms with the religious and cultural situation, this is all the more true in India. Our primary task is not to convince others about the reasonableness and credibility of Christian faith, but rather to immerse ourselves like Jesus, into the situation and enter into dialogue. Theology will follow from this encounter.

Modern science's shift from the immutable, unchangeable and universal laws, objectivity and deductive logicality to inductive observation, revision and reformulation, affirmation of probabilities and particulars and the acknowledgement of subjective and mental processes and personal knowledge also led to the serious reconsideration of theological methodology. Modern philosophical thought brought about a shift from cosmocentrism to anthropocentrism, and from the essentialist metaphysical theology and theological objectivism to the subjectivist and particular theologies, resulting in theological pluralism. Historical scholarship and anthropological studies of various cultures have led to historical mindedness, different from the classical world-view that was deemed to be permanent, uniform and universal, and to the acceptance of the pluriform world-views, diverse cultures and their evolving nature.

Meanwhile the II Vat. Council that resolved to respond dialogically to the diverse cultures and religions and to the various concerns and aspirations of the modern world and the oppressed peoples, called for the renewal in method that takes into consideration human experience and historical and cultural wisdom of diverse peoples. The growing awareness of the pluralism of cultures and religions prompted theologians to revise their theological methodology giving rise to the dialogical method. The change in the theological methodology is urgent for any kind of relevant theology that seeks the total liberation of people. Kurian Kunnumpuram says that the new method of theologising must be experience-based, praxis-oriented, dialogical, and interdisciplinary.[7]

Doing Theology in the Indian Way

It is commonly accepted that theology in Asia or India forms part of the quest for liberation (*moksha*); knowledge is sought for the sake of and in self-realization. George Pattery observes that "theology is not primarily an act of illuminating the mind as it is a committed listening to, deciphering, understanding and realizing God's word.[8] Theological activities are a way of life belonging to an ultimate human attitude. A theologian sees reality as a whole. The different disciplines are not seen in watertight compartments as sociology, science, philosophy, theology, etc., but as contributing to a holistic perspective. The theology of liberation in Asia is understood as "our way of sensing and doing things as revealed in our people's struggle for spiritual and social emancipation".[9] In the changed theological method, the focus is the dialectical reading together of the two poles, the pole of the Judeo-Christian tradition of faith experiences and the pole of our present day experiences in a specific cultural and historical matrix.[10] Theology as hermeneutics seeks critical understanding based on the socio-cultural analysis and challenges a culture that is de-humanizing, paving the way for a counter-culture which is life-affirming, liberating and communitarian.

The mystery of god will always be the central theme or the subject of theology. Theology sees everything with God's eye and theology's proper perspective is the faith perspective. While the mystery of God is the formal object of theology, its material object is everything: God and the world, the church, the society.[11] Theological methodology is here understood as a working principle, coherently formulated to arrive at the theological vision.

Every religion offers a variety of means for the quest for liberation from unjust structures and oppressive powers, humanisation and community building in view of a new society which is based on the ideals of human brotherhood, freedom, justice and peace. The slogan for this change of approach says, "theology has to be reborn at the 'grassroots', i.e. in the midst of life and lived experience of the people."[12] Contextual theology is "an intentional and thought-out effort to do theology in and for a given context, an effort, that, furthermore, is undertaken by people who belong to that context and make use of its own intellectual, religious and spiritual resources".[13] Contextual theologising is more than inculturation. While contextualisation includes the whole context, indigenisation and inculturation may be narrowly understood. "Inculturation and indigenisation are apologetic methods focussed on the translation/interpretation of a received text for a given culture, whereas contextualisation sees this translation/interpretation as a dialectical process in which text and context are interdependent."[14]

We reach such insights not merely by rhetoric but by committed search and action. "With those who want to change, not just to interpret, the world, like Phule and Ambedkar, the truth they seek is not just the object of an intellectual quest, nor merely a pragmatic technique, but rather truth as a reality, a *satya,* authenticated by its humanist and liberative potential."[15] Self-reflection and critique in the process of enlightenment can change the attitude, which presupposes strategic action capable of dissolving distortions and manipulations. It has to aim at living with a sense of justice and freedom in the economical, political, social, personal, cultural and religious realms. It is historical, inclusive and holistic. A holistic approach is needed to enter into the Indian world-view which insists on the interrelatedness of everything and a cosmic wholeness, avoiding any sort of dichotomy. Felix Wilfred referring to the holistic Indian approach states:

> Employing the traditional resources of the people, which resonate with their present life and experience, roots the liberation praxis in culture and thereby makes it effective. The Indian praxis of liberation must go hand in hand with the holistic and integral vision of reality, characteristic

of the traditional Indian culture and heritage. In this vision, the socio-political struggle for liberation is not simply a matter of the empirical order or of ethical concern. The Indian approach places the empirical and ethical concerns within a framework of a totality of reality, which comprises the divine, cosmic and human dimensions.[16]

Theologising in the Indian context has to take into account of the communal, critical, constructive, contextual and liberational aspects. In a society that is divided between rich and poor, powerful and powerless, exploiters and exploited, dominant and subaltern etc., Christian discipleship demands that we take the side of the poor. When people are placed poles apart, not only economically and politically but also socially, psychologically, culturally, religiously, etc., the role of the agents of liberation is to denounce the death dealing forces on the one hand and announce the dawn of a new age and establishment of a new world order inspired by the divine.

Dialogue and Counterculture

Every culture is capable of mediating God's presence in the language of its people. Any countercultural and theological discourse in India has to be rooted in the socio-cultural and religio-cultural realities, determined by poverty, religion and caste and be in continuous dialogue with as they represent different aspects of the Indian reality as a whole. About the hopeless and helpless situation of the present times in the world the Catholic Biblical Association of India states:

> One great characteristic of our times and the general mood of the present day world can best be described as demoralisation, despondency, disillusionment and despair leading to suicide as the 'Blue Whale' game discloses. But it is always the poor and oppressed who are the victims of 'structural sin'. They are crushed broken, disfigured and torn into pieces by the rich and the powerful to the extent that they undergo untold and endless sufferings and excruciating pain.[17]

Hermeneutical studies have made it clear that interpretation and understanding is accompanied by the pre-understanding and pre-options of the interpreter in a particular context, in a horizon of meaning, in a given historical and cultural situation. But it is not easy to give a clear-cut definition of the present socio-cultural situation in India. Kappen expresses the plural and complex nature of the Indian culture thus: "It is characterised by the interplay of diverse and conflicting factors: the superimposition of bourgeois culture over the traditional, the uneven development of capitalism and of the culture germane to it, the overlapping of caste and class, the rise of ritually inferior castes to economic and political dominance, the ambivalence of socialist ideologies."[18]

In India many subaltern socio-cultural movements emerged in the past because of the cultural crisis brought about by the cultural imperialism of Indian and Western origin.[19] Such movements can be called countercultural movements as they emerge from the discontent or the subaltern experience in different dimensions: economic, political, psychological, social, cultural, religious, etc. Self-reflection and a critique in the process of enlightenment can change attitudes. This presupposes strategic action capable of dissolving distortions and manipulations. People look forward to an alternative culture by rediscovering their cultural roots and heritage, and seek a new value system that paves the way to an egalitarian society. There is the need to develop a hermeneutics from the perspective of the victims or subalterns. Tribal identity is marked by their rootedness in land and by the egalitarian social structure. The tribal ethos based on the values of anti-greed and anti-pride offers a valuable alternative model for India today which is being devastated by the greed of consumerism and pride of caste. Soares-Prabhu beautifully shows the implications when these values are incorporated in the life of a community:

> Anti-greed and anti-pride are therefore not just individual virtues which Jesus demanded from those who wished to follow him. They are the structuring principles of the alternative community he sought to build. They are, therefore, meant to be community values. They are to be realised not just in individuals who strive to be 'poor' (Lk 6:20) and 'humble' (Mt 5:3; 11:28) but in the lifestyle and functioning of the community as a whole...That is, it [the Church] must demonstrate its poverty and its humility (its serviceability),

as well as its option for the humble and the poor, in its transactions within the community (bishop-priest; priest-laity; men-women; rich-poor; clean caste-dalit), as well as in its uncompromising prophetic stance towards the huge, immensely greedy, power-hungry, and status-conscious world outside.[20]

In the face of dominating and dehumanizing forces it is important to have a clear vision and a leadership with prophetic voices, which pave the way for a counter-culture. Such counter-ideologies, anti-hegemonic thoughts spun out of moral imaginations and critique, affect the historical development and change of culture, thus leading to social transformation. The counterculture brings about an all-round development and fulfilment of a human person and his/her needs in community, working against all that is oppressive and dehumanizing.

Contradictions and complexities do exist in the cultural situation of India, but this does not mean that there is no possibility for a radical cultural revolution. There is a longing for a free, egalitarian and just society and there were socio-cultural movements of protest in the past which challenged the logic of dominant code in the cultural ground. Religious traditions and cultures have been a major resource of the Asian peoples to situate themselves, to find their identity and ultimate meaning. The self-communication of God through the word is appropriated through interpretation. Hermeneutics is the way of understanding reality by interpreting the language, through which a perception of reality in a particular context is communicated in another context. As hermeneutics, theology seeks a critical understanding based on the socio-cultural analysis, and challenges any culture that is de-humanizing to pave the way for a counter-culture which is life-affirming, liberating and communitarian.

At the level of culture there is also a trend to transform the world into a monocultural zone. Though there are forces of division and fragmentation operative in the socio-cultural life, we also observe counter movements of unity and integration existing side by side. Felix Wilfred observes:

> In spite of many fragmentations characterising today's world, we also note, on the other hand, signs of hope. The human family is moving towards a unity, which was, perhaps, never before achieved in history. There is a deep aspiration to get out of situations of division and to reach integration. If fragmentation is self-destruction of humanity, the movement towards unity is the sign of its redemption….. The myth that the reality can be known by atomising it is giving way to holistic and integral approach that can unfold the web of relations connecting all parts of reality.[21]

The emerging movements of today such as the ecological movement and the feminist movement are a sign of this orientation and approach to unity and integration and at the same time a protest against fragmentation.

Dialogue and cultural Interpretation

All those who work for the creation of a better world by theological and pastoral action should be furnished with an adequate understanding of the cultural forces at work in society and enter into the world of values, motivations and attitudes. The dialectics between theology and culture is of great importance in theologising in India, as theology is faith seeking understanding. People today are realizing the need for dialogue and are ready to recognize the importance of pluralism in all areas of life. Felix Wilfred argues:

> Centralisation of every kind – political, economic, religious - will be forced to loosen its grip. Decentralisation of power, wealth, ideology, etc., will begin to happen keeping alive, in spite of many signs of divisions and conflicts, the dream of the unity of humanity in diversity. Pluralism is going to be the strongest antidote against all domination, control and regimentation. Its language is dialogue and its attitude and praxis is participation. For pluralism is based on the recognition of the otherness of the other. The liberation of the oppressed and the quality of the human life will depend very much on the measure pluralism will be practiced in the decades ahead.[22]

The interpretation of culture and tradition, a critical and creative process, is very much part of this theological activity. It is an option the gospel-community has to make in India in the theologising process, a challenge posed by the complex multicultural situation in India.

When Christians take part in this collective process of humanisation and integration in the socio-cultural milieu we call that inculturation. Dorr recalls that this process, as "the work for liberation, ultimately involves a *spiritual battle*, even though it is necessarily carried out in the economic, political and cultural level."[23] The struggle for the emancipation of the people and the transformation of society should aim at changes in the thought patterns, interests and values prevalent among the people. Simon Sebastian explains culture and argues that the Creation account in Genesis lays the foundation for a theological reflection on the nature of culture itself:

> If one understands culture in general as the prevalent thought-patterns and collective consciousness of a given society, or as the world-view that controls, shapes, animates, modifies and forms one's thought patterns and the collective consciousness, then the Creation account in the Bible is the world-view that informed the collective consciousness of Israel and was an expression of its culture.[24]

Human beings as co-creators relate with nature through their labour and culture. Culture is not simply the work place of God in continuing the work of creation, but as God collaborating with humans in the ongoing process of creation. This intimate relationship of God with the human community in and through culture explains the concepts of spirituality, faith, etc. Sebastian Painadath explains:

> Culture... articulates the world-view of a people. Spirituality keeps alive the orientation to the ultimate horizon of meaning in cultural perspectives. Spirituality is the ultimate source of creativity in the unfolding of a culture. Spirituality is the heartbeat of the myth of a culture. ....Spirituality gives rise to faith. The experience of being gripped by the divine Spirit evokes faith in the person or community. Faith is the surrender to the divine Spirit manifest in a particular instance.[25]

In the midst of poverty and misery of the vast majority of our people, culture plays a key role in the emancipation process, in realising economic development and political empowerment, and more importantly, in awakening the selfhood of people as they become the agents and subjects of history. Referring the role and the dynamics the culture play in the reconstruction of the lives of the people Felix Wilfred says:

> The culture of a people expresses its spirit, its collective unconscious. Like the trees of the forest which preserve the soil from erosion, the cultural roots of a people give them strength and selfhood to withstand the oppression and exploitation of the powerful. It is the living embodiment of its experiences transmitted from generation to generation. It is the specific way of peoples' knowing, feeling and perceiving the reality and interacting with it.[26]

In our encounter with any culture there is needed to discern it well and to fully cooperate with the Creator in growing in it. In this process, denouncing certain cultural expressions on the plea that they have become instruments and signs of oppression, without taking into account the objective value of these expressions would be unwise.[27] The resurgence of the Dalits and the lower castes in India constitute a new political force started to assert and organising themselves politically and socio-culturally, is threatening the dominant castes. "The consciousness of the marginalized dominated class-castes, subjected and subdued by the caste ideology for many generations, was roused out of their inferiority-complex and intellectual subjection, due to many socio-cultural changes taking place rapidly. The democratic revolution, the promises of political parties and governments, the exercise of power through the franchise, the constitutional guarantee of a casteless egalitarian socialist society, etc., led to the rising expectations of people."[28]

In this process of reinterpretation, besides the rediscovery of the socio-political history and religious and cultural resources and texts, the subalterns unearth rich theological mines such as the Dalit *Sahitya*, with its pathos and calls for praxis, folklore, myths, etc. The subaltern solidarity which is built upon the shared experience of powerlessness is the real milieu and power-centre for the creation of a counterculture similar to the one envisioned by Jesus, which is built not on hierarchy, inequality and competition but on cooperation, equality, fraternity and liberty of all sections of society. Questions should be raised about the credentials of any religion, culture or tradition, whether they respond positively and creatively to the challenges posed by the humanisation process, or the call to make this world a better place to live in freedom, justice and dignity.

Centrality of Dialogue in Doing Theology

Unlike other methodological tools, dialogue with the overall situation goes to the very heart of theology. It is based on the conviction that the dialogue of God with humanity and the world continues even today. Even more, it presupposes that it is starting from the present experiences that we begin to understand God's self disclosure. The very fact that people of different faiths come together to respond to the challenges of life, is itself a theological act. For from a Christian perspective we understand the divine mystery not so much as a substance, as relationship. The relationship fostered among human beings becomes the appropriate language to understand the Divine mystery, which is relationship. Sebastian Painadath explains the theologising process clarifying different terms:

> Faith is a response to the Spirit of God transforming the human spirit. Theology is the perception of the word of God transforming human culture. Hermeneutics is the way of interpreting the symbols of faith in a contextualised theological pursuit. Such a pursuit is always conditioned by the cultural fabric of the people. Hermeneutics is therefore an exploration into the dynamic elements of a culture by interpreting the format of myth and language. There is no abstract faith, no neutral theology of global validity. Faith and theological reflection are always in correlation with the culture of a people.[29]

Faith is manifested in the belief systems and spirituality in the forms of religiosity. Symbols unfold, identify, assimilate, and interrelate diverse levels of reality. The specificity each symbol upholds is to be understood in the horizon of the self-revelation of the divine in history. And the revelation of God to the humans happens through the medium of language that roots itself and emerges from culture. The revelation of God in history is the event gathered up in words. The word that opens the core of the person and integrates the community is the symbol of reality. About the word that emerges out of a world-view and its relationality and function in culture and interpretation. Raymond Panikkar explores the word, its vital relationship with the world and the universe of discourse: "Each word is a microcosm; it carries with it an entire universe, and when in freedom (when it is free) it reveals a whole world contained implicitly in a particular word. Words do not live in isolation; they are nurtured in a much larger universe of discourse."[30] The incarnate Word (Logos), God's self-communication, is understood as the theological foundation for inculturation. The incarnation of the Word is a "mystery [that] took place *in history*: in clearly defined circumstances of time and space, amidst a people with its own culture."[31]

Now the question is how can the Gospel community be carrier of good news when a large majority feel that they are at the margins? How does the Gospel community enter into dialogue with different cultures, both dominant and subaltern, when the gospel has a special option for the poor? Questions should be raised about the credentials of any religion, culture or tradition, whether they respond positively and creatively to the challenges posed by the humanisation process, or the call to make this world a better place to live in freedom, justice and dignity. Every religion has failed in more than one way in the challenge of humanisation, and contributed to the dehumanisation and enslavement of people, their subjugation and oppression.

In the light of these conflicts and the pluralities of cultures and traditions a theology that makes sense in India has to safeguard a dialogical character. Felix Wilfred explains:

> To theologise in India means to theologise within a great civilisation characterised by immense diversity; it means to do theology in the midst of contradictions and conflicts, and unprecedented challenges at all levels... Theology would make sense in India as service to life and it needs to be fostered through continuous dialogue. It is a way to bring the Good News of Jesus Christ closer to the lives of the people through concrete engagement. The importance of the theological task stands in bold relief against a serious crisis threatening and engendering life. Moreover, we are in the midst of a

serious conflict between the forces of life and the death-dealing powers of darkness. The dialogue indeed here is not something referring simply to intellectual discussion, rather relating to the realm of praxis.[32]

Theology, faith-seeking understanding, should be consistent with the faith praxis which enters into every dimension of God's salvafic action, including cultural, social, and historical. The dialogical inter-dependence of the literary-critical, the historical-critical and the social-scientific, is the ideal each offering and receiving correctives at each level. The truth is attained in a self-correcting, mutually enriching process of theological conversation.[33] Dialogue in theology is not simply a clarification of the knowledge of faith but a movement: "Dialogue is open-ended and it leads us into the depths of the mystery, to understand which we need to be in continuous journey with others. For, dialogue is not simply a means to achieve something. Every dialogue has mystery as its horizon. Silence is at the heart of all true dialogue. It is that which enables us to encounter in a deep spiritual manner the reality before which we stand and with which we interact. It is in silence that our words in theology acquire their power and energy, meaning and direction. This silence we refer to as the experience of God, and it is the origin of all our words. Silence reflects more closely than words, the ultimate mystery.[34]

Thus, the path of theology is not one which leads from faith to clarity of knowledge, but rather a movement from faith to its realisation in life through dialogue.[35] As a methodology, dialogue in the pluralistic situation, is the heart of theology which is based on the conviction that God is in dialogue with humanity and the world. It is important to understand that the starting point is the present day experiences where God discloses Himself in history.

Dialogue and Hermeneutics

Lack of rootedness in the human experience of the people and culture has precipitated a crisis in theology and interpretation. Culture that mediates God's presence is in the language of its people. The self-communication through the word in language is appropriated through interpretation. Hermeneutics deals with the interpretation of texts or of events gathered up in language. Painadath explains: "Hermeneutics is the way of understanding reality by interpreting the language through which the perception of reality in a particular context is communicated to another context. The experience of reality is communicated through *the word*: through symbols and scriptures, myths and folklore, ordinances and orientations, etc. Language is a primary medium of this self-communication of the author, which can be a person or a community."[36] In hermeneutics, as it is done in theology, it is very important to understand the dynamics and role of language, culture etc. Language, the primary medium of communication, is very much connected with the events taking place. It crystallizes and codifies the experiences of events into texts, which seek interpretation. Painadath goes on to explain:

> That through which a specific experience of reality is communicated may be called a **text**. The text evolves out of the experience of the author and hence the text is his/her progeny. It somehow embodies the spirit of the author. It is a living reality. As a living reality the text has to be approached and understood, respected and interpreted. Encounter with a text is encounter with the author in his/her context; however this encounter takes place in a new context which opens new possibilities of understanding in fresh horizons of perception.[37]

Standing within the Judeo-Christian Tradition which has received so many historical incarnations, we believe that a substantially identical Christian message can find expression in a plurality of embodiments corresponding to the new contexts of our contemporary world.[38] A hermeneutical reading of the text means, reading through the glasses of the reader's concerns. Simple as this may sound, it refers to a fourfold movement: (1) A new experience of reality (2) renders us suspicious of our understanding of reality; (3) this in its turn makes us suspicious of the way we go about the Bible; (4) Out of this emerges the attempt to re-interpret the Bible.[39] The pluri-dimensional aspect of the Indian reality and the mutuality between its different dimensions conceived in doing theology, envisaged in a dialogic dynamics, follow an ongoing hermeneutical movement. At the same time the interpretation process is not done from a neutral stand: there is a conscious bias in favour of the subalterns, the victims of the oppression. The method in use could be the explorative cultural analyses and interpretation done from a countercultural perspective. Both analysis and interpretation cannot be understood as two separate activities or functions distinguished in time and place, but as two aspects of a process of theologising and hermeneutics.

Hermeneutics is a re-reading based on a given concrete situation.[40] It is a participation in the creative process of the spirit, which demands a threefold dialogue:

> This creative exploration demands a threefold dialogue: (i) Dialogue between the reader and the author on the basis of the text. In this dialogue the original context of the author confronts the new context of the reader. There is a fusion of horizons taking place in this process. (ii) Dialogue among the readers, each interpreting the text in a specific context. The diverse perceptions of the readers interact in a critical and creative way so that the depth of the meaning is probed into and the relevance of the message is explored. Such a dialogue is the only way to safeguard the interpretation from manipulating the text by one or the other reader. (iii) Dialogue between the reader and the heritage of interpretation. The one who interprets, especially in the case of interpreting texts of faith experience, is part of a community (space) and heir of a heritage (time).[41]

There is no definitive singular interpretation. Interpretation has to convey meaning and meaning may be different in changed situations, in different cultures and traditions and in different periods in history. Text and interpretation belong together and understanding is seen to be linguistic. Painadath explains: "Being that can be understood is language. Language is not a mere speaking box; it is neither purely objective nor subjective. Language is a relational reality. It binds subject with the object and communicates depth to depth...... there is no hermeneutics without language and no language without hermeneutics. Language and interpretation coalesce in hermeneutics."[42] Theologising in India has to be in the Indian language as the language is the living expression of the culture of a people, which constitutes the understanding process. The concerns which will prompt an Indian reading will be those shaped by the basic orientation which underlined India's cultural pluriformity and which has led to a characteristically Indian way of experiencing reality which is (1) inclusive rather than exclusive (2) cosmocentric rather than anthropocentric (3) symbolic rather than empirical and (4) religious rather than academic.[43] But the liguisticality of understanding transcends the limits of any particular language and it explains the capacity of the language to say many things at one time and to have plurality of interpretations:

> It is the concrete use of the language in conversation that promotes the horizon of understanding, which thus emerges as transsubjective and dialogical. As dialogue, language is not the possession of the participant but the medium of understanding. Insight is possible in conversation because words, due to their relationality to the whole of being, have around them a "circle of the unexpressed", drawing the partners into the "infinity of the unsaid".[44]

At times we come to know that an insight has dawned in on us; at other times that our interpretations and theological discourses are distorted either as a justification of our own privilege, or as a reinforcement of our oppression. In a limited way we know that we have internalised structures of marginalisation either as oppressor or as oppressed. At the moment of insight we realize real changes are taking place in the very process of understanding. It is not simply the acquisition of more information or a mere clarification that is taking place between partners of dialogue with roughly equivalent perspectives. O'Brien says: "We experience, in short, that it [interpretation understood as dialogue between partners] is a therapeutic experience - whether structured or not – that involves a moment of vulnerability or liminality, during which we gain a precious insight into the psychological roots of our discourse and consequently its distortedness."[45] The integral and dialogical character of this process is basic to the way of doing theology and interpretation. We look for a privileged perspective for our theology and interpretation which views the socio-cultural reality from the standpoint of the marginalized in all realms of life. We evolve this perspective by entering into and dialoguing with other perspectives, which will contribute to a mutual correction and enrichment, creating conditions for the therapeutic function of the theological enterprise. This dialogal approach helps to discover in theology the partial rootedness in and relatedness to structures of oppression leading to a new methodological self-awareness capable of effecting counter-theologies and counter-ideologies. The dialogal approach aims at a conversion among the partners so as to bring about transformation and change in society.

Conclusion

We do theology today, keeping in mind that we are doing it in a particular situation, the Indian context, of its many poor, many cultures, many religions and many castes. We are called to interpret the meaning and exigencies of Christian faith viewing the socio-cultural reality from the stand point of the poor, identifying ourselves with their struggles. This gives theology a privileged interpretative perspective, which is always in dialogue with other perspectives. It does so because of the ability this perspective has to create conditions for other theologies to enter into dialogue with and discover their partial rootedness in, and relatedness to, structures of oppression, leading to a new methodological awareness for theology. The closeness of the subalterns to nature and their community sense will enable them to vibrate with the divine and respond to its call to fashion anew the world, society and culture, assuring better conditions for living in freedom, justice and love.

A community which embodies the *Abba* experience of Jesus will have the characteristics of radical freedom, radical universalism, radical sharing, radical service and radical equality. [46] This is because human beings are not perceived in isolation, but situated in the social milieu of their family and caste, and even humankind is understood to be part of the whole cosmos (the world as the body of God). Such an approach is holistic inclusive, integral and dialogal, and this is really the Indian way of thinking. As the holistic Indian mind has the passion for wholeness, it "thinks dialectically, is tolerant of ambiguity, and is able to hold together seemingly contradictory aspects of reality as complementary parts of a never fully to be apprehended whole."[47] This approach is needed to enter into the Indian world-view, which insists on the interrelatedness of everything and a cosmic wholeness, avoiding any sort of dichotomy. This integral and dialogal approach is basic for doing theology and interpretation in India, if it wants to meet the test of relevancy.

God acts in history, and this action finds manifold expressions in culture as the Spirit recreates the face of the broken earth. The theologian or the interpreter, if he/she wants to be relevant and adequate to the actual context responsive to its challenges, must discern the divine dynamics and take into account life-threatening and life promoting concerns of the people seriously. This spiritual empowerment with a new value system to commit oneself by way of dialogue in a plural world helps us to work for the establishment of a new society in the style of divine reign.

Endnotes

[1] Felix Wilfred, *On the Banks of Ganges,* Delhi: ISPCK, 2002, 2.

[2] Felix Wilfred, *On the Banks of Ganges,* Delhi: ISPCK, 2002, 3.

[3] Ibid, 4-5.

[4] Clodovis Boff, "Theological Methodologies", *Dictionary of Third World Theologies,* Virginia Fabella MM &R.S. Sugirtharajah (eds), New York: Orbis Books, 2000, 197.

[5] Soares Prabhu, "Indian Church Challenged by Poverty and Caste" in Isaac P. (ed), *Biblical Themes for a Contextual Theology Today,* Pune: JDV, 1999, 143.

[6] J. Constatine Manalel, "Original Vision of Indian Theological Association" in Theologising in the Context, Jacob Parappilly (ed), Bangalore: Dharmaram Publications, 2002, 6.

[7] M. Amaladoss, T.K. John &G. Gispert Sauch (eds), *Theologising in India,* Bangalore: TPI, 1981, 18.

[8] George Pattery, "Inculturation And/Or Liberation", *EAPR,* 30(1993) 3&4, 317.

[9] Ibid, 317-318.

[10] De Mesa, Jose M., & Wostyn Lode L., *Doing Theology,* Philippines: Claretian Publications, 1990, 17 ff.

[11] Virginia Fabella& R. S. Sugirtharaja(eds), *Dictionary of Third World Theologies*, Clodovis Boff, "Theological Methodologies", New York: Orbis Books, 2000, 197.

[12] J. M. De Mesa & Lode L.. Wostyn, *Doing Theology*,Quezon City: Claretian Pub., 1990, 3.

[13] R. Latourelle and R. Fisichella (eds.), *Dictionary of Fundamental Theology*, New York: Crossroad, 1994, 1098.

[14] R. O. Costa (ed), *One Faith, Many Cultures*, New York: Orbis Books, 1988, xii.

[15] Rudolf Heredia, "Subaltern Interrogations of Hindu Nationalism. Need for a New Hermeneutic (1)", *Vidyajyoti*, 66, 10(2002), …, 821.

[16] Felix Wilfred, *Leave the Temple: Indian Path to Human Liberation*, New York: Orbis Books, 1992, 5.

[17] Laurance Culas, "The Message of Hope to a World in Crisis, Statement of the annual Conference of CBAI, 2017, *Vidyajyoti*, 82(2018), 66.

[18] S. Kappen, *Jesus and Culture*, Delhi: ISPCK, 2002, 40.

[19] Cf. J.N. Farquhar, *Modern Religious Movements in India*, New York: Macmillan, 1967; M.S.A. Rao (ed.), *Social Movements in India*, 2 Vols., Delhi: Manohar Publications, 1978,1979.

[20] George Soares-Prabhu, "Antigreed and Antipride", in Isaac Padinjarekuttu (ed.), *Biblical Themes for a Contextual Theology*, Pune: JDV, 1999, 256.

[21] Felix Wilfred, "On the Threshold of the 1990's: Emerging Trends and Socio-cultural Processes at the Turn of the Century", *Jeevadhara*, XX(115), 1990, 61-62.

[22] Felix Wilfred, "On the threshold of the 1990s:..", 63.

[23] Donal Dorr, *Mission in Today's World*, New York: Orbis Books, 2000, 93.

[24] Simon Sebastian, "Inculturation as a Dialogue with the Poor", *Vidyajyoti*, Vol. 65, No. 6, 2001, 418.

[25] Sebastian Painadath, "Hermeneutics in Indian Theology, *Vidyajyoti*, Vol 62, No. 5,1998, 306.

[26] Felix Wilfred, "On the Threshhold of 1990s:...., 66.

[27] P. Puthanangady, "Which Culture for Inculturation: The Dominant or the Popular", *EAPR,* 30(1993), 306.

[28] A. Thumma, *Voices of the Victims*, Delhi: ISPCK, 1999, 11.

[29] Sebastian Painadath, "Hermeneutics in Indian Theology", *Vidyajyoti*, Vol 62, No. 5, 1998, 303.

[30] Raymond Panikkar, "The Power of Words" in Francis D'Sa (ed.), *The Dharma of Jesus*, Pune: Institute of Study of Religion, 1997, 411.

[31] John Paul II, *Ecclesia in Africa: Post Synodal Apostolic Exhortation of Holy Father*, Nairobi: Pauline, 1995, 45.

[32] Felix Wilfred, *Leave the Temple:*..... 4-5.

[33] John O'Brien, *Theology and the Option for the poor*, Minnesota: Liturgical Press, 1992, 56.

[34] Felix Wilfred, *On the Banks of Ganges*, Delhi: ISPCK, 2002, 16.

[35] Felix Wilfred, *On the Banks...*, 9.

[36] Sebastian Painadath, "Hermeneutics in Indian...", 309.

[37] Ibid.

[38] J. M. De Mesa & Lode L.. Wostyn, *Doing Theology*,Quezon City: Claretian Pub., 1990, 18.

[39] Francis X D'Sa, *Theology of Liberation: An Indian Biblical Perspective*, Pune: JDV Theology Series, xiv.

[40] John Sobrino, *Christology at the Crossroads*, London: SCM Press, 1978, 397.

[41] Sebastian Painadath, "Hermeneutics in Indian.....", 310-311.

[42] Ibid, 312.

[43] George Soares-Prabhu, "Interpreting Bible Today" in Francis D'Sa (ed), *Theology of Liberation: An Indian Biblical Perspective*, Pune:JDV, 2001, 9.

[44] John O'Brien, *Theology and the Option...*, 139.

[45] John O'Brien, *Theology and the Option....*, 136.

[46] George Soares-Prabhu, "Antigreed and Antipride", 243-247.

[47] George Soares-Prabhu, "Interpreting the Bible in India Today", in Francis X. D'Sa (ed.), *Theology of Liberation: An Indian Biblical Perspective*, Pune: JDV, 2001, 9.

Silver Lines on Samanvaya in Rishikesh

Davis Varayilan

As Samanvaya Vidya Dham celebrates the silver jubilee of its existence in Rishikesh, it has all the right to be grateful, joyful and hopeful. I wish Samanvaya to turn the silver into gold not just by being part of the history but by making history through its empowering presence, contextualization of theology and contributions to the Church and society. Looking back to 25 years of its existence and remembering people who have contributed for its birth and growth with gratitude is the greatest tribute we could pay to those who have gone before us and those who are carrying on in a commendable way what was bequeathed to them. History is in fact the backbone of any social institution to survive adverse situations and to flourish with new vigour and to bring out the hidden dynamics of an initial movement. History has to be interpreted from the point of view of God because the course of events in history is directed by God. This article is organized into three parts from a historical perspective: the birth, development the impact of Samanvaya in Rishikesh.

BIRTH OF SAMANVAYA IN RISHIKESH

Several deliberations and studies have gone through before the birth of Samanvaya. The deliberations primarily focused on the experimentation of theological formation already in context, the contextual realties of massive poverty and religious pluralism and the suitable places and methods of theological education and formation.

Theological Formation in Context

The Second Vatican Council came as a game changer in the understanding of priesthood, priestly ministry and priestly formation and opened the way for theological formation in context. Drawing inspiration from Vatican II Asian bishops clearly affirmed that "Seminarians and religious in formation should not be taken out of their cultural environment, but be in continual contact with their living traditions. Formation is not so much information about the past but an introduction into new possibilities for the future."[2] Ever since Vatican II, there have been concerted efforts taken by different seminaries in India to contextualize the content and method of theological education. The changing cultural, social and religious scenario of contemporary India, marked by acute awareness of the multi-religious experiences, awakening of the subaltern groups and the increasing influence of globalized world and media thrust upon seminaries to respond to them creatively by contextualizing the theological formation and revamping the existing paradigms of theological education. Thus Catholic Bishops Conference of India in its *Charter of Priestly Formation for India* emphasized the importance of having the formation of priests in the region, in the language and life style of the people and in small groups to receive personal attention and guidance, develop their character and be built up in team work and communion with others. It states, "Without prejudice to its "all India" dimension, priestly formation, as far as possible, must be done in the region and among the people for whom the seminarian is going to work and in the language of that people. This will make it possible for the seminarians to be thoroughly educated in the culture of the people of the region of his future ministry. The programme of priestly formation will, therefore, make its concern to respond more adequately to the joys and hopes, the griefs and anxieties of the people of the diocese or region for whom the seminarians are being prepared (3.1.6).

Syro-Malabar Major Archepiscopal Curia, 2007 in its *Charter of Priestly Formation in the Syro-Malabar Church* has underlined the need for the seminarians to have sufficient knowledge of the religious tenets of the believers of other religions and acquaintance with their practices to exercise the ministry of shepherding the flock (47), to inculturate theological categories, art forms, architecture, liturgical celebration, music, festivals, etc. for the people to feel at home with their fellow-citizens (48-49) and to give the seminarians sufficient exposure to mission realities, especially northern India (50).

At the emergence of various eparchies of the Syro Malabar Church in central and north India, five of them having been entrusted to the Carmelites of Mary Immaculate, the pioneering missionaries became convinced that the pluralistic situation of India, especially of North India, made it imperative that the candidates should be introduced well into the languages and cultures of the peoples of the respective regions which demanded them to have the formation of the future missionaries in the mission territories. This was the beginning of a new epoch in the formation programme in the congregation. It was from this fundamental missionary context and thrust in North India that the unfolding of the formation programme of the CMIs in the missions commenced and flourished.

In *"Our Vision: CMIs towards the Third Millennium,* General Synaxis of 1990-91 stressed the importance of an action-oriented and contextualised theology and training programme in the context of our congregation's growing involvement in the missions and the socio-cultural and multi-religious challenges we encounter today. "This calls for mission-oriented Theologates which the participation of competent people with field experience in different areas related to actual mission life and action. (p. 7). After several deliberations at various levels and study reports, the General Synaxis (XXXIII) in its third session in 1991 approved the proposal to establish a Regional Mission Theologate and informed the Congregation by Fr Thomas Mampra, then Prior General in his circular no. PG/CIR/No.08/93 dated 12-10-1993. Samanvaya

Theology College, Bhopal along with its Regional Centres is evolved and established as a fitting and timely response to the challenges encountered by the CMI missionaries in the evangelising mission of the Church in North India.

Samanvaya Theological Formation in Rishikesh

Responding to the signs of the times and according to the decision of the General Synaxis, the north Indian mission provinces launched Regional Mission Theologate in 1994 and christened it as "Samanvaya," which means "integration," integration of learning with doing theology, faith with life and personal development with community's mission. Its vision, thrusts and method is an outcome of the several deliberations and studies on the basis of the experiences of CMI missionaries in various parts of the country in the past decades and similar experimentations in other Regional Theologates.

To prepare the future religious missionary priests, Samanvaya chose two major contexts of India, namely, Tribal-rural context of Chattisgarh in Jagdalpur and religiously pluralistic context of north India in Rishikesh for theologization and for the integration of these contexts in evangelization and pastoral ministry, it chose the rural pastoral context of Bhopal and urban pastoral context of Bangalore. Accordingly the main thrusts of the years were set as God and the World for the first year, Christ and Human for the second year and Spirit and the Church for the third year.[3] This way of contextualized theological formation of Samanvaya is conceived as a movement that is dynamic, person-oriented, context-sensitive and experience-based. The outcomes expected of the students are faithful stewards of the people and nature, obedient servants of the Kingdom of God and good shepherds of the flock.

The second year of theology is conducted in the inter-religious context of Rishikesh because we are living in times when we witness religious pluralism as an undeniable fact and irreversible norm of today's global family. Moreover, India is the cradle of the world's major religions and the birthplace of many spiritual traditions. The plurality of religions is natural for the people of India where each one seeks out to know, engage and build relationships with the neighbours of another faith. It is also rooted in a tradition, which has approached the religious experience of other religions with respect and with a sense of sacred.

Religion is a force that has unifying and divisive powers. The unifying elements of religion promote peace, build up human community and foster fellowship while divisive tendency indulges in fighting, devalues the diversity and generates violence. Religion is a powerful force that influences the world-view, decisions and interpretation of Indian society. Therefore, Asian bishops suggest: "Diversity is not something to be regretted and abolished, but to be rejoiced over and promoted, since it represents richness and strength."[4]

The relevance of Christianity in the world of religious pluralism depends on how far it is open to journey with the followers of other religions. It is the clarion call for the Christians to shed their prejudices and recognize the presence and work of the Spirit in other religions and develop a culture of dialogue which will be the unique contribution of the Indian Church towards the Universal Church. St. John Paul says, "Contact, dialogue and cooperation with the followers of other religions is a task which the Second Vatican Council bequeathed to the whole Church as a duty and a challenge" (*Ecclesia in Asia*, 31).

Context of Rishikesh

Rishikesh is chosen as one of the three Regional Centres of Samanvaya Theology College because it is known as the sanctuary of great sages and saints and its surrounding areas are conducive for God-experience and serious theological reflection and learning from an inter-religious perspective. What makes the context unique is the increasing number of pilgrims coming both from India and abroad seeking spiritual experience and guidance.

Samanvaya is located in the foothills of lower Himalayan ranges and a walking distance to holy river Ganges, temples, hermitages and ashrams in Rishikesh. Rishikesh, literally means Lord of the senses, stands for Lord Vishnu. The root form of the name Rishikesh is *rsikesa,* the Lord of the senses, a name attributed to Lord Krishna (Bhagavat Gita 1, 21). Raibhyamuni performed austerities on the banks of river Ganga and conquered his senses and obtained the vision of the Lord. The place where performed his tapas was known as Hrsikesa because he became the Lord of his senses and obtained the vision of the Lord.[5]

Geographically, Samanvaya is located at an altitude of 360 metres in the Tehri-Garhwal region of Uttarakhand. The whole area of Rishikesh comes under four districts – Tehri-Garhwal, Pauri-Garhwal, Haridwar and Dehradun. Ecclesiastically, the first two districts belong to the Diocese of Bijnor which is entrusted to the CMI congregation. The Dehradun and Haridwar districts belong to the diocese of Meerut. The first Catholic presence in this area was Swami Abhishiktananda, a French monk, who reached in October 1968 and settled in a small *kutiya* at Gyansu (a kilometre away from Uttarkashi) followed by Vandana Mataji who came in 1977 and established Jeevandhara Kutir. The diocese of Bijnor bought the land in 1980 and established a mission station in 1982.

The context in which we live can deeply influence and radically change our outlook towards other religions. It can have a sacramental power to lead us to the Transcendental Mystery. Rishikesh, situated on the banks of the Ganges and surrounded by Himalayan ranges, is known from medieval times as the celestial abode. It is one of the gateways to the *Chār Dhām*: Gangotri, Yamunotri, Kedarnath and Badrinath. Therefore, it is considered to be a base for devotees on their journey to the *Char Dham Yatra*. The beauty of the surrounding scenery along with the holiness of the river Ganges makes Rishikesh a truly unique place. From ancient times onwards, sages used to retire into the forests of Rishikesh for prayer, meditation and spiritual practices. *Sannyāsins, sādhus, sādhakas, gurus* and pilgrims populate the place. Hymns, chants, *bhajans, kīrtans, mantras* and the sound of the bells reverberate everywhere in Rishikesh. The flowing river Ganges and the thick forests of Himalayan ranges energize the atmosphere. *Āśram*s, temples, hermitages and shops of religious articles occupy the locality.

Rishikesh vibrates with the peaceful energy created by all these elements. Coming to Rishikesh one experiences a special energy, inspiration and a disposition to mental silence. It is this spiritual vibration that attracts thousands of people to visit Rishikesh frequently.

Haridwar and Rishikesh are considered important places of pilgrimage. *Sādhus and sannyāsins* give spiritual life to the pilgrims who go to these holy places. Although some may put on saffron robes for worldly motive, there is no doubt that many of them are genuine seekers after the truth, who have cut off their relationship with the relatives and family members and lead a life of contemplation. Genuine *sannyāsins* and *sādhus* think beyond religion and caste and welcome anyone who is a genuine seeker of God. Rishkesh is renowned for numerous Yoga centers, and perfectly termed as the World Capital of Yoga, which offers training of Yoga and meditation. There are many water sports activities like rafting and adventurous activities like wild forest trekking that have attracted number of tourists to Rishikesh.

DEVELOPMENT OF SAMANVAYA

The development of Samanvaya could be seen in two periods: Samanvaya at Prithvipal Sadan from 1995-2008 and Samanvaya Vidya Dham at Tapovan from 2009-2019.

Samanvaya Mission Theologate at Prithvipal Sadan (1995-2008)

Prithvipal Sadan is one of the parishes of the diocese of Bijnor. It consists of a priest house, guest house and a Church with basement. It is located on the way to Laxman Jhula and a cluster of temples which are frequented by Hindu pilgrims. The six bheega land of Prithvipal Sadan was purchased by Fr. George Edathiparambil CMI on February 29, 1980 and registered at Devprayag Tahasil on August 11, 1980. He started staying in a rented building at Dehradun road and celebrated first Holy Eucharist for the people in Rishikesh on Sunday June 8,1980. The foundation stone of Priest House (Prithvipal Sadan) was laid on 27th July, 1980 was blessed by Mar Gratian Mundadan CMI on 7th February, 1982.

The first batch of nine students along with their Master Fr Prsanna Bhai accompanied by Fr Jose Chittooparambil, the dean arrived at Prithvipal Sadan for the first semester of the second year of theology at Rishikesh on July 3, 1995. Prithvipal Sadan housed Samanvaya for 13 years from 1995 to 2008. At that time the campus already had a guest house besides the Priest house. The brothers used the guest house for their stay, classes and meals. When the Church was built in 2003, a basement with a class room, hall and a guest room was added to it for the use of Samanvaya. Thanks to the thoughtfulness and concern of Bishop Gratian Mundadan.

The students of the first batch were: Kallookaran Jaison, 2. Karamel Xavier, 3. Kizhakkekara Noble, 4. Kuttiyanickal Cyril, 5. Moolayil George, 6. Muringathuparambil Francis, 7. Peedikathadathil Joseph, 8. Vadakkinezhath George and 9. Vazhappilly Denny. During the period of 1995 to 2008 there were 14 batches of students and 7 masters, namely, 1. Prasanna Bhai (1995-1998), 2. Davis Varayilan (1999), 3. Paul Vithayathil (2000), 4. Sebastian Elavathingal (2001), 5. Jose Chittooparambil (2002), 6. Sebastian Elavathingal (2003), 7. Antony Kalliyath (2004), Josin Kaithakulam (2005), Davis Varayilan (2006-2008). The parish priests of Prithvipal Sadan who supported and associated with Samanvaya staff were: 1. Fr. Varghese Koikara, 2. Fr. Peter Vallikavunkal, 3. Fr Varghese Kottoor, 4. Fr. Jose Chittooparambil 5. Fr. Jose Elamthuruthiyil, and 6. Fr. George Kachappily.

Samanvaya was well begun in Rishikesh with Fr Prasanna Bhai who was very much oriented towards inculturation and living in an Indian way. He could easily immerse himself in the context of Rishikesh because of his lifestyle, pleasing personality and knowledge of Sanskrit and Indian philosophy. He had to go through the initial struggles from within and without but he did give a momentum to Samanvaya way of life through his efforts to inculturate Samanvaya in the context of Rishikesh by introducing yoga, arati, Indian meditation, pilgrimage to holy places, and regular visits to the ashrams and meeting the pilgrims, etc.

Structural Development of Samanvaya

Samanvaya started as a movement but the steady increase of the number of students and for the effectiveness of Samanvaya formation, the staff members felt the need to have structure of its own. The platform in which they raised the need for structural development was the Samanvaya Managing Council (SMC) which was constituted in 2003 for the effectiveness of the formation given to the students of second year theology in Rishikesh and for the understanding and cooperation among Samanvaya, the Diocese of Bijnor and St. John's Province, Bijnor. The members of the SMC are Bishop of Bijnor, Provincial of St. John's Province, Rector and administrator of Samanvaya, Master of students at Rishikesh and Parish priest of Prithvipal Sadan. This meeting used to be held once a year when Fr Prior General comes for the canonical visitation. Fr Prior General presides over the meeting and the Master of students of Rishikesh functions as the secretary to the Council.

The thought for having permanent structure for Samanvaya was discussed in SMC and a contract was signed on October 14, 2004 with the diocese of Bijnor to construct a structure in the campus of Prithvipal Sadan when Fr Paul Vithayathil was the rector. According to the contract the structure will be used by Samanvaya for a semester and the rest of the months some courses will be organized by Samanvaya for other people. The plan was almost ready and was in the process of getting permission from the Haridwar Development Authority for which Fr Jose Elamthuruthy CMI, parish priest of Prithvipal Sadan took initiative. But during the Samanvaya Managing Council held at Prithvipal Sadan on August 7, 2006, Fr Davis Varayilan, Master of Students shared his observations in Rishikesh and noted that "the students appear to come here as guests and are not disposed to have a deeper reflection and personalization, since they are here only for a semester. Therefore, he proposed to extend the Samanvaya programme in Rishikesh for the whole year."[6] Rev. Fr Antony Kariyil, then Prior General also agreed with this proposal but asked to have thorough discussion with the staff of Samanvaya and Dharmaram.

The participants of Samanvaya Managing Council of 2006 "expressed concern about the feasibility of developing infrastructure for conducting Samanvaya programme at Prithvipal Sadan, since the atmosphere is not conducive for prayer and study. At that point, the Bishop spoke about the possibility of considering an option in which the land earmarked for the hermitages might be given for the use of Samanvaya after due consultations, provided the structures built there are used for the whole year." "He made it clear that if this plan is realized, the infrastructure built there would be managed by Samanvaya and the existing contract about the arrangement at Prithvipal Sadan would stand cancelled."[7]

Fr Prior General concluded the Council meeting by directing Fr Sebastian Elvathingal, then Rector "to take the necessary steps to make amendments in the Samanvaya programme in Rishikesh: (1) extending the Samanvaya programme in Rishikesh for the whole year, (2) in-depth discussion among the staff of Samanvaya regarding the changes required in the Samanvaya programme in view of this new arrangements in Rishikesh and to report to Fr Prior General, (3) organize another Council meeting if necessary to make amendments, and (4) define the role of Bijnor Province in the new contract."[8]

The staff of Samanvaya Theological College met on September 25, 2006 at Bhopal and discussed the proposal of Samanvaya Managing Council in detail and unanimously passed to conduct two semesters of second year theology in Rishikesh, seeing the present set up, the need and the scope in Rishikesh. This new proposal for Samanvaya, Rishikesh was presented by Fr Davis Varayilan in the Formation Council Meeting held in Bangalore on October 26, 2006 and decided to extend for one year of theology course at Rishikesh. The proposal for extending the training programme at Rishikesh to a full academic year was adopted after due consideration of the salutary benefits that can accrue from such a modification.

The potential areas of having more infrastructure facilities at Rishikesh was also identified and presented in the Formation Council, such as, to start a Centre for Inter-Religious Relations in the same campus for the individuals or groups even from abroad, who are interested in the study, research and experience of inter-religions relations, for the gatherings of the inter-religious nature, and for the field studies by the students of Missiology or Indian Spirituality or similar courses in Dharmaram Vidya Kshetram, Bangalore.

After getting the green signal from Samanvaya staff, General Formation Council and Fr Prior General, a contract between the diocese of Bijnor and CMI congregation was drafted for the use of the property where Samanvaya is now housed. The Samanvaya Managing Council held at Prithvipal Sadan on August 1, 2007 discussed the contract in detail and made necessary changes. It was signed after the Holy Mass in the Church and the signatories in the contract are Bishop Gratian Mundadan CMI and Fr Antony Kariyil CMI, Prior General of the Congregation.

The plot of land where Samanvaya is housed was purchased by Fr Augustine Keemattam CMI for Catholic Diocese of Bijnor from two persons, namely Mr Kumwar Singh Bhandari 40 Nali and 6 Mutti and Sri. Hargopal Aggarwal 18 Nali and 7 Mutti on December 30, 1983 and October 9, 1984 respectively. Later five cottages were constructed in this land and used by the hermits and fathers and sisters who wanted to spend longer time in prayer. According to the agreement the front part of the land from the entrance to water canal excluding four cottages was given to Samanvaya for the construction.

The foundation stone for the new building of Samanvaya was blessed by Mar Gratian Mundadan CMI on March 4, 2008 at Pastoral Centre, Nimbuchaur during the second session of the Provincial Chapter of St. John's Province, Bijnor and laid by Fr Mathew Thenamkalayil, Vicar Provincial of St. John's Province, Bijnor on June 3, 2008. The fund for the construction of the Samanvaya building was a major problem but trusting in the Lord Fr Davis Varayilan signed the contract with Mr. Takur Singh Gusain of Uttarakashi to start the construction work of the Seminary. It all began with seven lakh rupees given from Samanvaya Theological College, Bhopal. God's ways are mysterious.

As the work progressed, Fr Sebastian Elvathingal, then Rector made a memorandum of understanding with the Christ University and they gave 16 lakh rupees through Dharmaram College, Bangalore. Then with the recommendation of Fr Jose Panthaplamthottiyil, then Prior General, Fr Sebastian wrote to all the Provincials of the congregation and 9 provinces responded with their contribution.

The contributions from Samanvaya, Dharmaram, Provincials and other agencies were not sufficient to complete the work. At that moment a request was placed before Bishop Gratian for the loan from the diocese of Bijnor. With the consent of the Finance Committee of the diocese of Bijnor, Bishop Gratian offered 30 lakh rupees interest free loan for three years. Thanks to the diocese of Bijnor for the timely help and Bishop Gratian for his keen interest in the contextualized theological training programme adopted by Samanvaya. He has been instrumental in realizing this dream of Samanvaya Vidya Dham. He has taken personal interest not only in the Samanvaya formation through his creative suggestions and constructive criticism but also in developing the structure of Samanvaya Vidya Dham in Rishikesh in different ways. Thanks to Fr George Kachappilly CMI, the parish priest, for his generous support and cooperation for the construction.

The new Samanvaya building was blessed by Mar Gratian Mundadan CMI and inaugurated by Fr. Jose Panthaplamthottiyil CMI, then Prior General on October 6, 2009 in the presence of General Councillors, former Rectors of Samanvaya, many fathers and sisters from CMI communities and diocese of Bijnor and sadhus and sannyasis and residents of locality. The blessing ceremony was typically Indian style with an inter-religious thrust which was appreciated by all. Three more buildings were added to it with the support of funding agencies and benefactors. The administrative block, Vidya Bhavan, was built with the support of MISSIO, Aachen, the Archdiocese of Cologne and Diocese of Paderborn and blessed by Fr Raymond Mancheril CMI, the first Executive Chairman of Samanvaya Regional Mission Theologate on December 8, 2012. The Dining hall, Bhojanalay was built with the partial contribution of the diocese of Stuttgart and blessed by Fr Davis Varayilan CMI on October 15, 2012. The Namrata kutir with four rooms was built with the generous contributions of Dienytrabe family from Germany through Fr Joy Paul Manjaly CMI and blessed on September 08, 2010.

Samanvaya Vidya Dham at Tapovan

After functioning in the parish at Prithvipal Sadan until 2009, Samanvaya was shifted to its new site christening it as "Samanvaya Vidya Dham." It means the abode of wisdom through integration or an abode of integrated wisdom. Wisdom is the capacity to see life as God sees it. It is a grace from God built out of knowledge and experience. It calls us to act not just with mind but with the heart. From 2009 onwards with shifting of Samanvaya to the new site, the complete second year theology was also shifted to Rishikesh. The usual practice of having the second semester of the second year theology at Dharmaram Vidya Kshetram at Bangalore was shifted to the first semester of third year theology. During the period between 2009-2019, there were 11 batches of students who have gone through complete second year theology in Rishikesh and they were guided by 4 masters, namely, Fr Davis Varayilan (2009-2013), Fr Louis Malieckal (2014), Fr Josin Kaithakulam (2015-2016) and Fr Cyril Kuttiaynickal (2017-) and the animators were Fr Naiju Kalamabukattu, Fr Jose Kizhakkekutt, Fr Joshy Pazhukathara, Fr Cyril Kuttiayanickal, Fr Jose Chittooparambil and Fr Louis Malieckal.

Samanvaya Vidya Dham, the main residence has 21 self-contained rooms for the brothers, 4 rooms for the staff and a chapel, class room and a computer room. Besides the residence there are three more buildings, namely, administrative block with class room, library and a hall; dining hall; and a cottage with four rooms. Samanvaya welcomes guests and anyone who is genuinely seeking God to spent days and weeks. The location of Samanvaya Vidya Dham is very serene and conducive for prayer and study and very convenient to walk to the important places of Rishikesh. It is free from the noises of the street. The prayers and *bhajans* are usually conducted in Hindi and occasionally in English.

Weekly adoration is an integration of life in the context, class room and prayer. Indian motifs and other symbolic rituals such as *arati* are adapted to go along with Indian spiritual ethos. Their profuse use is meant to make the Christian spiritual sensitivity attuned to that of Indian spiritual climate. The life style is simple and the food is vegetarian.

The regular presence of the seminarians at Rishikesh from 2009 has helped to create an atmosphere of understanding and acceptance in the locality where Christian presence used to be looked upon with suspicion due to prejudices and misunderstandings. The seminarians visit the ashrams and hermitages on the banks of the Ganges to communicate with the inmates. The inhabitants of ashrams are always hospitable and in many cases eager to clarify their doubts about the Christian religion. Thus the presence of the seminarians gradually builds up an atmosphere of mutual trust and appreciation removing the traces of suspicion.

The life of Samanvaya students in the inter-religious context of Rishikesh is depicted artistically on three panels in the chapel.[9] It fosters an integral vision of God realization. The paintings are an integration of the Indian spirituality and Christian theology. The symbols used in the chapel have the vibration to resonate with the culture of the land as they explicitly perform a two dimensional task of pointing towards the Reality and elevating the human spirit into the sphere of Experience. The three panels in the chapel proclaim three aspects of the entire life on earth: creation (*Srushti*), sustenance (*Sthiti*) and integration (*Layam*). These panels present the Trinitarian dimension of Christian faith – the Father, the Son and the Holy Spirit. These three persons in the Trinity, though constitute the same Reality, are attributed with different roles in the entire process of life on earth, namely, creation, redemption and sanctification. The creation is depicted through *panchabuta*: ether, air, fire, water and earth. The redemption is portrayed as Jesus sitting in the meditating posture amidst the entire beings of the universe. The source of this representation of Jesus is the Book of Isaiah 11:1-9. Through his self-emptying and self-giving love, Jesus unites all differences in religions and shows the way to the Father. The third panel carries the symbols of Hinduism (*Aum*), Islam (the Crescent), Buddhism (*Darmachakra*), Sikhism (*Khanda*) and Taoism (Yin-yang). The Spirit, the eschatological gift, integrates all the elements and guides the entire creation to journey in harmony as co-pilgrims to the not yet of the Kingdom of God. The artist of these three panels in the chapel was Mr Suresh from Kalady, Kerala who reflected and meditated upon the passage Isaiah 11:1-9 and portrayed in an inculturated way. Thanks to Fr Sebeesh Vettiyadan CMI who designed the tabernacle and the altar.

On entering the Samanvaya Vidya Dham campus at the top of the residential building an artistic piece of Christ squatting on semi *padmasana* holding his right hand in *guru mudra* (symbol of a teacher) is clearly visible as welcoming you. The background canvas is suggestive of a number of religious contextualised thinking currently in vogue in the theological circles. What come first strikingly clear are the symbols of world religions. Along these symbols one will notice a few items used by the people around the area for worship. The unmistakeable message of the emblem specially designed for the Rishikesh unit is that everything that indicates the worshipping of the lord of all is certainly welcome for Christ and men and women of steady consciousness as in *padmasana* – lotus position. This piece of art on the wall is the creative work of Fr Joy Elamkunnapuzha CMI in 2012.

Contextualization of Academic Programme

Samanvaya stands for integration of learning with doing theology, text with context and faith with life. From its inception, Samanvaya has contextualized its theological formation and education. It follows the method of exposure-immersion, experience-reflection, and interpretation-action.[10] The exposures to the context, pilgrimage to holy places, live-in experience of Indian Christian Ashram were there from the beginning. Live-in experience of Hindu Ashram was included part of the academic programme from 1999. It was the choice of the brothers to find out suitable ashrams for the live-in experience. Thus they have lived in the ashrams like Paramarth Niketan, Madubhan

Ashram, Swami Rama Sadhaka Grama, Gita Bhavan, Dayanand Ashram, Chandra Swami's Sadhana Kendra Ashram, Vikas Nagar. Considering the effectiveness and the interest in the brothers who lived in Sadaka Grama, it was decided to send the entire batch to Sadaka Grama for yoga and meditation from 2009. Swami Ved Bharati, the founder and head of Sadaka Grama was very welcoming and generous to accommodate the brothers and conduct Christian meditation and classes on yoga and meditation were taught by renowned teachers in the Ashram. The vibrant presence of Swami Ved Bharati and his Christian meditations conducted for brothers were a source of inspiration for everyone.

The class on Bhagavat Gita and prayer in Vanamali Ashram by Vanamali Mataji was included as part of academic curriculum from the year 2000. A challenging week was given to some batches to experiment and experience the stark realities, creativity, risk and trust in God from 2009. Some of them went for one week trekking to Devprayag, as daily labourer from Rishikesh market, wandering sadhaka in Haridwar, etc. It was unforgettable and enriching experience for them. Sometimes some learned monks are invited to the seminary for spiritual discourses and discussions.

The academic year begins with the orientation to the context and religio-cultural analysis of Rishikesh. This orientation helps the students to begin their life in the context as tourists through meaningful exposure and move towards becoming pilgrims through immersion and finally oriented to become seekers of God experience. The students expose themselves to the context with the curiosity of **tourists** in the evenings to observe the customs and rituals of the place, to engage in conversation with *sādhus, sannyāsins,* hermits and pilgrims both Indian and foreign. Exposure brings the students closer to the contextual realities. The purpose of the exposures is not to diagnose problems in other religions and correct them but to get out of one's prejudices and enlarge our inner world and begin to understand and appreciate the goodness in other religions.[11]

As **pilgrims**, they immerse themselves in the context by participating in the *ārati, bhajans, kirtans, pravachans,* etc. and having one-week live-in experience of Hindu ashrams and night stay in gurudwaras during one week pilgrimage whereby the students are deeply moved by the fervor of worship, the deep devotion and the living faith of the people. The students make pilgrimage to different centres of Hinduism at Haridwar, Neelkanth and Badrinath; Sikkhism at Hemkund and Buddhism at Clement Town, Dehradun. Trekking 48 kilometres in two days to Hemkund and 28 kilometres to Neelkhant in a day is a challenging and enriching experience. The hardships along the way pull them out of their comfort zones and instil confidence in them to take up any challenging task in the future. The exposures to the mission stations of the diocese of Bijnor both in the planes and the hills are an added attraction and experience to the students. The bishop, fathers and sisters of Bijnor diocese and the Provincial and fathers of St. John's Province have been very welcoming and caring.

As part of the immersion programme the students also collaborate with a local NGO called "Clean Himalaya Movement" by spending two hours on Saturdays to pick up the plastic items and keep the town clean. The purpose of the immersion is to provide the students with an experiential knowledge of the other religions and to encourage them to enter into dialogue with the adherents of other religions to learn what the Holy Spirit has "taught others to express in a marvelous variety of ways,"[12] especially, the prominent values and their ways of prayer and worship.

In the second semester, the students move from the outer journey to an inner journey and enter into the depth of the realities around and live as **seekers** (*sādhakas*) to experience God who is present everywhere. Seekers are those who have already set the path for themselves. They search as Christian theologians to find new meanings in their faith and practices. The second year of theology which focuses on Christ and human is meant to facilitate the students to grow in 'configuration to Christ' by entering deep into the contemplation of the person of Jesus

Christ and develop an intimate and personal relationship with him. The more the students grow in Christ, the more they commit themselves to Christ; and it is no longer they who live, but Christ who lives in them (Gal 2:20). The seekers in other religions challenge the students to go beyond the customary routine prayers and practice of religion to experience God.[13] What is expected of the students from these method of moving from tourists to pilgrims to seekers is "to be on fire with the love of Christ and burning with zeal to make him known" (*Ecclesia Asia*, 23).

IMPACT OF SAMANVAYA

In his empirical study on 'Vocation and Formation of Priests and Religious in India', Paul Parathazham mentions that "data from several studies suggest that, in spite of the enormous investment of time, money and personnel, priestly formation in India today fails to deliver the goods, at least quality goods."[14] He distinguishes between the formation provided and the outcome from the same formation and recognizes that the outcome is not satisfactory. If I critically evaluate and compare the opportunities and the exposures provided to the students in Samanvaya and the outcome of the students after their ordination, the result is not up to the expectation. At the same time there are some areas where changes are visible especially in the attitude, sense of responsibility and the capacity to think critically and differently.

The success of Samanvaya formation depends on the openness and receptivity of students and constant accompaniment of the staff. Students who can mould their minds according to the needs of the time will manage change better and will be successful in their life and ministry. Samanvaya provides the context and opportunity for the students to mould themselves but the impact varies depending on their openness to the context and willingness to take up the challenges. The staff members have to work more than the established seminaries to accompany the students constantly and analyse their contextual experiences regularly to enlighten them.

Attitudinal Change

The strength of the Samanvaya formation in Rishikesh is the attitudinal change in the students towards other religions and cultures. The prolonged exposure and constant interaction with the followers of other religions destroys deep-rooted prejudices and helps them enter into the inner world of the "other" and appreciate and appropriate the richness of the other religions into their own spirituality. They begin to experience that plurality is not a threat but richness. They move from rigidity to flexibility. Students learn the art of flexible thinking to apply what they learn to new life situations. They show interest and openness to unlearn and relearn according to the signs of the times. This type of theological formation also enables them to be critical, creative, open, flexible and daring to take risk.

The exposure and immersion enriches, deepens and purifies their own faith and enables them to maximize the divine within them. It helps them to discover at a greater depth certain dimensions of the Divine Mystery and the teachings of Christ that have been communicated less clearly in the Christian tradition like hospitality, renunciation, simplicity, solitude, non-violence, etc. The students' dynamic presence in the context influences the people they encounter, especially in the Ashrams to shed some of their prejudices against Christianity.

Raising questions

"Questions provide the key to unlocking our unlimited potential," writes Tony Robbins, the American motivational speaker. It is not an abundance of answers that makes us creative and grow, but the quality of our questions. Albert Einstein says, "The important thing is not to stop questioning." The exposures and immersion in the unique context of Rishikesh provoke the students to raise new questions in the class which make the class more interactive and participatory. A well-asked question is already half the answer. It also helps the students to develop the skill to ask the right questions. The context challenges them to do what they have never done before or never existed before. George Bernard

Shaw says, "You see things and you say 'Why' ? I dream of things that never were and I ask 'why not'?" The radical changes are brought by the great people by asking the question "why not". Such questions lead to possibility thinking and make them more creative. The radicality of our call is to show the direction for the people by becoming a counter culture in today's society.

The students faced some fundamental and practical questions in the background of their experience in the ashrams with the holy men and women living there. Which is the most effective means to witness the message of Christ today – an institution or a holy charismatic person? Does the Church carry out its mission of radically transforming the society through its numerable institutions? What is the risk of projecting and promoting the individuals with great peoples following? What is the future of Church's mission in India if it continues the institutionalization of its talents and resources both spiritual and material to proclaim the good news?

Sense of Responsibility

The small size of the community in Samanvaya promotes more personal participation, responsibility, freedom and sense of belonging among students as they live, work and study together in different situations. The advantage of small community is informality which permeates the entire spectrum of life in Samanvaya – in the class room, during meals, in the liturgical celebration and in get together. There is a sense of concern for one another and team work. The students are challenged to make responsible choices and decisions in shouldering the household duties. Each one's effort and contribution is necessary for the life of the entire group. If someone fails, the failure cannot go unnoticed. This fact poses a great challenge to the daily decisions and patterns of behaviour one develops in Samanvaya. This sense of responsibility is a great asset as they move out of the seminary. The strong experience of community life in the seminary forms the seminarians to be men of communion, in the model of Trinitarian mystery.

Conclusion

The contextualized theological formation of Samanvaya is the right response to the changing needs of the Church and the context of the present world because there is sufficient flexibility in the system to adapt according to the signs of the times. The purpose of Samanvaya Vidya Dham in Rishikesh, where the main thrust of the academic programme is Christ and human, is to help the students to take Jesus seriously whose spirituality was thoroughly contextual. He read the signs of his times and taught his followers to do the same (Mt 16:3-4). We take Jesus seriously when we begin to read and respond the signs of our times with honesty and sincerity. The twenty first century is moving in the direction of becoming a century of dialogue because of the globalization and the alarming rise of religious fundamentalism, communal violence and terrorist activities in the world. Thus Samanvaya formation is envisaged in the mission for the mission to suit the evangelising mission of the Church engaging in dialogue with the cultures, languages, religions, and socio-economic realities of the land and people.

The context of Rishikesh challenges the students spiritually and theologically. The history of the Church proves that theology has developed when it faced challenges from the society or from the heretics. Facing challenges from outside the seminary, from the contextual realities is absolutely necessary to build up a contextual theology which is the need of the time. This formation programme offers an integrating and integral coaching in the light of the Christian faith, cultural diversity, religious plurality, and the economic poverty which the vast majority of Indians ecounter on a daily basis in their living and learning scenario.

Samanvaya intends not to domesticate the formation to a rigid set of rules and norms that make the students fit only for risk-free and routine tasks and follow the beaten path that perpetuates the status quo in the mission but to encourage the students towards a risk-taking, initiative and creativity so that they can take up creative and risk-involved ministries in the mission. Samanvaya is a courageous step in the field of theological formation.

Endnotes

[1] Louis Malieckal, "Contextualized Theological Education and Mission in India since Vatican II," in *God-Talk in Context: A North Indian Theological Experiment,* ed. Benny Thettayil (Bangalore: Dharmaram Publications, 2016), 50-75.

[2] FABC Office of Evangelization, "Conclusions of the Theological Consultation," 1991, in *For All the Peoples of Asia: Federation of Asian Bishops' Conferences Documents from 1970 to 1991,* Vol.1, eds. Gaudencio B. Rosales and C. G. Arévalo, Quezon City: Claretian Publications, 1992, 20. (Henceforth cited as *FAPA,*1).

[3] Davis Varayilan, "Theology on Wheels: A Movement for Samanvayam," in *Theology on Wheels: A Movement for Contextualized Theological Education,* ed. Davis Varayilan (Delhi: ISPCK, 2011), 11-20.; Davis Varayilan, "Samanvaya in the Inter-religious Context of Rishikesh," in *God-Talk,* 136-37.

[4] Statements of Bishops' Institute of Religious Affairs (BIRA) IV/II, in *FAPA,*1, 321.

[5] Augustine Keemattam, "Rishikesh and Theological Formation," in *Rishikesh and Beyond: Theology in Inter-religious Context,* ed. Davis Varayilan (Bangalore: Dharmaram Publications, 2007), 77.

[6] Report of Samanvaya Managing Council, 2006.

[7] Ibid.

[8] Ibid.

[9] Davis Varayilan, "Samanvaya in Inter-religious Context of Rishikesh," in God-Talk, 145-50.

[10] Davis Varayilan, "Theology on Wheels: A Movement for Samanvayam," in *Theology on Wheels,* 10-11.

[11] Davis Varayilan, ed., *Rishikesh and Beyond: Theology in Inter-religious Context,* Bangalore: Dharmaram Publications, 2008, 11.

[12] FABC II, 35, *FAPA,* 1:35.

[13] Varayilan, *Rishikesh,* 18.

[14] Paul Parathazham, "Vocation and Formation of Priests and Religious in India – An Empirical Study," in *Shaping Tomorrow's Church,* ed., Kurien Kunnumpuram, (Mumbai: St. Paul Press, 2006), 15.

Part Two

Christology, Soteriology and Scripture

Samaritans, Gentiles and Women in the Vision of Jesus According to Luke

George Kaniarakath

Introduction

"I am bringing you good news of great joy for all the people; to you is born this day in the city of David a Saviour, who is the Messiah, the Lord" (Lk 2: 10-11). And a multitude of angels sang: "Glory to God in the highest heaven, and on earth peace among those whom he favours" (Lk 2:14).This is how the third Gospel, known after Luke introduces the universal salvific mission of Jesus the Saviour, *Yeshua* (Heb). Of course, there is reference to the Messiah and David which are all part of the inevitable consequence of his incarnation or becoming man and inserting himself in human history.[1] In his birth he is limited and tied up to a Jewish family and its history; which of course was providential in the divine plan of human salvation; but in his mission, he is beyond all frontiers as declared about him also by the righteous and devout elderly Simon when as a child, Jesus was presented in the temple: "a light for revelation to the nations" (Lk 2:332). It becomes evident also in the theological presentation of the Genealogy of Jesus presented by Luke (3:23-38), which culminates with the statement, "Son of Seth, son of Adam, son of Enos, son of Adam, son of God" (3:38). This is to be seen in contrast to the Matthean presentation (1:2-16) which begins with Abraham and concludes with "Jacob the father of Joseph the husband of Mary, of whom Jesus was born, who is called the Messiah" (1:16).

In this essay, we analyse the relevant Lucan texts to find out the attitude of Jesus toward the Samaritans, people of other cultures and women. It is highly relevant in the Samanvayan way of reading, understanding, and interpreting the history of salvation in a wider and more realistic perspective, in a world of religious and cultural pluralism. Of course, Jesus is *the* Saviour of all and in this perspective we look at the unity in diversity found in the world reality. In this essay we deliberate on Samaritans, Gentiles, or better, people of other persuasions and Women.

Who are the Samaritans?

The name 'Samaritans' is from the Hebrew name '*Shomerim*' which means guardians/Keepers/Watchers (of the Law/Torah)" which was given by God through Moses. Ethno-religiously, they are Israelites or Hebrews living mainly in the area of Samaria and so known as '*Shamerim*' (Samaritans), who consider themselves as descending from the tribes of Ephraim and Manasseh who were sons of Joseph and who survived the destruction of the Northern Kingdom of Israel (Samaria) by the Assyrians in 722 BCE. The Samaritans claim that they are the true Israel who are descendants of the "Ten Lost Tribes" taken into Assyrian captivity. When the Assyrians captured the northern kingdom of Israel, some were taken into captivity while others who were left behind intermarried with the Assyrians and thus became half-Jews and half-Gentiles; thus neither fully Hebrews nor fully Gentiles. Their tradition of worship is based on the Samaritan Pentateuch which, they claim, was the original and that the Jews had a falsified text produced by Ezra during the Babylonian exile. They believe that their religion and worship, based on the Samaritan Pentateuch (Jer 41:5) is the true religion of the ancient Israelites from before the Babylonian captivity preserved by those who remained in the Land of Israel. They also believe that Mount Gerizim was the original Holy Place of Israel from the time of Joshua's conquest of Canaan. According to the Samaritans, it was on Mount Gerizim that Abraham was commanded by God to offer Isaac, his son, as a sacrifice. The Torah mentions the place where God 'chooses to establish his name' (Deut 12:5) and Judaism applies it to Jerusalem. However, the Samaritan text speaks of the place where God *has chosen* to establish his name, and identify it as Mount Gerizim, making it the focus of their life of faith (Jn 4: 20-21). They claim to have continuously occupied their ancient territory and to have been at peace with other Israelite tribes until the time when Eli disrupted the Northern cult by moving it from Shechem to Shiloh. For the Samaritans, this was the great «schism.» The Deuteronomic history, written in Judah, portrayed Israel as a sinful kingdom, divinely punished for its idolatry and iniquity by being destroyed by the Assyrians.In Chronicles 36:22–23 we read that the Persian emperor, Cyrus the great (559–530 BCE), permitted the return of the exiles to their homeland and ordered the rebuilding of the Temple (Zion). According to the Jews, the inhabitants worshiped other gods and that resulted in a syncretistic religion, in which they accepted the Israelite God and other gods and the Samaritans followed it. Hence they were considered heretical and schismatic and spurious worshippers of Yahweh, the true God of and detested even more than pagans.[2] Ezra 4 says that the local inhabitants of the land, including the Samaritans, offered to assist with the building of the new Temple during the time of Zerubabel. When the Jews were rebuilding Jerusalem (after the Babylonian captivity (606-536 B.C.), the Samaritans offered their services. They were summarily rebuffed (Ezra 4:1-3) and the Samaritans responded in kind (Ezra 4:4ff). The Jewish historian Flavius Josephus describes the Samaritans as idolaters and hypocrites.[3]

Among the Hebrews, there had always been a division between the north and the south. After David and Solomon there arose sectionalism that led to the division of the kingdom .The division caused the Judeans rejecting the offer made by the Samaritans to jointly rebuild the temple in Jerusalem.

According to the Samaritans there is one God, *Yahweh*, the same God accepted also by the Hebrew prophets. The Torah was given by God to Moses on Mount Gerizim which is the genuine sanctuary; Jerusalem is not the one true sanctuary chosen by Israel's God. Many Samaritans believe that at the end of days, the dead will be resurrected by the Taheb, a restorer (possibly a prophet, some say Moses). There is Resurrection and Paradise (heaven).The priests are the interpreters of the law and the keepers of tradition; scholars are secondary to the priesthood. They have a different version of the Ten Commandments (the 10th is about the sanctity of Gerizim).

The Samaritan Pentateuch differs from the Jewish Masoretic Text; one is doctrinal as the Samaritan Torah explicitly states that Mount Gerizim is "the place that God *has chosen*" to establish his name, as opposed to the Jewish Torah that refers to "the place that God *chooses*". Other differences are minor and seem more or less accidental. There are some 6,000 differences between the Samaritan Pentateuch and the Masoretic text; some see some 1,900 points of agreement between it and the Greek LXX version. Several passages in the ST would also appear to echo a Torah textual tradition not dissimilar to that is seen in the Samaritan text.

Jesus' Approach to the Samaritans in the in the Second Testament

In Mark, Matthew and John

In the Second Testament, the first written gospel according to Mark does not mention the Samaritans. According to Matthew, when instructing his disciples concerning the proclamation of the word, Jesus tells them not to visit any Gentile or Samaritan city, but instead, go to the "lost sheep of Israel (10:5; 15: 24), which was only a temporary adjustment (Mt 28:19), is absent in the corresponding Lucan passage (9:1-6). A Samaritan village rejected a request from the messengers travelling ahead of Jesus for hospitality, but did not oblige as the villagers did not want to facilitate a pilgrimage to Jerusalem, a practice which they saw as a violation of the Law of Moses. Strangely, this episode is present only in Luke (9:51-53) and Luke alone reports about seventy two disciples being sent out on a temporary mission and in the Bible seventy refers to all the nations (10:1-16).

In John 4:4-42 we have the story of the Samaritan women with four minor sections. First, there is the explanation why the Lord happened to pass through Samaritan territory (Jn. 4:1-4). Second, there is an exchange between Jesus and this woman (Jn. 4:5-26). Finally, here is the effect of that incident (Jn. 4:27-42). Jesus moves from Judea in the south, to Galilee in the north. The evangelist notes that "he must needs pass through Samaria." Some scholars, therefore, view this "must needs" language as referring to a compulsion other than mere convenience. Jesus had to confront the smoldering suspicion and enmity between Jews and Samaritans by ministering to all. [4] But there were other routes between the two provinces and it was not even the common one. One would travel to the east, cross over the Jordan, and thus skirt the Samaritan territory.[5] Jesus was passing through Samaria on the way to Galilee and at Shechem/Sychar Jacob, sat down at the well of Jacob being wearied, exhausted (*kopiaō*) with his journey (Jn. 4:6); while the disciples went in search of food. Then there came a Samaritan woman to draw water and Jesus asked her for some water which surprised her as a Jew was doing it. William Barclay even tells of a segment of the Pharisees who closed their eyes at the sight of a woman[6] approaching, they would close their eyes. And yet the Master said to the woman: "Give me to drink." Jesus ignored the sectarian question and spoke of a gift of God and living water that would quench thirst forever. When she requested that water, Jesus pointed to her life and she declared him a prophet and spoke about the mountain on which the ancestors worshipped in contrast to Jerusalem where the Jews worship. Jesus said, "But the hour is coming, when the true worshipers will worship in spirit and truth, for the Father seek such as these to worship him" (v.23). Jesus meant o say, "cult at both sacred sites will be replaced by worship in Spirit and truth."[7]

The Lucan Approach of Jesus to the Samaritans in the Parable of the Good Samaritan

In Luke Jesus is open to the non-Jewish Romans and others; he manifests a positive attitude and approach towards the ethnic and religious outcasts like the Samaritans. This is clear in the exemplary story of the Good Samaritan (Lk 10:29-37) - which is fund only in Luke - in which an expert of the Scriptures, one who knew the Law (*Torah*, law or instruction of Moses)[8] asks Jesus, what one should do to inherit eternal life and Jesus answered the question pointing to the great commandment of the Lord, "You shall love the Lord your God with all, and with all your soul, and with all your strength, and with all your mind; and your neghbour as yourself " (v.27; see Deut 6:5 and Lev 19:18b);it is similar to what we find in Mk 12:28-31. The lawyer then asks Jesus, "Who is my neighbor?" Jesus answers by narrating the story of a person who was going from Jerusalem to Jericho through a road that was notorious for danger and looting at in the time of Jesus; it was even known as the "Way of Blood" because 'of the blood which was often shed there by robbers.'[9] The traveler was striped, beat and left half dead. A priest passed that way by the other side when he saw the man; a Levite too did the same. May be because the priests were not to be defiled by contact with the dead except the next of kin (Lev 21:1ff.). The priest and Levite should have assumed that the fallen traveler was dead and so did not want to be ritually clean. Then there came a Samaritan who was 'moved with pity;' he bandaged his wounds, poured oil an wine on them, put him on his animal and brought him to an inn. He gave the innkeeper two denarii promising to give more later. And Jesus asked the lawyer, 'Which of these three,…was the neighbor to the man who fell into the hands of the robbers?' The answer from the lawyer was, "The one who showed him mercy."Jesus said to him: "Go do likewise."

The parable was understood and interpreted by Origen as an allegory in which the fallen man was Adam going down from Jerusalem, which is paradise to Jericho, the world. The robbers were hostile powers. The priest stood for the Law and the Levite for the prophets. The Samaritan, indeed, was Christ. The wounds were disobediences, the animal the Lord's body and the inn was the Church that welcomes all. The inn-keeper was the head of the Church, to whom its care has been entrusted. And the Samaritan's promise of return represented the Savior's Second Coming.[10] This sort of interpretation is seen also in John Chrysostom of Constantinople, Ambrose of Milan and Augustine of North Africa. However, this is not accepted by most modern scholars.[11]

In fact the question of the lawyer implied to whom the commandment of love was applicable and the answer of Jesus meant that "one can define only the subject of love, not the object. The Samaritan is chosen to illustrate a subject whose range is unlimited."[12] Here according to Jesus, the idea of a neighbor who is to be loved and helped, goes beyond blood, geography and even religion. In India the parable could be understood in the wider ecumenical and inter-religious contexts. For Jesus, humanity has priority over one's religion, race or caste. It sheds light also on the question of Dalits.[13]

The Healing of the Ten Lepers and the Thankful Samaritan (Lk17:11-19)
Again Luke alone reports the episode about the ten lepers that Jesus healed and in which only a Samaritan turned back 'praising God in loud voice' (17: 11-19). Jesus was going to Jerusalem passing through a Samaritan village (9:51-52), between Samaria and Galilee and ten lepers cried out from distance, "Jesus, Master, have mercy on us" and Jesus aid to them to go and show themselves to the priests. As they went, they became aware that they were healed and one of them went back praising God in loud voice; he prostrated before Jesus in thanksgiving. "And he was a Samaritan," one hated by the Jews as a schismatic, who returned and thanked the ord. In the Lucan Gospel and the Acts the approach to the Samaritans is very special and it goes well with the attitude of Jesus to the outcast in general as presented in this story of the thankful Samaritan.

Jesus' Approach to People of Other Nations

The healing of the Centurion's servant by Jesus (Lk 7:1-10) is fund also in Matthew (8:5-13) with some minor differences. Certainly in both the stress is on the faith of a Gentile.[14] At Capernaum in Galilee a centurion, an officer over 100 men, approached Jesus requesting him through some Jewish elders to heal his servant who was sick, who spoke to Jesus about the man who loved the people and even built a synagogue for them. Meanwhile, the centurion sent people to tell Jesus that he needed only Jesus speak the word that his servant be healed; the sick seek touch of Jesus to be healed, but the centurion has a deeper faith. Seeing this, in admiration Jesus turned to the people and said, "I tell you, not even in Israel have I found such a faith" (Lk 7:9; Matt 8:10). Authentic faith in God/Jesus is possible to all people of goodwill." The story contrasts a Gentile's faith-response to Jesus with the Jewish authorities' rejection of him."[15] The story suggests that the blessing of the Reign of God is for all who have faith and not only for the Jews (Acts 10: 34ff).[16]

Approach of Jesus to Women

In Luke In the Synoptics there are two stories involving women that we do not find in Luke, the story of the Syrophoenician woman and Mary's anointing of Jesus (Mk 7:26; Mt 15:22). Some other stories he shares with them. However, he records a surprising number of episodes involving women that are unique either in their entirety or in their extended focus on women. We know that

In the ancient Near East Women generally had no rights as free persons; they were always subject to a man, either her father or husband."[17] Women were active "In Hellenistic, Roman and Jewish societies in the domestic private sphere, while men were active in the public sphere. According to the class, time and place in which they born, women had the opportunities available to them. The everyday lives of mainly the upper class Hellenistic and Roman women were often in tension with the ideal. Some Jewish women occupied leadership positions in the synagogues of the Diaspora communities. Alongside these apparent anomalies the gender values of society characterised and influenced the life of most Hellenistic and Jewish women of the Second Testament period. The Jewish attitude toward women was less than ideal. While in some books of the First Testament afforded great dignity to womanhood (Prov. 31:10ff), we also see negative remarks especially in wisdom literature especially in Ben Sira (9:3-9;19:2; 25:16ff.) The Hebrews over the years were influenced by others and thanked God that one was neither a Gentile, a slave, or a woman![18]

In respectful and dignified ways does Luke treat women as those associated with Jesus' birth as Mary (1:27-2:52) and Elizabeth (1:5-2:66), and the notable widow Anna (2:36-38). Women accompanied Jesus in his public life (8:1-3); they were with him on the way to Calvary (23: 27-31) and were present at the crucifixion (23:49), at the burial (23:55-56a), and at the tomb (24: 1-12). That they found the body of Jesus, prepared it for burial, embalming and placed the body in the tomb are remarkable (24:13-56). Besides, they were the first to announce the resurrection of Jesus.

In the Infancy Narratives

While both Luke and Matthew present birth narratives of Jesus (Lk 1:5-2:52 and Matt 1:18-2:12), the announcement of Jesus' birth and the narrative of his infancy in their gospels are different. Luke's account places Mary at the centre of the story while Joseph assumes prominence in the Matthean account. There are significant differences between the two accounts and to be noted is that the announcement of Jesus' birth is made to Mary not to Joseph in Luke, unlike as is in Matthew 2:35. However, though Matthew and Luke have independent accounts, they share a number of common details. Jesus was born in Bethlehem, in the reign of King Herod. Jesus' mother, Mary is a virgin betrothed to Joseph, from the line of David. Jesus' conception is through the Holy Spirit and the name Jesus is given by the angel. However, there are a number of points distinctive to Luke who has clearly portrayed Mary as recipient of God's announcement of the birth of the Saviour. Luke has also included and the story of Elizabeth and the birth of John the Baptist. While Zechariah is a priest, from a priestly family of the division of Abijah (Lk 1:5), Elizabeth, his wife, was from the priestly family of Aaron. To be noted is that Luke introduces both Elizabeth and

Zechariah as characters of equal importance. Every statement made of Zechariah is matched by what Luke says of Elizabeth. The priestly lineage and the names of both are given (Lk1:5). Both are righteous before God, both are childless, and both are getting on in years. Elizabeth with her husband are said to be righteous (*dikaioi*). In the scriptures this adjective is rarely used to describe a woman. Elizabeth is the only woman to whom the term is applied. This is significant in the light of the way Luke uses the term in respect of Jesus.

Elizabeth had passed the child-bearing age and to be childless in Judaism was a disgrace, a great misfortune, a sign of divine punishment and a source of shame. In the Lucan narrative, Zechariah and Elizabeth are placed within the tradition of Abraham and Sarah (Gen 16:1), Isaac and Rebecca (Gen 25:21), Jacob and Rachael (Gen 30:1).The world of F.T Judaism is focused on the Temple as Zechariah, the priest, takes his place in the temple cult and, according to the custom, wins the lot to burn incense. When Zechariah, was alone at the altar of incense, an angel of the Lord speaks to him about the birth of a son to him. Zechariah fails to recognise God and God's messenger and asks for more knowledge, a sign. He also fails to remember the biblical tradition of the faith of Abraham. He fails to interpret correctly the initiative of God and asks for a sign and he is struck dumb. The sign given to him is that of silence. Although Elizabeth did not experience directly the angelic appearance, her interpretation of the sign of God's visitation is in contrast to Zechariah's response of unbelief. The narrative takes us from the Temple to the private home of Zechariah and Elizabeth (Lk 1:23). The promise, made to Zechariah, finds fulfilment as Elizabeth finds herself to be pregnant. She, in contrast to Zechariah, understands this to be an expression of the compassion of God and interprets her pregnancy in the light of the First Testament precedence. Elizabeth, in contrast to Zechariah, recognises God's grace. It is Elizabeth who announces her pregnancy as the gift of God. "This is what the Lord has done to me when he looked favourably on me and took away the disgrace I have endured among my people" (Lk 1:25). Zechariah comes out unable to speak, the people understand that he had seen a vision. The Lucan narrative places the response of a woman, in the home whose response of faith sharply contrasts with Zechariah's response of unbelief. Luke positions the narrative in the Jewish context, in the Temple sanctuary. In the second epiphany Gabriel appears to Mary to announce the birth of Jesus (Lk 1:26-38). This second scene of annunciation is closely aligned with the first. Although there are contrasts in form and language between these two passages, the contrast here is between the characters Zechariah and Mary. Luke has obviously portrayed women as equal to men in dignity before God by the paralleling of events involving men and women, which is seen repeatedly.

Women in the public Life of Jesus

In the context of the public life of Jesus, Luke gives the stories different women as the privileged widow at Zarephath (1 kings 17:9; Lk 4:25-30), Jesus healing Simon Peter's mother-in-law (4:38-39); the story of the widow of Nain (7:11-17); he healed Jairus' daughter and the woman with the hemorrhage (8:40-55); heals He healed a woman who had been crippled 18 years (13:10-17). There are women who were sick or sinners who were healed by Jesus: the account of a woman of the city, a sinner who came to Jesus at the Pharisee's house (7:36-50)is an expression of love, devotion and thanks to Christ. Unhindered by self-righteous Pharisees, this repentant woman entered the house during a meal to show her indebtedness to Christ for his unconditional pardon of her sins. She wept on his feet, washed them with her tear and anointed them with precious oil and wiped them with her hair. Christ made it an occasion to teach the great lesson that those who love most are those who are conscious of the debt and bondage from which they are released and liberated.

The haling of a woman who was a cripple (13:10-17) is another example Jesus concern for men, the main issue is the observance of the Sabbath. The parables about the kingdom include the parable about the woman and leaven and the woman and the lost coin (15:8-10).

We have also the enlightening stories about Mary listened while Martha worked (10:38-42), the parable about a woman in a parable found a lost coin (15:8-10); a widow persistent in I going to a judge to obtain justice (18:1-5) and a poor widow gave two small coins to the temple (21:1-4). There were Women who ministered, and who obeyed Jesus' words and some who travelled with Jesus (8:2-3); Mary and Martha who were visited by Jesus (10:38-42), the women along the road who declared Mary's womb and breasts blessed (11:27-28). Jesus declared that those who hear the word of God and do it are his mother and brothers (8:19-21). Anna, a prophetess, blessed the child Jesus (2:36-38).

Women at the Crucifixion of Jesus Women

There were women among those who observed the crucifixion (23:27, 49).Two groups of women are identified in the context of the crucifixion and death of Jesus, the daughters of Jerusalem and the women from Galilee. Through the narrative of the daughters of Jerusalem Luke presents the consequences of Jesus' death for Jerusalem. In contrast, it is through the narrative of the women from Galilee that he announces that Jesus is alive and depicts the hope of the new community of faith. The daughters of Jerusalem (23:27-31) are located in the narrative as part of the crowd following Jesus to his execution. According to Luke, Jesus turns to these women and prophesies that they will come to praise as blessed 'the barren, the wombs that never bore and the breasts that never gave suck' (23:29). Jesus' words to the daughters of Jerusalem reveal the fate awaiting the people of Jerusalem who failed to recognise Jesus for who he is. In these verses (23:27-31). Luke presents a situation similar to that of the woman in the crowd in Luke 11:27 where 'Jesus' words to the daughters of Jerusalem (23.27-30) include a negative form of the beatitude' spoken by the women in the crowd in Luke 11:27. Jesus' words drew attention to the priority of listening to the word of God as the foundation for blessing.

The daughters of Jerusalem are similar to the women from Galilee in that both groups of women follow Jesus as he travels to the cross. However, while the daughters of Jerusalem are caught into the life and conditions of family and responsibility in the city that has failed to recognise Jesus as the prophet from God, the women from Galilee are among those who constitute Jesus' followers, the community of his disciples. The women from Galilee re-enter the narrative in Luke 23:49. In addition to Luke 8:1-3, the Lucan narrative identifies the women from Galilee on three occasions: at the crucifixion of Jesus (23:49), at his burial (Lk 23:55) and at the empty tomb (24:6). The women from Galilee provide a critical linkage among Jesus' Galilean ministry, his crucifixion, burial and resurrection. The reference to the women following Jesus from Galilee is noteworthy. They play a central role in the narrative of the human response to Jesus' death as they are the first to proclaim his resurrection; they become the nucleus of the new believing community, and they are commissioned as witnesses along with the twelve and the others in Luke 24:48. The apostles are absent but the women from Galilee are present. It is probable that Mark 15:40ff in Luke's text has been distributed over both Luke 23:49b and 8:2ff. Luke has chosen not to follow Mark's account (15:39), but has drawn on a tradition L. In Luke the male disciples did not flee at his arrest, so Luke relates 'a great number of people followed him and among them were women who were beating their breasts and wailing for him" (23:27). Though he does not specifically refer to disciples or apostles in this regard, he notes that "all his acquaintances, including the women who followed him from Galilee stood at a distance, watching these things" (23:48-49); it is the women who are the witnesses to the crucifixion. The women from Galilee are mentioned again in Lk 23:55 in connection with finding Jesus' body. Although first-century culture usually minimized the importance of women, Luke portrayed women as good examples in the early church as we see in the book of Acts whose author he is.

The Women on the Third Day

Luke ch 24 provides a very special account of 'the third day when Jesus' departure (9:31) is completed, he is raised to life (24:6-7), and finally departs from the eleven and those with them and is carried up into heaven in glory (24:26, 51). The centrality of Jerusalem in the Lucan narrative is clear. It is the city in which Jesus' destiny is reached and from which he enters his glory. Women are witnesses of Jesus' death; their function is not that of the idle crowds 'gazing at' the spectacle. The account in Luke follows that from Mark. Luke's redaction clarifies that Jesus' crucifixion and burial were occurring on the day of preparation and it was almost the Sabbath (23:54). Luke omits the names of the women, and adds that the women went back home to prepare spices and ointments before the Sabbath (23:56a).

Women at the Empty Tomb

Luke's account of the empty tomb (4:1-12) follows that of Mark (16:1-8) and finds parallels in Matthew and John. The Lucan narrative builds on the element of surprise by detailing the preparations of the women (23:56-24:1). The women who had seen the tomb where Jesus' body had been laid (23:55), who were prepared to complete the services for his burial (23:56-24:1), are confronted by an empty tomb. They respond in bewilderment. The women are first to hear the message of resurrection. The announcement of Jesus' resurrection confirms the discipleship of the women. In the empty tomb, in the midst of their perplexity, the women from Galilee are addressed by two men in dazzling apparel who announce the initiative of God (Lk 24:5). The two men invite the active response and participation of the women in God's initiative. The two men regard the women as disciples. They address the women as those who themselves have received Jesus' teaching in Galilee and they invite the women to remember the words of Jesus. Through this invitation to remember the prediction of Jesus, the narrative strengthens the identification of the women as disciples in their own right. The women were part of the community of followers referred to in Luke 8:1-3. In Luke's account the message of heavenly messengers has been changed. The query in Luke 24:5b is unique to Luke, "Why do you look for the living among the dead?" The assurance given to the women in the Matthean and Marcan accounts, 'do not fear, do not be afraid' has been replaced in Luke with the characteristic Lucan emphasis on life as one of the effects of the Christ event; Jesus is risen, he is not there.

Finally in the Acts of the Apostles, which is also from Luke, we have several references to women which go well with the gospel in which there is some focus on the attitudes, actions, responses and responses of omen. In the Acts we have the phrase' both men and women often repeated as they prayed (1:14), believed (5:14), were baptised (8:12), were imprisoned (8:3; 22:4), were persecuted (9:2) and so on.

Jesus' Disciples to Preach to All

Luke begins his second volume known as Acts: "In the first book I have narrated all that Jesus began to do and teach until the day he was taken up, after he had given instruction through the Holy Spirit to the apostles whom he had chosen" (1:3) to bear witness to him to the ends of the earth. The Acts begin with Jerusalem to end up in Rome (Acts 28). On the Pentecost what the disciples spoke was understood by Parthians, Medes, Elamites, residents of Mesopotamia, Judea, Cappadocia, Pontus, Asia, phyrigia, pampyhylia, Egypt and the parts of Lybia belonging to Cyrene, and visitors from Rome, both Jews and proselyts, Cretans and Arabs.."(2:8). The idea here is that the Spirit makes the language and life-style of the disciples become intelligible to all the nations.

General Conclusion

The evangelist Luke who was born in Antioch and converted to Christianity was well-educated in classical Greek was a highly talented writer who did not have Jewish background. Some see Luke as the most theological of the Synoptic gospels and that "he writes as a Gentile Christian, when the first generation of the Church was well advanced."[19] Some typically Jewish practices found in Mark are absent in him. The universalism and the comparatively prominent roles given to women in the Infancy narratives; A Samaritan resented as a model of mercy (10:25-37), and gratitude (17:11-19) the gentiles as model of good conduct and openness to faith (7:9). To be noted is that appear more women with some important roles in this gospel than in the others.

Even more remarkable is that the Third Gospel is less hostile to Jews than Matthew, Mark or John.[20]

Endnotes

[1] Anything historical is essentially bound to time and space which create diversity.

[2] J.L. McKenzie, *Dictionary of the Bible*, London-Dublin, 1965, p. 765.

[3] *Antiquities of the Jews*, 9, 14, 3.

[4] Tenney, M.,*The Expositor's Bible Commentary*, Vol 9, Frank Gaeblein, ed. Grand Rapids, Zondervan, 1981, p. 54.

[5] Josephus, *Antiquities of the Jews*, 20.6.1.

[6] Barclay,W. *The Gospel of John*. Philadelphia, PA: The Westminister Press 1956. pp. 142-143).

[7] R.E. Brown, *An Introduction to the New Testament*, p. 343.

[8] In Greek a *nymikos*, 'lawyer' which is equivalent to *grammateus*, 'scribe' who is a Scripture scholar. (Francis Wright, *The Gospel According to Matthew*, Basil Blackwell, Oxford, 1981. p. 442.

[9] F.H. Wilkinson, "The Way from Jerusalem to Jericho," *The Biblical Archeologist.*, Vol 33, No.1, 1975, pp. 10-24.

[10] Origen, 34.3, trans. J.T. Lienhard, *Homilies on Mark, Fragments on Mark*,1993, p. 138.

[11] J.L. McKenze, *Dictionary of the Bible*, p. 635.

[12] R.E. Brown, An Introduction to the New Testament, TPI, Bangalore, 2000, P.245.

[13] M.Ganavaram, "Dalit Theology" and the Parable of the Good Samaritan,: *Journal for the Study of the New Testament*, Vol 15, No. 50, 1993, pp. 59-83; Vermes Geza, *The Authentic Gospel of Jesus*, London, Penguin books, 2004, pp. 152-54.

[14] F.W, Wright, *The Gospel according to Matthew*, p. 209.

[15] R.E. Brown, *An Introduction to the New Testament*, p. 240.

[16] *The New Community Bible*, Revised Text, St Pauls, Bombay, 2008.

[17] J.L. McKenzie, *Dictionary of the Bible*, Geoffrey Chapmann, 1965, p. 935.

[18] http. www.Yehuda Mirsky, "*Three Blessings*," The Jewish prayer book (*siddur*) has three lines in the opening of morning prayer known as *birkhot ha-shahar* or the "dawn blessings" that begin "Blessed are you O God, King of the Universe, Who has not made me...a Gentile, a slave, and "a woman." See the Talmud Berakhot 60b.

[19] J.L. McKenzie, *Dictionary of the Bible*, p. 525.

[20] J. L. MaKenzie, *Dictionary of the Bible*, p. 526.

Interfaith Encounter for our Day
Biblical Approaches and Paradigms

Benny Thettayil

Introduction

Vatican II has served as a turning point in the Church's relationship with other religions. For the first time, official magisterial documents opened the way and manifested an appreciation for interaction with other religious traditions. In *Nostra Aetate*, the Church brought in a positive outlook toward other religions: "The Catholic Church rejects nothing that is true and holy in these religions." The document claims that the Church has a high regard for the way of life, precepts and doctrines of other religions. Although they might be different from the way of life, precepts and doctrines of the Church, they nonetheless "reflect a ray of that truth which enlightens all people." (NA 2).

Various statements of Vatican II on other religions are particularly important in the multi-religious contexts like that of India and of several other Asian countries where the Church exists as a numerically insignificant minority. These statements have been the basis and inspiration of the Church as it has sought to be faithful to the Gospel and to the people it has been called to serve and to live with. The immediate result of the Vatican II in the Asian setting was the foundation of the Federation of Asian Bishops' Conferences (FABC), which consistently and successfully laboured to deepen and foster the sense of being Church among other religions of Asia. The primary concern of the FABC has been to bear witness to Christian faith in a context that is characterized by a diversity of cultures and a plurality of religions.

Religious intolerance, communal violence, caste division and atrocities perpetrated by religious terrorists in India in the recent past have harmed the very legacy of its pluralistic existence. However, a nonviolent interracial existence, peaceful intercultural living, a harmonious interfaith meeting of people and a pleasant interreligious existence are a challenge to humanity.[1] As Hans Küng observes regarding the interfaith encounters, "There can be no peace among the nations without peace among the religions. There can be no peace among the religions without dialogue between the religions."[2]

Interfaith Encounter of the Church

In December 2004, the Pontifical Council for the Pastoral Care of Migrants and Itinerant People wrote about the *People on the Move* and titled the document *Inter-Religious Dialogue in the Migrants' World*. The document made a clear and positive statement regarding how a Christian is to regard people who belong to other religious traditions: "Even though there are similarities and differences among religious faiths, the main purpose of each religion is to make every human more spiritual. We must view different religions as essential instruments in developing a good heart with love and respect for others. This will not only encourage people to live with greater appreciation for one another, but it will also help eliminate prejudices and false perceptions."[3] It is a fact that in the last few decades, the society has become more pluralistic than previously was the case. Some of these new forms of religious expressions are inevitably influencing the Church.

All these have an impact on the Church's life. In the parish work, the ministers and members of the parish community increasingly come into contact with those of other faiths in their midst. It is a development which challenges us to consider the relationship of Christianity with other religions, especially those faiths that are surrounding us.

The occasional interreligious services that we organize or are invited to attend, present the minister one place of encounter with other faiths which raises a new kind of pastoral challenge. If a family circle has members who belong to more than one religious tradition, the most important moments of its members' lives will bring this encounter to the surface through the ministry of the Church. To a non-conservative minister, the new trend that allows the members of a family to practice different religious beliefs, raises new questions: How should a wedding be conducted if one of those getting married is a Hindu? Is it possible to include Buddhist elements in a Baptism if the father or the mother is a Buddhist? Is it possible for a funeral to be based on both Islamic and Christian traditions if the deceased had converted from Islam just before his death? All these questions have theological implications and to a minister with a pastoral mind, the answers will involve far more than the CIC and the CCC. For a pastor, all the answers should follow the principles of Christian love and hospitality, at the same time, one should be careful to maintain sufficient distance from some of the practices of other religions so that the wrong kind of syncretism could be avoided.

Biblical Interfaith Encounters

Any Christian religious expression must be subordinate to the Christian Scripture, which is the foundation of Christian faith. The Bible is a collection of diverse books whose gestation spans a period of about a thousand years in its written form and far more years in the oral form. Throughout these varied texts, the common thread is the recognition of the saving work of God in human history, culminating in Jesus Christ.

When we look for interreligiosity in the Bible, we do not find an unambiguous answer there to all our questions in this regard. Some of these books contain conflicting perspectives on interreligious encounter relative to their age. The Christian attitude to the sacred texts, which played a formative role in its development requires the consideration of different perspectives in order to arrive at a balanced overall understanding.

On the one hand, very often, Christians read God's word in isolation. Depending upon the text that we read, we form a theology of interreligious encounter. There has been a critical approach to other religions based on the concern of the prophets of Israel with the religions of the surrounding nations (cf. Is 46:1-7; Jer 10:2-5). The prophets make stern declarations based on the Decalogue, according to which the people of Israel should not bow down to other Gods or make idols for themselves (Ex 20:2-5). Texts like this are reminders to Christians that they are called by the law to practice single minded devotion to the Lord.

On the other hand, the Bible tells us that the saving acts of God are not limited to his chosen people. The Scripture refers to a number of occasions when God was actively involved outside Israel. In particular, this is seen in the accounts of God blessing his chosen people through external agents like Melchizedek (Gen 14:17-20) and Balaam (Num 22-24). The status of Israel as the chosen people of God does not rule out the possibility of his positive involvement in other nations. In Amos, God is so generous to consider the Ethiopians as important to him as the children of Israel and reminds the people that it was he who led the migrations of the Philistines and the Aramaeans also (Amos 9:7). Why else would the God of Israel employ an Israelite prophet to bring a non-Israelite nation like Nineveh in Assyria even against the will of the prophet himself (Jonah)?[4]

The Gospels tell us of how Jesus was prepared to recognise the example of the faith of a non-Israelite Canaanite woman[5] (Mt 15:21–28). There are examples of faith among the Gentiles that surpasses that of the Jews and Jesus does not make a secret of the fact (Lk 7:9).[6] There are far more righteous and godly people among the Samaritans than among the

Israelites whom Jesus makes a paradigm worth emulating (Lk 10:29–37). For Jesus, "your neighbour is anyone in need and with whom you are thrown into contact."[7] Later on, in his well delivered contextual speech at the Areopagus, Paul understands and places on record the fact that the Greek religion is a sign of the Athenians reaching out towards God. Their prophets have already told them part of what Paul wanted to tell them (Acts 17:16-30). Paul also reminded the inhabitants of the city of Lystra that God had not left them without a testimony concerning himself and it was he that gave them from heaven rains and fruitful seasons, satisfying their hearts with food and gladness (Acts 14:17).

When we consider that the kingdom of God is a far larger reality than the Church, and that like the Church, many other realities subsist in the kingdom, we make our vision broader and make place for all peoples in our heart. Some of the elements of the eschatological vision present in the prophetic books encompass the notion that the riches and beauties of the non-Israelite nations will find their place in the kingdom of God (Is 60:4-11). It is an invitation to consider that peoples and nations in fact "seek the Lord of hosts in Jerusalem" (Zec 8:22). In the Apocalyptic eschatological vision, the nations and the kings of the earth are to walk in the light of the lamp that is the Lamb (Rev 21:24-26), because, Christ is the new light, which enlightens *everyone* (Jn 1:9).

The command of Jesus obliges the Church to make disciples of all nations (Mt 28:18-20). Hence, the pursuit of interfaith encounter has been mission and evangelization. According to these teachings of the Bible, Christians can engage boldly and confidently with their neighbours of other faiths. The fact that God is already present wherever we proclaim the gospel of Jesus Christ challenges us to overcome cultural boundaries and expectations.

Creative Tension in the Encounter

Generally, faith traditions address universal human concerns and questions and come up with many common answers. Depending upon these answers, there are considerable differences between various religions. When a faith tradition encounters another, these differences and the way these differences came about must be kept in mind. The lack of such a consideration does a disservice to both faith traditions. Meaningful and respectful interfaith encounter must address and honour both the narrow particularistic and broad universalistic elements of both the faith traditions,[8] as depicted in the story of the interaction of Jesus with the Samaritans in chapter 4 of the gospel of John.

When one focuses on the *particularistic* elements of a faith tradition, one tends to focus on and emphasize the differences that are found in religions. This inevitably leads to a hostile encounter and dialogue of argument. It disrespects the commonality of humanity that leads to common themes of religious inquiry and answers. The particularistic view focusses on the tree so intently that it tends to lose sight of the grandeur of the forest. In the Samaritan episode of John 4, Jesus transcends his own tradition to a greater reality that is far beyond the particulars of both the Samaritan and Jewish sacred traditions (Jn 4:23-24).[9]

When one focusses on the *universalistic* elements of a religious tradition, one tends to emphasize the commonalities that often lead to a peripheral encounter and a dialogue of relativization. One tends to overlook the faith experiences that led to the various answers that made one particular faith different from another. It disrespects the unique foci and answers of other faiths. However, the universalistic view is so panoramic and sweeping that when this view is adopted, one misses those particular elements, the trees that made such a grandeur of the forest. Hence, in John 4, Jesus underscores certain historical facts as true and does not want to dilute them even to win the whole of the Samaritans (Jn 4:22).

Too much of a focus on either *particularistic* elements or *universalistic* elements is disrespectful of the faiths and the faithful of another religious tradition in one manner or another. However, there is a third way to navigate the encounter between various faith traditions. It is to embrace a creative tension where the commonalities are seen to provide context to the particularities. In the same way, the particularities provide nuances to the commonalities. The ensuing dialogue does not seek understanding by deemphasizing either elements. It respects both the elements without underplaying or overplaying differences inherent in both these, but the tension between these is recognized and made creative to bring out something that is totally new in the new light that is found in the process: "Woman, believe me, the hour is coming when neither on this mountain nor in Jerusalem will you worship the Father... God is spirit, and those who worship him must worship in spirit and truth." (Jn 4:21-24).

Open to Religious Encounters
Familiarity of other faiths helps to identify the nature of that faith. Often, distant observation and second-hand information do not inform, it tends to misinform and confuse. Many faith traditions utilize similar terms but with very different meanings. Some utilize very different terms but with very similar meanings. Both of these are difficult to recognize without practice and conversation. The Johannine mountains of Gerizim and Zion are mountains, but with a great difference.

The knowledge of other faith traditions helps one to understand one's own faith better as all the faiths are linked in the supernatural. To a great extent, we learn this fact through comparison and contrast. For example, in the Sermon on the Mount, when Jesus taught, how the Kingdom of God operates, he provided a series of contrasts. He illustrated how the world tends to operate in contrast to how the Kingdom works. Perhaps, without presenting any contrasts, Jesus could have said that the Kingdom of God is loving, kind, forgiving and so forth. However, by employing contrasts, we discover how far we are from God's ideal.

The acquaintance of other religious traditions helps one gain a sense of what are the key differences and what are not. The main differences between Christianity and other religions are commonly in areas of Soteriology that deals with the nature and process of salvation (cf. Jn 4:22). However, there are several things that we might think are key characteristics of Christianity, but are also shared by most other faiths. Consider the fruits of the Spirit like love, joy, peace, gentleness, goodness, faith, meekness and self-control (Gal 5:22-23). These are qualities that Paul identifies in a growing Christian. All these qualities, in various ways are also promoted by other religious traditions. Paul notes that against these, there is no law. That would mean that people in general, think these are good, or at least not bad.

It is often in contrast with other religious traditions that we gain a clearer understanding of the broadness of our faith. When our understanding of faith is limited to our own, and when we do not have a broader faith perspective, often we end up majoring on minor issues. By learning about other faiths, it is possible that we come to understand the possibility of variety within varied valid expressions of Christianity.

In reality, many of our assumptions regarding other faiths are made without any interaction with them. By knowing other religions better, we can also understand that we as Christians often share far more in common with them than we hold different.

Biblical Paradigms of Interfaith Encounter

According to Alan Race, there are a few basic paths that lead to interfaith encounter: Exclusivism, Inclusivism.[10] To these, as we take a look at the various biblical scenes of interfaith encounter, Universalism could be added.

The Canaanite Exclusivism

In the beginning of the story of Jesus's encounter with the Canaanite woman, Jesus' apparent attitude is exclusivistic, as he tells her clearly that he is sent only for the people of Israel[11] (Mt 15:24). In the modern world, a Christian Exclusivist believes that only those who are Christian in their faith, embracing Jesus as their Saviour will be saved. In some circles, the term Particularist is used in order to describe a narrower version of the exclusivist. In his answer to the woman, "the strongly particularized character of Jesus' mission is clearly seen."[12] An Exclusivist believes that salvation is mediated only through his own faith tradition. As such, people can only be saved by Jesus, and it is only available to those within their own specific sect, or those who embrace a certain unique doctrine, or have participated in a special ritual like.

The Areopagan Inclusivism

Paul peacefully encounters the Athenians at Areopagus and considers that they are already worshippers of the same God that Paul had come to them to speak about, but they do not know him (Acts 17:16-31). An Inclusivist Christian would hold the view that Jesus is the means to salvation, but there may be some people who are saved by Jesus although they do not necessarily know Jesus. Some believe that Jews can be saved through their faithfulness to the Mosaic Law even if they reject Jesus. Others say that Muslims can be saved by Christ even though they reject His role as Saviour because they worship the same God who is the God of Abraham, Isaac and Jacob.[13]

The Greek Universalism

In the encounter between Jesus and the Greeks in John 12, both Jesus and the Greeks dance around with an attitude of universal religious acceptance. The Greeks come in search of him and he welcomes them and has a hearty dialogue with them. The Universalists are found at the other extreme side of the spectrum. They believe that God immediately or ultimately saves everyone. A universalist Christian might believe that Jesus' salvation is available to all, and effective for all. It is in this shade of thought that theologians like John Hick, Raimon Panikkar, and others operate. To some, they are Relativistic and do not support any kind of proselytization. In some of these circles, conversion is considered an anathema, or at least very inconsistent with interfaith encounter.

Any of the shades that is present in the spectrum of interfaith encounter gleaned from the New Testament that is given above, does not point to any particular directive to engage with other faith traditions. In every encounter, the believers always look for a transcendence based on the creative tension that is presented by the new light that is received.

Biblical Approaches in Interfaith Engagement

In addition to the biblical paradigms of interfaith encounter, the Scripture is strewn with various kinds of encounters between protagonists of various faith traditions. Jesus himself and his disciples, as they ministered to the Word of God, encountered individuals of various faith persuasions and traditions and in spite of the fact that they did not always end up having their way, they left a positive influence on the members of other faiths who met them. The following are a few examples of such biblical approaches.

Samaritan Apologetic Approach

There is a beautiful example of an apologetic attitude in what Luke presents in 9:51-55. "When the days drew near for Jesus to be received up, he set his face to go to Jerusalem. And he sent messengers ahead of him, who went and entered a village of the Samaritans, to make ready for him; but the people would not receive him, because his face was set toward Jerusalem. And when his disciples James and John saw it, they said, 'Lord, do you want us to bid fire come down from heaven and consume them?'" James and John are not able to tolerate any other way to respond to the Samaritans.[14] In this view of James and John, the purpose of interfaith engagement is to convert those of other faiths to one's own faith. Anyone with a different view point is not tolerated. Argument and confrontation become the most valid forms of conversation. Typically, people who take recourse to this approach, emphasize the differences between faith traditions and overlook or deemphasize similarities. The goal is always to correct the wrong beliefs of the other; in this case the Samaritans. O. Cullmann,[15] who argues for a strong Samaritan connection, supports the view of J. Bowman,[16] who holds that 'the Gospel was written for the Samaritans', who are even considered to be Gentiles.[17]

For the Jews like Jesus, there were two routes to travel from Judaea to Galilee: one through Samaria and the other, via the other side of the Jordan. The eastern route along the Jordan valley avoiding Samaria was a longer one. The Jews who believed that they would be polluted by walking through Samaritan regions, avoided this route via Samaria. The hostility that was prevailing between the Jews and the Samaritans was another reason for them to avoid this route. The route through Samaria was shorter and it was also considered safer as it was under the unified administration of the Romans that time.[18] In spite of all these, Jesus chose to go to Galilee via Samaria.

Christians who are more Particularist or Exclusivist in terms of Interfaith encounter, often gravitate to an apologetic approach. In some circles, this kind of engagement is also described as the *confessional* approach. This perspective presents a blurred view of realities. When one emphasizes only the differences, one ignores valuable similarities, which in turn, leads to a distorted version of the other religion. This is what is happening to James and John when they looked at the Samaritans who refused to welcome Jesus. A distorted view of another faith hampers the possibility of a genuine interfaith encounter and lead one to an impasse and block all the future possibilities of engagement.

Samaritan Solidarity Approach

A solidarity approach is made by Jesus in his encounter with the Samaritans (Jn 4), as he takes the initiative to engage with a foreign people. Many scholars consider 'the Samaritan connection'[19] crucial to the understanding of the interfaith encounters in the gospel of John. G.W. Buchanan holds that 'the author (John) came from another Semitic group, namely the anti-Judean, Samaritan Christian Church'.[20]

In spite off the geographical considerations given above, the peculiar use of the Greek word *dei* (Jn 4:4) highlights some kind of *necessity* of Jesus to pass through Samaria. This necessity is understood by some scholars as 'geographical necessity'[21] and by other commentators as "divine necessity"[22] and others opine that God had willed it.[23] In the gospel of John *dei* is usually associated with the plan of God (cf. Jn 3:14,30; 9:4). Even if the journey through Samaria was demanded by geographical consideration, his life for two days among the Samaritans was guided by divine necessity.[24] His interaction with the Samaritan woman on the way and his openness and readiness to engage with the Samaritans who were held in contempt by the Jews (Jn 4:9) is a paradigm for Christian engagement. It showcases his attitude of openness and readiness to reach out to people on the peripheries or to respond positively to those who wanted to reach out to him.

Despite the debilitating social conventions of his own Jewish community, Jesus asks for a drink facilitating a dialogue with the Samaritan woman. Had not Jesus opened the conversation, an enlightening and fruitful dialogue would not have ensued; probably she would have gone away in silence; probably the opportunity of the engagement of Jesus with the Samaritans would have been lost. This attitude of openness to reach out to the Samaritans led Jesus to a wider horizon of his mission; it was his first mission to the non-Jews.

When the cultures or faith traditions come together in solidarity, the encounter can be of great advantage. All those who are engaged in such a meeting, search for the truth together and in solidarity with each other. When the seeking becomes a corporate endeavour, the truth that is found is far more profound than the one that is initially sought after. The truth is neither of the existing options, but something that is quite new (Jn 4:24). Jesus respected her search for the right place of worship and the Messiah and was able to reveal to her not only the great truth about right place but also the person who deserves to be worshipped. Neither the Jews nor the Samaritans had the monopoly and ownership of the truth. Any claim of monopoly tends to sabotage the very spirit of effective religious encounter. Hence, Vatican II rightly teaches: "Let Christians, while witnessing to their own faith and way of life, acknowledge, preserve and encourage the spiritual and moral truths found among non-Christians, also their social life and culture." (*Nostra Aetate*, 2). The journey towards the Ultimate Reality becomes more meaningful and fruitful when we make it in solidarity and fellowship with other believers.

Jewish Relativistic Approach

John 8:1-11 is a beautiful story of a profound faith encounter. On the peripheral level, a few elders of the Jews who bring an unfortunate girl to Jesus are seeking after truth on the basis of which they are sure to take an action, which they had decided upon. However, they come to Jesus in dialogue. At least outwardly, they are truth-seeking in attitude, and not confessional. That is, outwardly, they have bracketed their own beliefs (injunction by Moses) or even tossed them aside so that they were better prepared to learn from those of other opinions or faiths. They are apparently raising Jesus to the level of Moses to emphasize at least the possibility of similarities with other views. Had they been genuine, they could be classified as more Pluralistic or Universalistic in their approach, as they had left room for the possibility of some truth to be found in Jesus.[25]

On the one hand, in this approach of the elders, they are on a quest for truth, but they are relativizing truth they have received from Moses. On the other hand, although they begin with relativizing, as in a good interfaith engagement, respect for each other prevails. Gradually, the elders arrive at a firm standpoint in their own faith, and enter into dialogue with self-confidence and leave with a better understanding of the Law of Moses. Each goes on to live the truth they have found in their own way.

Without this openness, any engagement becomes shallow. Only if we are at home in our own faith, we shall be able to honestly encounter the faith of someone else. The person who falls victim to relativism of the multicultural society may be capable of dialogue, but that person does not benefit from the encounter.

Hellenistic Availability Approach

Breaking the narrow confines of the ethnic and religious walls, Jesus makes himself available to a group of the Greeks and welcomes them to a space that is usually reserved for his people, the Jews. Towards the end of the ministry of Jesus, these Greeks come to meet Jesus. This meeting of the Greeks follows the Pharisees' concern regarding the ovation Jesus received as he approached Jerusalem before his triumphal entry into the city: 'You see that you can do nothing; look, the world has gone after him' (12:19). Immediately the author notes: 'among those who went up to worship at the feast were some Greeks' (12:20). Since these Greeks came to Jerusalem for the festival, some interpreters have identified them as proselytes; others have seen them as Greek-speaking Jews in the Diaspora.[26]

Hengel's view regarding Jesus going to the Greeks in 7:35 and the Greeks coming to Jesus in 12:20-22 is note-worthy. Hengel argues that the statement of Jesus in 7:35 'here probably means "Greek-speaking Gentile" rather than "Greek-speaking Diaspora Jew"' and in 12:20-22, regarding the Greeks who want to see Jesus, Hengel observes: 'That means that now even proselytes or Gentile sympathisers are coming to Jesus'.[27] Similarly, Koester argues that there are good reasons to think that the Greeks represent Gentile interest in Jesus. 'The use of the term Greeks, which regularly designated non-Jews in sources of this period, and their arrival at precisely the moment when the whole "world" was going after Jesus, indicate that they should be understood to be people who were not of Jewish background, even though they had come to Jerusalem for the festival.'[28]

The esoteric language that Jesus uses when he is conversing with the Greeks shows that Jesus was crossing both the ethnic and linguistic boundaries to accommodate the Greeks who had come in search of him. The incident points to two prerequisites in faith encounter: First of all, of a presence that is so impressive that others are attracted to you and secondly, your availability to those who approach you, no matter what faith tradition they belong to.

Nicodemian Illumination Approach

In the beginning of John 3, there is an unfinished story of a great teacher who comes to Jesus by night and holds a dialogue with him. Nicodemus, who is also a teacher as Jesus was, wants some illumination because of the difference that he finds in this maverick teacher – "God is with him" (Jn 3:2).[29] Although the setting is contrived and one does not know what happens to Nicodemus at the end of the story or when does he leave the scene, or who is actually speaking towards the second half of the purported answers of Jesus, it is a great story to follow as the interlocutor of Jesus is employing an illumination approach in interfaith encounter.

In this approach, one neither embraces another confession nor give into another argument. One does not relativize one's beliefs either. The focus is on mutual understanding. No one is subsumed into another; each has questions to ask and clarifications to be given. Based on the sustainability of the side of the argument Nicodemus eventually falls silent as one listens to the profound way in which Jesus presents the truth as he had experienced it (Jn 3:11).

Risk of Religious Diversity

Interreligious matters are quite divisive. While in many non-religious cases, taking a position that is inclusive is a good idea, but in religion, that is risky. On the one hand, there are those who consider anything that has to do with interfaith encounter problematic (cf. Jn 7:45-52). What they are comfortable with is really proclamation and argument because they are sure of themselves and they assume that they are deeply rooted in their faith (cf. Jn 7:46-48). However, they fail to gauge their own faith by means of encounter with others. On the other hand, there is a tendency to relativize truth in interfaith encounter, as some people are only looking for a common ground. Anyone who professes his or her faith as true and practices it, can and should desire people to share a similar commitment and should meet them. These meetings pave the way for mutual understanding, which is foundational to breaking down barriers that have been built across hearts.

Interfaith engagement is not preaching, which is a one-way communication to change someone's mind; nor is it apologetics, which is a two-way communication to do the same. A genuine engagement focuses on understanding, but not by trying to win arguments. It is by bringing about mutual understanding that builds trust, and opens the door for more effective sharing of one's own beliefs that the engagement on an interfaith level is made effective. For a person from a radically different faith tradition, steps like ready-made presentations, clever arguments and polemics are likely to create a hostile response, not the desired one.

When we consider interfaith communication, we need to be aware of the following practical aspects: (1) Each Christian has a toolbox of skills associated with serving God as he/she shares faith with others. Some tools may be related to spiritual disciplines such as prayer, witnessing and mediation. Other tools may be related to less specifically religious disciplines such as teaching, argument, encouragement and counselling. Having a wide variety of skills and disciplines is important, but that is not enough. (2) One must know how to use each tool. A blacksmith may have a lathe, which is a versatile and powerful machine, but still he needs considerable training to use it well. A minister may know how to preach, but still, there is a great distance between this and preaching *effectively*. (3) One must have the wisdom to know the right tool to use in each specific circumstance. Some people are very skilled in prayer, but important as prayer can be, there are times when prayer is an inadequate tool. A hungry neighbour needs more than prayer. There are times when preaching is needed, and times when it is inappropriate or unhelpful (cf. Jn 6:5).

Conclusion

Often, as far as interfaith communication is concerned, we are like the disciples of Jesus who were incredulous when they returned from the town with some food and saw Jesus speaking with a woman (Jn 4:27). They were unable to see the immense possibilities of life and relationship as they overlooked and downplayed them. Like the disciples, we hasten to shove people into labelled religious boxes. Sometimes, we are also like the angry and frenzied men who could have pelted that stone without a moment's hesitation because all they saw was the sin and not the *person* they were accusing (Jn 8:1-11).

Unless one is sure of one's stance and is not rooted in one's own faith, one tends to lose ground. If one is approaching the scenario of encounter with confidence, even at the possibility of giving into a more profound presentation of the truth, one does it with clarity, albeit it might take place a few years after the encounter (cf. Jn 7:50; 19:39-42). However, if the exclusivists who are on one extreme of the spectrum make a swing toward the apologetic approaches, and the universalists who are on the other extreme of the spectrum make a swing toward relativistic approaches, then the clarification approach must be most attractive to the inclusivists. Anyone, irrespective of one's point on the spectrum, is invited to engage in the clarification approach as it leaves room for freedom to respond one way or another.

Exclusivists often proselytize. They seek to share their faith with others with hopes that others will convert to their faith. This is what the Sadducees hoped that Jesus would do when they encountered him with an extremely stretched scenario of the seven brothers marrying a woman in a sequence and dying childless (Mt 22:25). Additionally, this was an "attempt to make Jesus look ridiculous."[30] However, relativizing one's beliefs would not be conducive to conversion because, in the same way, at a later point in time, he can be converted again. Seeking understanding from each other and of each other tends to reduce misunderstanding and leaves the person free to choose as the Spirit works in him as in the case of Nicodemus who made a researched decision to stand up for Jesus, although it took a long time for him to come to such a stance.[31]

Interfaith encounter is as crucial as ever in the life and mission of the Church in India today. Indian churches live in situations where they are a minority and their contact with believers of other faiths is a part of daily life. The call of *Nostra Aetate* to encounter peoples of other faiths as well as to discern those "rays of truth" found in them is more urgently to be answered today.

On the theological level, India calls for an endeavour to understand and respond to the reality of religious pluralism. John Paul II states that the Church's relationship with other religions is dictated by a twofold respect: Respect for man in his quest for answers to the deepest questions of life, and respect for the action of the Spirit in man. Excluding any mistaken interpretation, the interfaith meeting held in Assisi confirmed his conviction that "every authentic prayer is prompted by the Holy Spirit, who is mysteriously present in every human heart."[32] Given the contemporary misunderstandings and conflicts between religions in India, the task of interfaith encounter is all the more critical in building a more peaceful and just society as the Church's response to the Spirit of God who urges us to build the Kingdom of God in collaboration with one another.

Respectful exchange of spiritual experience with anyone from any faith tradition, is the biblical approach as we considered various paradigms above. We need to consider the fact that the places on earth that are mono-cultural and religiously monolithic are rapidly decreasing. Hence, a minister of the word of God cannot say that he is competent in his ministry without the skills in interfaith communication. Samanvaya primarily aims at ministers who work in cross-cultural or religiously pluralistic settings in the North Indian missions. As a tool, interfaith communication is practiced and is ever made sharp through its constant interaction with those of diverse opinions on spirituality, faith and religion.

Endnotes

[1] M.D. Bryant, "The Inter-Religious Future: Reflections on the Horizon and Way", in A. Kalliath (ed.), *Pilgrims in Dialogue: A New Configuration of Religions for Millennium Community*, Bangalore: Dharmaram Publications, 2000, p. 147.

[2] Hans Küng, *Global Responsibility: In Search of a New World Ethic*, London: SCM Press, 1991, p. 105.

[3] *Inter-Religious Dialogue in the Migrants' World*, 6, Pontifical Council for the Pastoral Care of Migrants and Itinerant People, December 2004.

[4] H.W. Wolff, *Obadiah and Jonah*, M. Kohl (trans.), Minneapolis: Augsburg Publishing House, 1986, p. 76.

[5] A. Stock, *The Method and Message of Matthew*, Collegeville, MN: Michael Glazier-Liturgical Press, 1994, p. 256, notes that the beneficiaries of the acts of Jesus are those who "count for nothing in Israel's society... the disenfranchised persons as a Gentile woman."

[6] J.A. Fitzmyer, *The Gospel according to Luke*, vol. 1 (AB), Garden City, NY: Doubleday, 1981, p. 650.

[7] J.A. Fitzmyer, *The Gospel according to Luke*, vol. 2 (AB), Garden City, NY: Doubleday, 1981, p. 884.

[8] Harvey Cox, "Many Mansions or One Way? The Crisis in Interfaith Dialogue", in *The Christian Century* (August 1998). pp. 731-735. See "Two Poles in Dialogue" in https://munsonmissions.org/2018/08/15/two-poles-in-dialogue/. Access 03.02.2019.

[9] See Benny Thettayil, *In Spirit and Truth: an Exegetical Study of John 4:19-26 and a Theological Investigation of the Replacement Theme in the Fourth Gospel* (Contributions to Biblical Exegesis and Theology 46), Leuven, Dudley, New York: MS, 2007.

[10] Alan Race, *Christians and Religious Pluralism: Patterns in the Christian Theology of Religions*, Maryknoll, NY, Orbis, 1982. See also Alan Race, "Threefold Typology, and a Defence of Pluralism," In http://files.constantcontact. com/b0804459001/401ecd06-5a3d-41da-abdc-4d27c97deffa.pdf. Access 02.02.2019. The third element that he speaks of is Pluralism, which will not be given much consideration in our discussion.

[11] Stock, *Method and Message of Matthew*, p. 257, notes that the answer of Jesus is an answer to the controverted question whether the Gentile mission can be justified; he knows that he was sent to Israel... as he had first sent his disciples only to Israel (10:6)."

[12] Stock, *Method and Message of Matthew*, p. 257.

[13] However, it is a fact that even those who normally call themselves exclusivists, may have some inclusivistic views. For instance, they may believe that infants who die are saved by Jesus even though they do not know him. The same might go with those who are too mentally disabled to understand the gospel message and respond to it. Others may go further and say that those who have never heard the message of Christ may still be saved by Christ based on their response to the truth as they know it.

[14] Fitzmyer, *The Gospel according to Luke*, p. 827.

[15] See O. Cullmann, *Der johanneische Kreis. Zum Ursprung des Johannesevangeliums*, Tübingen: Mohr Siebeck, 1975, pp. 49-52.

[16] See Bowman, J., *Samaritan Studies*, in *BJRL* 40 (1958) 299-327.

[17] According to M. Hengel, *The Johannine Question*, Philadelphia, PA: Trinity Press International, 1989, p. 122; 216n., the Samaritans who are 'half Gentiles' are presented as representatives of all Gentiles.

[18] But according to Josephus (Ant. 20.118; War 2:232) this route also posed a lot of dangers and difficulties. See Josephus, *The Complete Works*, W. Whiston (trans.), Nashville, Thomas Nelson Publishers, 1998, p. 639.

[19] J. Ashton, *Understanding the Fourth Gospel*, Oxford: Clarendon, 1991, p. 295.

[20] See G.W. Buchanan, "The Samaritan Origin of the Gospel of John", in *Religions in Antiquity: Essays in Memory of Erwin Ramsdell Goodenough. Studies in the History of Religions*, ed. J. Neusner, Leiden: Brill, 1968, p. 163.

[21] C.K. Barrett, *The Gospel According to St John*, 2nd ed., Philadelphia: Westminster, 1978, p. 230.

[22] R.E. Brown, *The Gospel According to John*, vol. 1 (AB), Garden City, NY: Doubleday, 1966, p. 169.

[23] G.R. Beasley-Murray, *John* (WBC), Waco, TX: Word Books, 1987, p. 59.

[24] E. Keck, *Luke, John* (NIB), Nashville: Abingdon Press, 1995, p. 565.

[25] J. Maniparampil, *The Gospel according to the Beloved Disciple*, Bangalore: Claretian Publications, 2011, p. 293.

[26] J.A.T. Robinson, *The Destination and Purpose of St. John's Gospel*, in NTS 6 (1960) 117-131, p. 120, insists that the Greeks in John 12 are not Gentiles but Greek speaking Jews. However, R.E. Brown, *The Community of the Beloved Disciple*, New York, NY: Paulist, 1979, p. 55, suspects that 'it was particularly when the Johannine Christians of Jewish descent were rejected by Judaism and no longer thought of themselves as "Jews" that they received numbers of Gentiles into the community'.

[27] Hengel, *Johannine*, 122. R.E. Brown, *An Introduction to the New Testament* (ABRL), New York, NY et al.: Doubleday, 1997, p. 80, holds that the Greeks in chapter 12 are Gentiles. However, according to Wilson (*Related Strangers*, 74) 'the Greeks (*hellenes*) who came to worship in Jerusalem at Passover and ask to see Jesus (12:20-21) might be God-fearers, proselytes, or Diaspora Jews'.

[28] K.A. Koester, *Symbolism in the Fourth Gospel: Meaning, Mystery Community*, Minneapolis, MN: Fortress, 1995, p. 21. Among the scholars, there is a dispute regarding the real identity of the Greeks. Brown (*John*, lxxvii) observes that 'the role of xii 20 in the plan of the gospel cannot be explained unless 'Greeks' means gentiles'. From the context H.B. Kossen, *"Who Were the Greeks of John X11 20?"* Studies in John presented to Professor Dr J.N. Sevenster on the Occasion of His Seventieth Birthday (NovTSup 24), Leiden: Brill, 1970, p. 108, understands that they were the representatives of the Gentiles. J. Beutler, 'Greeks Come to See Jesus (John 12,20f)', *Bib* 71 (1990) p. 346, likewise opines that the 'coming of the Greeks to Jesus is the coming of those who had not seen' i.e., the Gentiles. B. Lindars, *The Gospel of John* (NCB), London: Oliphants, 1972, p. 192, sees the coming of the Greeks as pointing to a universal mission. T. Okure, *The Johannine Approach to Mission: A Contextual Study of John 4:1-42* (WUNT 2, Reihe 31) Tübingen: Mohr Siebeck, 1988, p. 64, agrees with Lindars

regarding the universal mission seen in the episode. See also Brown, *Community*, 55-58. Brown, *John*, pp. 29, 314, 318, 466, 470, holds the view that 'Greeks' refers to persons of Gentile origin. Likewise, J.L. Martyn, *A Gentile Mission that Replaced an Earlier Jewish Mission?*, in R.A. Culpepper et al. (eds.), *Exploring the Gospel of John* (FS D. Moody Smith), Louisville, KY: Westminster/John Knox Press, 1996, 124-144, p. 131, is convinced about the fact that the Greeks in John 12:20-24 'are surely Gentiles'. Similarly, K. Berger, *Im Anfang war Johannes: Datierung und Theologie des vierten Evangeliums*, Stuttgart: Quell, 1997, p. 156, speaks of the 'Heidenmission' in John 12. B. Klappert, *The Coming Son of Man Became Flesh: High Christology and Ant-Judaism in the Gospel of John*, in R. Bieringer, D. Pollefeyt and F. Vandecasteele-Vanneuville (eds.), *Anti-Judaism and the Fourth Gospel: Papers of the Leuven Colloquium, 2000* (Jewish and Christian Heritage Series 1), Assen: Royal Van Gorcum, 2001, 159-186, p. 183, also notes that the Greeks in 12 are 'god-fearing Non-Jewish Greeks, making a pilgrimage to the Passover'. However, it is to be noted that the presence of a significant Gentile Greek component in Johannine Christianity is disputed by J.L. Martyn, *The Gospel of John in Christian History: Essays for Interpreters*, New York, NY: Paulist Press, 1978, p. 120, because there seems to be no trace in the gospel of conflict over their inclusion in the community.

[29] S.B. Marrow, *The Gospel of John: A Reading*, New York: Paulist Press, 1995, p. 36.

[30] Stock, *Method and Message of Matthew*, p. 339.

[31] Marrow, *The Gospel of John*, p. 34.

[32] John Paul II, *Redemptoris Missio* 1991:28.

The Christian Transformation into the Image of Christ

Thomas Srampickal

T he idea of our adoption as children of God in Christ Jesus through the working of the Holy Spirit is discussed in Gal 4:5 and Rom 8:14-16. In Gal 3:26-27 and Rom 13:14 Paul explains further that this adoption as children of God takes place in baptism where we actually put on Christ, the new man or the new Adam. The deeper implications of putting on the new man who is Christ are explained in Col 3:1-17. It implies at the same time our putting away of the old nature of sin (Col 3:5). On the other hand putting on Christ involves adorning ourselves with the divine characteristics like compassion, kindness, lowliness, meekness, patience, love etc. which Christ possessed (Col 3:12). This incorporation into Christ results in the destruction of all the distinctions and enmity among the humans. It unites mankind as one body or one person in Christ (Gal 3:28; Col 3:11). Paul discusses the deeper implications of this transformation in texts like 2Cor 3:18, Rom 12:2, Gal 4:19, (Col 3:10), etc. 2Cor 3:18 contains a brief and comprehensive presentation of Paul's idea of Christian transformation. It offers us a clear idea with regard to Paul's vision of the Christian transformation into the image of Christ and the process involved in it. We may discuss it here in some detail. First of all we propose a translation for the verse 2Cor 3:18, which we deem more exact and present better Paul's original vision of Christian transformation contained in the verse, *"We all with unveiled face beholding the glory of the Lord as in a mirror are being transformed into the same image from glory to glory as it comes from the Lord's Spirit."*[1]

In the vision of the New Testament, Jesus Christ, the Incarnate Son of God who assumed our humanity in order to manifest the invisible face of God, our Heavenly Father, is not only the most exemplary model for our pilgrimage of life on earth in search of the Father's House, but also the prime spiritual source from which flows the divine power from the Father for the salvation of all humanity. This concise and important statement indicates Paul's vision of the Christian God-experience as well as the right spiritual process to be followed in realizing our transformation into the image of Jesus our Lord. We have in 2Cor 3:18, a culminating statement which in a summary from presents the glorious condition of the new covenant where people are progressively transformed.[2] This new state of affairs is presented in sharp contrast with the situation under the Mosaic Law, where the Jews were blindly succumbing to its enslaving power. Several authors see v. 18, the last verse of the pericope, as a recapitulating sentence that brings to conclusion the whole discussion in 2Cor chapter three.[3] Let us have a close consideration of this theologically important statement of Paul, discussing the verse part by part in order to have a clear understanding of the process of our internal transformation into the image of Christ as envisaged by the apostle. Every part this verse contains some significant insights into the mystery of Christian God-experience and transformation. We shall consider also the other related pronouncements of Paul in the discussion, so that we may have a more comprehensive understanding.

"We All"

The initial words of v.18 'we all' (ἡμεῖς δὲ πάντες) show that Paul is introducing a general statement, in the final verse of the pericope of 2Cor 3:7-18. The emphatic character of the expression implies a contrast. When we regard the expression in the light of the discussion in the pericope, the contrast naturally appears to be with Moses and the children of Israel referred to in 3:7-15. Paul presents the fully confident behaviour of the Christians as they participate and grow into the glorious image of the Lord.[4] They stand in full contrast with the Jews who failed to accept the revelation in Jesus, just like their ancestors who were blind before the glory of God revealed through Moses and failed to grasp God's words and obey him at Sinai (Ex 34:29-35).

Authors in general agree that the use of 'we' (ἡμε ῖς) closely defined through 'all' (δὲ πάντες) indicates not only Paul and his co-workers but all Christians. Paul praises the glory of the New Covenantal existence and explains that this surpassing glory is present to everybody who belongs to Christ. According to Bultmann the generalization to all Christians is already opened up in v. 16 and is explained further in v. 17. In v. 18 the general Christian self-consciousness is expressed.[5] A tone of triumph present in the emphatic use of 'all' (δὲ πάντες) and this exultation is due for the believers in Christ who share in the victory of the self-giving love of the crucified and Risen Lord.

"With Uncovered Face"

The expression **"With Uncovered Face"** (ἀνακεκαλυμμένῳ προσώπῳ), contains an allusion to the veil over the face of Moses and to the unbelief of the people of Israel at Sinai (Ex 34:33-35) as well as an allusion to the unbelieving Jews of the Pauline times. Their unbelief is contrasted with the faith of Christians[6] who opened their hearts to God, believing the gospel and accepting the salvation offered to humanity in Jesus Christ (2Cor 3:14-15). This symbolic expression implicitly glorifies on the one hand Paul's own new experience of faith in Jesus Christ as he surrendered himself to him through the experience of conversion which removed the veil of unbelief from his heart and gladdened his face in opening his eyes of faith in the Lord. On the other hand, it also implicitly glorifies the faith of the Christians who open their hearts to believe in Christ accepting with open minds the proclaimed gospel and commits their lives to God in Christ.[7] This new awareness of faith rejoices their minds and removes the veil of spiritual darkness of their hearts gladdening their faces as well. They joyfully relate themselves to

God and enjoy the fellowship with all believers with open minds and hearts (Acts 2:46-47).[8] Paul could summarily present the new experience of Christian openness through the short phrase, "with unveiled face" implicitly referring to the Sinai story and contrasting it with the Christian experience of spiritual freedom. [9] The usage implies a contrast of the Christians with the Jews and to their representative, Moses. What the expression connotes would be; *'we are neither diffident like Moses nor misconceived and close minded like the Israelites.'*

"Beholding the Glory of the Lord as in a Mirror"

The statement, "Beholding the Glory of the Lord as in a Mirror" (τὴν δόξαν κυρίου κατοπτριζόμενοι), points to the indirect aspect of our present God experience. At the same time it provides us a glimpse into the deeper implications of the process of our spiritual transformation. If, thanks to the privileged experience of Moses, the Old Covenant has been marked by a contemplation of the divine glory, the new covenant is characterized by a much higher contemplation of the glory. Since Paul uses a verb which signifies an indirect vision in a mirror, the superiority of this contemplation is not because of a more direct vision but because the Christian contemplation is not transitory as that of Moses and also because it is extended to all the believers.[10]

What is the contextual meaning of the Greek verb 'katoptrizomai' (κατοπτρίζομαι), which means, *to behold as in a mirror* or to *reflect as a mirror*? Is the mirror-notion which was contained in the classical use of the verb still maintained in Paul?

a. Reflecting or beholding?

It is generally observed that the extant Greek literature of the classical or of the New Testament times, provides us with no example of the middle verb *katoptr-zōmai* (κατοπτριζόμαι) in the active sense, *to reflect as a mirror*. It was always used with the meaning to behold as in a mirror. Still, a few authors have strongly argued that the context supports an active meaning, though it was comparatively, of later origin.

b.   Beholding as in a mirror

The majority of the authors believe that the participle *katoptrizōmenoi* (κατοπτριζόμενοι) is to be interpreted as beholding as in a mirror. The principal argument in favour of this is that the Greek verb *katoptrzō* (κατοπτρίζω) in the middle form does not have the meaning to reflect but only to contemplate or behold as in a mirror. Several authors (Godet, Kent, Collange, Bultmann and Feuillet) consider this as the strongest argument. Though the verb *katoptrzōmai* (κατοπτριζόμαι) generally means to behold or show as in a mirror, it can, in the active voice, sometimes mean to reflect as a mirror. Some authors have observed that in the Koine Greek active voices and middle voices are often confused and so the middle form of the verb could have gained the active meaning as well. Against this, others (Godet, N. Hugedé, Feuillet and Collange) point out that in the Greek literature no example of this verb in the middle having an active meaning has been found.[11]

Another argument in support of this position is that the ancient versions provide only the meaning of 'beholding as in a mirror.'[12] The Fathers of the early times (Origen, Tertullian, Augustine, Primasius, Chrysostom and Theodore) and especially the Greek Fathers favoured this meaning (refer. Godet, Feuillet and Collange). The context of the verse in 2Cor chapter three supports this position.

According to Ex 34:33-35, (which is behind our pericope) Moses unveiled his face before the Lord rather to behold the glory of God and not to reflect it. In the background of 2 Cor 3:18, (as pointed out by Barrett, Bultmann and Kruse) the idea of *being changed into the likeness of the Lord from one degree of glory to another*, is better understood to occur while believers are beholding rather than reflecting the glory of the Lord. Bultmann holds that the idea of transformation through reflection is not intelligible while indeed the idea of transformation through beholding is. It is to behold the glory of God and receive the knowledge of him that transforms. In support of this position Feuillet and Kruse indicate that in 2Cor 4:6 it is the beholding of the glory that Paul has in mind.[13]

Basing on the context, Barrett, Bultmann and Furnish argue that Christians are contrasted here not with Moses but with the unbelieving Jews and that this supports the meaning beholding as in a mirror. According to Bultmann, Christians can certainly not be compared with Moses, but only with Jews and "with uncovered Face" should be construed in terms of unveiled heart. The translation 'we reflect' would remove the contrast of the Christians with the Jews who, because of their veil, cannot behold the glory of the Lord (2 Cor 3:14-15).[14] Godet and Windisch argue in this direction basing on the context of the Pauline theology. As Paul indicates in 1 Cor 13:12, in this life we are not contemplating the glory of the Lord directly and face to face. This mode of contemplation will only be possible in the 'parousia.' One should not forget that, for Paul, to see the Lord means to have an indirect vision of the Lord (*katoptrzein*), rather than seeing face to face.[15]

It is also asked whether the Greek verb in the middle voice *katoptrzōmai* (Κατοπτρίζομαι) has retained in Paul its mirror-notion. In the later Greek, especially in the later Patristic usages, the image-value has been weakened and eroded and the verb often signified only *to see* or *to contemplate*. Most of the commentators do not accept such a possibility as early as the period of Paul. Several authors argue that such a verb which was used very rarely in the literature cannot have easily lost its sense of the mirror image.[16] It is indicated that some 15 usages of this rare verb in the middle voice so far noticed in the Greek literature always maintains its image-value.[17]

In fact, Moses unveiled his face in order to behold the glory of the Lord and not to provide a reflection of it to the Israelites. The veil as such did not stop the reflection; his face was reflecting the divine glory under the veil. What the veil hindered was the beholding of the glory by the Israelites. Also theologically speaking nobody can reflect the glory of the Lord without beholding his glory and receiving it from him. A mirror reflects only what it absorbs first. Therefore majority of the authors are for the meaning **to behold as in a mirror**. Also the early Fathers and ancient versions in general favour this line of interpretation.

c.   The Implied Metaphor of the Mirror

The next point to be considered is how the notion of the mirror is present in Paul's use of it. The general approach of the Pauline theology with regard to our vision of God, favours an idea of mediation just as the verb Katoptrvizomai with its implied metaphor of the mirror, indicates. Paul never claimed that he or the Christian community have a direct vision of God. 1Cor 13:12a: **"For now we see in a mirror dimly, but then face to face",** clearly shows Paul's approach in this regard (ref. 2Cor 5:6-7).

How can the mirror-notion implicit in our vision of the Lord be explained? The basic question here is - "what does the mirror represent?". There are suggestions to interpret the mirror either as Christ or the Gospel or the Christian community.[18] Paul believed that in the New Covenant, God revealed himself in Christ. According, to 2Cor 4:6 God's glory is manifested in the face of Christ. In 3:18 Paul speaks about our beholding the Lord's glory and about our Christian transformation. The question here is whether we have now a direct vision of the Risen Lord. In 5:6-7 Paul has expressed his mind in this regard. "We know that, while we are at home in the body, we are away from the Lord." So we do not have a direct vision of God nor of the Risen Lord, rather *we walk by the faith* revealed through the Gospel. In this regard the question whether the mirror is *the Gospel* or *the Christian community* does not seem to make much sense. For Paul, the Gospel was certainly not represented by a written book. It was rather the one which is proclaim*ed, believed and is living* in the Christian community. In 2Cor 4:4 he views the Gospel as the light of the glory of Christ and in 2:14 it is seen as the fragrance of the knowledge of him (Christ) that is being spread everywhere through the apostles.

"The Glory of the Lord"

Let us also consider whose glory is reflected in the mirror or whom Paul indicates by the term 'lord' (κυρίου) in the phrase 'the glory of the Lord' (τὴν δόξαν κυρίου). Christ can be regarded at the same as the mirror that reflects to us the glory of God as well as the image of God that is reflected. We do not have today direct vision of the Risen Lord, but only an indirect vision. Hence in the context of 2Cor 3:18, what is considered as the mirror is rather the Gospel, in which we behold Christ who is the image of God. The expression 'the glory of the Lord' (τὴν δόξαν κυρίου) in 3:18 appears parallel to the use 'the glory of Christ' in 4:4 where the Gospel is seen as the light of Christ's glory. His glory is manifested through the Gospel, which contains his teachings, and the ideals and values of the kingdom that he preached. It presents before us the witness of his life, his suffering, death and resurrection. It is the glory of God himself manifested in the face of Christ (4:6) and beheld by the Christians now in the mirror of the Gospel. In other words, when we behold Christ's glory in the mirror of the gospel, we gain a true glimpse of the glory of God.

"We are transformed"

The aspect of the Christians' growth into Christ or their transformation into the image of Christ that Paul expresses through the Greek verb *metamophōw* (μεταμορφόω) deserves our special attention. Paul has used this composite verb only twice (here and in Rom 12:2). What does Paul actually say concerning growth of Christian life through the use of this verb or what is the real nature of the Christian transformation?

Since Paul has used the Greek verb in the middle voice *metamophōw* (μεταμορφόω) only very rarely, its appearance in this context has aroused much interest. Initially we may indicate certain philological observations made by Bultmann and Plummer. Bultmann points out that the verb *morfōw* comes from the noun *morfē* (μορφή) which means that which appears towards the outside. It is contrasted with the essence for which the Old Testament and Paul lack a term. In fact, shape is the very expression of the essence. It is worthy of note that in Hellenistic Greek *morfē* (μορφή) is the term used to denote the divine essence. The compound verb *metamorfosthai* (μεταμοφοῦσθαι) implies change into a new shape i.e. a new essence.[19] Plummer indicates that *metamorfoùmetha* (μεταμορφούμεθα) is better translated as 'are transformed' than 'are changed'. For there exists another Greek verb, *allassesthai* (ἀλλάσσεσθαι) which means *'to be changed'*. He prefers to translate the verb as 'to be transfigured' because it expresses better a parallel with the synoptic use of *metamorfōw* (μεταμορφόω) (Mk 12:2; Mt 17:2).[20]

One main point authors discuss with regard to *metamorfosthai* (μεταμοφοῦσθαι) is the influence behind its use here. Is it the synoptic tradition about Jesus' transfiguration or the Moses-parallel from Exodus that influenced Paul in the use of the term? Or is there a Hellenistic influence or a Palestinian Jewish-motif behind it? Another important consideration is the nature of the transformation implied by the use of the present tense.

a.   The influences behind

Several authors have raised the question whether Paul was influenced by the conception of the Hellenistic mystery religions in putting forward the notion of a metamorphosis by vision. Recently Murphy-O'Connor has earnestly argued in favour of such an influence. He thinks that Paul might have been influenced by the widespread Hellenistic belief that the vision of a god or goddess has a transforming effect on the spectator. In his view the Pauline opponents in Corinth who are referred to in 2Corinthians, as those having received a different spirit (2Cor 11:4) must have been naturally subject to Hellenistic influence and they must have interpreted the glory of Moses in terms of metamorphosis. Against these people Paul insisted the transitory character of the Mosaic glory and highlighted the ever-intensifying transformation of the believers due to the effect of the gospel. Paul has consciously corrected the Hellenistic mystery-religions' conception of transformation making clear that believers are not transformed into gods but are progressively conformed to Christ.[21]

Against the background of the suggestions favouring a Hellenistic influence we may refer to the other position that the Palestinian Jewish motifs are sufficient to explain a concept of transformation by vision.

J. Fitzmyer offers several examples from the Qumran literature and from the Old Testament that express the idea of the illumination of the countenance and of the heart indicating a transformation. In his opinion though a specific idea of reflecting as a mirror (κατοπτριζόμενοι) cannot be found in these texts, the concept of transformation by vision could be seen as a Palestinian Jewish motif.[22]

E. Larsson raises the question whether Paul, in his exposition in 2 Cor 3:18-4:6, is not influenced by the tradition of Jesus' transfiguration on the mountain before his three disciples.[23] A basic difference between the synoptic tradition and Paul is accepted, as at the occasion of Jesus' transfiguration the disciples did not experience any transformation. Still there exists a resemblance in certain basic vocabulary between the synoptic narration and Paul, which cannot be explained by a common dependence of both on the Exodus narration of the Mosaic transfiguration. The Greek verbs metamorfosthai (μεταμοφοῦσθαι) and lmpein (λαμπειν) and the substantive dōxa (δόξα) are absent in the Exodus story, while they are common both to the Synoptics and Paul. Hence Larsson concludes that the story of Jesus transfiguration joined with the Exodus narrative is at the starting point of the Pauline conception of the Christian metamorphosis thanks to the contemplation of the divine glory. This dual background is considered sufficient to explain the Pauline formulation, making unnecessary any reference to extra-Biblical religious parallels. Feuillet and Lambrecht believe that the possibility of such an influence cannot be ruled out, even though they do not openly endorse the Larsson-theory. However Lambrecht finds the parallelism with Moses discussed in 2Cor 3:7-13 as the immediate reason to bring in the idea of transformation in 3:18.[24]

b.   The Nature of the Christian Transformation

It is in contrast to the physical transfiguration of Moses discussed in 2Cor 3:7-13, that Paul develops his conception of the intrinsic nature of the Christian transformation in 3:18. In the apology (2 Cor 2:14-7:4), Paul stresses the value of the spiritual and intrinsic realities. The idea of inner renewal and spiritual conformation to Christ is part of Paul's basic thought on baptism and Christian life. The primary source for this conception is nothing other than his own conversion experience and his inner realization of the spiritual renewal through the working of the Spirit. In 2Cor 4:7-5:4, he speaks of his weak physical existence and compares it with an earthen vessel. He carries the death of Jesus in his body through persecution, afflictions and through all kinds of sufferings. In several places in his epistles, Paul reminds us that our growth into Christ has to take place in the present life itself. In Gal 3:27, Paul says that in baptism Christians have put on Christ. Later in 4:19, he adds that Christ is to be formed in them. In 2 Cor 4:16, he speaks of his confidence because of the inner nature being renewed every day. Here it is clear that what he intends is their further growth into Christ after the baptism. All these indicate that the transformation in question is of an intrinsic or spiritual nature and that it is to happen in the context of the earthly life. In these texts and in 2 Cor 3:18 Paul seems thus to speak of the same act from two aspects, a moral transformation and a spiritual union with the Lord. The spiritual union itself involves a double process. We are being transformed into Christ and Christ is being formed in us (Gal 4:19).

c.   Moral Transformation

Paul's vision on the nature of the Christian transformation becomes further clear in Rom 12:2b, "be transformed by the renewal of your minds". The Christian transformation cannot be reduced to an accumulation of merits for the future glory. It happens rather through the inner illumination of hearts by the knowledge of God that comes to us through the Gospel of Christ (2 Cor 4:4-6). In Phil 1:9-11, Paul indicates that the Christian must grow in love and knowledge, and become pure, blameless and filled with the fruits of righteousness. In Gal 5:16-26, Paul beautifully discusses the moral transformation needed in the life of a Christian. In 5:19-21, he offers a list of negative things which are the works of the flesh and which bar a person from inheriting the kingdom of God. On the other hand, in 5:22 Paul offers a list of positive characteristics or virtues, which are the fruits of the Holy Spirit and which results from crucifying our negative desires and the passions of the flesh. Those who follow Christ should live by the Spirit and then there will be manifested the true fruits of the Holy Spirit in their lives: – love, joy, peace, patience, kindness, goodness, faithfulness, gentleness and self-control. These positive qualities belong to those who live according to the inspirations of the Holy Spirit, and they need no other law to walk in the ways of God. (Refer, Rom 6:13 and Col 3:1-15).

d.   Spiritual Union

The Christian transformation is understood by Paul really as a transformation into Christ himself or as a deeper spiritual union with Christ. In Rom 8:9-10 Paul writes: "But you are not in the flesh, you are in the Spirit, if in fact the Spirit of God dwells in you. Anyone who does not have the Spirit of Christ does not belong to him. But if Christ is in you, although your bodies are dead because of sin. Your spirits are alive because of righteousness." In Gal 2:19c-20 Paul beautifully explains his experience of the life of faith in Christ as a life of self-abandonment and as an experience within him of the living presence of Christ who is total self-giving love: "*I have been crucified with Christ; it is no longer I who live, but Christ who lives in me; and the life I now live in the flesh I live by faith in the Son of God, who loved me and gave himself for me.*" In Gal 4:19 he points to this living presence of Christ within us, as a simultaneous act. It implies that the transformation is a double process, i.e. we are being transformed to Christ and Christ is being formed in us. In 1Cor 6:17 Paul states, "But he who is united to the Lord becomes one spirit with him." These words point to the deeper aspect of the Christians' spiritual union with the Lord. Of course, this union with the Lord comes to the level of a profound realization in this life, only in the mystical experience of that union. (Reference may be made to the lofty writings of the great mystics like St. John of the cross or St. Theresa of Avila. See also Jn 6:56-57; 14:23; 15:1-10 etc.).

"The same Image"

When we consider the implication of Paul's usage of the phrase, **"The same Image"** (τὴν αὐτὴν εἰκόνα), we have to take into account his Jewish background. The Torah strictly prohibited the making of an image of god or of anything else and its worship (Ex 20:4; Deut 5:8). What lay behind this prohibition was the fear that the Israelites would be tempted to follow the idolatry practices of their neighbours. In spite of this unfavourable background, we still find that Paul is applying the term to Christ. In the vision of Paul as expressed in 2Cor 4:4 and Col 1:15, Jesus Christ is truly the Son of God, the image of the invisible eternal One, who is our Heavenly Father. In the fullness of time, through the incarnation of God's Son, the invisible of face of the One God is revealed for the salvation of all humanity, in the historical person of Jesus of Nazareth. The Gospel presents before us the beautiful example of Jesus life as our ideal to be imitated. God's will for humanity is that we should renew our lives according to the unsurpassing model given to us in Jesus Christ and should really become his image seeing his glorious face manifested in the gospel, and thus we should really bear the image of God, our Heavenly Father.

> To the modern mind, the use of the expression, *"image of God"* may appear to be a contradiction. How can there be an image of God who is invisible and formless? The expression is to be understood in the light of the approach of the ancient Greek philosophy which did not limit the meaning of the term *'image'* to a functional representation present to the human senses, as we often conceive of it today. They thought of it in terms of an emanation, of a revelation of the very being with a substantial participation in the original object. In the Platonic Cosmology, the world as a whole is the visible image of the invisible, yet intelligible *'World of Ideas'* (αὐτοζων). In this approach, the image is understood not as a reality present only in the mind or imagination. It has a share in reality, indeed it is the reality. Thus, the image (εἰκών) does not imply a weakening or a feeble copy of something; it implies the illumination of the being's inner core or essence. When Paul describes Christ as the image of God all the emphasis is on his equality with God. It is another way of talking about him as the Son of God. In the New Testament usage of the term image, the original is always implied and present. This aspect is clearly

expressed in Heb 10:1, which sharply distinguishes image (ε ι κών) from shadow (σκιά), which indicates only a shade or a faint outline, while *image* (ε ι κών) speaks of the substance: "Since the Law has only a shadow of the good things to come and not the substance of those realities ... ..."

One of the problems the authors face with regard to the expression, "The same Image" (τὴν αὐτὴν εἰκόνα) is the use of 'the same' (τὴν αὐτὴν) as if the term has already been introduced before.[25] In interpreting the sense of "The same Image" (τὴν αὐτὴν εἰκόνα) authors are somewhat evenly divided between two main ways of understanding. Many see it as a direct reference to the image of God which is Christ himself. Others think that the image spoken of is that of Christ and so only indirectly it alludes to the image of God.

Two different solutions are offered to explain the special meaning of the expression, *"the same"* (ε ἶκων with the qualification τὴν αὐτὴν). Some (Feuillet, Barrett, Lambrecht and Wong)[26] point out that the notion was already implied in the use of the Greek participle (κατοπτριζόμενοι) which means *'beholding as in a mirror'*. Both possible meanings of the term 'beholding' or 'reflecting' denote this idea.[27] Lambrecht and Wong indicate another possibility too. The Greek middle participle *'katoptrizómenoi'* (κατοπτριζόμενοι) has a direct object, *'the glory of the Lord'* (τὴν δόξαν κυρίου). In Paul the terms 'glory' and 'image' are very closely related. To be God's image is to manifest his glory. Hence the reference of "The same Image"(τὴν αὐτὴν εἰκόνα) could be to the previous use *'the glory of the Lord'* (τὴν δόξαν κυρίου). Wong goes even to the extent of identifying the use of the term 'the glory' with Christ and thinks that *'the glory'* and *'the image'* are parallel usages referring to the same person.[28]

It is generally accepted that, "The same Image" (τὴν αὐτὴν εἰκόνα) is a reference to Christ as the image of God which the believers behold as reflected in the mirror. In general they regard the mirror and the image as denoting one and the same person, Christ. Lambrecht interprets *'the mirror'* as the gospel and still holds that the

'the image' referred here is the image of God: " *...by the phrase in 2Cor 3:18 and Rom 8:29 Paul does not point to the image of Christ which the Christians are, but to the image of God which Christ is.*"[29] *Barrett explains that by Christ as the image of God what is meant is not a speculative personification as in Wisdom hypothesis but the historical person of Jesus in whom the invisible God becomes visible to man.* [30]

Godet clarifies that the reference is to the image of Christ, the glorified Lord whose divine beauty which believers behold in the gospel and which impresses itself on their hearts and lives, becomes their proper nature. As he points out, the image of Christ which we contemplate and try to conform ourselves with, is not a model exterior to us. The goal or object of our transformation in spiritual life, the *'image of the Lord,'* that we behold in faith, is not an exterior reality, but an internal presence. The specific sense is that we should undergo a transformation by which the image in question should become in a sense our proper moral being. Van Unnik thinks that the tenor of the whole passage and especially the expression "The same Image" (τὴν αὐτὴν εἰκόνα), indicate that the allusion is to *the image* of the One, whom we all have in common, namely *'the image'* of Christ to whom we with all our differences are transformed.[31]

Against the tendency to identify exactly *'the* image' referred to, Furnish comments that the question is wrongly posed when one asks whether *the image* mentioned is Christ's or God's. Paul is thinking of Christ as the image of God, the one in whom God's glory is disclosed. Then one has to say that the concept of *'the same image'* has a Christological and theological dimension simultaneously.[32]

Christ, the son of God in whom God is beheld, and the image of Christ into whom believers are being transformed, is one and the same Lord whom we see mirrored in the gospel manifesting the invisible face of God, our Father. By the expression *'the same image'* what Paul means, is that image of Christ we behold, as we reflect on the most beautiful model of his life present in the Gospel. According to Gal 4:19, 'Christ is to be formed in us.' As we accept the Gospel through faith and live it,

Christ is not outside us but inside us. The Gospel mirrors his image or somehow objectifies Christ for us, so that we may more and more perceive his glory. This beholding of the Lord and the transformation into him happens within us. The direction of the movement in the process of our transformation is not to the model of an external one, but to the image of Christ present within us, as we adore him in faith in our hearts.

"From Glory to Glory"

The basic discussion with regard to the expression "From Glory to Glory" (ἀπὸ δόξης εἰς δόξαν) is concerning the exact connotation it adds to the nature of transformation in question. Does it indicate a continuous progressive sense, or a causal sense, or does it contain a transitional sense? Some of the Fathers of the Church preferred a transitional sense that would indicate a movement from one kind of glory to another. St. Ephrem interpreted the sense of the expression '*from glory to glory*' as from the lost glory in paradise, to the heavenly glory gained through Christ. St. Augustine offered the explanation - from the glory of creation to the glory of justification.

In modern times Héring has offered an interpretation opting for a causal sense:- from the glory of God (as the source) to our glory (as the effect). According to him, "from glory" or 'by glory' (ἀπὸ δόξης), indicates the source, and "to Glory" (εἰς δόξαν) points to the result of the transformation, 'for' or 'towards glory'.[33] Such an interpretation in the causal sense denoting the glory of God or of Christ as the source of our glorification appears to make a better sense. But the difficulty with this interpretation is that the idea is already expressed otherwise in the verse. Furnish and Godet also see the possibility to have a causal sense for the expression in co-relation with the final phrase of the verse, "As it comes from the Lord's Spirit" (καθάπερ ἀπὸ κυρίου πνεύματος). It would imply that Christ's glory is the cause and principle of our transformation. But Godet offers two arguments to reject this option as less probable. First of all, in the present form the expression is subtle and unclear. Paul could have expressed it more clearly with the addition of (his - ἀτου) = "From his glory to glory" (ἀπὸ δόξης ἀυτου εἰς δόξαν). *Secondly the expression understood in this way only repeats the ideas that have already been expressed: ".. beholding the glory of the Lord as in a mirror" (cause), and ".. are being transformed into the same image" (effect).*[34]

The idea of a continuous progression in the process of our transformation appears to be the best sense possible in the, context. This meaning is quite appropriate because it brings the Christian transformation into sharp contrast with that of Moses which was by nature passing one. If Moses' glory was only transient and fading away after each renewal, our glory which is intrinsic and permanent, continuously grows. Such an idea of a present progressive transformation is considered as the best option by many modern authors.[35] The idea of a gradual progress is regarded as more natural in the context. It adds a new element to the sense: in opposition to the brightness of the face of Moses which was diminishing, the glory of Christians is not only permanent but increasing. In contrast to the simple reflection of the brightness which was exterior and temporary, the transformation is organic, vital, and consequently lasting. Plummer, Feuillet and Bultmann point out that a special aspect of the Christian transformation is underscored here.[36] It is a continuous and gradual process, and not a sudden change completed as if by magic in an instant. What results from a sudden change might end in stagnation. But the change in the Christian progresses from strength to strength and shines more and more unto the perfect day. According to Bultmann this is a process occurring in stages and without cessation. That this happens in the eschatological present follows from the fact that the beholding is a present activity. The transformation does not take place as a magical process but as the divine power coming into effect in the historical life of the believer.

"As it comes from the Lord's Spirit"

The concluding phrase of the pericope "As it comes from the Lord's Spirit" (καθάπερ ἀπὸ κυρίου πνεύματος)[37] *yields a variety of inter-pretations.* The complication in deciding the exact meaning of the Greek phrase (καθάπερ ἀπὸ κυρίου πνεύματος) comes from the structural and the grammatical peculiarities of the phrase,[38] as well as from the difficulty in deciding the exact contextual meaning of the polysemous word '*spirit*.'

In our opinion, in the phrase, "as it comes from the Lord's Spirit" (καθάπερ ἀπὸ κυρίου πνεύματος), the object of the Greek preposition '*apo*' (ἀπό=*from*) should naturally be '*the Spirit*' (πνεύματος - in the genitive case), and the other genitive, '*of the Lord*' (κυρίου) might be a possessive genitive. Then the phrase could be translated: '*from the Spirit of the Lord*' or '*from the Lord's Spirit*.' This reading goes quite in tune with the general approach of the theological vision of Paul as we find in the genuine Pauline letters. The Risen Lord works in the mind and heart of the believers through his Spirit. It is the Holy Spirit who touches hearts, converts them and renews the lives. Genuine transformation of life, is always the function of the Holy Spirit, as Paul explains in Rom chapter 8 and Gal chapters 4 and 5. In Gal 5:25 we read, "If we live by the Spirit, let us also walk by the Spirit." Accordingly we are spiritually alive because of the working of the Holy Spirit and we have to continue to grow spiritually living or walking according to the inspirations of the Holy Spirit.

The source of our Christian life and the power behind the ongoing spiritual growth and transformation is the Risen Lord who works in us through his Spirit and recreates us into his image as we behold him in the mirror of the Gospel. In Paul's view, the Risen Christ works in us always through his Spirit. The Holy Spirit who is the Spirit of God (Rom 8:9a) or of the Father is at the same time the Spirit of Christ (Rom 8:9b) or the Spirit of the Son (Gal 4:6). Therefore the interpretation or translation, "as it comes from the Lord's Spirit," appears to be fully in tune with the Pauline line of thought and richly meaningful. It is the Holy

Spirit who continuously works in us and transforms us internally drawing within us the image of Christ. In Rom 8 and Gal 4-5, Paul beautifully presents the Christo-centric and Trinitarian aspects of Christian life and spirituality. In Gal 4:4-7 we read, *"When the time had fully come, God sent forth his Son, born of woman, born under the Law, to redeem those who were under the Law, so that we might receive adoption as children. And because you are children, God has sent the Spirit of his Son into our hearts, crying 'Abba! Father.' So you are no longer a slave but a child, and if a child then an heir, through God"* (Refer also Rom 8:14-17). These verses summarily explain God, the Father's function of sending his Son to offer us salvation and to make us his dear children, and Father's gift of his Spirit to provide us the sense of children and to enable us to cry from the heart, *"Abba! Father."*

It is the Holy Spirit who provides us the New Life in Christ, enabling us to be born as children of God in Christ in the sacrament of baptism (ref Jn 3:5). It is the H. Spirit who acts in every sacrament and showers upon us all graces earned by Christ through the Salvific Act of the Cross. It is the Spirit who distributes all spiritual gifts and empowers everyone for every good work. Paul experienced the power of divine grace in the event of his conversion and all through his life. He was quite sure that his achievements in the apostolate were not really his own merit, but only the work of God's Spirit. (Rom 12:3; 15:15; 1Cor 3:10). Paul explains the function and importance of the H. Spirit in Christian life and how we have to live following the guidance of the Spirit, in Rom 8:2-16 and Gal 5:16-26. The best way to live according to the Christian faith is, to listen to the inner voice of the H. Spirit who speaks in the depths of the soul and follow it faithfully. He reminds us that the right way to overcome the passions of the flesh and to live the 'law of Christ' (Gal 6:2; 1Cor 9:21) or 'the law of love', is 'to walk according to the Spirit' (Rom 8:4; Gal 5:16).

The person who through total self-surrender places oneself or rather abandons oneself into the hands of God is certainly led by his Spirit and is enabled by grace to do whatever God wants from him. Paul was convinced that the success of the proclamation does not depend on human erudition or eloquence, but on the power of God's Spirit, who alone can touch the hearts and convert them. In the Pauline vision, the essence of Christian religion is grace and a good Christian life is our response of gratitude to God's self-gift to us in Jesus Christ. One who is compelled by the love of Christ and empowered by his Spirit, does the will of God from the heart. The fundamental basis of our hope and confidence should be in God's salvific love manifested in Jesus Christ (Rom 5:7-10). Paul had full confidence in the everlasting love and unwavering faithfulness of God and in the benevolent guidance of his Spirit. With deep trust he depended on the power of God's love and this enabled him to face challenges he had to encounter in the proclamation of the gospel and to overcome the oppositions and difficulties with courage and patience. Certainly it was from his deep personal experience that Paul could narrate so well the fruits of Holy Spirit in Gal 5:22, "*But the fruit of the Spirit is love, joy, peace, patience, kindness, goodness, faithfulness, gentleness, self-control; against such there is no law.*"

The statement, "as it comes from the Lord's Spirit" (καθάπερ ἀπὸ κυρίου πνεύματος) is to be seen as parallel to 2 Cor 3:17b, which points to the salvific function of the Holy Spirit. Together with Hering[39] (and also Lenski and Furnish) we consider the meaning: '*from the Lord's Spirit*' or '*from the Spirit of the Lord*' as the best probability.[40] It is evident that the term 'Lord' used here is a reference to Christ. In 2 Cor 3:14, Paul clearly says that it is Christ who removes the veil of stubbornness from our hearts. From there on wards, in verses 15-18 the antecedent of the term 'Lord' is Christ and Paul is consistent in his use of language. We have to live our Christian life carefully listening to the inspirations of Spirit and accomplishing God's will as the Spirit guides us and this openness to the illuminations of the Spirit will renew our lives and transform us truly to become the real image of Christ our Lord, making us to be the beloved children of God our Father.

Conclusion

In Paul's theological vision as indicated by 1Cor 15:45-49 and Rom 8:29-30, the goal of the salvation process for every human being, is to become the image of the Son of God. According to God's eternal plan of our salvation revealed in Jesus Christ, we are "... *predestined to be conformed to the image of God's Son, in order that he might be the first-born among many brethren*" (Rom 8:29). According to 1Cor 15:47-49, the goal of the whole process of the history of salvation is that all humanity should become conformed to the image of Christ. Paul has his own deeper vision in interpreting the use of divine image employed in Gen 1:27. In understanding the human beings' relationship with God the OT tradition emphasized Gen 2:7 and not 1:27. The central point in OT anthropology is that man is dust and ashes before God and that he cannot stand before God's holiness (Psalm 103:14; Eccl 3:20). In 1 Cor 15:45-49, Paul makes a comparison between Adam and Christ who, in the New Covenantal perspective, is the last Adam or the eschatological Adam. He applies only Gen 2:7 to the sinful humanity, which is represented by the first Adam. Gen 1:27 presents only God's plan for humanity in Christ. He is the last Adam, the eschatological Adam who fulfils within himself, what is intended by Gen 1:27. "*The first Adam was a man of dust, but the last Adam is a man from heaven who became the life-giving spirit ... ... Just as we have borne the image of the man of dust, we shall also bear the image of the man of heaven* (1 Cor 15:47, 49). God's plan for humanity is that they all should become conformed to the image of Christ the last Adam and thus should be transformed into the glorious, holy image of God. This, in the divine plan, is the marvellous goal of the whole salvation history.

What Paul explains in 2 Cor 3:18, is his vision concerning the process of our transformation, in realizing in us God's plan of salvation to make us conformed to the image of his Only Son, Jesus Christ our Lord. Interpreting in the light of his epistles in general, Paul's vision of Christian transformation contained in 2 Cor 3:18 could in brief be paraphrased thus: We Christians are to be neither diffident like Moses nor misconceived like the Israelites, but with trust, confidence, freedom and love, we have to behold the glory of the Lord in the mirror of the Gospel. This beholding would effect a real transformation of life in us, when we contemplate the sublime beauty of the loving and merciful face of God manifested in the incarnate Son of God, Jesus Christ as mirrored in the gospel. When the Gospel is made alive before us in the liturgy, or through meditative personal reading of the Scriptures or the proclaimed word, and as it renews our ways of life, we behold the glorious face of the Lord in contemplation. We are then being increasingly transformed into the image of the Lord which we behold. This happens especially when we celebrate the mysteries of faith in the liturgy, where the Lord manifests himself and acts in us to transform us and unite us with him.[41] This contemplation touches our hearts and challenges us to renew our lives; it transforms us morally and spiritually. A double process is involved here; we are transformed into Christ, as Christ is formed in us, lives in us. The Gospel offers us a new vision, a new value system and attitude, a new approach to life and makes us internally free through the indwelling presence of the Spirit. It effects in us a deeper spiritual or personal union with God in Christ. We are transformed and united with the Lord as the Lord unites himself with us; we live in the Lord as the Lord lives in us (Gal 2:20, 4:19). This is a process which begins in baptism and is to continue unto the last breath of life. And it is a conscious and free process that takes place in us, as we surrender ourselves to the Lord in love and admiration and walk in God's ways freely cooperating with the inspirations of the Holy Spirit (Rom 8:4; Gal (5:16), who dwells in our hearts (1 Cor 3:16; Rom 8:9) and unites us with Christ providing the sense that we are children of God, our Eternal Father (Gal 4:6-7; Rom 8:15-17).

Endnotes

[1] We cite here the original Greek text of 2Cor 3:18 for reference:- ἡμεῖς δὲ πάντες ἀνακεκαλυμμένῳ προσώπῳ τὴν δόξαν κυρίου κατοπτριζόμενοι τὴν αὐτὴν εἰκόνα μεταμορφούμεθα ἀπὸ δόξης εἰς δόξαν καθάπερ ἀπὸ κυρίου πνεύματος.

[2] In Furnish's view, the themes of the preceding verses are both integrated and assimilated to the new affirmation in v. 18. The themes of splendour (vv. 7-11) and of veiling (vv. 14-16) are explicit here and the related themes of boldness and freedom (vv. 12-13, 17) are implicit. See. V.P Furnish, *II Corinthians*, (Anchor Bible), Garden City, New York, 1984, 1985, p. 238.

[3] According to Windisch v. 18 leads the midrash (vv. 7-18) to a proud and jubilant confession. In it we may notice at the same time a continuation of v. 12, a positive completion of v. 13 and a building of an antithesis to vv. 13-16. The demonstration of freedom indicated by the expression, "With Uncovered Face" (ἀνακεκαλυμμένῳ προσώπῳ) shows that v. 18 also brings v. 17 to completion. H. Wisndisch, Der Zwite Korintherbrief (KKNT), Göttingen,1924, 1970; P. 127. We do not agree with Windissch in considering the text of 2Cor 3:7-18 a midrash. 2 Cor 3:7-18 does not serve the purpose of a midrash to Ex 34:29-35. Paul does not interpret the Scriptural text for the emulation of the present generation nor apply it to a new context. He refers to the Exodus text which describes the institution of the Mosaic ministry and the promulgation of the Law and declares that these institutions are no longer valid. Their glory is now surpassed and superceded by the gospel which proclaims the establishment of a New Covenant and a new ministry. Should we call such a composition a midrash?

[4] A midrash or a pesher is never written on a Scriptural passage to declare that the function of what is said there is cancelled and that the people have to look for a new scheme of salvation by which the plan provided in the Scripture is nullified and replaced. This indicates a fundamental difference from the midrashic form of interpretation.

[5] The emphatic character of the expression 'we all' is often noted by the authors. They generally express some unanimity with regard to the basic meaning of this expression though certain diversity of opinion could be observed with regard to the particulars. Plummer and Furnish opine that the particle *d'e* (δὲ) used here is not adversative but transitional. It means 'and' rather than 'but'. It expresses transition from the state of liberty indicated in v. 17 to those who are set free as described in v. 18. A. Plummer, A Critical and Exegetical Commentary on the Second Epistle of St Paul to the Corinthians (ICC), Edinburgh, 1915, p.105.

[6] Schlatter argues that if Paul had intended only himself and other ministers it would have resulted in a self recommendation which he emphatically denounces in the beginning of 2 Cor 3. He would have darkened the new covenant if he had praised only his dignity. A, Schlatter, Paulus der Bote Jesu. Eine Deutung seiner Briefe an die Korinther, Stuttgart, 1934, 1969. p. 519. Plummer points out that the contrast with Moses would be greatly weakened, if the 'we' is limited only to the ministers of the gospel. A. Plummer, p.105. R. Bultmann, Der Zweite Brief an die Korinther (KKNT), herausgegeben von E. Dinkler, Gẍttingen, 1976; (tr.) by

R.A. Harrisville, The Second Letter to the Corinthians, Minneapolis, 1985, p. 90. Acording to Collange, here the underlying contrast however is not between Israel and the Christians, but between the pseudo-apostles and the Christians. Against those pseudo-apostles in Corinth who claimed privileges for themselves Paul underscored the experience common to all Christians. See, J.F. Collange, Enigmes de la deuxième épître de Paul aux Corinthiens. Etude exégétique de 2 Cor. 2:14-7:4 (NTS MS 18), Cambridge, 1972. p. 115.

[7] While some authors see here a negative comparison or contrast with Moses others point to the Israelites and still others speak of a double contrast. Plummer finds here a contrast expressed with Moses whose face was veiled. The phrase indicates that the veil is now removed and there is no concealment in the case of the Christians. Collange and Kruse read a comparison with Moses in the positive sense. Collange argues that the mention in the pericope refers mainly to Moses and it is not the question of Israel except in vv. 7 and 13b. The reference to the face (πρoσώπoν) indicates that the allusion to Moses is positive and not to a Moses from whom the Christians should differentiate themselves but to the one who gives the example. According to Kruse, if Moses may have lacked boldness before the Israelites and so veiled his face, when he went in before the Lord he did it with confidence and freedom symbolized by his unveiled face. The believers too approach God in the same way. See Plummer, p. 105. Collange, pp. 115-116. C.G. Kruse, The Second Epistle of Paul to the Corinthians   An Introduction and Commentary (TNTC), England, 1987, p. 100.

[8] Lenski and Murphy-O'Connor find in the Christian behaviour a contrast as well as a comparison with Moses. Lenski points out that Moses veiled himself sometimes, but the Christians never veil themselves. As Moses' face reflected the divine glory, so our faces ever reflect the glory of God. There it was in a transient outward way, but in the new covenant, it is in an inward and permanent way. According to Murphy-O'Connor the contrast in 3:13 indicates that the Christians have the confidence (παρρησία), which Moses lacked and they possess the freedom given by the Spirit. But Moses was not always veiled. At times he went before the Lord and removed the veil to speak with him. Like Moses, the Christians have privileged access to God and in this they are contrasted with the Israelites whose hearts are under a veil. R.C.H. Lenski, The Interpretation of St. Paul's First and Second Epistles to the Corinthians, Minneapolis/Minnesota, 1937, 1963, pp. 947-948. Refer also, J. Murphy-O'Connor, "*Pneumatikoi and Judaizers in 2 Cor 2:14-4:6*", in Australian Biblical Review, 34 (1986), p. 53.

[9] According to Schlatter, as long as the veil remains over the hearts its effect remains also over the faces. If the heart does not feel, think and will, the eye

is blind and then the mind is blinded. In the opinion of Furnish, the term 'face' suggests a contrast to Moses while the context suggests a contrast to the unbelieving Jews whose hearts are veiled. This second option appears more probable because of the statement in v. 16, "when they turn to the Lord the veil is taken away". Here the face is equivalent to the hearts in v. 15. Schlatter, pp. 519-520. Furnish, pp. 213-214.

[10] Van Unnik observes here rather the influence of a Semitic usage where a veiled face symbolises lack of confidence and conversely the unveiled face confidence and openness. W.C. Van Unnik, *"The Semitic Background of* ΠΑΡΡΗΣΙΑ *in the New Testament"* in Sparsa Collecta II, (Supplements to NT,30), Leiden, 1980, pp. 290 306.

[11] A. Feuillet, Le Christ sagesse de Dieu d'après les épîtres pauliniennes (EBib), Paris, 1966. p. 138.

[12] G. Godet,., La seconde Épître aux Corinthiens, Neuchatel, 1914, p. 124. H.A, Kent, A Heart Opened Wide. Studies in II Corinthians, Grand Rapids (MN) 1982, pp. 63-64. Collange, pp. 116-118. Bultmann, p. 90. Feuillet, pp. 137-138. N. Huged ', La m'taphore du miroir dans les 'pntre de saint Paul aux Corinthiens, Neuchʌtel/ Paris, 1957, p. 23.

[13] Godet, Feuillet, Barrett, Bultmann, Collange and Furnish hold this argument. Godet, p. 124. C.K. Barrett, A Commentary on the Second Epistle to the Corinthians, London, 1973, p.125. Bultmann, p. 91. Collange, p. 117. Furnish, p. 214.

[14] Windisch, p. 128. Feuillet, pp. 141-142. Barrett, pp. 124-125. Collange, p. 118. Bultmann, pp. 91-92. Kruse, p. 100.

[15] The following authors have offered this argumentation. Refer, Barrett, p. 125. Bultmann, p. 91. Furnish, pp. 213-214, 239.

[16] Godet, pp. 124-125. Windisch, p. 128.

[17] R.P.J. Dupont, "Le Chrétien, Miroir de la Gloire divine d'après II Cor III,18", RB 56 (1949) 392-411. Feuillet, p. 142.. Collange, p. 117. J. Lambrecht, "Transformation in 2 Cor 3,18", Biblica, 64 (1983) 243-254. See esp. pp. 246-251.

[18] Hugedé, p. 23.

[19] Several authors interpret Christ as the mirror. Feuillet, p. 143; Collange, p. 118; Furnish, pp. 239-242. On the other hand some authors explain that the Gospel is the mirror in which we see the image of the Lord. See Godet, pp. 125-126; Kruse, p. 100; Lambrecht, p. 250. A few writers prefer to see the Christian Community as the mirror. Schlatter, p. 520; Carrez, p. 102. Lambrecht thinks that there need not be made a distinction between the Gospel and the Christian community. The Gospel in the context is to be understood as one being proclaimed by the apostles and accepted by the community in their lives, in other words a living Gospel.

[20] Bultmann, p. 95.

[21] Plummer, pp. 106-107.

[22] J. Murphy-O'Connor, "Pneumatikoi", pp. 54-55.

[23] J.A. Fitzmyer, "Glory Reflected on the Face of Christ (2 Cor 3:7-4:6) and a Palestinian Jewish Motif", TS 42 (1981) 630-644, esp. 639-644.

[24] E. Larsson, Christus als Vorbild, Eine Untersuchung zu den paulinischen Tauf- und Eikontexten (ASNU 23), Uppsala, 1962, pp. 282-284.

[25] Feuillet, p. 144. Lambrecht, p. 251.

[26] Plummer, p. 106. Bachmann, p. 177. Allo, E.B. Seconde Épître aux Corinthiens (EB), Paris, 1956. p. 96. Windisch, p. 128. Godet, p. 126. Lenski, p. 949. Feuillet, p. 144. Another diffaculty is the accusative use of the expression as if it were the object of an active verb while the Greek verb used here is in the passive "We are transformed (into) *the same Image* (τὴν αὐτὴν εἰκόνα μεταμορφούμεθα)." Several authors attempt to find an explanation for this accusative use with a passive verb. Plummer points out that in the past some have considered a preposition like '*to*' or '*into*' (κατά or εἰς) as understood. But he rejects such a hypothesis and states that such a verbal form in Greek used here (μεταμορφούμεθα) meaning 'to change,' need not have a preposition. By themselves they imply 'to change to' or 'to change into.' Bachmann and Allo think that the accusative without preposition is an accusative of internal object and denotes the purpose or aim of the movement. See Plummer, p. 106. Bachmann, p. 177. Allo, E.B. Seconde Épître aux Corinthiens (EB), Paris, 1956. p. 96. Windisch, p. 128. Godet, p. 126. Lenski, p. 949. Feuillet, p. 144.

[27] Feuillet, p. 145. Barrett, p. 125. Lambrecht, p. 245. Wong, p. 67.

[28] Feuillet has argued that if we accept the sense 'to behold as in a mirror' instead of the other meaning 'to reflect as mirror' the whole difficulty would fully disappear: *We are transformed into the same image that we contemplate.* But we think that both meanings can help us equally in this case: *We are transformed into the same image that we behold or reflect.* See Feuillet, p. 145. Lambrecht too has expressed this view. Ref. Lambrecht, p. 245. See also Barrett, p. 125. Wong, Emily, "The Lord is the Spirit (2 Cor 3, 17a)", in ETL, 61 (1985), p. 67.

[29] Lambrecht, pp. 245-246. Wong, "The Lord is the Spirit", p. 67.

[30] Lambrecht, pp. 245-246.

[31] Barrett, p. 125

[32] Godet, p. 126. Van Unnik, "With Unveiled Face", pp. 167-168.

[33] Furnish, p. 215.

[34] Héring, pp. 27-28.

[35] Furnish, pp. 215-216, 242. Godet, p. 126. Goudge thinks that either of the interpretations, a causal sense or a progressive sense could be adopted with equal probability. The thought is either that the transformation proceeds from the divine

glory and brings glory to us, or that the glory instead of fading, grows from more to more. See Goudge, p. 33.

[36] Plummer, p. 107. Lenski, p. 950. Allo, pp. 96-97. Feuillet, p. 145. Bultmann, p. 95. Wong Emily, pp. 67-68.

[37] Plummer, p. 107. Feuillet, p. 145. Bultmann, pp. 95-96.

[38] Schmithals. views the closing words of v. 18: καθάπερ   ἀπὸ   κυρϱ ου   πνε΄ υματος (together with v. 17) as a Gnostic gloss added by one of the Corinthian opponents of Paul as a marginal comment in the original epistle itself. Later, in copying the marginal gloss crept into the text itself. Schmithals, Gnosticism in Corinth, an Investigation of the Letters to the Corinthians, (tr.) J.E. Steely, Nashville/New York, 1971. pp. 321-324.

[39] The Greek preposition ἀπό   takes genitive case for its object. In the phrase the nouns κυριοs and πέυμα are used in the genitive κυρϱου   πνε΄ υματοs. Hence one of them should be object of the preposition and the other may be a possessive genitive. This complexity brings a variety of possibilities for the interpretation. If κυρϱου is the object of the preposition ἀπό, the term πνε΄ υματοs can be considered either as a possessive genitive with the meaning: *'from the Lord of the Spirit'* or πνε΄ υματοs can be considered as used in apposition with κυρϱου with meaning: *'from the Lord, the Spirit* or *'from the Lord who is the Spirit.'* If the direct object of από is πνε΄ υματοs, and   κυρϱου is a possessive genitive, it could mean: *'from the Spirit of the Lord'* or *'from the Lord's Spirit.'*

[40] *Héring has strongly suggested the translation, the Spirit of the Lord. For it is the Spirit who produces the transformation. Lenski and Furnish as well propose this rendering as a good possibility.* Héring, p. 28. Lenski, pp. 950-951. Furnish, p. 216.

[41] *But Bultmann has rejected this option saying, for such a rendering the Greek text should have been* ἀπὸ   πνεύματοs κυρίου   = *'from the Spirit of the Lord'; the present form can scarcely be read thus.* See Bultmann, p. 96. But we find several usages of Paul himself to justify the rendering *'from the Lord's Spirit'* or *'from the Spirit of the Lord.'* In Romans 8:11 we find Paul is using the expression ἀτου   πνευματοs in the sense of *'his (God's) Spirit.'* In 1Cor 2:7 Paul is using expression – Θεοῦ   σοφίαν meaning *'God's wisdom,'* as we have in 2Cor 3:18f – ... Κυρίου   πνεύματοs = Lord's Spirit.

[42] Our participation in the liturgical celebration of the Eucharist is discussed in 1Cor 10:16-17; 11:23-30; and Baptism in Rom 6:3-23; 1Cor 6:11; 12:13 etc.

Secularism and Christians: Biblical Perspectives

Joy Philip Kakkanatt

Introduction

The word 'secularism' and other semantically related terms like 'secular,' 'secularization,' are understood differently in different parts of the world. Especially the term 'secularism' connotes seemingly divergent nuances. In the West, secularism basically means having no religious affiliation, and to be secular means to be a free-thinker, to relegate faith to a private and personal sphere, etc. To be secular, in this sense, implies saying no to the supernatural, reducing everything to this world, and to deny anything and everything beyond human reason as myth and fiction. As Pope Benedict XVI points out, western secularization "has relegated the Christian faith to the margins of life as if it were irrelevant to everyday affairs."[1] This tendency has even developed a positivistic and *secularized hermeneutic* ultimately based on the conviction that the Divine does not intervene in human history. According to this hermeneutic, whenever a divine element seems present, it has to be explained in some other way, reducing everything to the human element. This leads to interpretations that deny the historicity of the divine elements.[2] It even leads to the denial of divine intervention in human realm as a truthful reality, and rejects it as a matter of faith. The effect of such a secular outlook is the divorcing of faith from life, both in the individual and social realms, as seen in the legalization of gay marriages, etc. The danger of this understanding of secularism is the reduction of faith and the Church or of any religion as a matter to be decided by each individual without having any communitarian implications and objective norms. As Pope Francis summarises:

> The process of secularisation tends to reduce the faith and the Church to the sphere of the private and personal. Furthermore, by completely rejecting the transcendent, it has produced a growing deterioration of ethics, a weakening of the sense of personal and collective sin, and a steady increase in relativism. These have led to a general sense of disorientation, especially in the periods of adolescence and young adulthood which are so vulnerable to change.[3]

In short, this understanding of secularism implies no norms based on faith and religion, freedom from all religions and religious things and reduces faith to a totally subjective and private affair without having any repercussion on the state, the policies, etc.

Differing with this western understanding of secularism, by secularism we in India mean equality and respect of every human being, irrespective of caste, creed, gender and race. It implies the acceptance of all religions as equal and the equal treatment of all religions by the state. It also includes the legal measures that will not tolerate public intolerance to minorities.[4]

The difference in the understanding of secularism can be illustrated by an example: In the West, to be secular means removal of all religious symbols in the name of religious neutrality. In India, secularism means to have the broad mindedness to permit all the religious symbols to co-exist. As one scholar says: "Secularism in the Indian context should imply respect for pluralism and a non-coercive and a voluntary recourse to change. Respect for diversity not only embodies the democratic spirit, it is the real guarantee of unity. We should value democratic, not fascistic, unity."[5]

Now the questions for us to consider are: What does it mean to be secular as a Christian? Or are there possible secular perspectives we can derive from the Bible? Or to put it in a slightly different way, what are the biblical values that help us to be secular in our Christian living? Some important dimensions of secularism, in my opinion, are the freedom and space that are given to others to make their own choices in life, the magnanimity shown in helping a person to live well, and the tolerance of co-existence despite differences. This becomes all the more relevant today, when facisit forces with extreme right political and religious ideologies try to reduce the freedom of movement and expression to people to think differently and have a different religious affinity than the one they uphold as valid to be an Indian.

The right to be Free - the Message of Exodus

A very fundamental value of the event of Exodus is the right to be free. If slavery is the coercive limiting of one's freedom of existence and movement, the Exodus teaches that the God of the Bible is somebody who does not tolerate oppression of slavery and that God is a dynamic force who engages actively in human history to guarantee freedom of expression and service. "Let my people go so that that they can have a free space to worship me" (see Exod 5:1) is a call to grant freedom of movement. While Egypt and Pharaoh symbolize the forces that curtail the right of freedom, Moses represents the mediator and intercessor who facilitates the liberation to freedom of worship, decision making, and freedom of movement. The Exodus as a liberating movement towards freedom from all kinds of slavery has many implications when we speak of secularism as basically permitting others space to exist while safeguarding our own right to exist. We Christians in India can become agents and mediators of facilitating the fundamental right of every human being "to be free" to exist with the dignity of a human being. All life negating elements – be it fundamentalism, discrimination based on caste and creed, gender, corruption, denial of religious freedom, gender injustice, child labour, etc.– are contemporary forms of slavery, which hinder human freedom.[6] Here an observation of W. Brueggemann is well in place. He warns against the danger of "spiritualizing the Exodus language" by reducing the slavery merely to sin and the liberation as liberation from sin, and he insists that "it is simply wrong to refuse the material dimension of slavery and freedom."[7] He continues:

> The world of bondage, so well-known by Israel, persists in our time. The power of deathliness, which resists the liberating intention of Yahweh, continues powerfully, perhaps in more clever form than in ancient times. In the face of that enduring threat, Israel's testimony continues to be recited in hope and courage. This testimony is about the resolve of Yahweh and the work of Yahweh's recruited human agents.[8]

In the New Testament, this value of freedom of existence with dignity gets a new thrust in and through the words and deeds of Jesus. The sum and substance of Jesus' proclamation is liberation, which is all-encompassing, covering both material and spiritual. It is not to let any dominant power throw a stone at a poor marginalized person, even if sinful, and in that way to help a bruised reed and a dimly burning wick to find space and freedom to rekindle and live (Isa 42:1-4). At the same time, it is to help experience an inner transformation or *metanoia* of leading a morally better life by avoiding sinful paths (Jn 8). As the famous Nazareth manifesto clarifies, the ministry of Jesus is total liberation of humanity (Lk 4:18-20). The "liberating attitude," as Jesus documents in the Gospels, helps us to develop a secularized hermeneutic to live the Christian faith in radically new ways by giving value to the humanness of the marginalized in this globalized era.[9]

Such an understanding of Exodus as active engagement to create a better freedom of existence, has universal significance and helps us to go beyond a too spiritualized and sectarian understanding of freedom and to involve with greater commitment in the struggles of the oppressed and the marginalized for liberation and freedom of expression.[10]

Solidarity vs Individualism and Exclusion

An important challenge of Christian secularism is to promote a culture of co-existence and proactive living together to counter the threat of the atheistic secularism which advocates individualism, relativism and consumerism. As Pope Francis points out, "We should recognize how in a culture where each person wants to be bearer of his or her own subjective truth, it becomes difficult for [the]citizen to devise a common plan which transcends individual gain and personal ambition."[11]Solidarity in essence means "to think in terms of the community and priority of the life of all over the appropriation of goods by a few."[12] Both the Old Testament and New Testament stress this aspect. The very character of God of the Bible is communitarian. The God of the Bible is One who involves actively in the human life situation through his active intervention in history, especially in solidarity with the powerless and less privileged of the society. The basic tenant of the covenantal relationship, which is central to biblical faith, is reciprocity and commitment towards the well-being of the other. The prophetic understanding of justice and righteousness as taking care of the marginalized - the poor, the widow, the orphan, the alien of the society - is derived from the covenantal understanding of community. What prophets criticized as injustice is "a life of self-protection, self-sufficiency and self-indulgence."[13] The prophetic advocacy to seek the Lord, not by going to the sanctuaries and the performing cults but rather by doing justice and righteousness, may help us grasp the meaning of living the faith in a secular way (Isa 1:11ff.; Jer 7:4-7; Amos 5:21ff; Micah 6:8 etc). It is to imitate the God of the Bible not only in liturgy but also in solidarity with the voiceless of the society.

When we come to the New Testament, Jesus teaches us to show solidarity by being as merciful as the good Samaritan (Lk 10: 25-37), as merciful as the father of the prodigal son (Lk 15: 11-32), as merciful as Jesus himself who was through and through compassionate in his words and deeds. There is not even a single episode in the Gospels where Jesus turned a deaf ear and blind eye to the request of a any needy person, whether material, physical or spiritual. Rather, he was actively merciful in seeing the misery of the people and in doing something to alleviate it. He not only identified the hunger of the people, but provided food for them. As Tomas Halik writes:

What Jesus had to say about the last judgment assures us that God will accept *implicit, anonymous* faith, displayed in *acts of mercy*, in service to the suffering and needy... It is clear from Jesus' description that the justified will also include those who have no "pious" motive at all-they simply do it on account of the suffering people themselves.[14]

The socio-cultural and religious implications of this are very clear: In the Indian scenario, where human dignity is often challenged based on caste, gender, etc. we are called to be merciful by helping people who suffer from loss of dignity to regain it, by being actively compassionate to them. In the Indian context, I think that we need to be more secular in living our faith because we still practice a faith which is piety and cult-oriented and less action-oriented.

To be Tolerant and Broad-minded to Others

When one is convinced of one's own faith and is totally committed to its practice, there is a danger of intolerance to other faiths. This becomes all the more problematic in monolithic cultural contexts such as that of Europe. If one is familiar with only one's own faith, that person may become so circumscribed by it that he/she cannot see anything positive about others' faith and then naturally becomes very suspicious and critical of it. In this context, especially in our multi-religious and multi-ethnic context, is there any viable attitude possible which would safeguard our faith, but at the same time maintain a healthy tolerant dialogical relationship to other faiths? Here I would like to bring to your attention some passages, one from the OT and another from the NT which may help us in this regard.

Micah 4:1-5 is a beautiful text, which speaks of the universal attraction of the Torah coming from the mountain of the Lord, Jerusalem. The Torah becomes a point of reference not only for Israel but for all peoples and the result is shalom, well-being resulting from the harmony of relationships. The point I want to highlight is the language of welcoming invitation to all to accept the Torah. There is no coercion, but only a proposition. The text insists that, while we follow our own religious convictions with total dedication and commitment, we should be broad-minded in recognizing the freedom of others to have their own convictions. Micah 4:5 says, "For all the peoples walk, each in the name of its god, but we will walk in the name of the LORD our God forever and ever." It is a tolerant openness we rarely see in the OT. It means to avoid exclusivism and absolutism of beliefs to the extent that we leave no space and freedom for the other to exist.

The same openness is visible in the *kerygma* of the Gospel. A notable feature of Jesus' proclamation of the Kingdom of God is that he never compels, but only proposes.[15] When some of the disciples found the words of Jesus hard to grasp they left him. Jesus does not compel them to follow him, rather, he offers even to his closest circle of twelve the freedom of choice of departing from him (Jn 6:66-68). "Come, follow me" (Mark 10:21) and "Come and see" (Jn 1:39) is a loving invitation of discipleship which one is free to accept or decline.

In his reply to the Samaritan woman, Jesus shows openness to and recognition of the Samaritans (Jn 4:1-42) with respect, without forgetting their difference. It is a great virtue to recognize the goodness of others, even while one may not be fully in agreement with them. Jesus showed the courage to avoid animosity created by exclusions, thus bridging the fissure between Jews and Samaritans by walking across the territories of the Samaritans to reach Galilee from Judea. Jesus' attitude towards the Samaritans, which advocates avoiding contrasts and divisive approaches and by promoting common ground, is a great lesson of Christian secularism.

Universality of God's Mercy

In the Book of Jonah we see a great theme of the availability of God's mercy not only to the chosen people but to all those who are receptive to God's initiatives. The Book teaches the universal character of God's forgiveness, and in that way demands that humanity respect the freedom of God to show mercy and compassion to all whom he wishes. Man cannot put terms on God's nature. Jonah challenges us to have a broadminded attitude to the mercy of God. While we wish to receive God's mercy and forgiveness for our sins and flaws, we need to let others, too, enjoy the same mercy and forgiveness.

If we had to answer the question of the most unique value of the gospel of Jesus Christ, I consider it would be reconciliation effected through merciful love and vicarious suffering. The cross of Christ, which is the essence of the gospel,[16] being the ultimate symbol of reconciliation, is the best answer to the culture of animosity, atrocity, division and violence. If the culture of violence results from a mentality of contradictions and contra-positions, on the Cross we see biblical revelation proposing a model of reconciliation achieved through loving participation and immersion into the situation of a malady to transform it. The greatest newness of the gospel message is God's self-communication in the form of self-giving for the betterment of humanity. "For God so loved the world that he gave his only Son, that whoever believes in him should not perish but have eternal life" (Jn 3:16).

Here, we should not miss the universalism of Jesus' death on the cross. Jesus died on the cross not for a particular group, but for the whole humanity. St. Paul in Rom 10:12-13 says: (For there is no distinction between Jew and Greek; the same Lord is Lord of all and bestows his riches upon all who call upon him. For, everyone who calls upon the name of the Lord will be saved.

Christian Vocation: to be a Living Gospel of God's Mercy

Jesus' discourse on the final Judgment in Mt 25:31-46 can be considered as a commentary on the fifth beatitude "Blessed are the merciful, for they will receive mercy" (Mt 5:7). The final judgment will be the good news of salvation for those who practiced mercy towards the needy. It consists of active commitment and forgiveness. To be merciful means "to be sensitive to other people." As Pope Francis remarks: the lack of mercy is visible in the indifference to the plight of the other and in the culture of comfort. In his words:

> The culture of comfort, which makes us think only of ourselves, makes us insensitive to the cries of other people, makes us live in soap bubbles

which, however lovely, are insubstantial; they offer a fleeting and empty illusion which results in indifference to others; indeed, it even leads to the globalization of indifference. In this globalized world, we have fallen into globalized indifference. We have become used to the suffering of others: it doesn't affect me; it doesn't concern me; it's none of my business![17]

Christian mercy is universal:[18] There is no religion for basic human needs like food, shelter, human dignity, health, forgiveness, etc. When the heart is moved with pity, one can transcend the prejudices of segregation to become a true neighbor to a person or community in need. Jesus establishes the norm of Christian mercy in his teaching: to be ready to serve anyone who has need of us along the road of life and to become that person's sister or brother, whatever his or her political ideology, social class, or moral condition.[19]

In this way, universal charity, which is mercy in action, can become an effective means for evangelization as a witness to the style of Jesus.

Work for Uplifting the Cause of the Deprived People: The Best Way to live Christian faith in a Secular Way

An important component of Jesus' teaching is the ethical demand of living the Christian faith, which is essentially taking care of the poor.

A secularized spirituality is one that is other-oriented as that of the Good Samaritan of the parable. The priest and Levites maintained a religiosity which was self-centered. For a Christian, every needy person becomes a neighbour. Jesus modifies the question from who is my neighbour to what is to be done to be a neighbour to a person in need. One becomes a neighbour to a person by caring for him/her in his misery. One becomes a neighbour when one's heart and bowels recoil when confronted with suffering and misery, which would prompt him/her to change his/her itinerary and do what is necessary to alleviate the predicament. The whole of the activity of the Samaritan is understood as an expression of the sentiment of mercy. The same can be seen also in the parable of the Pharisee and Tax Collector in Luke 19:9-17.

Christian Secularism: A Call to be a Counter-Culture

If we want to make Christianity credible, we must present it as a cultural alternative to the dominant culture of today which is insensitive to the cry of the marginalised and the middle class and caters only to the management of a surplus balance sheet. In a culture where the majority are side-lined for the benefit of a few privileged minorities, it is good to revisit the God of the Bible who presents himself as the One who leaves the ninety-nine in the desert and goes after the lost one.

This means, as Walter Kasper [*Mercy: The Essence of the Gospel and the Key to Christian Living*] writes, to use the biblical understanding of God "who suffers [*mitleidet*] with his creatures, who as *misericors* has a heart (*cor*) with the poor and for the poor (*miseri*)" as the starting point for theology, rather than use metaphysical notions.[20] If the theological academia and the *magisterium* had focused on the central revelation of the Bible as a merciful God who listens to the cry of the poor and the less privileged, and at times cries with the poor, no Christian would have sat quietly watching the anti-rape demonstration in Delhi few years ago. They would have been at the fore-front of such initiatives, in order to highlight the cultural alternatives to the dominant culture of today.

Jesus showed through his life and ministry an alternative for the self-centred power structure which reduces authority to being served rather than to serve. He resisted the temptation to make use of his power for his own glorification and gratification, but rather, exercised that power to feed the five thousand hungry.

In his miracles we see Jesus constantly in solidarity with the marginalized of the society. The shift of focus of the Christian culture is clear in Jesus' teaching in the words of Mt 25:40: "Truly, I say to you, as you did it to one of the least of these my brethren, you did it to me." He is careful to protect the cause of the weak, when he warns not to harm any of the little ones (*paidia*) of the community. We can identify here a core value of the Christian: to act as a cultural alternative to the culture of contemptuous disconnect to the minority concerns and voices and to develop a new culture of interface with them. It is important, because, as Felix Wilfred says, "The vision and world-view of Jesus and his praxis is one of helping to construct the suppressed identities of the *anawim* relegated to the backyard of history by the power centers of Palestine as well as of the Roman Empire."[21]

In the present day culture of economic and financial globalization, Jesus' vision of attention to the little ones on the margins becomes even more pressing. When the dominant culture is poised to dance to the tune of a profit-oriented market economy, and when 'the common man feels cheated, robbed and waits embittered as he perceives that he is excluded from the mainstream,'[22] the Christian vision should insist on the principles of subsidiarity and solidarity.[23]

Another feature of the Christian culture which stands in contrast to the prevailing worldview is the attitude of humility. Jesus in washing the feet of his disciples (Jn 13) sets an example of the virtue of humility and demonstrates the meaning of his saying: "But it shall not be so among you; but whoever would be great among you must be your servant, and whoever would be first among you must be slave of all" (Mk 10:43-44). He symbolically enacts his readiness to empty himself (*kenosis*) for others. He teaches us that humility is a willing self-sacrificial service for others, and it is essentially an attitude of regarding the other and not a self-regarding act.[24]

St. Paul writes in Phil 2:4-11 that Jesus, knowing his elevated status of being equal to God, showed a humble attitude in emptying himself (*kenosis*) in order to elevate humanity to a loftier status. An aspect of true humility, as manifested by Jesus Christ in the incarnation, is the ability to empty oneself to identify with the less privileged of humanity in order to lift them up. The altruistic self-emptying of Jesus in the incarnation reaches its utmost limit in his undergoing death on a cross, the most degrading death of all, in order to save humankind from the wretchedness of sin.[25] Paul suggests the self-emptying and self-sacrificing humility of Jesus Christ for the well-being of others, as the ultimate model for Christian behaviour and action.[26]

Conclusion

What I have been trying to present is to identify a few biblical themes which help the Christians to provide a new interpretation to the idea of secularism. The Bible presents a spirituality rooted in the revelation of God who communicates himself through His words and deeds. The God of the Bible is One who actively involves in human history with compassion; a God who suffers within Himself to save humanity from its maladies both material and spiritual (Hos 11:8-9); a God who relents from punishing because as Ezekiel proclaims, God has "no pleasure in the death of the wicked, but that the wicked turn from his way and live" (33:11). A true Christian faith-living means to imitate the nature of God as revealed in the Bible, especially in imitating Jesus Christ, the supreme culmination of Divine revelation, who continues to challenge us to re-examine our Christian living and to promote a spirituality which engages in bringing Good News to many lives because that is the ultimate message of Jesus Christ (euvaggeli,ouVIhsou/ Cristou/). It means to make a pilgrimage to the Sanctuary of God in cultic prayer and to recognize the needy person at the pool of Bethsaida of human existential predicaments and to help him/her to get up and go home. As we can all agree, "Deprivation and misery cannot be papered over with rhetoric, which is notoriously counterproductive when words and deeds part company."[27] This is true for faith-living. If Christianity wants to remain relevant in a scenario of growing insensibility to the ills of unbridled globalization and capitalism, it should live its faith in a secular way by being active in creating alternative trends for better human and ecological co-existence. Finally, Christian secularism is to be practised in building bridges of solidarity and facilitating accommodation of estranged sojourners generated by war, ethnic and religious conflicts, poverty etc, rather than building walls of separation that will lead to unrest, hatred and alienation.[28]

Endnotes

[1] Pope Benedict XVI, *Sacramentum caritatis*, 2007, 77.

[2] Pope Benedict XVI, *Post-Synodal Apostolic Exhortation Verbum Domini*, Trivandrum: Carmel Publishing House, 2010, # 35.

[3] Pope Francis, *Apostolic Exhortation Evangelii Gaudium*, Trivandrum: Carmel Publishing House, 2013, # 64.

[4] See Dipankar Gupta, "How to Secularise Secularism", *The Times of India* (Monday, November 30, 2015), 14.

[5] http://www.civilserviceindia.com/subject/Essay/secularism.html, accessed on 09.03.2015.

[6] See Mani Chacko Modayil, "The Biblical Jubilee: Culture as Social Dream and Protest" in *Liberation Hermeneutics in the Indian Interpretation of the Bible*, K. Jesurathnam et al, ed., Thiruvalla: CSS, 2012, 177 for a detailed description of slavery.

[7] Walter Brueggemann, *Theology of the Old Testament*, Minneapolis: Fortress Press, 1997, 180.

[8] Brueggemann, *Theology of the Old Testament*, 180.

[9] See J Severino Croatto, *Exodus a Hermeneutic of Freedom*, Maryknoll, New York: Orbis Books, 1981, 48-66.

[10] See Croatto, *Exodus a Hermeneutic of Freedom*, 8.

[11] Pope Francis, *Evengelii Gaudium*, # 63.

[12] Pope Francis, *Evengelii Gaudium*, # 188.

[13] Brueggemann, *Theology of the Old Testament*, 422.

[14] Tomas Halik, *Patience with God*, New York: Doubleday, 2009, 200.

[15] Jeffrey Bloechl, "Christianity in a Secular Age: Beyond the Zero-Sum Game", http://www.abc.net.au/religion/articles/2014/09/17/4089705.htm accessed on 88.03.2015.

[16] Kazoh Kitamori, *Theology of the Pain of God*. London: SCM Press, 1966, 140.

[17] http://www.vatican.va/holy_father/francesco/homilies/2013/documents/papa-francesco_20130708_omelia-lampedusa_en.html, on 14.08.2013.

[18] Pope Benedict XVI, *Deus Caritas Est*, Mumbai: St. Pauline Publications, 2006, #25

[19] Segundo Galilea, *The Beatitudes: to Evangelize as Jesus Did*. Maryknoll, New York: Orbis Books, 1984, 56.

[20] Walter Kasper, *Mercy: The Essence of the Gospel and the Key to Christian Living*. New York: Paulist Press, 2013, 11.

[21] Felix Wilfred, The Sling of *Utopia*, Delhi: ISPCK, 2005, 42.

[22] Valson Thampu, "Misreading Meaning of 2014 Lok Sabha Poll Mandate", *Deccan Herald* (Friday 19 February 2016), 11.

[23] Pope Francis, *Evangelii Gaudium*, #189-190; also Kasper, *Mercy*, 187-189.

[24] Ben Witherington III, *John's Wisdom*, Louisville, Kentucky: Westminster John Knox Press, 1995, 240-241.

[25] Peter T. O'Brien, *The Epistle to the Philippians: A Commentary on the Greek Text*, Grand Rapids, Michigan: William B. Eerdmans Publishing Company, 1991, 227-229.

[26] Gerald F. Hawthorne, *Philippians*, Word Biblical Commentary, vol. 43, Nashville: Thomas Nelson Publishers, 1983, 79.

[27] Thampu, "Misreading", 11.

[28] See http://w2.vatican.va/content/francesco/it/speeches/2016/february/documents/papa-francesco_20160217_messico-conferenza-stampa.html accessed on 20.02.2016.

Part Three

Practical Theology

Wandering with the Master:
A Theological Learning Experience

Sebastian Elavathingal

WANDERING – THE SCHOOL OF JESUS

Wandering with the Master and learning from experience, instruction and reflection are integral features of contextual theological formation. The model and inspiration of this theological wandering is the three years of itinerant life of the disciples with Jesus.[1] In fact, wandering from place to place is the typical method of instruction employed by Jesus to explain the meaning of God's reign and to foster the faith of the disciples in a fatherly God. The disciples learned from direct experiences of life as well as from the timely instructions given by Jesus. They reflected on the Master's words and tried to grasp the divine mystery as much as they could. Learning was for them a personally transforming experience. Their feet were moving with hope, hands were doing good with love and eyes were seeing wonders with faith.[2] Along with the physical wandering, the disciples dared to undertake an adventurous journey into the divine Mystery, guided by Jesus. They attained the realization that the Jesus who walked with them is the Word made flesh, the Son of the living God, the Lord and the Messiah.

From the Gospel narratives it becomes evident that wandering from place to place was the typical method adopted by Jesus for the spiritual and theological formation of the disciples. "Jesus went about all the cities and villages, teaching in their synagogues, and preaching the gospel of the Kingdom and healing every disease and every infirmity" (Mt 9:35). In fact, Jesus imparted to the disciples the most important truths about God, when they journeyed with him. Their wandering with dusty feet on the roads of Galilea and Judea, meeting people of all sorts in the surrounding villages was for them a journey of faith.[3] Their physical wandering coincided with an inward spiritual journey by which they underwent a thorough transformation in their way of thinking and behaviour. They became the convinced messengers of Good News all over the world.

No doubt, in contextual theological formation the Master who accompanies the students is primarily Jesus Christ. He dons on himself the mantle of a teacher, when he says, "You call me Teacher and Lord; and you are right, for so I am" (Jn 13:13). This role is taken secondarily only by the guide of theological formation who is designated as the master of the students to accompany their action and reflection programmes. The master has an inalienable role in the learning process through wandering. The constant presence of the master denotes the purposefulness of wandering that it is not to be seen as a lazy "aimless" motion or an activity of recreation and relaxation.

WANDERING AND THE UNFOLDING CONSCIOUSNESS

Wandering means not only physical mobility, but also the activity of an exploring mind with intellectual eagerness and emotional vitality. It is a process of the unfolding of consciousness that takes place progressively at different levels of human experiences in actual life contexts. While wandering, Jesus the Master imparted the knowledge of God through his words of truth, actions of goodness and images of miraculous power and glory. Words, actions and images correspond to all the levels of active human awareness. It can be seen as a holistic and experiential way of learning, involving the whole person – mind, hands and heart.

Following Jesus as a disciple is often compared to ascending to the top of a mountain. Ascending implies the physical and spiritual movements, demanded by the challenging vocation of following Jesus. Physical ascent implies an ascetic process of renunciation and consequently a return to the original perfection.[4] The mountain is shown in the Bible as a place of spiritual enlightenment. There are many instances in the Gospel, in which Jesus felt closer to the heavenly Father and moved by the power of the Spirit, when he was on a mountain to teach or to pray. From this, it can be assumed that the movement of ascending to the heights implies the revelation and clarification of the Trinitarian mystery. It elucidates the life of the Son, his relationship to the Father and to the Holy Spirit.[5] That is why on some occasions, Jesus' self-revelation takes place in a spectacular manner on mountaintops.[6] He reveals the mystery of his Trinitarian life by returning to the heights from where he descended (Jn 3:13). During the Transfiguration on Mount Tabor the heavenly Father authenticates the person and the mission of the Son. "He was still speaking when, behold, a bright cloud overshadowed them, and a voice from the cloud said, 'This is my beloved Son, with whom I am well pleased; listen to him'" (Mt 17:5).

WANDERING AND SEEKING THE KINGDOM OF GOD

Throughout the three years of their wandering Jesus tried to drive home one truth, one core message, which would transform and characterize the lives of his disciples. He summed up his entire teaching under the umbrella concept of the "kingdom of God". It was an entirely new vision of life and reality. It was however, not simply an ideology nor a theory to be reflected and grasped conceptually. In order to realize the message of the kingdom of God, the disciples were asked to set out in search of it. "Seek first his kingdom and his righteousness, and all these things shall be yours as well" (Mt 6:33). It required a "conversion" of the person, in order to grasp its mysterious nature.

Jesus' wandering life began after announcing the kingdom of God as his life's mission on earth. "Jesus came proclaiming the good news of God and saying, 'The time has been completed and the kingdom of God has drawn near; repent and believe in the good news'" (Mk 1:14-15). In Luke's Gospel the beginning of Jesus' ministry is in Nazareth. In the synagogue, he read from the scroll of Isaiah chapter 61, "The Spirit of the Lord is on me, because he has anointed me to preach good news to the poor. He has sent me to proclaim freedom for the prisoners and recovery of sight for the blind, to release the oppressed, to proclaim the year of the Lord's favour". Then he proclaimed solemnly, "Today this scripture has been fulfilled in your hearing." Thereby Jesus hinted at the inauguration of the reign of God with its programme and action plan.

The concept of the kingdom of God is not defined by Jesus anywhere. But he describes its nature with various images, stories and parables. The Pharisees asked Jesus, "when is the kingdom of God coming?" To this question Jesus responded quickly and clearly, "the kingdom of God is not coming with signs to be observed; nor will they say, 'Lo, here it is!' or 'there!' for behold, the kingdom of God is in the midst of you" (Lk 17:20-25). Jesus tried to explain the silent and hidden nature of the kingdom of God, when he compared it to a tiny mustard see which would grow into a tree (Mk 4:30-32; Mt 13:31-32; Lk 13:18-19). It is like the seeds sown in a field. The sower goes to sleep. Nobody knows how the seeds grow, because God grants growth to the seeds (Mk 4:26-29). It is like a hidden treasure in a field or a fine pearl sought after by a merchant (Mt 13:44-46). Underlining the slow and silent nature of the kingdom of God, Pope Francis says, "The Kingdom of God is not a spectacle."[7] It is won through a process of life, beset with hardships, humiliations and rejections, leading finally to blessedness, peace, comfort and joy (Mt 5:3-12). It is not by theorizing but by confronting the harsh realities of life that the mystery of the kingdom of God is revealed and experienced.

WANDERING WITH JESUS, THE TEACHER

Jesus wandered among the people, in towns and villages, in their different life situations preaching and healing (Mt 9:35). People considered him as a respectable teacher *(Rabbi)* and approached with questions, sometimes approvingly and sometimes skeptically. Nicodemus, himself a teacher, asked Jesus calling him Rabbi, "How can anyone be born after having grown old? Can one enter a second time into the mother's womb and be born?" (Jn 3:4). Jesus clarified his doubt by showing the need of being born of the Spirit as spiritual persons. The Samaritan woman asked Jesus, "Sir, you have nothing to draw with, and the well is deep; where do you get that living water?" (Jn 4:11). Jesus enlightened her saying that water can well up in each one who approaches the source of the living water, Jesus himself. To the question "Is it lawful to cure on the Sabbath?" (Mt 12:10) Jesus gave the interpretation of the law of the Sabbath with the knowledge of a teacher. The Sadducees raised the question of resurrection to test Jesus (Mt 22:28). Jesus corrected their ignorance of the scriptures and taught the true meaning of resurrection. The rich young man addressed Jesus, ""Teacher, what good deed must I do, to have eternal life?" (Mt 19:16; Mk 10:17; Lk 10:25). Jesus taught him the way of renunciation. Similar questions which raised by the people and disciples were answered by Jesus clarifying their doubts about right living (Jn 6:28, 30) and human relationships (Mt 18: 21). Jesus interpreted the law in terms of mercy and forgiveness (Jn 8:15).

What distinguished Jesus from other teachers of his time was his wandering. "Foxes have holes and birds of the air have nests; but the Son of man has nowhere to lay his head" (Mt 8:20; Lk 9:58). Jesus is found in the desert (Mk 1:12) beside the sea (Mk 2:13), in the fields (Mk 2:23), on the mountain (Mk 3:13) among the crowds (Mk 4:1), in the villages (8:27) and in prayerful solitude (Mt 14:23). The Gospel of Mark traces Jesus' itinerary from Nazareth to Jerusalem. "Jesus wanders from Nazareth to the Jordan, then stays in the desert near the lower course of the Jordan (Mk 1:1-13). Afterwards he goes to Galilee (Mk 1:14-9: 50) and undertakes two side-trips into the land of the Gentiles (Mk 5:1-20; 7:24-28), then he returns to the lower course of the Jordan to the oasis Jericho (Mk 10:1-52) and ends his journey in Jerusalem (Mk 11:1-16:8)."[8]

The words spoken by Jesus were responded by his hearers not in the same manner. Jesus would compare the fate of his words to the fate of the seeds sown by a farmer in his field. As he sowed, some seeds fell along the path, the birds devoured them. Other seeds fell on rocky ground. They sprang up immediately, but in the scorching sun they withered away. Some seeds fell upon thorns, and the thorns choked them. Those seeds that fell on good soil brought forth plenty of grains (Mt 13:3-9). Sometimes his words were beyond the grasp of the disciples, especially when he spoke about the suffering and death ahead of him. Peter tried even to detract him from the way of suffering (Mk 8:32-33). Still they believed in the truth and authenticity of his words. Simon Peter said, "Lord, to whom shall we go? You have the words of eternal life" (Jn 6:68). The recognized in Jesus the truth, the life and the way (Jn 14:6). They were to attain the fullness life, listening to his words, imitating his actions and following his path.

Listening to the Word of God consists not in the grasping of an idea, but in meeting the person of Jesus and learning from him what it means to be human. "Being Christian is not the result of an ethical choice or a lofty idea, but the encounter with an event, a person, which gives life a new horizon and a decisive direction. Saint John's Gospel describes that event in these words: 'God so loved the world that he gave his only Son, that whoever believes in him should ... have eternal life'" (3:16).[9] Jesus himself is the Word of eternal life. What he teaches is more than the words of wisdom. It is the "bread" that nourishes and gives life. His words are not only to be heard and understood, but also to be tasted and experienced by body and mind at the same time. Jesus said, "The words which I have spoken to you are spirit and are life" (Jn 6:63). Jesus would remind the tempting devil, quoting from the Scripture (Deut 8:3) that what nourishes a person is the Word of God. "Man shall not live by bread alone, but by every word that proceeds from the mouth of God" (Mt 4:4). The intimacy of the Word of God was experienced by prophet Jeremiah as he ate the words coming from God's mouth. They became to him "a joy and the delight" of his heart

(Jer 15:16). Prophet Ezekiel was given a scroll with the Word of God. "And he said to me, 'Son of man, eat this scroll that I give you and fill your stomach with it.' Then I ate it; and it was in my mouth as sweet as honey" (Ezek 3:3). The Word of God is his kindness that can be tasted as milk (1 Pet 2:2) and relished as honey (Ps 19:10; 119:103).

WANDERING WITH JESUS, THE MAN OF THE SPIRIT

The active life of Jesus among the people was impelled by the power of the Spirit. At the beginning of his ministry, as he was baptized by John in Jordan "the heaven was opened, and the Holy Spirit descended upon him in bodily form like a dove" (Lk 3:21-22). He was led by the Spirit to the desert to be tempted. "Then Jesus, filled with the power of the Spirit, returned to Galilee, and a report about him spread through all the surrounding country" (Lk 4:14). In the synagogue at Nazareth, after reading from the scroll, Jesus applied to himself the words of prophet Isaiah, "The Spirit of the Lord is on me, because he has anointed me to proclaim good news to the poor. He has sent me to proclaim freedom for the prisoners and recovery of sight for the blind, to set the oppressed free, to proclaim the year of the Lord's favor" (Lk 4:18-19). It was the formal inauguration of his ministry among the people.

Wandering with Jesus participating in his ministry among people living in all conditions of life offered the disciples possibilities to learn from his actions. His way of behaviour while dealing with people taught them many practical lessons of life. They observed and learned from his attitudes, values and preferences in human relationships (Mt 5-7). Jesus was decidedly on the side of the poor and the weak. He condemned hypocrisy (Mt 23: 1-39). He was kind-hearted towards the sick (Mk 1:41; Lk 7:12-14) and merciful towards sinners (Lk 15:1-2). He appreciated the faith of the people, irrespective of their social and religious background. As shown in the Gospel narratives, Jesus did not hesitate to approve the compassion of the Good Samaritan, the deep trust of the Centurion (Mt 8:10) and the undaunted faith of the Canaanite woman (Mt 15:21-28), even though they were non-Jews. Jesus even approved the good works of a stranger, whom the disciples wanted to prohibit. He said, "Do not stop him ....for whoever is not against us is for us" (Mk 9:39-40). Jesus included in his circle all those who are of good will. The universal outlook of Jesus is expressed, when he says, "Whoever does the will of my Father in heaven is my brother, and sister and mother" (Mt 12:50).

The miracles of Jesus were overwhelming experiences of life for the disciples. They were spellbound at the wedding in Cana, when Jesus showed the first sign of his divine power (Jn 2:1-11). The miracle of Transfiguration on Mount Tabor was for them such a "shattering" experience that they fell down on their faces (Mt 17:1-8). It meant for them a "shocking" awareness change, which transposed them to an ecstatic state of mind. Jesus touched and raised them. From their "fallen state" they were "corrected" in their body and mind with a renewed awareness of the reality around them. All the other miracles of healing, feeding, exorcising and resuscitating which Jesus performed on the way were also moments of self-transcendence, in which the disciples were raised to higher realms of spiritual awareness, which extended beyond the physical limits of seeing, doing and reflecting. The climax of Jesus' wandering with the disciples is his solemn entry to Jerusalem. It highlights the glorious image of Jesus as the King and the Lord. "Throwing their garments on the colt they set Jesus upon it. And as he rode along, they spread their garments on the road. As he was now drawing near, at the descent of the Mount of Olives, the whole multitude of the disciples began to rejoice and praise God with a loud voice for all the mighty works that they had seen, saying, 'Blessed is the King who comes in the name of the Lord! Peace in heaven and glory in the highest!'" (Lk 19: 35-38; Mt 21:6-9; Mk 11:7-10).

WANDERING AND SPIRITUAL TRANSFORMATION

Walking with Jesus was for the disciples a learning process resulting in a spiritual transformation. It involved a new theological understanding, a new awareness of God and humanity, which "corrected and perfected" (Mt 5:17) their previous notions. It was more than mere theoretical or discursive learning. The education of the disciples through wandering with Jesus was experiential, that is, comprising the sensitive, intellectual and emotional levels of awareness, touching and transforming the whole person.

Transformation can be seen in their changed awareness of God, which is characterized by an understanding of God as a loving Father, inviting to an intimate personal relationship. The stories and parables of God's love narrated by Jesus instilled in them the love for God the Father so deeply that they yearned to see the Father immediately. Philip said, "Lord, show us the Father, and we will be satisfied" (Jn 14: 8). The pursuit of knowledge shown by Jesus finally reaches God the Father. It consists in a spiritual regeneration of becoming the children of the loving Father (Jn 3:3). It is important to note that in the teaching method of Jesus the Master, the contextual experiences of the disciples are braided and integrated to their knowledge of God and the world. Jesus takes the disciples through the entire gamut of human experiences. From fishermen in the Sea of Galilee they were transformed into fishers of men (Mt 4:19). It was a long journey, which began with the call, "come and follow me" at the shores of Galilee (Mk 1:16-18; Mt 4:18-19). After traversing many different terrains of experiences, it came to an end on the Mount of Olives with Jesus' ascension into heaven. (Lk 24:50-51; Acts 1:6-9). He promised them the Holy Spirit to continue his mission.

Wandering with Jesus involves a transition from stability to mobility in theological search, understanding and experience. It reveals a God who is loving, merciful and forgiving. There is a theological position which holds that the truth of God is immutable. Monotheistic faith sometimes absolutizes a monolithic God-Image, which admits no change. The divine absolutism represents the tyranny of the Law which terrorizes and enslaves. It scares the mind and stagnates the spirit with fundamentalist instincts. But Jesus Christ comes preaching a Gospel of freedom from the Law. "For all who rely on the works of the law are under a curse; for it is written, 'Cursed is everyone who does not observe and obey all the things written in the book of the law'.... Christ redeemed us from the curse of the law by becoming a curse for us" (Gal 3:10-13). Jesus liberates humanity from the oppression of the Law by showing a new perspective.

It is not by blindly observing the Law, but by responding sensitively to human situations that one can fulfill the Law. Jesus taught this new understanding of the Law by narrating the story of the merciful Samaritan, who proved to be a good neighbour to the wounded traveller (Lk 10:25-37). The law-abiding priest and the Levite passed by quietly on the other side of the road, in order to avoid the man in need. Again, there are instances of interpreting the Sabbat law. According to Jesus, the Sabbath is to be subordinated to human needs (Lk 14:3; Jn 5:9; Mk 3:4). In judging the sinful woman Jesus did not apply the Mosaic Law of stoning a sinner to death. Instead, he appealed to the conscience of the accusers and let the woman go free without any word of condemnation (Jn 8:1-11). Jesus gives in all these instances a contextual interpretation of the Law, showing the mind of the Law-Giver, God.

THE WANDERING WITH THE "LOGOS" IN HISTORY

The physical wandering of the disciples coincided with an inner spiritual adventure which took them to the depths of the divine Mystery. The Mystery unfolded before them, revealing gradually the true identity of Jesus as the Word of God, the Son of the living God and the Messiah. The teachings and the actions of Jesus naturally raised questions about his person (Mt 13:55; Jn 6:42; Mk 6:3) and his authority (Mt 21:23-27; Mk 11:27-33; Lk 20:1-8). Who is Jesus? What is his source of authority?

Jesus' wandering in the world began, as he was sent by the Father. He revealed the origin of his mission, when his authority was questioned. "All things have been delivered to me by my Father; and no one knows the Son except the Father; nor does anyone know the Father except the Son, and anyone to whom the Son chooses to reveal Him" (Mt 11:27). At this point, the journey of faith needs retrospection, a looking backward to the origin of Jesus' mission. It can take the form of an "unfolding" of awareness from within. The journey outward is simultaneously a journey inward. It is delving deep into the divine Mystery from which the "history" of Jesus originates and unfolds in the world. Jesus takes us to the origins, when he claims that his authority is from the Father who sent him (Jn 3:35; Jn 17:2; Mt 28:18-20).

At some point of their wandering, the disciples heard the voice of the Father from heaven, which confirmed their faith in him (Mt 3:17; Mk 1:11). Jesus is the abiding presence of God with his people, "Emmanuel" (Mt 1:21), fulfilling the messianic prophesy of Isaiah (Is 7:14). Simon Peter was inspired to recognize Jesus as the Messiah, when he confessed, "You are the Christ, the Son of the living God" (Mt 16:16). It is only after seeing the resurrected Jesus with his wounds that Thomas exclaimed "My Lord and my God" (Jn 20:28). It was a gradual realization for the disciples that the one who wandered with them in the lifestyle of a "servant" is the Son of God.

In his Gospel John traces the person and the authority of Jesus to the timeless beginnings. He is the "Word made Flesh". John recognizes in Jesus the "Logos," hidden in God and operating with him, when the heaven and earth were created. "In the beginning was the Word, and the Word was with God, and the Word was God. He was with God in the beginning" (Jn 1:1-2). The Old Testament speaks of the Logos as a hidden associate of God's work, taking pleasure in the creation of the world (Prov 8:23-31). John would corroborate this Old Testament understanding saying, "Through him all things were made; without him nothing was made that has been made. In him was life, and that life was the light of all mankind. The light shines in the darkness, and the darkness has not overcome it" (Jn 1:3-5). John alludes to God's self-revelation beginning with the creation of light. God uttered his Word, "'Let there be light,' and there was light" (Gen 1:3). Referring to this primordial event, John would see Jesus as light and life. The Word who is the life and light of the world took the human form in the Incarnation and became the life and light of the world (Jn 8:12; Jn 14:6).

The notion of Logos in creation has been developed by the Fathers of the Church to show the evolutionary unfolding of the universe as the progressive revelation of Jesus Christ in his glory.[10] The Holy Spirit is the power that draws each human person and the universe to fullness in Christ through all the vicissitudes of history, which evolves in the course of time.[11] The insight into the authority and authenticity of Jesus as the Word of God, the Logos of creation is, therefore, not only a "retrospect" of Jesus Christ's preexistence and preeminence, but also a "prospect" of his future manifestation in the fullness of glory. "The Word became flesh and made his dwelling among us. We have seen his glory, the glory of the one and only Son, who came from the Father, full of grace and truth" (Jn 1:14).[12] It gives us a vision of the fulfilment of the creation in the glorification of the Son. What holds these two moments of "beginning and fulfilment" together is the vibrant and creative tension of history.

THE CREATIVE PROSPECT OF WANDERING IN THE UNFOLDING OF THE "IMAGE OF GOD"

Imago Dei, the Image of God is, like the Logos, another biblical expression which has inherent in it a creative and evolutionary dynamism. In St. Paul's letter to the Colossians we read, "He is the image of the invisible God, the first-born of all creation; for in him all things were created, in heaven and on earth, visible and invisible, whether thrones or dominions or principalities or authorities—all things were created through him and for him" (Col 1:15-16; 2 Cor 4:4). This text shows the pre-eminence of Christ, his centrality in creation and his "exemplary" role in salvation.

Jesus Christ is the Exemplar of creation. It is after his model and according to his "measure" that everything in creation has come into existence. The mention of the exemplary role of the image of God is already in the creation account of the Book of Genesis (Gen 1:26-27; 5:1; 9:6). St. Paul recognizes in Jesus Christ the divine "design" embedded in the creation and manifested in humanity through the works of salvation. He writes, "He is before all things, and in him all things hold together. He is the head of the body, the church; he is the beginning, the first-born from the dead, that in everything he might be pre-eminent.

For in him all the fullness of God was pleased to dwell, and through him to reconcile to himself all things, whether on earth or in heaven, making peace by the blood of his cross" (Col 1:17-20). The reconciling role of Jesus in the world is an ongoing process, in which all are called to participate through their respective ministries, contributing to the building up the body of Christ. The finality of this process is the growth of everyone "to maturity, to the measure of the full stature of Christ" (Eph 4:13). It is also the task of realizing a human community which grows up in every way "into him who is the head, into Christ, from whom the whole body, joined and knit together by every ligament with which it is equipped, as each part is working properly, promotes the body's growth in building itself up in love" (Eph 4:15-16).

From the vision of a universe which attains progressive fulfilment, moving towards the realization of fullness in Jesus Christ, who is the "Word" and the "Image," ensues the itinerant nature of our theological endeavour extended in space-time, in human history. Theological search is to be undertaken with sensibility to the creative tension in history and readiness to participate in it. The incarnate Word appropriated human history with all its spatial and temporal limitations. He walked his way through the varied terrains of his living space, weathering all kinds of experiences proper to human nature. As one among the humans, it was necessary for him to suffer many things. "He must be rejected by the elders, chief priests and scribes, and he must be killed and on the third day be raised to life" (Lk 9:22; Lk 24:26; Mk 8:31).

The disciple who wanders with Jesus must also participate in his suffering. Inviting to discipleship, Jesus says, "If anyone wishes to come after me, he must deny himself, and take up his cross and follow me" (Mt 16:24; Mk 8:34; Lk 9:23). The Evangelist Mark shows the following of Jesus not only as a growing awareness of his Messiahship (Mk 8:27-30), but also a corresponding awareness of his Servanthood (Mk 10: 45). His itinerary begins from Galilee and leads to Jerusalem. Jesus goes with the fullest awareness of the impending sufferings in

Jerusalem (Mk 8:31; 9:30-31; 10:32-34). Finally, the way of the cross and death (Mk 14:1-15, 42) takes its upward course to reach its climax in his resurrection (Mk 16:1-20). The lot of the disciples is not different from that of Jesus, whom they follow on his way.

The formative period of suffering will culminate in the realization of joy at the revelation of glory. Apostle Peter writes, "Beloved, do not be surprised at the fiery trial that has come upon you, as though something strange were happening to you. But rejoice that you share in the sufferings of Christ, so that you may be overjoyed at the revelation of his Glory" (1 Pet 4:12-13; 2 Cor 1:5; Phil 3:10). The great things that are awaiting us after this period of suffering are far beyond human imagination. "For this slight momentary affliction is preparing for us an eternal weight of glory beyond all comparison, because we look not to the things that are seen but to the things that are unseen; for the things that are seen are transient, but the things that are unseen are eternal (2 Cor 4:17-18).

The spiritual transformation of the disciples has an evolutionary nature. It is like the gradual manifestation of a hidden potentiality in an ever more surprising manner. The apparently weak and insignificant disciples can draw their latent capabilities from within, assisted by the grace of God. The personal evolution of the disciples has to be seen in relation to the cosmic process that is taking place around them. St. Paul writes to the Romans, "We know that the whole creation has been groaning in labour pains until now; and not only the creation, but we ourselves, who have the first fruits of the Spirit, groan inwardly while we wait for adoption, the redemption of our bodies (Rom 8:22-23).

The spiritual transformation assumes the pattern of an artistic procedure. An artwork comes into existence not in a haphazard or casual manner, but through a planned and willed procedure in view of an imagined or real exemplar. The evolutionary process of history leads us the fullness of Christ, who is the "Exemplar" of the universe, in whom all things will be summed up, "recapitulated" in the fullness of time.[13] It is the expression and fulfilment of God's plan for us and for the entire creation. He chose us before the foundation of the world and destined us in love to be his sons in Christ. "For he has made known to us in all wisdom and insight the mystery of his will, according to his purpose which he set forth in Christ as a plan for the fullness of time, to unite all things in him, things in heaven and things on earth (Eph 1:9-10).

FOLLOWING THE PATH OF BEAUTY

The "imitation of Christ" implies in its comprehensive sense a conscious self-transformation in view of the "truth" of Christ, his incarnate reality. The truth of Christ is his rootedness in the reality of suffering and death, his deformity and ugliness, his wounds and his sorrows (Is 53:3-5). But the process of the transformation to the truth of Christ is continued until it is clarified and enlightened by his "beauty" revealed in his Transfiguration and Resurrection. He can be then acclaimed as the "fairest of men" (Ps 44). Certainly, it is not merely the physical beauty of the Saviour's appearance that is glorified, but the beauty of Truth that shines forth in him. Beauty is a superior form of knowledge and it reveals the greatness of truth. "The beauty of truth also embraces offence, pain, and even the dark mystery of death, and that this can only be found in accepting suffering, not in ignoring it."[14] In this sense we can speak of the "beautiful wounds," which are signs of the human longing for the final realization and perfection.

The longing in separation is the characteristic of genuine love. It is nostalgia, the intense desire that impels a quest for attaining the original state of union in love. The cause of nostalgia in human beings and in the creation is Jesus Christ himself. "When men have a longing so great that it surpasses human nature and eagerly desire and are able to accomplish things beyond human thought, it is the Bridegroom who has smitten them with this longing. It is he who has sent a ray of his beauty into their eyes. The greatness of the wound already shows the arrow which has struck home, the longing indicates who has inflicted the wound."[15] Discipleship, therefore, is walking the *via pulchritudinis* (the way of beauty) with relentless yearning for truth, justice and goodness.

In the spiritual transformation of a disciple, the experience of beauty plays a decisive role. Beauty can "speak directly to the heart, turning astonishment to marvel, admiration to gratitude, happiness to contemplation. It is unlikely to result in indifference; it provokes emotions, it puts in movement a dynamism of deep interior transformation."[16] It entails an emotional "shock," which breaks all inhibitive shells and liberates the person from within. With enthusiasm, it takes the course of confronting reality directly, rather than depending on "second hand" knowledge through instructions. It seeks knowledge through personal experiences, through a direct relationship with reality. "Being struck and overcome by the beauty of Christ is a more real, more profound knowledge than mere rational deduction. Of course we must not underrate the importance of theological reflection, of exact and precise theological thought; it remains absolutely necessary. But to move from here to disdain or to reject the impact produced by the response of the heart in the encounter with beauty as a true form of knowledge would impoverish us and dry up our faith and our theology. We must rediscover this form of knowledge; it is a pressing need of our time."[17] These words of Pope Benedict underlines the importance of contextual theological formation.

WANDERING AND LEARNING THEOLOGY

The classical method of learning theology is confined to class rooms or university campuses. Specialized teachers are available for different subjects and the centralized library functions as a great source of knowledge. Class room learning presupposes some fixed questions and fixed answers to those questions. The questions derive from texts and not from the changing contexts in which human life evolves through struggles and conflicts. It is likely to ignore the problems of life as they are confronted in actual human situations.

As far as priests and missionaries are concerned their theological learning is not purely an academic exercise, but a pastoral experience. Their concern is primarily the people for whom they are anointed. Pope Francis reminds in his Homily on Holy Thursday in 2013 that those who are anointed are destined to serve the poor, the prisoners and the oppressed. He quotes the verse 2 of Psalm 113 and explains that it is a fine image of "being for" others. "'It is like the precious oil upon the head, running down upon the beard, on the beard of Aaron, running down upon the collar of his robe' (v. 2). The image of spreading oil, flowing down from the beard of Aaron upon the collar of his sacred robe, is an image of the priestly anointing which, through Christ, the Anointed One, reaches the ends of the earth, represented by the robe."[18]

Evidently, the message of the anointed ones has to reach the peripheries of the world, the least and the last. The "unction" of the preached Word of God touches the daily lives of the people, "when it runs down like the oil of Aaron to the edges of reality, when it brings light to moments of extreme darkness, to the 'outskirts' where people of faith are most exposed to the onslaught of those who want to tear down their faith."[19] Hence Pope Francis appeals to all priests to "go out", to the "outskirts" where there is "suffering, bloodshed, blindness that longs for sight, and prisoners in thrall to many evil masters."[20] The vocation to be a priest and a missionary is not to settle down and relax. It is a call to involve in the day to day lives of the people and to be identified with them. "This I ask you: be shepherds, with the 'odour of the sheep', make it real, as shepherds among your flock, fishers of men."[21]

According to Pope Benedict, faith is not a burden, it does not enslave us. Faith gives wings to the believers, so that they experience freedom. He affirms: it is beautiful to be Christian.[22] It is Christ's beauty, the splendor of the revelation of truth that inspires us to follow him. Pierced by the arrow of the beautiful, the mind seeks restlessly until it attains the vision of truth.

Endnotes

[1] "The view on Jesus as a wandering teacher and prophet shows that 'wandering' means more than that, that wandering is a basic concept of theology". See D. Dormeyer, "Jesus as wandering prophetic wisdom teacher" in *HTS Theologiese Studies/Theological Studies*, Vol 4, No.1-2 (1993), p. 102; at https://www.ajol.info/index.php/hts/article/view/148318/137822, accessed on 25-10-2018.

[2] Fernando Belo in his materialistic reading of the Gospel of Mark shows that theological experience has an indispensable relation to the bodily practice of "feet, hands and eyes". He puts this idea in the three phrases, "The practice of feet or the hope", "The practice of hands or the love of neighbour" and "The practice of eyes or the faith". See Fernando Belo, *Das Markusevangelium materialistisch gelesen,* Stuttgart, 1980, pp. 306, 312.

[3] See A. J. Swoboda, *The Dusty Ones: Why Wandering Deepens Your Faith,* Grand Rapids: Baker Books, 2016: Examining the theme of wandering in the Bible, A. J. Swoboda shows in his book *The Dusty Ones* that some of God's most important truths are revealed to those whose feet are dusty from the road.

[4] Ascent presupposes a descent. "No one has ascended into heaven but he who descended" (Jn 3:13). The ascent-descent (*exitus-reditus*) pattern of salvation was first shown by the 6th century theologian Dionysius the Areopagite. It implies a theological method of knowing God by shedding all prior knowledge (*apophatic* method), as one goes upward closer to God. It is like the experience of Moses on Mount Sinai, plunging into the mysterious darkness of unknowing. See Paul L. Allen, *Theological Method: A Guide for the Perplexed,* London: T&T Clark International, 2012, p. 93.

[5] See Fr. John Nepil, "The Ascent of Assent", quoting Adrienne Von Speyr, "There is no better way of clarifying his [Christ's] relationship to the Father, then by the image of ascent" at https://thosecatholicmen.com/articles/the-ascent-of-assent/ accessed on 17-11-18.

[6] Matthew has in his Gospel some significant mountain scenes: Jesus' temptation (Mt 4:8), Sermon on the Mount (Mt 5:1-12), healing the sick (Mt 15:29-31), the Transfiguration (Mt 17:1), Jesus' final discourse (Mt 24:3) and the commissioning of the disciples (Mt 28:16-20).

[7] Pope Francis, "In the Kingdom of God with 50 cents in their pocket", Morning Meditation in the Chapel of the *Domus Sanctae Marthae, Thursday, 13 November 2014, L'Osservatore Romano,* Weekly ed. in English, n. 47, 21 November 2014; https://w2.vatican.va/content/francesco/en/cotidie/2014/documents/papa-francesco-cotidie_20141113_in-the-kingdom-of-god.html accessed on 30-10-2018.

[8] D. Dormeyer, "Jesus as wandering prophetic wisdom teacher" in *HTS Theologiese Studies/Theological Studies,* Vol 4, No.1-2 (1993), p. 109; at https://www.ajol.info/index.php/hts/article/view/148318/137822, accessed on 25-10-2019.

[9] Benedict XVI, *Encyclical Letter Deus Caritas Est,* 1 ; http://w2.vatican.va/content/benedict-xvi/en/encyclicals/documents/hf_ben-xvi_enc_20051225_deus-caritas-est.html, accessed on 15-11-2018.

[10] St. Irenaeus is credited more than anybody else for developing the biblical notion of the recapitulation of everything in Christ. See *Encyclopedia.com*, "Recapitulation in Christ" at https://www.encyclopedia.com/religion/encyclopedias-almanacs-transcripts-and-maps/recapitulation-christ accessed on 15-10-2018.

[11] Justin the Martyr, "For next to God, we worship and love the Word who is from the unbegotten and ineffable God, since also He became man for our sakes, that becoming a partaker of our sufferings, He might also bring us healing. For all the writers were able to see realities darkly through the sowing of the implanted word that was in them. For the seed and imitation impacted according to capacity is one thing, and quite another is the thing itself, of which there is the participation and imitation according to the grace which is from Him" (II Apology Chap.13). See *Catholic Encyclopedia, New Advent*, s. v. "The Second Apology of St. Justin Martyr" at http://www.newadvent.org/fathers/0127.htm accessed on 15-10-2018.

[12] The Stoic idea of *logos spermatikos* (seminal word) which means the law of generation in the universe was adopted by Justin the Martyr. In his II Apology he writes that the seeds of reason (the Logos) is implanted in every race of men (II Apology, Chap. 8). See *Catholic Encyclopedia, New Advent*, s. v. "The Second Apology of St. Justin Martyr" at http://www.newadvent.org/fathers/0127.htm accessed on 15-10-2018.

[13] The Church Father Irenaeus (140-202) has explained his vision of "Recapitulation" in the following manner: "He has therefore, in His work of recapitulation, summed up all things, both waging war against our enemy, and crushing him who had at the beginning led us away captives in Adam ...the enemy would not have been fairly vanquished, unless it had been a man [born] of woman who conquered him. ... And therefore does the Lord profess Himself to be the Son of man, comprising in Himself that original man out of whom the woman was fashioned, in order that, as our species went down to death through a vanquished man, so we may ascend to life again through a victorious one; and as through a man death received the palm [of victory] against us, so again by a man we may receive the palm against death." See Irenaeus, *Against Heresies* 5.21.1 in A. Roberts and J. Donaldson (eds.), *The Writings of Irenaeus* Vol. 2, Edinburgh: T & T Clark, 1869, pp. 110-111

In modern times, Teilhard de Chardin has developed an evolutionary vision of "Recapitulation." His cosmic vision presents the evolution of the universe through different stages to its fullness in Jesus Christ, the Omega point. See H. Paul Santimire, *Nature Reborn: The Ecological and Cosmic Promise of Christian Theology*, Minneapolis: Fortress Press, 2000, pp. 47-59.

[14] Cardinal Joseph Ratzinger (Benedict XVI), "The Feeling of Things, the Contemplation of Beauty", Message to the Communion and Liberation (CL) Meeting at Rimini (24-30 August 2002) at *http://www.vatican.va/roman_curia/congregations/cfaith/documents/rc_con_cfaith_doc_20020824_ratzinger-cl-rimini_en.html* accessed on 10-11-2018.

[15] Ibid., Cardinal Ratzinger quoting the 14th century theologian Nicholas Cabasilas from his work, *The Life in Christ,* the Second Book, 15; See Nicholas Cabasilas, *The Life in Christ*, New York: St Vladimir's Seminary Press, 1974.

[16] Pontifical Council for Culture, Concluding Document of the Plenary Assembly 2006, "*Via Pulchritudinis,* Privileged Pathway for Evangelisation and Dialogue" at http://www.vatican.va/roman_curia/pontifical_councils/cultr/documents/rc_pc_cultr_doc_20060327_plenary-assembly_final-document_en.html, accessed on 15-11-2017.

[17] Cardinal Joseph Ratzinger (Benedict XVI), "The Feeling of Things, the Contemplation of Beauty", at *http://www.vatican.va/roman_curia/congregations/cfaith/documents/rc_con_cfaith_doc_20020824_ratzinger-cl-rimini_en.html* accessed on 10-11-2018.

[18] Pope Francis, "Homily of Pope Francis" on Holy Thursday, 28 March 2013, at http://w2.vatican.va/content/francesco/en/homilies/2013/documents/papa-francesco_20130328_messa-crismale.html accessed on 20-10-2018.

[19] Ibid.

[20] Ibid.

[21] Ibid.

[22] Pontifical Council for Culture, Concluding Document of the Plenary Assembly 2006: Pope Benedict XVI said this in his interview with Vatican Radio on 14 August 2005 just before leaving for the World Youth Day at Cologne. This idea is developed by Enzo Bianchi in an article in which he writes that in a society with a strong presence of non-believers and followers of other religions Christians must know to witness a presence humanly beautiful, enriched by the joy of friendship, surrounded by the harmony of creation; Cf. E. Bianchi, "Perché e come evangelizzare di fronte all'indifferentismo," in *Vita e pensiero* 2 (2005) 92-93.

Contextual Theologies

After the Model of Jesuan Pedagogy

Naiju Jose Kalambukattu

Introduction

Contextual theological endeavours with appropriate Christological foundations are of prime importance. Such undertakings necessitate appreciation and assimilation of the characteristic features of Christ, the Word became flesh, in whom we find the perfect integration. The Word, which was with God and was God (Jn 1:1) became flesh and pitched his tent among us (Jn 1:14). John is pleased to allude to the sacred tent that served as the sanctuary for the Hebrews in the desert. It was a tent where God was present beside the people (Ex 33:7-11). Jesus the Son of God, the Splendor (Heb 1:1) and Image (Col 1:15) of the Father became human and he is the true temple of God among people (Jn 2:21). In pitching his tent among us, the incarnation, God has entered through his Word into the history of humankind to fulfill the mission of the Father (Jn 20:21).

Jesus adopted new forms and new approaches in carrying out his saving mission[1] and espoused the style of sincere and serious expressions of immersion into and assimilation of the culture.[2] Now the mission of the Church is the continuation of the mission of Jesus taking into account the life situation and context of the people. Mission is the incarnation of Christian faith in other cultures; rather it attempts to understand Christian faith in terms of a particular context, which according to Bevans is a theological imperative.[3] This article is an attempt to explore the relevance of theologizing in context and highlights the pedagogy of Jesus as the model to be imitated.

Redefining Contextual Theologies

There is an urgency to redefine the mission attuned to the needs and aspirations of the people in the margins.[4] Therefore, it presupposes exposure to the lives and contexts of the people, for it takes the context and the *sitz im leben* seriously. In exposure, one is still an outsider of that which one experiences, but in immersion, one enters into and becomes united or identified with the reality of other persons: However both exposure and immersion are real life encounters with the reality.[5] Such encounters initiate the theologians to the real life-situations and urge them to reflect in the light of the gospel, and therefore, contextual theological reflection starts from live-in experience of life, history, struggles, pains and hopes of the people through participation and immersion, for the experience enables us to theologize in context.[6] In other words, the relevant theologizing consists in the dialectical interaction of the Word and world,[7] i.e., it prompts to "interpret the Christian faith in the light of the events and experiences of today as well as to understand the events and experiences of today in the light of the Christian faith."[8] The concern for an ongoing hermeneutic of the dialogue of the gospel with the contexts, cultures and religions is relevant and opportune,[9] and today the Church, especially in India, takes serious efforts "marked by significant breakthroughs and shifts alternating with long periods of non-contextual, non-creative repetitive scholastic theology."[10]

The gospel by its very nature is intended for all peoples, all ages, land and context and therefore is not bound exclusively to any particular culture, for it pervades all cultures and illumines them all with the divine light. The gospel must be adapted to different cultural contexts to develop meaningful contextual theologies, for it is an articulation of the message of the gospel in the cultural categories of the people. Hence, the missionaries should take into consideration the existing socio-cultural and religious situations and have a genuine love and respect for all peoples, cultures and religions; and the gospel is to be preached. The evangelization is neither vanquishing the culture and faith experience of the people nor recounting them that they are erroneous in what they believe and do, but consists in respecting local cultures, ethos and faith expressions.[11] It is the incarnation of Christian faith in other cultures; rather it attempts to understand Christian faith in terms of a particular context, which according to Bevans is a theological imperative.[12] In this pursuit of theologizing in context, Jesus sets a unique style and his disciples are invited to "have the same mind of Jesus" (Phil 2:5).

Jesuan Style of Theologizing

Jesus who entered into and got united to the reality of human beings in their poverty-stricken and unjust context and preached liberation, and appeared to the disciples in "secular" contexts of life like fishing (Jn 21:4-6), travelling (Mk 16:12; Lk 24:15), and wanted them to find him in the ordinary events of life, and communicated the Word in the language and idiom of the people is the model in theologizing in context. He adopted new forms and new approaches in carrying out his saving mission[13] and espoused the style of sincere and serious expressions of immersion into and assimilation of the culture.[14]

The incarnation is immersion into history and by incarnation Jesus became the perfect exigent of God.[15] "He is the visible image of the invisible God" (Col 1:15). The solidarity of Jesus with the poor and the outcastes is evident in the incarnation (Jn 1:14). Pope Francis states, "Unafraid of the fringes, he himself became a fringe (cf. Phil 2:6-8; Jn 1:14). So if we dare to go to the fringes, we will find him there; indeed, he is already there. Jesus is already there, in the hearts of our brothers and sisters, in their wounded flesh, in their troubles and in their profound desolation."[16] Kudilil delineates the dynamics of incarnation, "A hitherto unknown and far away God became near to humankind, took on the limitations of time and space unto himself, began to speak their language and share their life with all its dimensions."[17] The Word made flesh integrated both heaven and earth. Furthermore, Jesus was a victim of insults, mockery and contempt due to his immersion in the context of common people. He was called "a glutton and drunkard and a friend of tax collectors and sinners" (Mt 11:19), "a mad man" (Mk 3:22-30), "the carpenter's son" (Mk 6:3) and "a Samaritan…possessed by a devil (Jn 8:48-52).

Jesus preferred to be in solidarity with the powerless and the voiceless poor, bring them life-transforming good news and liberate them from suffering and exploitation.[18] The identification of Jesus with the poor and the needy is clearly visible in his Nazareth manifesto (Lk 4:18). There is a radical shift from the values of the clever and the wise of the world to the wisdom of the marginalized and the downtrodden in the society. He is the liberator of those who expected a saviour, who are vulnerable and kicked to the outskirts of the society due to poverty, illness, handicaps and other deprivations. Jesus' mission was "holistic in nature, voice for the voiceless, accepting the outcasts and downtrodden."[19]

Jesus was always sensitive to the context where he lived and was eager to reach out to the people, especially to those at the periphery (Lk 8:1-3), and confronted the reality in the form of sin, sickness, injustice, hypocrisy, love, fear, pain, etc. There he proclaimed the Word and fulfilled it. He confronted the reality and interpreted the context of sin with forgiveness (Jn 8:11), sickness with healing (Mt 8:3; Mk 1:40; Lk 13:12-13; 18:42; Jn 5:8; 9:6-7), evil spirits with driving them out from persons (Mk 9:25; Lk 8:29), injustice with denouncing (Lk 12:45-46), hypocrisy with condemning (Mt 23:13; Lk 11:39), and worry, fear and pain with instructing (Mt 6:25; Lk 12:22-23) and praying. Being totally available at the service of the marginalized, he gave them freedom, hope, wholeness and new orientation to their lives and transformed them. Jesus envisaged the restoration of humanity and its total well-being.[20]

Jesus befriended tax collectors and sinners (Mt 9:9-11; Lk 5:27-32), reached out to lepers (Mt 8:2-4; Mk 1:40-42; Lk 5:12-15), associated with women (Lk 8:2-3), he was favourable towards gentiles (Lk 7:1-10) and Samaritans (Lk 10:30-37) and had special love and concern for the defenseless of society.[21] He visualized true liberation of humanity, a setting where everyone lives in solidarity, freedom and justice, for his "mission was to lead humans to realize true freedom by their becoming authentic humans."[22] He stood against the powerful ones who perpetuated injustice, religious abuse, down-play of women and misuse of political structure, and societal abnormalities such as injustice, oppression, exploitation, and visualized an alternative society consisted of justice, love, equality and peace.[23] The credibility of Jesus lies in his solidarity with the poor, the marginalized, spiritually poor, socially outcast, religiously downtrodden, and culturally separated, honored/dishonored by gender, etc. Hence, for the one who proclaims Jesus who was poor and stood for the cause of the poor, has no better option than to be in solidarity with them which in turn adds his or her credibility and integrity.[24]

Contextual Theologies after Jesuan Style

According to J. Massey, every theological expression has to pass two tests, which are based on the two divine interventions 'God takes the side of the oppressed' (Ex 3:7-9), and the message that 'God liberates the oppressed' (Lk 4:18-19), and these two messages have to be the spirit behind all theological expressions.[25] Therefore, theologizing in the Indian context necessitates addressing itself to the liberative praxis of the oppressed, exploited and marginalized people, taking a serious note of stark realities within social, cultural, political, economic and religious pluralism to help the people in their struggle to alter their situation of injustice and oppression.[26] Therefore, "contextual approach should start from the scratch, from below, from the concrete life of the people, and then should strive at a new interpretation of the messages and ideals of Jesus in the gospels and the Christian tradition."[27] This understanding might have urged a number of contextual theologians like Rahner, Lonergan, and Gutierrez to reiterate that theology is not really done by experts and then "trickled down" to the people for their consumption, rather, done by people themselves who are subjects and agents of culture and its change.[28]

The contextual theologies emerge through encounter, exposure and experience. They create a positive and open attitude to life and realities. There is a contextual and experiential in-take of knowledge, which converts them into effective sharers of the good news. The message of the gospel, to be effective, must be adapted to the local culture and lifestyle, which in turn demands "a deep understanding of the aspirations, feelings, thought patterns, outlook, etc., of receiving culture and shows genuine concern and sensitivity to those factors. Thus the good news becomes intelligible, acceptable and realistic for the hearers."[29] It also means the reasonable and harmonious development of all faculties of the students helping them to become genuinely human. Bevans rightly captures that theologizing in context takes into account not only the gospel message and the tradition of the Church, but also the culture of the one who is doing theology and social change within that culture.[30]

Life-experiences in the contexts and theologizing them will enable the students to cherish the "vision of Church as a correlative, cooperative, collaborative, collegial, and co-inclusive People of God with its task of 'mystery of moon,' and really radiating the light of her Master, outgoing and evangelizing the world."[31] In the spirit of *Gaudium et Spes*, the exposure and immersion programmes make "the joy and hope, the grief and anguish"[32] of the people their own, and establish a deep solidarity with the them.

The experiences of encounter and immersion are to be geared to a process of sound theological reflection. The teacher facilitates and guides the students in reflecting the experiences and assimilating new information, for "experiences, duly reflected upon, can certainly be much more formative than mere information or knowledge."[33] The students become critical co-investigators in dialogue with the teacher promoting dialogue and a healthy teacher-taught relationship.[34] The theologizing becomes a process of making one's faith alive, meaningful and contextual, i.e., discovering the divine in the concrete life situations. Aykara expounds, "Experience is the fertile field of mature thoughts. Original, healthy and unique thoughts are born from the sedimentation of personal experiences; and not from borrowed ideas and undigested theories swallowed from others."[35] The experiences help the students to develop into a person of compassion, competence and commitment to be at the service of the least ones in the society. The theological education and formation "rooted in the life-situation of the people should also affect the *life-style* of those who theologize, especially by living the simplicity of the poor."[36]

The theologizing in context clarifies the logic of self-giving and inspires the students to volunteer and to serve the poor with the 'Smell of the Sheep.' To phrase it differently, they are challenged to become the 'People of Heart' who can feel with the people and commit themselves for their cause,[37] and as the Good Samaritan (Lk 10:33-35), they become the good news to the people. The contextual formation and education enable the students to be in the shoes of the carpenter of Nazareth who was always at the periphery and inspire them to take a stand with the marginalized who are at the periphery of human existence. Hence the exigency of the formation of priests and religious adapted to the cultural contexts, where they are to witness and proclaim the good news. This will lead to the realization of the ardent wish of Pope Francis: "I want a Church which is poor and for the poor...We are called to find Christ in them, to lend our voice to their causes, but also to be their friends, to listen to them, to speak for them and to embrace the mysterious wisdom which God wishes to share with us through them."[38]

The theologizing in context enables the students to accept and appreciate themselves and others leading them to an integrated or comprehensive growth, which is the need of the challenging situations, they are placed in. It enables the students to live together with different people and get identified with them in various contexts, and helps them to grow into a new life-style by experiencing the life of the weak and the poor, the sick and the marginalized (1 Cor 9:22-23). It enables them to respect all and to have a sense of justice, for the live-in experience with the poor in the context equips and enables the students to engage in the works of justice and the tasks of human development and liberation.[39] It also enables them to be people of integrity, for "if the human qualities are lacking in the life of a priest who is supposed to witness to Christ, he will fail in his mission."[40]

Presbyterorum Ordinis invites the priests to live as instruments of Christ, the eternal priest,[41] who invites the disciples to follow the alternative style of life and witnessing he has taught. Theologizing in context has to be a process through which the students are gradually guided to reach greater heights of understanding the person and message of Jesus Christ and assimilating it into the life situations. It inspires them to touch and be touched by the miserable lives, and helps them to become prophetic leaders following the example of Jesus and his preferential option for the poor as well as his courage to break down the social and cultural barriers. Students become keenly sensitive to the diverse contexts and dare to take prophetic steps for the mission of the Church and the well being of the people, for the prophets have both a sense of God and a sense of human beings, denounce the evil,[42] and cry out for justice and care of the poor.[43] It aims at a holistic theology of knowing, loving and doing (*jnana, bhakti* and *karma*).[44] It is "a holistic and harmonious experience of integration in which knowing, loving and doing, that is, *jnana, bhakti* and *karma* are united. Such a process of integration must begin with direct experience (*anubhava*), through involvement and active participation (*karma*/action). It is then reflected and meditated upon (*jnana*/knowledge). The realization that follows is personalized and expressed creatively in love, devotion and selfless service (*bhakti*/love)."[45]

Theologizing in context requires leaving the comfort of one's nests and structures, to get acquainted with the life-experiences of the people at the periphery.[46] The encounters, immersions, experiences, reflections and interpretations constantly challenge the students to leave the security, which the institution provides in order to embrace the insecurity that Jesus offers. They spur them on to equip themselves with sound theological reflections to prepare themselves for the future ministry. Therefore, it is essential to do theology through a programme of action-reflection-action ensuring the notional knowledge of divine truths become possessive and transforming one.[47]

The students are to be encouraged to articulate their theological insights and reflections by way of symbols, poems, write-ups, parables, music, paintings, etc. Thus they are initiated to do theology in line with the style and manner of Jesus who shared the profound mysteries of the kingdom through the parables and made them intelligible to the people. As Karokaran expounds, there is an "affirmation of solidarity and identification with a people in the process of the contextualization of the Christian faith."[48] It is not exporting Jesus from outside to the people in a particular cultural context, but presentation of him from within a people, and getting identified with them.[49]

Conclusion

The very dynamics of incarnation by which Jesus entered and got immersed into the human history constantly challenge the disciples to get in his shoes, for the integrated person and mission of Jesus, the good shepherd is the bedrock of theologizing in context. The contextual theological education promotes a radical option for a life of simplicity and identification with the poor. It creates a universal vision among the students and enables them to stand with and for the people. It helps the students to preserve and promote the cultural, social and religious diversities of the tribals, aboriginal, dalits and other ethnic and religious minorities to nurture the pluralistic spirit of India. It triggers an ongoing process making the message of salvation incarnate in the specific and living cultures of the people.[50] "Widen the space of your tent, extend the curtains of your home, do not hold back!" (Is 54:2) is true to the task of immersion and getting exposed to the various cultural realities of the context.

The task is to interpret the context and assimilate the text critically in freedom, and St Paul who "opposed Cephas" (Gal 2:11-14), the greatest paradigm in contextualization, adaptation, inculturation and articulation of revelation and faith,[51] and proclaimed the good news without disturbing the existing system and understanding in the Athenian society (Acts 17:22-23, 28) sets an example to imitate. And for that as Pope Francis instructs, it is essential to "... Strip away the fear of opening the doors and going out to encounter all especially the poorest of the poor, the needy, the remote, without waiting..."[52] Thus, theologizing in context becomes a serious imitation of the style of Jesus, the Word became flesh and dwelt among us (Jn 1:14). It is taking a step forward in realizing the vision of a 'Church of the poor', articulating a liberative spirituality (Lk 4:18-19) drawn from Jesus, and achieving a structural change in the life of the Church returning to her original roots to meet the present world in mission with its challenges and promises. It is following the stand point of Jesus with determination in responding courageously and creatively to the challenges, especially, in transcending all that prevent people from becoming better humans in various contexts.

Endnotes

[1] A. Shorter, *Toward a Theology of Inculturation*, London: Wipf & Stock Publishers, 1991, 62.

[2] S. Athappilly, "Inculturation in the Model of Incarnation," in S. Chackalackal, ed., *New Horizons of Indian Christian Living: A Festschrift in Honour of Prof. Dr Vadakethala Francis Vineeth CMI*, Bengaluru/Coimbatore: Vidyavanam Publications/ Preshita Communications, 2009, 440.

[3] S.B. Bevans, *Models of Contextual Theology*, Maryknoll, NY: ORBIS Books, 1992, 1.

[4] J.K. Ravela, "Mission for the Margins: Nehemiah 5 as a Paradigm Shift for Mission," in P.J. Titus – D.S. Maben, ed., *Bible and Mission: Biblical Perspectives for Doing Mission in Contemporary India*, Bangalore: SBSI & Tiruvalla: CSS, 2015, 51.

[5] D. D'Sousa, "Exposure-Immersion Programmes: From Concern to Solidarity with the Poor," *Third Millennium* 3, 2 (April-June 2000), 35-36.

[6] S. Arokiasamy, "Towards Contextual Theology: Reflections on the Development in the Indian Church," in J. Massey, ed., *Contextual Theological Education*, Delhi: ISPCK, 1993, 50.

[7] N.J. Kalambukattu, "Introduction," in N.J. Kalambukattu, ed., *Theologizing in Context: A Hermeneutic of Living Dialogue between the Word and the World*, Bangalore: Dharmaram Publications, 2019, 1.

[8] K. Kunnumpuram, "Theological Method in Vatican II," in M. Jayanth, ed., *Indian Theologies: In Search of Methods and Models for Theologizing*, New Delhi: Christian World Imprints & Pune: Jnana-Deepa Vidyapeeth, 2017, 2.

[9] J. Saldanha, *Exploring Frontiers*, 2016, 13, 97.

[10] S. Arokiasamy, "Towards Contextual Theology: Reflections on the Development in the Indian Church," in J. Massey, ed., *Contextual Theological Education*, Delhi: ISPCK, 1993, 50.

[11] J. Mariadas, "Institutionalization Paralyses Evangelization," *Ephrem's Theological Journal* 21, 2 (October 2017), 29.

[12] S.B. Bevans, *Models of Contextual Theology*, Maryknoll, NY: ORBIS Books, 1992, 1.

[13] A. Shorter, *Toward a Theology of Inculturation*, London: Wipf & Stock Publishers, 1991, 62.

[14] S. Athappilly, "Inculturation in the Model of Incarnation," in S. Chackalackal, ed., *New Horizons of Indian Christian Living: A Festschrift in Honour of Prof. Dr Vadakethala Francis Vineeth CMI*, Bengaluru/Coimbatore: Vidyavanam Publications/ Preshita Communications, 2009, 440.

[15] S. Athappilly, "Inculturation in the Model of Incarnation," 435.

[16] Francis, *Gaudete et Exsultate*, 135.

[17] G. Kudilil, "Mission Approaches in Evangelizing Process – With Special Emphasis on Human Promotion in the Missionary Context of India," *Ephrem's Theological Journal* 21, 2 (October 2017), 14.

[18] J. Jerald, "Philanthropic Mission of Jesus: Kingdom Values as Paradigm for Doing Mission in Contemporary India," in P.J. Titus – D.S. Maben, ed., *Bible and Mission: Biblical Perspectives for Doing Mission in Contemporary India*, Bangalore: SBSI & Tiruvalla: CSS, 2015, 153.

[19] J. Jerald, "Philanthropic Mission of Jesus: Kingdom Values as Paradigm for Doing Mission in Contemporary India," 155.

[20] J. Jerald, "Philanthropic Mission of Jesus: Kingdom Values as Paradigm for Doing Mission in Contemporary India," 152.

[21] J. Jerald, "Philanthropic Mission of Jesus: Kingdom Values as Paradigm for Doing Mission in Contemporary India," 153.

[22] J. Parappally, "Christian Leadership and the Praxis of Jesus," in A. Kalliath, ed., *Christian Leadership: The Shifting Focus in Theological Education*, Bangalore: Dharmaram publications, 2001, 79.

[23] J. Jerald, "Philanthropic Mission of Jesus: Kingdom Values as Paradigm for Doing Mission in Contemporary India," in P.J. Titus – D.S. Maben, ed., *Bible and Mission: Biblical Perspectives for Doing Mission in Contemporary India*, Bangalore: SBSI & Tiruvalla: CSS, 2015, 154.

[24] G. Kudilil, "Mission Approaches in Evangelizing Process," 18.

[25] J. Massey, "Christianity to be Renewed? Rethink Theology," in J. Massey – T.K. John, ed., *Rethinking Theology in India: Christianity in the Twenty-first Century*, New Delhi: Manohar, 2013, 28.

[26] K.C. Abraham, "Contextual Theologies," in J. Massey, ed., *Contextual Theological Education*, Delhi: ISPCK, 1993, 18.

[27] J. Chittooparampil, *A Christian Vision for a New Society in India: Theological and Countercultural Perspectives*, Delhi: ISPCK, 2014, xiii.

[28] S.B. Bevans, *Models of Contextual Theology*, 13.

[29] G. Kudilil, "Mission Approaches in Evangelizing Process," 14.

[30] S.B. Bevans, *Models of Contextual Theology*, 1.

[31] A. Pushparajan, "Embracing the Laity: The Vision of Pope Francis," in K. Pandikattu, ed., *Pope Francis: His Impact on and Relevance for the Church and Society Commemorating Five Years of His Papacy*, Pune: Jnana-Deepa Vidyapeeth/New Delhi: Christian World Imprints, 2018, 134.

[32] *Gaudium et Spes*, 1.

[33] J. Saldanha, "Formation in Context," *Third Millennium* 6, 4 (October-December 2003), 34.

[34] L. Fernando, "Doing Theology in Context, Teacher-Student Partnership," *Third Millennium* 6, 4 (October-December 2003), 9.

[35] T. Aykara, "CMI Legacy of Ecclesiastical Education and Mission: Dream for the Future," in P. Kochappilly, ed., *Contextual Ecclesial Education and the Evangelizing Mission of the Church: Proceedings of the CMI Philosophers' and Theologans' Forum on "CMI Legacy of Contextual Ecclesiastical Education and the Evangelizing Mission of the Church*," Bangalore: Dharmaram Publications, 2018, 68.

[36] P. Arockiadoss, "Regional Theology Centres and Formation of Christian Leadership," in A. Kalliath, ed., *Christian Leadership: The Shifting Focus in Theological Education*, Bangalore: Dharmaram publications, 2001, 289.

[37] L. Fernando, "Doing Theology in Context, Teacher-Student Partnership," 9.

[38] Francis, *Evangelii Gaudium*, 198.

[39] D. Varayilan, "Contextualized Theological Formation in Samanvaya: Vision, Orientation and Impact," in B. Thettayil, ed., *God-Talk in Context: A North Indian Theological Experiment,* Bangalore: Dharmaram Publications, 2016, 35.

[40] J. Bala H., "A Paradigm Shift for Integral Human Formation of Priests," *Vidyajyoti Journal of Theological Reflection* 82, 4 (April 2018), 291.

[41] *Presbyterorum Ordinis*, 12.

[42] B. Haring, *Sin in the Secular Age*, Slough-England: St Paul Publications, 1974, 114.

[43] W.T. Murma, "Poverty: A Catholic Social Teaching Perspective," *Asian Horizons* 11, 3 (September 2017), 564.

[44] Prasann Bhai, "Goal, Vision and Identity of Samanvaya," in C. Kuttiyanikkal, ed., *Theological Formation in Context: Samanvaya – A CMI Initiative*, Bhopal: Samanvaya, 2009, 108.

[45] S. Elavathingal, "Integration (*Samanvayam*) in Theological Formation: A CMI Experience," 313.

[46] R. Joseph, "Reinventing Religious Life: The Challenge of Pope Francis," in K. Pandikattu, ed., *Pope Francis: His Impact on and Relevance for the Church and Society Commemorating Five Years of His Papacy*, Pune: Jnana-Deepa Vidyapeeth/New Delhi: Christian World Imprints, 2018, 145.

[47] A. Karokaran, *Mission: An Alternative Model*, 179.

[48] A. Karokaran, *Mission: An Alternative Model*, 138.

[49] A. Karokaran, *Mission: An Alternative Model*, 138-139.

[50] J. Pathrapankal, "Scribes Trained for the Kingdom of God," in P. Kochappilly, ed., *Contextual Ecclesial Education and the Evangelizing Mission of the Church: Proceedings of the CMI Philosophers' and Theologians' Forum on "CMI Legacy of Contextual Ecclesiastical Education and the Evangelizing Mission of the Church,"* Bangalore: Dharmaram Publications, 2018, 45.

[51] B. Thettayil, "Conclusion: Caricaturing the Face of God," in B. Thettayil, ed., *God-Talk in Context: A North Indian Theological Experiment*, Bangalore: Dharmaram Publications, 2016, 409.

[52] Francis, *Meeting with the Poor Assisted by Caritas*, Assisi (Perugia), 4 October 2013.

Local Church of Bijnor:
Phases of Growth and the Vision for the Future

Gratian Mundadan

S amanvaya was and is a great dream of several people, people who have seriously and genuinely reflected and have known and have realized what it really means to evangelize in the words of Jesus, namely, to bring the Reign of God **here and now on earth** (not simply looking forward to the end times for a realization, though the fullness and perfection of this realization happens only at the end times, according to Vatican II GS, 39) among humanity, building up of a **New Society**, which Jesus envisaged. Samanvaya was not a challenge, but a humble initiative to rediscover and employ the methods/ways/means/ procedures Jesus Himself appropriated when He became a human being, bringing the Father's Eternal, unconditional, boundless **Love and Mercy,** in order to re-establish the conditions and atmosphere when He decided to create Man and Woman in the well-ordered, well-furnished, perfectly equipped Cosmos. He created them to be the crown of all His creation, to increase and multiply and to form a Family of Humans living in mutual love, brotherhood/sisterhood, in the ways of real Justice, Truth and Peace. He also appointed them to order, govern, work upon, utilise the whole cosmos in accordance with His Will, which always is the **All-Round and Perfect Well-Being and Happiness of**

His Children, living in real, genuine Joy, in flowering Fellowship and fullness of Justice – the Kingdom of Heaven on Earth: "Thy Kingdom come! Thy Will be done on earth as it is in Heaven."

There was an attempt and proposal, earlier, to have a seminary for the missions just as the one in Bangalore – Dharmaram, as the CMI Mission 'Ad Gentes' began to spread in the North India. But the way it was proposed and presented, it looked like a copy of Dharmaram in North India. The Seminar in which it was proposed did not accept that proposal at that time. Instead it proposed 'Poornodaya' to train the CMI missionaries in North India and to be a research Centre for Mission in general and of the CMI mission in particular. One wonders if Poornodaya is fulfilling its original *mission and vision*. Samanvaya, on the contrary, was a new vision; it was altogether a new project; it was a concrete realization of many who started with 'adaptation' and 'inculturation', may not be properly realizing and discerning the true meaning of these terms, and dreamed further aiming at creating an Indian Christology, Indian Theology, Indian Liturgy to Worship the Father, Son and the Holy Spirit, appropriating the Worship Jesus might have offered to the Father in the situation of India at various times, various cultures, its thinking pattern, the ambience of the people's way of life, their world vision, amid the many Religions and Ideologies of India, moving from alienation to identification following the manner of Jesus, seriously and genuinely making an attempt for an Indian Interpretation of the Bible (for the present and for the future), a Dalit reading of the Bible, a Poverty-ridden peoples' reading of the Bible, an exploited and suppressed people's reading, against an oppressing and suppressing people's ways, an expansionist, greedy, maliciously ambitious people's schemes. Samanvaya is envisaged as a genuine attempt to seek Christ in the aspirations and traditions of the people of India whom God, in His Great Plan for humanity, wanted to make agents of change - change in the society, change in world vision, change in social vision and change in approaches. Samanvaya wanted to form the seminarians in a process of theologising in various Indian situations in order to help Jesus to re-incarnate in those situations for those people and their culture, their life situations, their thinking patterns, their way of life, their daily needs and requirements, their true freedom, their efforts for realization of what God wanted them to be when He created them.

Contextualized theology – Text applied to Context - has been referred to as a theological method or a way of theologising. But the question is if there is any theology without a context. The so-called Western Theology, is a theology that developed and grew against the background of the context of those countries, their times, their culture, their traditions, their way of life, their vision of life and world and the human society, their situation, their social and political set up, just like the Hindu Theology, which was developed and grew against their thinking pattern regarding the human society, the world, culture, traditions etc. They extol caste system; the Western theology was extolling the 'slavery' and 'human labour as obligation, having no rights for themselves' and many other unjust traditions and situations, till recently and even today. There is no Absolute Theology, like the Word of God, which is absolute, applicable everywhere and at all times. It is a crime to impose a theology, developed in one place at a time and a particular context, on the people living in other places, in altogether a different context and at different times. Worse is enforcing the style, words and phrases and sentences, attitudes, dispositions, sentiments, methods, rituals, in prayer that developed among some other people, in a different context, at a different time, in a different atmosphere for other people. How can it become really one's own prayer? No wonder our prayers and rituals become a kind of *Manthrocharanam*! Content is great, part of our Faith, the Christ-experience of many people. Adapt these into one's own style, one's own words and phrases, suiting to one's own context, situation, atmosphere, times instead of transliterating, swallowing, even without understanding the proper meaning. Samanvaya is, I firmly believe, a humble attempt to initiate this process. How far *Samanvaya* has achieved this vision is a matter to be discussed.

All these are not perhaps the area of this article, according to the Editor. This paper is on **Local Church of Bijnor: phases of growth and the vision for the future**. May be, other articles will deal in detail with these points. All the same, these are an indication to the second part of the proposed title of the article. This will be dealt with later.

Part I:LOCAL CHURCH OF BIJNOR: PHASES OF GROWTH

Some things Special about Bijnor Church

a. It was, on the arrival of the missionaries, a purely virgin land with no Catholics, no Catholic institutions, no presence of the Catholic Church in any form whatever. It is remarked that the then Archbishop/Bishop Joseph Evangelisti OFM Cap. of the diocese of Meerut never wanted to part with any area where the diocese had established the presence of the Church, mostly through institutions and also through small communities of faithful. It was a barren land, just like those places where the Apostles, after the Ascension of Jesus and Pentecost, went to preach the Good News. They had in most cases the presence of Jews, the remnants of the Israelites. Here too we had a few Methodist Christians. Evangelization work had already been done in this area. The American Methodist Missionaries arrived in this part of the country in early 20th century and they did a lot of work in this area. As a result there were around five thousand Methodist Christians within the area of the Exarchate of Bijnor. But, with the missionaries gone back, and the local pastors not being zealous in catering to these Christians, they were all like 'scattered sheep', never wanting to go back to their original faith and their old way of life. Several groups among them were more or less inclined to join the Catholic Church if they were given a chance. It must be acknowledged that the first group of Catholics in Bijnor Mission were these Methodist Christians who came over to the Catholic Church. Already a movement in this line was going on in the whole of the diocese of Meerut. This was a piece of hope, which Fr. John Chamakkala, the Finance Officer and Chancellor of the Diocese of Meerut, gave the missionaries when they met for the first time.

b. The land comprising the diocese of Bijnor, especially the hilly area, known as Garhwal, is the '*holy land*' of the Hindu brethren, with the sources of the holy river Ganges and also of Yamuna, the 'Devbhumi' with the presence of 'chardham' – the four most important pilgrimage centres of the Hindu brethren, namely Badrinath, Kedarnath, Gangothri and Yamunothri and several other holy places connected to their ancient tradition, like Rishikesh, Haridwar, Devaprayag, Rudraprayag, Karnaprayag, all of which have become very much alive today, with greater momentum after the rise of RSS in the country. Adi Sankaracharya reached these remote areas in the 8th century A.D. walking all the way from Kalady in Kerala and preaching the Advaitha Vedanta for a revival of Hinduism,which was almost disappearing due to the influence of Budhism. He re-established the Temples of Badrinath and Kedarnath, and started the first of the four Shankar Maths/Ashrams, namely Jyotir Math in Joshimut. The CMI missionaries, the disciples of Jesus, monks of 'Mount Carmel', now, followed him in the 20th century to preach and teach the real Advaitha – God is one and only One, the Father of all. Our mission is to make people understand that this God is our Father and we all are His beloved children who are supposed to live as members of the same family - free children of God - in true fellowship and work together for the progress of the world, God's precious Gift, for the benefit of every single human being and all together, enjoying together all that this Beloved Father has provided for us all, without any distinction or discrimination, to be distributed in a just way according to the needs of everyone; fight against the systems of the society that has overturned this situation with oppression, suppression, discrimination, distinctions, with classes of poor and rich, with classes of high and low, with classes of hierarchy, clergy and laity etc., to actively participate, following Jesus, in transforming the present world and the history of humanity into what it should have been according to the Father, as He created the world and mankind.

c. The whole area of Exarchate of Bijnor, especially the Garhwal hills, was the most 'underdeveloped area in the most underdeveloped region of the most underdeveloped state' in the whole country with literacy percentage at that time below 15 among men and below 13 among women, with12 hospital beds for hundred thousand people, per capita income very low compared to other parts of the country, land not properly used as there were no people to give them instructions how to make use of land more productively, what kind of cultivation or what kind of orchards to be developed, destroying all the forest in the Himalayan mountains which is the 'Fort' of our country, which causes rain and fertility on the land, with frequent landslides, which cut of all kinds of communication between the various parts of the area. Even the plain area within the exarchate, the most fertile Gangetic plains, was not yielding as much it could, because of frequent floods, destroying complete villages and forcing the people migrate to other areas to settle where the river has changed its course and formed fresh land strips.

d. It, excluding the hill districts, was also an area notorious for its communal riots, dacoity, murder, exploitation of the poor and the landless, caste discriminations, clan fights, etc.

e. The Garhwal is also famous for many things, apart from the shrines and temples, the famous Valley of flowers – a frequented Tourist spot, perhaps the highest peak in the country, Nandadevi, deep valleys, with beautiful, gorgeous flora and fauna, real attraction for tourists.

There could be more!

The Beginning

The beginning was obviously very difficult. To start from scratch in an altogether new place where the missionaries were totally strangers, was indeed a challenge. Staying in one of the Parishes of the diocese of Meerut, they had to commute every day to Bijnor to find a place on rent to start with. In this matter, the parish priest of Raja ka Tajpur, where they were staying, was very helpful. He had contacts with the district authorities of Bijnor and through the influence of the district magistrate, Mr. Biswas, with the promise to start a convent school, they managed to get two houses on rent, one for the school and for the Sisters' residence, the other for priests to stay. Even though we started a school and Sisters were serving in the school, which was well appreciated and made use of by the majority of the people around, there were some who were very unhappy about the missionaries' presence and work. They started writing in some of the local newspapers cautioning the people about the intentions of the missionaries: to convert all into Christianity. We never bothered to react to it and carried on with our work. To find land and buy it was a herculean task, as we were strangers and the people did not have trust in us if we would continue or not. It was through the direct intervention of God, through the several miracles He worked, we have been able to carry on. Many incidents come to mind, both fearful and joyful. There are many events, which when one looks back later and reflects upon, make one shiver. So dangerous was the situation. But the Lord was with us and He helped us very generously and saved us from many dangers, many traps laid by people to catch us red-handed, robbers and dacoits and the result of all that is what we see in this Bijnor mission today. I appreciate with deep gratitude the sacrifices the first missionaries went through with great joy and satisfaction; their tireless efforts to establish the Church in this new area, managing with the bare minimum facilities they had.

Our dream as we began

When I was appointed the Apostolic Exarch of the newly established Apostolic Exarchate of Bijnor, I said to myself: Ten thousand Catholics in ten years' time (I have been hearing that the number of Catholics in Exarchates of Chanda and others grows, especially in the Andhra area, to ten thousands, twenty thousands, and people all over glorify the missionary work of CMIs, in this matter of growth of the Church, both in numbers and establishments). I was questioned persistently - no one to be blamed as that was the only criterion of the success of the mission according to the temper in the Church as a whole, and with greatest concern to spread the Christendom, under the guise of Kingdom of God - every time I went back to Kerala and other places in the South: how many conversions have taken place? How much land has been acquired? How many Institutions have been established? What are your plans to build up the Church in that area – meaning how many institutions, how many churches, how many workers, how many charitable activities….? I myself used to ask every missionary invariably whenever they came to visit me from the mission stations: How many baptisms have taken place. It was a desire or a dream, not realized yet, even after 46 years – the kind of expansion of and strengthening of the *Christendom*, conceived and propagated by theologians and by the Church, interpreting the Gospel of Jesus to suit to the power-mongering, royal-minded, ruling-ethos, big powers and the clerical community, the institutionalised hierarchy created by the same group, the privileged sections, which was in collusion with the same group for their own material profits, authority, power, position, fame and name etc. What I want to say is that the impression of all the people at that time about mission was expansion/spreading of *Christendom,* growth of the Church, meaning adding more and more members to the Church, bringing everyone into its fold – *one fold and one shepherd*, again Gospel and instructions and teachings of Jesus Christ, perhaps misunderstood and misinterpreted to a great extent, following the so-called traditions, man-made traditions of the Church, for the *salvation* of the people, *saving the souls*, which they would not have if they don't get baptized and become members of the Church. For a long time, mission was undertaken with the assumption that acceptance of the Christian Faith was essential for salvation: *nulla salus extra ecclesiam.* Therefore, numerical growth was crucial, and could be achieved through any means even with the help of colonial powers. – Missionary crusades and *Requerimiento,* guilty of contributing to the destruction of entire cultures; even fellow-Christians were not spared. Today the history of Christian mission evokes in the minds of many people negative feelings, in spite of the immense good done by the missionaries. Mission is usually characterized by slogans such as imperialism, colonialism, paternalism, intolerance and lack of credibility – mission closely related to the centuries of colonial depredation that has created a crucified Third World – colonial mission was not a mission conducted in the powerlessness and poverty that Matthew recommends (Mt 10:9-10) – it was an aggressive mission, carried out under the patronage of colonial powers, who in Latin America caused the greatest 'demographic collapse' in history…and in Africa and Americas were responsible for the most massive and brutal slave trade that our planet has seen – in spite of whatever qualities of dedication and compassion individual missionaries might have lived and worked with.

But I am not disappointed at all. I am sure that we did rather well in evangelizing this region, these people. Just to mention one instance, our work to make the people to become aware of their situation and condition through our attempts in conducting non-formal education, and many other development schemes, in the many villages have borne fruit. Even though initially the people not knowing our intention and not becoming aware of the results, strongly resisted, gradually through these non-formal education programme and others we have been able to bring in a total change in the attitudes of the people. They became very cooperative and began to see the changes that have happened in the children. They realized the need of education for their liberation from all those dehumanising conditions and started demanding quality education for their children. That was indeed a very remarkable change of attitude, which in turn helped them to achieve growth in every respect. Our first mission is to make people really human, as designed by God when He created mankind – man and woman; if we all, the poor and rich, the high and low, privileged and under-privileged, the main line and marginalized become real human beings then God's Kingdom will come with it. And that is our Mission, Jesus' Mission – perhaps a different and the true meaning of Mission as against the so-called mission of the proponents of *Christendom*.

The letter of Abhishiktanada Swamy

Abishiktananda Swamy, a beginner in the attempt to Indianize the Christian living, Christian Sanyasa, Christian Prayer, wrote a letter to the then Prior General, asking him not to bring all the institutions into this land of prayer and contemplation, rather start prayer centres only. He was then living in Uttarkashi, in disguise. I personally did not have any chance to interact with him. I have read his books and I have great appreciation for his person and for his writings, and his vision and proposals for a genuine growth of the Church in India. Yet I thought that his advice was a bit extremely placed and was a one sided vision. I thought a mixture would be the best. It is not only prayer and contemplation, however valid they are in a country like India which is well known for renunciation, asceticism and contemplation, it was equally important that we, following Jesus, work also for the liberation of the people in all aspects and provide them an experience of the Kingdom of God here and now, while preparing them to wait for the flowering of it in Heaven at the end times.

What did we do to begin with?

Inspired by the then style of missionary work prevailing at that time everywhere, we started schools. And they said that it was the best way to get into the area and create confidence in the people about us, from where we would be able to launch our programme. The first Bishop of Ahmadabad, Charles Gomes S.J., told me that it was by opening schools they – the Jesuits – started their mission in Gujarat, and became successful – and encouraged me to open schools. When we started, that was a great demand also of the people, in the small towns with the educated aristocracy – the officers and the bureaucrats. We never had any idea that the schools – English Medium – would bring in monetary profits, but wanted to get a foothold in the area. And so the effort was to start schools in the small towns. We did not have any cities or big towns with more than ten thousand people at that time. And our concern was to expand, spread all over with whatever means we are able to make use of. Incidentally, one of our group while talking to a person, who appeared to be a real estate businessman said in one breath: we want to buy land in Kotdwar, in Njibabad, in Pauri, in Sreenagar, in Rudraprayag, Karnaprayag....That man was really surprised. Later when we were negotiating the sale of a piece of land in Najibabad, with the intention later to establish a hospital, the owner of the land told me: *The talk among the people over here is that you will buy up all our land and then you will bring the British people back, again to rule the country and will make all of us Christians.*

Having no attraction at all for any one to make any profit running schools in this most underdeveloped region or any other institutions, no religious congregations came forward to start their own institutions. Religious Congregations of men came and made surveys, but were not happy as the chances at that time to establish themselves and run profitable institutions was less, and so went to other dioceses, even Latin dioceses, forgetting their outspoken position that the Syro Malabar priests and Religious should work only in places where Syro Malabar Rite could be followed. Now after 30-40 years several of the same Religious Congregations want to start their own institutions within the area of the diocese of Bijnor, which I predicted at that time. Some of them even regret that they have committed to the institutions directly under the diocese, instead of starting their own for several reasons. But now the diocesan priests also do not seem to be happy to invite them, unless they are ready to work under them.

When we started opening schools, I proposed to have only three or four schools at the most to have a foot hold in the five districts so that we could with the support of the bureaucracy in the district headquarters start working in the remote villages. If needed some elementary schools could be started in other places. But that dream did not realize when apart from the demand of the people, our priests and sisters were insisting to raise the elementary schools to high Schools and then to Higher Secondary level.

Also I said that the buildings of our institutions – schools, dispensaries or such – as well as the facilities there should be excellent, while our own houses shall remain simple and moderate, with a witnessing mission, not to give an impression of building up an empire, which again was an unrealized dream, as the missionaries who were so happy with the very minimum facilities in the beginning, started building priest houses and convents with all the most modern facilities possible.

The Development of the Mission

We have succeeded, in certain sense, to establish the Church in this holy land of the Hindu brethren, even though we have not succeeded making many followers of Jesus Christ among these people. But I am not at all disappointed. Ours was, as I used to say, clearing the land, ploughing, preparing the field and sowing the seed, which is the hardest of all. It is left to the future generations of missionaries to nurture these seedlings for their healthy and fast growth so that they bear an abundance of fruits. Our work, in the education field or development field or socio-economic field was and is well appreciated by the local people. They express their appreciation in many ways. And as such, we did not have to face any serious troubles in the past years. Even when people from outside and who do not know any thing about our work over here make efforts to create trouble, the local people would say: Don't do any thing with these people, you do not know what they have done for us. The government authorities and the officers were very helpful, unless they were mindfully biased.

Yet the response in the way of becoming members of the Church was not very encouraging. Not knowing what to do and how to do to execute our commission, we started erecting the Tabernacle in as many places as possible. Like the Israelites, who were instructed to go around the City of Jericho with the *Ark of the Covenant of the Lord* in order to capture it, we also were inspired to spread the Holy

Presence of the Lord all through the land establishing the Tabernacle in many places.

I firmly believe that the atmosphere at present is very conducive to go ahead, even though things are fast changing and a real challenge to our presence and work here is growing. If we understand the proper meaning of our mission as entrusted to us by the Lord and dedicate ourselves to work in that line, we will succeed, even though we will have to face many challenges and difficulties and dangers.

Primacy of Witnessing

The missionaries were firmly convinced that our missionary work has always to be primarily through witnessing. In this matter, my thoughts were very much supported and influenced by '*Evangelii Nuntiandi*', the post Synodal Document promulgated by Saint Pope Paul VI in December1975, which is being hailed as the *Magna Carta* of evangelization in the modern world. All through the document Paul VI repeats many times the term 'life witness'. He starts with '**Witness and mission of Jesus**' (6); he speaks of primary importance of **witness of life** (21): Above all Gospel must be proclaimed by witness. Take a Christian........Searching for suitable means he comes back to **witness of life.** He says: "...for the Church, the first means of evangelization is the witness of an authentically Christian life.......'. Modern man listens more willingly to witnesses than to teachers, and if he does listen to teachers, it is because they are witnesses'....It is therefore primarily by her conduct and by her life that the Church will evangelize the world, in other words, by her living witness of fidelity to the Lord Jesus – the witness of poverty and detachment, of freedom in the face of the powers of this world....." (41). To evangelize is first of all to bear witness – witness given to the Father's love (26). "...the present century thirsts for authenticity. Especially in regard to young people it is said that they have a horror of the artificial or false and that they are searching above all for truth and honesty. These "signs of the times" should find us vigilant. Either tacitly or aloud – but always forcefully

- we are being asked: Do you really believe what you are proclaiming? Do you live what you believe? Do you really preach what you live? The witness of life has become more than ever an essential condition for real effectiveness in preaching. Precisely because of this we are.......responsible for the progress of the Gospel that we proclaim". "What is the state of the Church, ten years after the Council?".......Does she testify to solidarity with people and at the same time to the divine Absolute?....Is she ever more committed to the effort to search for the restoration of the complete unity of Christians, a unity that makes more effective the common witness committed.........We exhort the religious, witnesses of a Church called to holiness and hence themselves invited to a life that bears testimony to the beatitudes of the Gospel.........We say to all of them: our evangelizing zeal must spring from true holiness of life, and, as the Second Vatican Council suggests, preaching must in its turn make the preacher grow in holiness, which is nourished by prayer and above all by love for the Eucharist ....the world .....is nevertheless searching for Him in, unexpected ways and painfully experiencing the need of Him ....The world calls for and expects from us simplicity of life, the spirit of prayer, charity towards all, especially towards the lowly and the poor, obedience and humility, detachment and self sacrifice.....Without this ...our word will have difficulty in touching the heart of modern man. It risks being vain and sterile" (76).

Ultimately Evangelization means to become true disciples of Jesus and make others His disciples. This aspect of 'becoming true disciples and making others true disciples of Jesus', which was the essence of Christian Life and Mission for the Early Christians, has been slowly displaced with the zeal for expansion, for concentration of power, which was perhaps the greatest mistake that happened in the growth of the Church. Also, I believe that the Church gradually left or minimised the importance of *ortho praxis*, meaning living the discipleship of Jesus and concentrated on *orthodoxy*, which divided the Church, and as such became a scandal for others, instead of becoming a powerful witness of *Unity, Identification, Solidarity.*

Here I want to refer to the thoughts of Father Dr. George M. Soares-Prabhu, the renowned Scripture Scholar and Professor of Scripture in JDV, expressed in several of his artices.. He says that the Great Mission Commission (Mt 28:16-20), which according to him is a composition of the Evangelist rather than a saying of Jesus, is not a 'mission command' – 'going' instead of 'go' - rather an instruction how to make people **disciples of Jesus**. It is an editorial masterpiece which weaves together the Christological (28:18), ecclesiological (28:19-20a), and eschatological threads (28:20b) of the gospel into a theological text of great power, is now read as a simple (even simplistic) 'Great Command', purporting to come from Jesus Himself [GEORGE M. SOARES_PRABHU: *FOLLOWING JESUS IN MISSION: Reflections on Mission in the Gospel of Matthew;* J. KAVUNGAL and F. HRANGKHUMA (eds.), *Bible and Mission in India Today* (Bombay: St. Pauls, 1993)]. For him the real mission command is in Mt 5:13-16, in which mission is described not so much in terms of verbal proclamation as of witnessing. The command is to be 'the Salt of the earth and Light of the world' and it was given in the context of the Sermon on the Mount, which spells out in detail what to be a 'follower of Christ' means [THE CHURCH AS MISSION: A Reflection on Mt 5: 13-16; GEORGE M. SOARES-PRABHU. *Jeevandhara* 24 (1994)].

We were eager to build up our small Christian communities in different places to be ideal communities, just as the 'early Christian communities'. And we had an advantage, namely, that we did not have any existing Catholic Community to influence them in a different way. I used to inspire the missionaries to build our communities up in the fashion of the early Christian Community, the most ideal community for the purpose of carrying on with the mission of Jesus. They worked really hard for that and so our faithful whenever they went to other dioceses in the region they were specially noticed, because of their behaviour different from others. Because we took special care to educate their children, these few families that we have are well placed in the society now, thank God and thanks to all, who collaborated with us. I don't claim that these communities are what we wanted them to be in the full meaning of it. Real Evangelization will be done through these communities when they become true replicas of the Kingdom of God, where God Reigns, a community where there is true solidarity, fellowship, concern for each other, stand for Truth and Justice for everyone.

We were interested not only in the small Catholic Community we had, but our services were rendered, perhaps many times more to the general public in the villages. Our social work department started working from the very beginning of the Exarchate and several effective schemes for the all round development of the people, who were otherwise in a very pitiable condition, have born good fruits.

Our non-formal Education Scheme

One among them is our **non-formal Education Project**. It has very effectively changed many things among the people. When, in 1979 UNO declared the 'Year of Literacy", we started this project and went to the villages with non-formal education project, neither the parents nor the children were interested. We had many setbacks. For the parents one more child meant only two more hands to work. Children were happy spending time at home with the parents and the village people, go into the field where their parents were working, go after the cattle grazing them. Education did not mean anything for them. Our many earnest attempts through non-formal education to help them to learn at least to write and read and count, which we and many thought was the only way for them to emancipate themselves from their poverty, their backwardness, bonded labour systems equalling to slavery, discriminations meted out by the rich and high in the society etc., was strongly resisted against. The government also was pushing non-formal education among the illiterates through teachers, professors, college students and other paid teachers, spending a lot of funds. All that came to an end within a very short time. Our work continued.

Gradually things began to change. There were demands from several villages to start (they thought it is school) non-formal education centres. We had in those days around ten to fifteen villages attached to the various mission stations, where non-formal education was conducted. And we saw to it that the children were made to write their examination in some schools for the fifth grade and then continued in the same school for their further studies. Our children from the non-formal Education Centres scored very high marks compared to the regular children in those schools and the teachers began to advise the children to come to our non-formal education centres instead of simply wasting their time in the school. We also started Adult Education, which brought in a kind of revolutionary change among the people. The women started writing letters to their husbands who were working in defence or other places, which surprised them. With all these there came a significant change in the attitude of the people in the villages, who began to demand for quality education for their children. Now they are not satisfied with the education, which the government schools provide. People even from the remotest villages began to purchase small portions of land any where near our schools and put up a small house so that their children could study in those schools.

As we found that government is trying to thwart our attempts by organising mid-day meal, ration etc. to attract the children to the schools, but with practically no teaching at all, thus taking away all our children, we reduced the number of such centres. There are a few still. The result was very pathetic: children enjoyed their life in their own way, but did not get educated until people began to realise the situation, and through many of our awareness-building programmes, became interested to provide proper education for their children.

Walking village doctors and midwives Scheme
Our Social work department along with the Medical department started training some selected leaders from the villages in elementary treatment of sickness common among the people in the villages. They were equipped with a kit of medicines and other needed instruments and equipments. In the same manner lady leaders were trained in mid-wifery and they began to go around the villages to help the pregnant

ladies, checking their condition during pregnancy and helping them for a safe and hygienic delivery. They also instructed and helped the mothers how to take care of their newborn children. These and our other attempts made the people sensitive about their health needs and they look for facilities where they receive good health-care. Today the situation is that people are looking for Super Speciality Hospitals for treatment, delivery etc.

Our *Satsanghs* in the Villages – prayers, bhajans, and discussions

These were aimed at bringing people closer to God and at the same time to work along with them to relieve them of the oppression, exploitation and poverty, chalking out plans together and working for it. People in the villages were extremely happy about these and they used to come in big numbers. But due to the intervention of the RSS, their people visiting every family and threatening them of such participation in programmes organised by Christians, slowly the number of people began to reduce and villagers were not as interested as they used to be, mostly out of fear of the RSS people. At the same time there is new a phenomenon that has emerged, the Khristbhakta movement. In almost all our mission stations, especially in the plain areas, many people come to the church or chapel in rather big numbers to hear the Word of God and get relieved of the pain and sufferings. They have deep faith and they witness to it daringly in front of people who question them.

Fight against Corruption

The missionaries insisted that we should never give bribe for getting things done by the government officials. Several Fathers and Sisters had very difficult times to get non-objection certificates, recognition to the schools, going to the offices in Moradabad, Lucknow, Allahabad etc. many times with no positive results. Disappointed they came asking permission to give some bribe. But I tod them: we may not be able to have many baptisms from among these people in this area (as they are non-responsive, very much rooted in their religion – we don't have tribal people except a very few in the hills, who are very sophisticated and in spite of our many attempts they never responded), but standing up for the gospel values and fighting against wrong practices, thus witnessing to the values of the Kingdom of God is all that we can do in this place. And all the missionaries continued firmly in this position for a long time. Unfortunately in course of time, when it became very difficult to get things done without bribe, our own Fathers, and may be Sisters too, began bribing in order to get things done easily and urgently. Now it has become impossible to get recognition or non-objection certificate without under the desk dealings.

What is Mission

I hold that evangelization is not transplanting a well organised, and perfected, as some would think, Church from its original place to new places, which I always considered detrimental to real evangelization. Rather we must be instrumental to make a Church grow in a new place where we are sent. It has to be done chiefly by sharing our own intense personal Christ experience with the people to whom we are sent, not so much by preaching or proclaiming, but through our life and sharing with them. Once we share our intense Christ experience, which we have received from our ancestors and which we live, those who come into contact with us will be inspired and will positively respond. They will naturally respond in their own way, not necessarily in the way we have been practising. These expressions of their positive response will be in their own cultural background, their way of perception, their way of life, in their own terminology. And that will be a 'new Church' with its own spirituality, its own theology, way of worship, administration etc., of course all derived and formed from the Gospel of Jesus. It is for the missionaries to lead and guide them in this process, in the proper way so that they don't in any way compromise with any of the fundamentals of Faith - faith in God and in Jesus Christ as the Saviour, and also faith in the Church, the community Jesus instituted to continue his mission, and be at the service of the Kingdom of God which he wanted to establish here and now on earth – Jesus' Vision of a New Society, the fullness of which will be realised in the end times as Vatican II says: "already present on this earth in mystery," but which, "when the Lord returns, will be brought to full flower" (GS, 39). This Church is the only visible sign, for the people, of the promised salvation, meaning freedom from every kind of bondage. And such a Church will be simply attractive to the right-minded people. Christian mission is concerned with fostering what Vatican II has called "the body of a new human family, a body which even now is able to give some kind of foreshadowing of the new age" (GS 39) – because the Church is the community of Jesus which continues his active presence in the world and is entrusted with his mission, its ordinary task is to further the process and help to bring Reign of God to its fullness – by becoming the symbol and the servant of God's Reign (see MICHAEL AMALADOSS, "Religious and Mission", SEDOS Bulletin 25 (1993), 208) – the new **'contrast community'**, in the place of the Israelites whom God called to be a 'contrast community', with the same mission as He has given to us, who because chiefly of their desire and demand to be like others utterly failed to be so. God called them, and us too to replace the failed Israelites, so that by living out the values of Jesus, make God's love present in the world and so prepare it for its transformation into the new heaven and the new earth – primary mission: to lead humankind and cosmic history to its fulfilment, in the full realization of God's Reign.

Inculturation

In the same line of thought, inculturation, I believe is an essential component of mission strategy. Taking inspiration from Jesus himself in his Incarnation, the Church has to be inculturated or rather incarnated in a new place and among the new people. The 'foreign' garb that we carry on with us is because of the lack of inculturation. If the Church were to grow in a place it has to take roots in that place. If the starting and growth of the Church in different places were according to what have been described above, there would not have been any need for inculturation at all. (Unfortunately the effort always has been to transplant, instead of making Jesus' Community grow in a new place in a new garb, assimilating and appropriating the new culture, new vision, new perception of the new people there). Such a Church is already their own and according to their culture, and will be fully owned by them.

Our missionaries were in general, with a few exceptions, convinced of the need for inculturation. But their concern was rather superficial and confined to Liturgical adaptations rather than the substance of inculturation in its true meaning. Abhishiktanada Swamy says that inculturation has to take place first in the life of the people who are making efforts for it, before venturing any kind of inculturation in the Litrugy. Incutluration in the Liturgy and other practices of our Faith will have to grow from our inculturation in our person and life.

Naturally we made some attempts at inculturation in the Liturgy and they were very much appreciated even by those people who do not compromise in any way regarding "paithrukam", more important for them than even faith and mission, as *Tradition* was more important to the Israelites than the *command of God*, about which Jesus accuses them and corrects them. For such people mission is simply transplanting the Church from where the missionaries come and enrol more and more people in the new areas to follow the same way, in the same manner, and in the same spirit. Otherwise it is not mission work for them. People fail to realize that it is impossible for people to change their life-long traditional habits, way of life, culture etc. If at all they are baptized and become members of the Church, they are Christians in the church and prayers, but not at all so in their lives. Many do not seem to be bothered about it as long as they are regular in their church attendance and devotional practices. It is here that we have to follow Jesus: He was born poor among the poorest of Israelites, identified himself fully with the sinners, outcastes, tax collectors, became one among them through his table fellowship and sincere compassion and concern for them and so he could stand for them and even fight for their rights. Thus the life of Jesus and his spirituality could be summarised in terms of perfect identification with the lowest among the people and constant struggle against the establishment, which caused such a situation of differences and discriminations, whether political, societal or religious, to make them privileged, deeply aware of the rights of these outcastes, and secure their rights for them, Free Children of God equally along with others.

The pressure from the mother Church in Kerala to keep up the 'paithrukam', while having not any other interests in the missions at all, stood very strongly on our way of trying several experiments in Inculturation and dialogue. In spite of that we dared to initiate something, which were appreciated.

Language

Mastering the language is the most effective means of inculturation, and of effective evangelization. If we have mastery in the language of the people we will be able to understand them well and in turn we will be able to share with them our experience of God, of Christ in a very touching and meaningful way. With this in view we initiated certain steps: One year after our arrival in the mission we started bringing the CMI Aspirants from Kerala to the mission to study in the schools over here along with the children of the place. And they picked up both English and Hindi languages marvellously well. They could handle the language very well. Local people were really appreciative of their ability to communicate with them in their language, in their ways of communication. Several of the missionaries started living in the villages among the people, really identifying with them in every thing, living a very simple life like the villagers themselves – proper identification. When we started the Minor Seminary for the Diocesan Clergy we chalked out a new programme of sending them, after an year of orientation in language, spirituality and vocation for priesthood, to the mission stations to attend the nearby Inter Colleges for their 'plus two' studies. This way of training the beginners in the language, life style and cultural expressions was very well appreciated by all and it really was very effective. Those who went through this process give powerful witness to its effectiveness.

Indian Christian Ashram Movement

When we came here there was Abhishiktananda Swamy living in Uttarkashi, Vandana Mataji and Isapriyaji living in the Shivanada (Divine Life) Ashram taking initiatives in Indian Ashram movement. Being more inspired and receiving a very positive push during the All India Seminar on 'Church in India Today' – an attempt to adapt the II Vatican Council Vision to Indian Church, 1969, they were already in that line, and wanting to be close to the source of Hindu Ashram Life. They became 'chela's of Chitananda Swami, the Acharya, in the Shivanada Ashram and also of Krishnanada Swamy, equally competent as the Acharya himself and the Secretary of the Ashram. They were having initial lessons of how to plan and build up an Indian Christian Movement through Ashram life. They were constantly under the special care of Abhishiktananda Swamy, initiator of this movement. I had several sessions with Vandana mataji and Isapriyaji with regard to what we should do to promote this movement. Their first request was to secure some land in Rishikesh. None of us could realize it at that time as we did not have any contact with people or civil authorities. They, with the help of Krishnanda Swamy, managed to secure a small plot of land in Rshikesh and built up a small Ashram with a few rooms for sadhakas and the common facilities for prayer cum satsangh hall, dining hall and kitchen. In subsequent discussions I proposed to Vandana Mataji that we need not restrict to Rishikesh where it is difficult to acquire land. She accepted my proposal to start an elaborate Ashram in Jaiharikhal where the diocese had sufficient land and an old building. They developed it and the Jeevan Dhara Ashram functioned successfully for a long time until they found themselves difficult to continue due to old age and could not find successors for themselves. It was lying vacant for a few years until our dear Acharya Thomas Kochumuttom took over the responsibility to be the animator in the Ashram in the same line. It is still serving many people, mostly people from within India rather than foreigners as in the time of Vandana Mataji. In this Jeevan Dhara Ashram in Jaiharikhal started and still continues some experiments in the way adapting our prayers, life style and also liturgy to the Indian situation. I am not sure if these will bear any real fruit, with lot of resistance from many places, with an indifferent attitude among the missionaries, and declining interest in these initiatives.

Dialogue

In the multi-cultural and multi religious situation of our country, Dialogue is very important. The official Church both globally and in India were concerned about living together and participating together in several projects of establishing peace, harmony. I had a vision different from that regarding Dialogue. I thought that real dialogue, on the level of religion, must be on matters of faith. My conviction was that such open, unbiased dialogue and discussions will help us to reach the Truth, and Truth, we know, is God, the loving and caring Father revealed by Jesus Christ. On my first visit to Dharmaram College after becoming the Exarch, I met Rev.Fathers Thomas Kochumuttom and Augustine Thottakara who were going for studies in Indology. I told them that they should come to help us here one semester each, engaging the students in Dharmaram during the other semester. Within three months of my being here in this area I developed certain ideas of mission in the line of inculturation and dialogue. I wanted to open up a very good Dialogue Centre in Rishikesh. God gave us some land, miraculously, I must say, in Rishikesh and we could start living there and working. Krihnanada Swamy of Divine Life Ashram in Rishikesh told me after being present for the blessing and inauguration of the small little house in Rishikesh: 'Bishop we must make this an International Dialogue Centre.' I thought that was a great dream. I had very concrete plans also made – a good library, some decent kutiahs, and other facilities. What I lacked was the availability of interested and competent personnel. I appreciate certain initiatives taken by Rev. Rev. Father Augustine Keemattam, in consultation with Vandana Mataji and her group and some others who were interested in such a project. For some reason or other, it did not materialise. When Rev. Father Davis Varayilan came up with the proposal to hand over some part of the land in Rishikesh, belonging to the diocese, for building up the Regional Centre, Samanvaya Vidya

Dham, of Samanvaya, the one and the only condition I made was that while establishing this Centre of Samanvaya in Rishikesh, efforts must be made to build up, side by side, a 'Dialogue Centre', with facilities for people to make in-depth studies on Religions and foster discussions and satsanghs to promote Inter-religious Dialogue. Unfortunately no one has taken these conditions seriously, while 'Samanvaya' became another seminary almost in the Traditional lines.

The contribution of Sadharmyam in Sreenagar, Garhwal, initiated by the CMI Province has been very impressive and fruitful in this line of Dialogue and Inculturation. Under the guidance and management of those who have been appointed in charge of this Centre, very effective steps have been taken to foster the spirit of Dialogue, especially among the educated group of people like the Professors of the Garhwal University. The problem one sees is that the genuine interest in these kinds of new initiatives in the line of proper evangelization gradually disappear, or at least diminish. The tendency is to go back to the traditional ways.

Flowering

Whether our efforts in the mission of Bijnor flowered and how it flowered and born fruit is for others to judge. Well, if you ask me to speak about it, I will very reluctantly say that it has flowered if one judges according to the standard, as understood and practised, of our Missionary/Evangelization work. We have a few Catholics and still some baptisms are taking place almost every year. We have one local priest, also a few seminarians, from among the locals, in various stages of formation, a few nuns from among our new families, a few very active 'catechists'. We have a few very sought after institutions, mostly for education, both English Medium and Vernacular Medium, though the demand for vernacular medium schools is diminishing drastically, a growing hospital, also very much sought after, apart from small number of centres to take care of, educate the disabled children, street people, unwanted and thrown-out, where the objective is to empower them and give whatever training possible to rehabilitate them into their own villages where they will be able to stand on their own feet, lead a rather normal life earning for themselves, not entirely dependent on others. We have a very efficient and active 'Karuna Social Service Society', intervening in the needs of the marginalised, poor sections of the society, with a number of projects for empowerment, development, growth. Our youth are very active and growing in their interest for evangelization. But the system continues without any change or rather getting worse everyday, the poor and the underprivileged not able to get justice done to them, with no voice to raise and fight for their rights, promises remaining only in the air. With all these, where are we? What are we? How the mission, the mission of Christ, the mission of the Church entrusted by Christ, the mission we have received and accepted from God, through Christ and through the Church – a Mission to establish the Kingdom of God/Reign of God here and now among humans - is being carried out? These are indeed questions one has to ask oneself and answer if one takes mission seriously.

I have a great worry. Did we build up another Welfare Society, whose main beneficiaries are the missionaries themselves, though a lot has been done on a compassion basis for the poor, illiterate, neglected people? Have we properly understood the real meaning of the mission Jesus has entrusted to us? Have we been committed to identify ourselves with those for whom we work and face struggles and conflicts in order to free them from the many bondages under which they are crushed and persecuted? Many such questions arise in the mind. Yes we have accomplished many things; we have built up much for the glory of God and for the good of His people. Can we console ourselves with these complacency feelings?

Part II: Local Church of Bijnor: Vision for the Future

This is a question to be answered by those who have inherited the work of Mission in Bijnor. As mentioned above in this paper, the initial work of the early Missionaries was to till the land, remove weeds as much as possible and prepare it for good crop. In that way Bijnor has been to a certain extent prepared well now. The atmosphere is very conducive at present, even though there are several serious threats facing us. A kind of situation has been created where people in general appreciate and accept whatever the missionaries have done for their betterment and as such it could be a very responsive situation, provided the missionaries keep up the close contact with, identification with the people and work hard with new initiatives, much more useful than perhaps what have been already experimented for the real good of the people. The mission has a strong foothold in the region and among the people. The missionaries have to give very close attention to the developments that are taking place in the social, political, economic aspects of the people and creatively interact to it. If this is realised, then the prospects for Evangelization of this land and people are very positive.

The Christbhakta movement that is picking up momentum in almost all the places where Missionaries work is a very positive sign. Weather many will become members of the Church is not very sure. But it is certain that the deep faith and intense experience of these Christbhaktas is certainly a sign of the presence of the Kingdom of God, as have been the miracles worked by Jesus and His disciples. It is indeed a matter of great contentment that the missionaries are very earnest in fostering and encouraging this movement. That will bear fruit in its own time. In what way this will bear fruit depends on the insights of the missionaries regarding their commission of evangelization. At present the Christbhaktas are interested mostly in the alleviation of their infirmities, in which they have great faith. This could certainly be upgraded to a movement to change the inhuman situation that is prevailing in many places and become a strong struggle for real freedom and true fellowship, which exactly is the goal of evangelization.

When I seriously reflect on this, **vision for the future**, my thoughts go in the following lines: We the true disciples of Jesus are gathered by Him and sent out by Him in order to work relentlessly in the spirit of Jesus Himself for bringing God's Reign here and now on earth, rather than merely aiming at the expansion of the Church community or its power position in terms of more mission stations, more institutions, more activities, more personnel. Our presence must spread and it must spread through our deep and intense God-experience and Christ experience. And this has to be done in a spirit of quite extraordinary freedom from material possessions (Mt 10:9), depending on local support, but no monetary rewards (mission shall not become a source of material gain), empowered with spiritual power, effectively imparting 'peace' (wholeness, health, healing) and an absolute trust in divine providence, in powerlessness, self-emptying, suffering, as proposed by Jesus in Matthew chapter 10. I don't deny the need for more people in the community to work for the achievement of this goal. That shall never become the goal. The goal must be: to establish true fellowship among the people, bring in the rule of love and compassion, justice and peace. In short it is to attempt sincerely and humbly to realise the dream of God the Father when He created human beings, namely the building up of a **New Society** where every human being can live in true fellowship with others, in deep communion among all, with justice practised and meted out to every one, in true joy and happiness.

As has been pointed out earlier, "The ultimate basis of Church's Mission is the witness of its community life and praxis. It is through its fidelity to the Christian *dharama*, with its antigreed and its antipride, that the Church remains 'salt' that has not lost its saltiness and 'light' that has not been hidden under a measure (Mt 5:14-15). Mission is a communication of life (of 'saltiness' or 'light'), and not merely enrolment into a club or conscription into an army, it must emerge spontaneously from the life of a witnessing community, and spread as it were by infection. Any verbal proclamation if it is to be authentic and not a form of what Matthew and (and Jesus) would call hypocrisy (Mt 7:5; 15:7), must first be lived out in the Christian life of the community. A Church that does not have a conspicuously Christian life (a Church, for instance, that is ridden by caste, or devoured by consumerism, or caught up in struggles for status or power) can no more engage in authentic mission than can a bad tree produce healthy fruit (Mt 3:8-10; 7:16-20; 12:33). Its mission sours into 'conquest', propaganda, or 'Church growth'; and the communities it engenders are not spirit filled Churches but infected reproductions of itself" [GEORGE M. SOARES-PRABHU, *The Church as Mission: A Reflection on Mt 5:13-16; Jeevandhara* 24 (1994)]

One of the essential requisite for this is encouraging and establishing sincere dialogue and cooperation among the various groups of well-disposed people, in order to establish Harmony and Peace among all people. In a situation where hatred is increasing and taking dangerous dimensions, this is very important. In spite of the world becoming a global village, the conflicts between groups and hatred among them is on the increase all over. This is indeed the power of evil, which has to be eradicated in order to create the New Society of peace, harmony, fellowship, justice and communion. The human tendency is always to resist the initiatives of God for their welfare as evidenced in the story of the original sin. People do not trust in God who has provided everything for them in abundance and guaranteed their welfare, provided they make use of God's creation faithfully as he has ordained them. A mistrust of God and also a mistrust of others! Consequence is violence and disharmony. The aim of every missionary has to be to change this situation and establish the Reign of God.

Poverty Eradication

Jesus claims in the Gospel of St. Luke (4:16-21) that he had been anointed by the Spirit precisely to proclaim good news to the poor and he solemnly announces that that the poor are blessed because of the Kingdom of God, which he has come to proclaim is truly theirs (Lk 6: 20-26). Well, Jesus in his Manifesto at his inaugural sermon in Nazareth announces that his task of 'evangelizing' is proclaiming the good news of liberation to the poor, of heralding freedom to captives, sight to the blind, liberty to the oppressed and so of inaugurating a time of salvation. His is thus a *social manifesto,* though the spiritual dimension is not denied. The salvation Jesus announces here is primarily a liberation from the pressures of social, economic and societal oppression. We cannot have a different task than that of Jesus in continuing his mission. This means that we have to be prepared to live by the values of Jesus and commit ourselves to the building up of the kind of community of freedom and fellowship that he envisioned, where spiritual poverty (anti-consumerism) will flourish and oppressive poverty (destitution) will vanish from our lives. For in a community that is truly Christian there can be no greed and no destitution, just as it was in the First Christian Community. Unfortunately that is not what we see in our Christian Communities at present. Even in our parishes where the parishioners are very active in all pious activities and organizations, we fail to see such a situation. Holy Father Pope Francis has spoken of the sin of 'indifferentism', the rich and powerful not concerned about the poor and marginalized in the same community.

In a country like ours, more especially in an area like Bijnor, where only a 15% or so of the population are adequately housed, clothed and fed, our attention has to be focussed on this aspect of our mission. We do work for the poor people, true. We help them to grow in every respect. But our attention has to be very much in the direction of changing the situation where there is distinction between the rich and the poor, the powerful and week. That kind of a society is the one that Jesus has envisioned.

Condition for Mission

The essential condition for mission is **a foundational experience of God and of human condition,** without which no one can be an effective missionary.

Resulting: in full freedom from all things to trust in God and trust in others.

Enabling: to love as God loves us – a beloved-oriented love as in the Holy Trinity.

Inspiring: working for the liberation of all people, rich and poor, powerful and powerless, discriminated and discriminating, hated and hating, oppressed and oppressing, under-privileged and privileged from all bonds to make all people fully free and love.

Aiming at: bringing God's Kingdom/God's Reign here and now on earth – the New Social order.

Making: people wait for the full flowering in the end times **New Heaven and New Earth.**

Upon These We Shall Build our Social Questioning A Search for a Theological Basis and Method in our Social Engagements

John Chathanatt

Introduction

Faith gives vision and grace. A vision of a social order based on faith and truth built on justice and cemented by merciful love was preached through the symbol of the 'Kingdom of God' by Jesus and called for repentance (Mk 1:15) to achieve the same. This indication of the Reign of God along with its imperative of repentance was given to us at the beginning of His mission and preaching (Lk 4: 18-22). As disciples we are called to respond to this revelation of Jesus and in our faith response we are given the energy of grace to respond as well as to carry out this mission of establishing such a graced social order, because of the very person who is making this announcement and initiating this process. In the presence of Jesus and in the light of the scriptures available to us, we reflect on the social realities to respond and to transform.   With the arrival of *Gaudium et Spes* (*The Pastoral Constitution of the Church in the Modern World*), the most influential document of Vatican II, a biblically based theological reflection on social issues and problems appeared among Theologians. Today we need to continue that reflection especially when we are confronting very many life negating experiences in the given social order the world over.

In this paper I am looking for a theological basis and a method of theological reflection and questioning on social realities especially in the Indian context. In other words, it is an attempt at theologizing in a social context. How to theologize in a social context? When I say social, I mean all the six dimensions of our life, namely, social, economic, political, religious, cultural and personal/psychological aspects of our life. Doing theology, in the Indian context of plurality and differences and life-negating experiences, is a challenging task. Theologizing in the Indian context and identifying a method in that process is important to do an adequate approach to doing theology in the India of diversities. A new way of being a Christian in India today, continuing the Church's mission of promoting the Kingdom of God, implies and even demands that the Church be involved in and have a critical engagement with the socio-economic, religio-cultural and political realities of our society. The very mystery of incarnation invites the Church to be a catalyst, the salt and the leaven in this process. The very mission of promoting the Kingdom values and announcing this reign of God in the existential life of the Church in the world demands an involvement in the mundane realities of our life today.

Theologizing in a Social Context

We have moved beyond the description of theology by St. Anselm, i.e., theology understood as 'faith seeking understanding'. In the Indian context, we speak of many theologies, like Dalit Theology, Tribal Theology, Feminine Theology, and Contextual Theology. Here an attempt could be made to describe the understanding or even the very definition of theology by various theological writers.

DESCRIPTION OF THEOLOGY BY DIFFERENT THEOLOGIANS

G. GUTIERREZ*	A critical reflection on Christian praxis in the light of the word of God.
S. KAPPAN ***	A human reflection on the negativity of human existence.
M. AMALADOSS***	A critical and dialogical reflection on faith and life, mediated by culture.
A. PIERIS*	A contextualized reflection on human existence in the light of faith.
M.M. THOMAS***	A Christian reflection on secular anthropology
RUETHER*	Contextualized experiential reflection on reality as a woman
NIRMAL*	A critical reflection on the experience of oppression, in the light of Christ-experience, as a *Dalit.*
S. RAYAN***	A reflection on the situation in the light of faith.
R. CHOPP**	A critical reflection on massive suffering, in the context of secularism and modernity, with the dangerous memory of Jesus.
D. TRACY**	A philosophical reflection on human experience in the light of faith
J. H. CONE*	A critical reflection on the oppressive situation, in the light of gospel, as a black.
G. MAR OSTHATHIOS	A pastoral reflection on the implications of Trinity for a classless society. (It is a

	pastoral exhortation with citations from the Bible)
E.SCHILLEBEECKX**	A critical Christian reflection on the intelligibility of the symbols (for a universal salvation).

* emphasize on the particularities for the adequacy of theology.

** emphasize on the universalities, for the intelligibility of theology.

*** emphasize on the particularities with a universal slant, for adequacy and intelligibility of theology.

A Possible Description of Theology

In the light of the above understanding, a possible description of theology could be attempted.

Theology is a critical and dialogical reflection on historical actions and our living in the light of faith (Word of God, Revelation, Tradition), and done in the presence of God, in the company of Jesus, oriented to transformation and involvement onto a process of further analysis, reflection and action.

This process leads to a deepening of faith and to a more faith-filled action and commitment to a spirituality in the world, in an effort of transformation and discovery of the divine presence in and to history and the universe, ultimately leading to salvation to have an experience of full Divine Presence.

In short, theology could be described as *'a critical and dialogical reflection on historical actions and our living in the light of faith oriented to transformation and action.'*

QUESTIONING ON SOCIAL ISSUES THEOLOGICALLY

We reflect and question on social issues and problems (eg. Poverty/ Destitution, Fundamentalism, Violence, Terrorism, Caste and race problems, Corruption, etc.). When we face crisis in the social order, nationally or internationally, we look for explanations and guidelines which give a human (Christian) perspective on these issues, problems and events. We need to create *Adequate* (confirming to reality, going into the *esse*, the beingness of reality, authentic), *Consistent* (being free of contradictions – eg. love and hatred cannot go together), *Coherent* (standing together – relationality), and *Comprehensive* (universality in time and space; all aspects taken together), horizon to see, judge and act correctly on social issues and social questions.

Social questioning (SQ) arises from *four strands* of our faith: 1. The Dignity and Sacredness of the human person. 2. Human Person as a Social, Relational, and Corporate Reality. 3. Our relationship with the Earth (the Earth and we belong together, and together we belong to Christ). 4. Our Concept of God.

SQ discloses the **horizon** of one's angle of vision. It discloses a **spirituality** (a way of walking, a way of being; *the hallmark of an authentic spirituality is to respond creatively to a real context*). The nature, the layers, the bricks of this horizon, this matrix, this viewing point (the elements that form this horizon), makes a difference in our way of "seeing" social issues and social realities. And for a believer it is the horizon of God that is fully *truthful, comprehensive, consistent, coherent* and *adequate*, in viewing a reality. And our attempt is to make God's angle, His view **our** view; to make His way of looking and seeing, **our way of looking and seeing**. It is in the meeting of the human horizon with that of the divine that we humans get our true authenticity (Incarnation becomes our paradigm, and a necessity for this). It is in this attempted union that we get to know the truthfulness of our truth, as one could say that *truthfulness of truth is truth itself.*

For a believing Christian it is in this horizon of God that the mission of Jesus is presented and manifested (Repent: Mk 1:14-15; Lk 10:9; Mk 1:4; Parables Mt. 20 onwards. The Mission: Lk 4:18-19; see Is. 61:1-2; Ps.146). At the moral dimension it is the establishment of *freedom, fellowship, equality, justice, truth, love, harmony, mercy, communion*, etc. St. Paul gives the intuition at the religious level (1 Cor 1:30): *wisdom, Righteousness, Sanctification, & Redemption*. The implication of this is that our *Social involvement has taken a sacramental significance because of the life of Jesus*. The neighbour is anyone *in need* (Mt 25:45). In his Abba experience, Jesus understands the fullness of his mission. It is in the mission of Jesus that we find our mission. Giving humans priority over Sabbath, he disclosed a spirituality of response-ability – the ability to respond to realities.

Hence the basis of our mission, social doctrine and social concern, our involvement and commitment, is *Jesus*, the **CHRIST EVENT**. Christ Event is the totality of the experience of Jesus: the incarnation, living the life, the death, resurrection and ascension of Jesus. Christianity is a person, a discipleship, then, not just a set of rules and regulations, rituals and cults, doctrines, authorities and commands. It is the centrality of a person. Hence it is that Jesus came:

- to form a community of god, women, men and the earth

- to lay a fresh accent on love; giving a newness to the love-commandment

- to place bread at the centre of his prayer, making service as the focus of his actions

- to give the human person and human needs and human possibilities priority over Sabbath, fasts, laws, traditions, temples, authorities, empires, rulers, customs

- the Sabbath is for the human person, he emphasized; and so are our parliaments, industry, technological research, the economy, the resources, the state, schools, universities, the employment bureaus, hospitals, the religious congregations, our assemblies, and our goods and services

- to disclose a spirituality of response-ability, the ability to respond to the divine murmurings and to the human realities of sin and grace.

In his Abba experience, He becoming the righteousness of God, manifests the Father to us – i.e., being *faithful to the demands of relationship* as a Son to the Father – being obedient unto death, even death on a cross fulfilling the will of His Father (Col. 2:13-15; 2Cor. 5:17-21; Rom 3:24; Col. 1:15-21; Gal 3:13; Phil. 2:5-11). This is the righteousness of Jesus. As the image of the Triune God we are one human reality, one human family, in many personal realizations.

Jesus goes where people are, not where they ought to be.

So the social questioning is a help to re-member each person to the one family of humans in many personal realizations. This is what working for peace implies.

In God's family we are one caste – cast in the same mould. In deep interdependence we live *from* and *for* one another. This implies that no action of ours is neutral, including our silence and our words. The earth and we belong together and together we belong to God. This is the source of our faith and the basis of our social questioning.

But we will **miss** understanding. We misunderstand. Contingent human beings that we are, limited and limiting that we are, as humans, we will miss *full* understanding. So we misunderstand. This realization should make our manner of questioning humble and non-moralizing. Question we must; question firmly and relentlessly; but always with a sense of deep serenity and searching mind without giving the least hint at moral judgement; firm but gentle is the key.

Social questioning then reveals to us what is *lacking*. It discloses the *negativities*, so that our journey could be continued by negating the negativities (repenting, i.e. turning back, taking a hundred and eighty degree turn) into the company of Jesus, unto the establishment of the reign of God.

THE CHALLENGE FROM JESUS

Jesus challenged the established social order reinforced by religion and guarded by the political power. The two vital aspects of Jesus's life and ministry, viz., healing and table fellowship, challenged the religious order of the day. Jesus struggled to the establishment of a loving and caring community of free and equal persons (Mt 25: 31-46). The central aspect of the society was sharing. Paul's institution narrative of the Eucharist witnesses to this (1 Cor 11:23-26). When the sharing was absent, Paul even seems to be angry. It is in that mood of holy anger, frustration and disappointment of their lack of understanding and non-communitarian action that he narrates the Eucharistic institution done at the Last Supper.

Our social involvement and attempt at transformation, thus, attains a sacramental significance in and through the life of Jesus. We see in the last supper the words and actions of Jesus: take, break, share and eat (Mt 26:26-28). These are the essential items to bring about social transformation, and to establish loving communities of free persons. Jesus went around doing good, challenging all that denied and hindered the establishment of the kingdom of God (i.e. reign of God). This necessitated Jesus to go where people are, as mentioned earlier, and not where they ought to be. As a teacher he came down to the level of the people - meeting tax collectors and sinners, challenging scribes and Pharisees, being with the poor of his times, even allowing prostitutes to meet him, so that he can grace them and take them to His level, washing their sins, pouring grace onto them, to form a community of equals pleasing to His Father. He has taken pains to re-member all the peoples of his time, jews and gentiles alike, back into a family of equal fellowship. In the breaking of the bread he has broken our brokenness. Thus we see that engagement in social issues and social questioning is a theological engagement oriented to action leading to transformation.

So our social questioning involves a **Theologizing Process** oriented to **Transformation and action**.

OUR MODE OF QUESTIONING

We do the questioning as a follower of Christ. Remaining in the presence of God we reflect on social issues and problems; and question them in order to bring about social transformation. Remaining in the presence of God – in the horizon of the Absolute – we look at our double commitment: 1. to faith (God) and 2. to the contemporary situation (history). It is the experience of two presences. They are not separate, because the world, history and our situation are included in our commitment to God. Though they are distinct, they cannot be separated, like the head and tail of a coin, forming one coin, but distinct in its entity.

Hence a theologian (a student of theology) is always in the presence of God. Social questioning is done in the presence of God to ascertain God's way of looking at reality. Hence the method of theology is a method of correlation and dialectic. There is a paradigm shift from top down to going up (an irrupting) – an inversion of theological methodology.

One would be formally doing theology if critical questions are brought to the living of faith in a situation at the time of reflection. Hence doing theology is a *second act*, as Gustavo Gutierrez, the father of liberation theology, says – the first act is our experience, involvement, commitment. Discussion on the negativities is meant for the creation of a wholeness and oneness.

So our faith tells us that for us Christians socio-economic, politico-cultural and religious issues are theological issues. Why? I shall take that up later.

With the above understanding of theology and theologizing process along with a questioning mind, a new method could be evolved. The following is an attempt in that process. I am indebted to Gustavo Gutierrez, the father of liberation theology, James Cone, our late Fr.

Samuel Rayan particularly, and many other theologians with a liberation mind-set, for the formulation of the following method.

TOWARDS A POSSIBLE METHOD

Theology is an effort to understand (probe, fathom) the Faith by living it in our situation and reflecting on this lived reality and returning critically to both Faith and the Situation. The following structure could be created:-

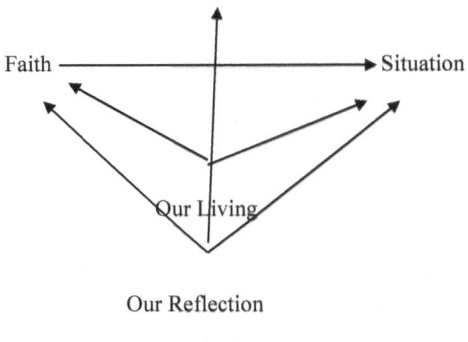

Our Reflection

Fig. 1

Here our reflection is on the living of faith in a situation of praxis (a clockwise movement in the figure above). Within the living/praxis, faith and situation meet. Here the situation challenges our living of faith. There can be a counter-clockwise movement too. Here we reflect on our living in a particular situation in the light of faith. Faith, then, challenges our living in a particular situation. We are challenged here; our practices are challenged here; our particular living process is challenged here by the faith that we ought to practice. There is a dialectic here between faith and situation.

Reflection shows the challenge that comes from the one to the other, the failure or success/readiness of the one to respond to the other. This reflection, then, is a second act - the living of our faith, namely, our living process and experiences, is the first act. Reflection may reveal that certain strands of faith-tradition fail to be lived, to reach and touch the situation though the situation seems to call for them. Reflection may also show faith trying to accommodate itself to given situations and be silent on certain aspects of the situation when a vigorous challenge seems to have been called for – Christians practicing slavery would be a very good example to this. Reflection will show that faith can discover itself partially or wholly in the situation, though anonymously. Reflection will show that in a divided and conflict-ridden world living the faith will mean making an option and taking sides. It will show that important aspects of reality can be missed if reality is not viewed from where the victims are: realities which the victimizers are keen of covering up or legitimizing in actual situations. Reflection brings us back to both faith and situation with critical questions seeking for answers. Theology, then, is an effort to explore faith's implications for life here and now in concrete situations. It is to explore the demands faith makes on our actual situations in order to "realize" the faith historically. Theology, then, becomes an effort to understand the situation, life, history, in the light of faith from the point of view of God, of ultimate meaning or destiny or hope or utopia. Here there is a double commitment: to faith and to contemporary situation or historical actions or the world of our actions - the two are not fully separated, because the world and history and our situation are included in our commitment to God. Loving God by loving the neighbour is the new commandment given to us by our Master. The world and history are God's initiative, God's concerns and God's love. Hence, there is no authentic faith commitment to God, our Creator and Saviour, the Lord and perfector of history, which does not include the processes and promises, pains and sufferings, aspirations and hopes of our historical process that God is making with us. This inclusive commitment is the starting point: commitment to God, God's design for the world, and to a just society and social order which could be epitomized as the kingdom on earth. So the starting point is our commitment, a point of our life at a moment of history. So the starting point is our experience at that moment.

Therefore the commitment to struggle against whatever contradicts or hinders God's purpose are discerned from the history of God's dealings with us under the guidance of the Spirit. The method is to bring our faith and contemporary situations face to face within a committed praxis of the faith in a particular situation. We attempt to make the two meet. We make the two question each other. We interpret each other contributing to a more humanizing praxis and to the construction of a more humane, gentler, peaceful and just world. This is possible because they (faith and situation) are related realities; the world is God's work. It is God's creation, concern and love. God is in the creation and is affected by what happens to it. So we can say that theology, then, is the effort to discover the divine presence in history, in contemporary events and experiences and thus to enable contemplation of the living and present God in history. It is an effort to discover what God is doing here and now. This enables us to challenge and to be challenged thereby to join God and collaborate with God 'in doing great things for the lowly, in routing the arrogant of heart, in pulling down mighty from their thrones, in exalting those of low degree, in filling the hungry with good things, in sending the rich away empty, in bringing good news to the afflicted, in proclaiming liberty to the captives, in giving sight to the blind, in setting the downtrodden free, in proclaiming a year of favour from the Lord'.

Hence one can even say that it is impossible to have faith if we are indifferent to the quality of history and the shape of the world. Because they are focus of God's concern. God so loved the world that He sent his only Son to the world. The world and history are also our work, the product of our loves and hates, our achievements and failings. To live our faith and reflect on the praxis is to question the forces and structures that are anti-life and against God. We are invited to reflect and discern where and how faith has been distorted, where important dimensions of faith have been muted, and even where faith tradition has been used to cover up oppression legitimizing domination.

This makes suspicion, and hence questioning, as part of our method. It is ideology – critique. Anti-god and anti-life values and views can subtly influence and distort our faith interpretation. Hence the importance of listening to the totality of the Word of God: not only the written but also unwritten, heard in prayer and obedience; not only in bible but also in other religious traditions – not only in "religious" texts and realities but secular moorings as well.

THEOLOGIZING PROCESS

The following figure can help us understand the whole process, in our theologizing attempt. Starting with our experience/commitment/involvement we move on to reflect about our context in the light of the text/faith or we reflect on the living of our faith (the nature of our text) in the light of our situation experience. Herein analysis of the situation becomes important. A re-reading of the text may become necessary; a re-look at our faith-practices may become inevitable. A change and elevation may be called for. Our commitment, involvement and our action and living process may need a transformative change in the light of a critical thinking. Our **attitudinal** (to have a new set of values), **behavioural** (to have a new way of acting) and our **cognitive** (to have a new vision of life) change may become an inevitable necessity. The transformation of my own self, and the change in the societal behaviour and life may need change and transformation. A further elevation, a dimensional change takes place here. And we continue the process with further analysis and with more critical reflection. A deeper faith-filled action would be the result. Now this elevated dimension of our action, this new experience, and deeper commitment and critical involvement become the starting point of another process of reflection. Thus we see a hermeneutic circle of reflection-action process taking place. This we call the theologizing process. A depiction of the same is attempted below.

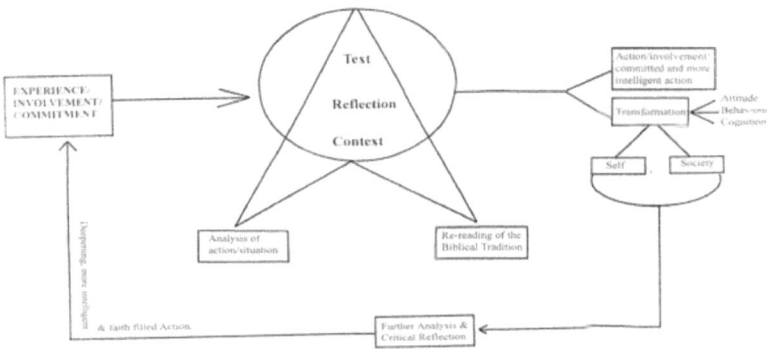

Fig. 2: Theologizing Process

The above figure 1 in repeated contextual reflection becomes figure 2. And making the figure 2 a repetitive habit will take us to the figure 3, a spiralling process of theologizing in a multidimensional form. This spiralling effect could be depicted in figure 3 below:

Fig. 3: The Spiralling process in Theologizing

A multidimensional elevation takes place here in our process of theologizing. We move from a lower level onto a higher level. The movement is always in the company of Jesus, perfecting ourselves, negating our negativities in the process, we move on to a new and higher dimension.

THE METHODOLOGICAL INVERSION IN THEOLOGIZING PROCESS

We can think of a short comparison of the Classical as well as the New Process of Theologizing.

The methodological Inversion in Theologizing Process

Classical Theology	The New Process of Theologizing
I. Trickling down	I. Erupting
II. Reflection upon the given - Word of God, notion of God - notion of Christ	II. Theology has a critical task
III. Starting point Traditional loci of Reflection: - Scripture/Revelation, - Tradition	III. The new contexualized, inculturated, Indigenous experience - based task of theologising, has its loci in: experience, context, culture, world events,pastoral activity, social change, "signs of the times" in the light of Scripture, traditions
IV. "Truth packets" are given. One has to unfold the given package and understand. "Faith seeking understanding" - could become a "theory" about God. - the task of theology is unfolding, understanding the given (truth).	IV. Truth is to be discovered in constant interaction with realities and events The task of theology is transformation Creation of a spirituality
V. The content of theology is fixed and given - a universal approach (One theology)	V. It emerges in historical processes. Theologizing process in many contexts. Eg. Theologizing in the Tribal, Dalit, feminine etc., context

VI. Role of theology: Application to - spirituality, morality Christian tradition and the Norms are to be applied to human experience. They are applied to events in history. Social Ethics/Moral Theology are realms of application. Hence a search for more and more of rational knowledge and the tendency to find universal norms.	VI. Human experience and Christian tradition (other traditions too) are to be read together dialectically. No uncritical acceptance of any tradition. Hermeneutics of scriptures is very important. Social ethical and moral poles are part of the living process of theologising; without action the process remains incomplete
VII. Implications: Compartmentalization of life possible	VII. No separation of Sunday from Monday in religious living, secular is sacred; no double life, i.e. one for the office and another for home and friends. - Methodological Invesion
VIII. Exclusively "formal," "discursive" intellectuality/understanding, emphasis on "standard"; critical acumen	VIII. A Paradigm shift. To a form that may be: - poetic, hymnal, - dance, artistic/painting, story - sermon/homily, drama, cinema (these could become valid form of theologizing)
IX. Could become closed, dry and purely discursive to maintain its "scientific character" - hence impersonal.	IX. Openness to reality, response-ability Loving knowledge (Gen 4.1) relational process. Hence life becomes a process of discovery of the self and the other, self in the other, and the other in the self in a continuum that ends only in the discovery of the other (you in me, and I in you) in an immersion without lose of identity.
X. Keeps its autonomy "the crown of sciences"	X. Inter-disciplinary

AN INTER-DISCIPLINARY APPROACH COULD BE DONE IN SEVEN STEPS

I.   Experimental (Phenomenology)

II. Scientific Enquiry.

-- socio-economic-political; historical affinity and manifestations in various religious traditions, cultures and societies; cultural interpretation.

III. Philosophical Reflection

-- the meaning of being human in the world; ethical/moral aspects; various interpretations in various tradition

IV. Religious/Scriptural interpretation and legitimisation.

V.   Critical Reflection in the light of Faith

-- Christic dimension; new creation, new humanity; kingdom values; situation of sin and redemption;

--ecclesial dimension.

VI. Response

-- of various people, of churches, sects, of peoples

VII. An adequate Christian Response oriented to Action which, in turn, is open to further critical reflection and more faith-filled action.

SOCIAL QUESTIONING: REFLECTION ON REALITIES

In way of summary one can say that social questioning (SQ) is done from a *horizon*, a *viewing point*, a *platform*, a *ground* where I stand/sit to view the reality. This makes a difference in our SEEING, JUDGING, and ACTING. The starting point is EXPERIENCE – our touch with a reality. Social questioning involves a theologising process and it is oriented to transformation. SQ springs from the Christian view of human reality. SQ discloses a spirituality of responding and response-ability, i.e., the ability to respond, and a particular "way of walking" in the Lord. SQ discloses the inseparability of the sacred and the secular. SQ is done in the presence of God to ascertain God's way of looking at reality (Mtt 25:45). In the reflection and action process, remaining in the divine presence (in the horizon of the Absolute), we look at our double commitment to a) faith (God) and b) to cotemporary situation (history). It is the experience of two presences. These are not separate, though they are distinct. The world, history and our situation are included in our commitment to God. Hence this reflection process is to create a spirituality. We reflect on the living of our faith in the situation. So our effort becomes an attempt to discover the divine presence in history. Discussion on the negativities is meant for the creation of a wholeness and oneness. SQ is oriented to transformation: 1. Cognitive change=to have a new vision of life. 2. Attitudinal change=to have a new set of values. 3. Behavioural change=to have a new way of acting.

Our faith tells us that all economic, social, political, religious or cultural issues have a moral/ethical dimension; and they should be under theological scrutiny. So, social questioning is a faith-search for the fullness of life, to find and attain the fullness of humanity, and, in that process, a search for the authentic God of Jesus Christ.

THE FOUR-FOLD FAITH CONVICTIONS

It was mentioned above that our four-fold faith conviction tells that for us Christians socio-economic, politico-cultural and religious issues are theological issues, and that they are under theological scrutiny. It is because of the following four religious convictions.

1. The dignity and the sacredness of the human person.

2. The view of the human person as a relational, social and corporate reality. This implies that we are interdependent. We build each other or we break each other. No action is neutral, including our words. We are in the image of a triune God, implying that we are communitarian in our very making.

3.   The earth and we belong together and together we belong to Christ.

4.   Our concept of God.

These four-fold faith convictions form the basis for our theological scrutiny in the realities around us.

CONCLUSION

So far we have been reflecting on the theological methods and the foundational aspects of our social involvement. It is very important to emphasize that our social involvement takes a sacramental significance because of the life and work of Jesus. The Christ event finally gives significance to our very process of involvement. It is very clear from our analysis that our involvements and contextualized approach gives rich meaning to our theological endeavour as such. Remaining in the presence of God, in the company of Jesus, we reflect on the present realities and question them for their negativities with the hope of transformation. Experience of acute problems around us and our commitment for the eradication of the same become the starting point of this new way of doing theology. Interpreting such experience in the light of the Gospel, and Christ Event, and questioning them in the presence of God with the intent of negating the negativities and transforming ourselves and the other including the structures that negates and dehumanizes become the process of our theologizing endeavour. This implies that the religious and ethical resources we have at our disposal along with the utilisation of the resources and methods of social sciences can be brought together for mutual enrichment in the process of doing theology. The latter together with philosophical method as tools of analysis is intrinsic to the new method that we are embracing in our attempt of a new quest in our way of proceeding for our methodology. The main concern is the word of God. It should interact with the human situation in our attempt at theologizing through reflection and action aiming always at transformation and conversion to Christ.

We know that socio-cultural analysis of the human situation is a sine qua non for a correct entry into and adequate analysis of the human situation. Hence the insistence on the human science and philosophical methods as intrinsic to our theological search. The port of entry of the Word of God is through the optic of the oppressed, the afflicted and marginalized section of the vast humanity, as the Biblical insights present to us. The Master of the Universe is hovering over us in our endeavour. We are not alone. In our journey of life, in the process of our reflection and action oriented to transformation, Our Master is with us with us in His Spirit gracefully guiding, challenging, correcting, assisting, and enabling us so that our journey is complete unto our union with His Father, i.e. ultimately leading to salvation to have an experience of full divine presence.

Shape of the Church to Come:
The Dimensions of the Coming Church
in a Pluralistic Context

Cyril Kuttiyanikkal

Introduction

The structure, shape and the form of church has undergone profound changes over the centuries. Recent years has witnessed to a growing awareness of the religious and cultural plurality of the present world. It is not for the first time that the church had to adequately respond to the plurality of religions and cultures. In general, the Christian churches assumed and emphasised discontinuity between Christianity and other religions.[1] However, the Catholic Church through the Second Vatican Council has now looked at its continuity and relationship with other religions and cultures. It has come up to say that God's plan of salvation extends to all. The openness brought about by the Council has initiated new encounters and relationships between different religious communities in India. Both Hinduism and Christianity have evolved and developed over centuries in different cultural contexts and contain within them gems for the future generations. Their mutuality and interaction might proof beneficial for both. "In the multi-religious context of India what we need today is an inclusive and interreligious vision based on the best of her spiritual insights, values and cultural traditions".[2] Nevertheless, the lack of ecclesial models for such fecundated formation. "What is lacking is a feasible notion of what it means to be a modern Catholic Church in the future, one that is not overwhelmed, but rational and appealing. There is need of an energetic metaphor that, as it were, attracts the future, motivates spiritually, convinces ecclesiologically, and works both culturally and operationally".[3] In this small articles I would like to draw some possible signposts for a model of being Church relevant and meaningful for India. First of all I shall present the status quo, the way how Indian Church comes across to people of other faiths. It will be followed by a description of the importance of models and a presentation of the necessary characteristics of such a model for the Indian context. This will take us to the Christ devotee model which seems to gain the imagination of Indian mind as well as which enables the Christian proclamation of Jesus Christ welcome in India. After presenting the life of the Christ devotees, I shall conclude with my remarks.

However before I venture let me concretely affirm some principles:

1. We should not be too quick in dismantling the existing models of church.

2. Existing churches need to embrace new paradigm-

3. In my opinion there is no final, once and for all, immutable standard model of being church

4. The Bible does not project or present a correct model that we are to follow always.

Waypoint of Navigation

Jesus Christ in his ecclesial manifestation has been present here in India from the apostolic times. This church had a variety of expressions and forms in several places. The image of the church as presented or visible in India is what many theologians and thinkers call as 'institutional model'. To make it clear let us just have a glance at how the church comes across to the people of India at large. It is enough to take the perspective of the people outside the Christian circle and look at the church from their place. The life style, mission and presence of the church as visible to them have the following features which could be summarized for a quick overview;

1. The church community is being seen India at the moment as a service provider: the services are mainly in education, health care, orphanages and other social or charity organizations.

2. It comes across to the larger community in India as a community which is different from others. Mostly the people come in contact with the church in the context of reception of the service. Apart from receiving those services, they do not have either much communion or communication with the church-community.

3. As is heard from several quarters, its rituals, its gorgeous feasts, its ethos, religious expressions etc., are not in tune with the cultural sensitivity of other Indian communities.

4. It is a minority community trying to protect itself, trying to build up institutions after institutions for itself, for providing services while desperately searching for its own space, role and recognition. It is trying to preserve its identity against and not in relation to other communities. The church is perceived as a foreign body and sometimes seen as a threat to national integration, religious and cultural identity. The church, they say, is foreign in its lifestyle, in its institutional structure, in its rituals and worship, in its western-trained leadership and in its theology.[4]

5. I would finally say that the church community in India did not make a spiritual impact, nor it became a trumpet blower for a social change or a voice of change of conviction. It did not turn to be a truly religious movement.

Now this is the normal situation of the church. "Normality is a paved road: it is comfortable to walk, but no flowers grow in it." Said Vincent

Van Gough. Therefore conceptualizing passionately and taking the road less travelled is not a luxury, but a choice. With that choice we need to reimagine the shape of the church suitable for the present day context of plurality of cultures and religions. It is important to take the unchartered terrain and go where there are no guarantees.

The Importance of Models

Avery Dulles introduced the term 'models' in ecclesiology in order to describe different realizations of being church. He uses this term because Church as a mystery cannot be spoken of directly. He further says that in the case of the Church "any analogy will never be perfect because the Church as a mystery of grace has properties not paralleled by anything knowable outside of faith"[5]. In order to speak about the mystery we need analogies afforded by our experience of the world and these analogies provide us with models[6]. "When an image is employed reflectively and critically to deepen one's theoretical understanding of a reality it becomes what is today called a model"[7]. At different points of history, different images or models emerged as a kind of key to offer a synthetic vision of the church[8], but none of these models says everything about the church. However, they say something about it, and manifest the development of church's self-understanding at a particular time.

Dulles speaks about the heuristic function of models in ecclesiology when he elaborates on the two-fold functions of the models in ecclesiology. In computer science a heuristic is a technique designed for solving a problem when classic methods are too slow, or for finding an approximate solution when classic methods fail to find an exact solution. The models of church has two fold functions. One is the explanatory function and the other is the exploratory function. On the explanatory level, the models synthesize what we already know about the church, while on the exploratory level they have the heuristic function of leading us to new theological insights. Or, as Hahnenberg puts it, 'the heuristic function of models, offer an accessible pattern for addressing important questions'[9]. These models are assessed by living out the consequences to which they point[10]. Since the correspondence of each model with the mystery of the church is only partial and functional, they are inadequate; therefore, the use of a combination of irreducible distinct models is advised. "The models that emerge are an insight into those questions and issues facing the community; they are the shorthand for the concerns of the time"[11]. New models emerge because of their capacity to solve certain problems which the predecessors could not deal with sufficiently.

Since no clear and successful model of ecclesia relevant for the inter-cultural and inter-religious context of India is visible on the horizon, let us now look at what should the possible contours and conditions of such a future church.

The Shape of the Church to Come; Some Preliminary Observations
Although all the major religions of the world are represented in India, it is predominantly Hindu in religious ethos. Hinduism has a basic openness as Rig Veda prescribes, 'Let noble thoughts come to us from all directions' (.89.9). India also has within her several, social, ethnic, linguistic and religious groups. Diversity and unity has become the cornerstone of the society. The earlier church model with its focus on discontinuity has not been able to achieve the acceptance of the people. According to Dayand Bharti the growth of Christianity was marked by a development in opposition to existing communities and thus becoming itself thoroughly communalized which is one of the greatest tragedies of mission history in India[12]. The religious ethos Christianity has not won the imagination of the Indian mind set. Primarily it is imperative to replace the existing mind-set which looks for conquering people and for snatching people out of their parent culture with a new model, new paradigm and a new mind set. The church has to imagine herself as the leaven which has to be permeated into the fabric of the society and not as Noah's arch to which everyone must be carried into. The church has to be imagined as salt which looses itself in order to preserve the community, in order to be at the service of the society and not an institution who has clear cut boundaries to keep some

inside and others outside. With the background of discontinuity, the idea of membership in the church with begins by baptism does not fit into the fabric of Indian culture and thought pattern. For the western thinker the either/or dichotomy is the only path of logic, which is basically Aristotelian. This type of binary logic helps one to determine whether something is true of false through affirmation or negation. However there are other modes of envisioning the reality. The Jain vision of *saptabhangi*(sevenfold prediction) incorporates affirmation, negation and the inexpressibility along with their combinations. The strict binary mind set has to be set aside to allow the birthing of the idea of belonging. People can belong to the church through definitely baptism, but by faith as well. Although we may not be able to make a blueprint for a successful model, we shall now draw some contours of a possible model for the future.

An Incarnated Church with a Focus on Jesus

Presently the church is seen as a foreign entity by the Indians at large. Its structures, spirituality, rituals, the very way of life of its members and so on do not resonate with the Indian mind set. What is required is a model of church that can be seen as well incarnated amidst the Indian reality. The wall that separates the church from the people of India is to be dismantled. The structure, the rituals, the spirituality and the very being of church needs to be incarnated into the Indian framework. The incarnational model needs to be taken seriously. The incarnational model suggests that God accepted humanity in its fullness and Jesus became fully human. Similarly Indian church has to become fully incarnated. It is not that first God redeemed humanity and accepted humanity, but he accepted humanity while redeeming it. Similarly, the focus should not be on what is negative or positive in the culture, but accepting its totality while assuming, but redeeming of its negativities in the process.

The spirituality of Christianity, the religious life and renunciation of its thousands of nuns, monks and priests, the charity and selfless service of its members, its vision of one universal family of god's children as brothers and sisters are not comprehended by the Hindus as these expressions are not in tune with their framework.

The church is to project an open ecclesiology, incarnated amidst the villages bringing the message of peace and love. There has to be direct encounter of people with the church and its members and thus church has to pitch its tent in their midst.

The locus of attention has to be Jesus. People in India already do have a high regard and respect for Jesus. No one shall be forced to change their religion. What is to be proclaimed is Jesus and the Gospel. The focus has to be on the kingdom values and the centrality of Jesus. People can be advised to listen to Jesus and become his true devotees. There shall be no pressure on them to discard their culture and religion. They shall be allowed to remain culturally within their family and village which mark their identity. The very identity of church as Indian church will enable the members to present an Indian vision of Christian life.

Church as a Praying Community

India is known for its spirituality and many people from outside come here for spiritual fulfilment or even spiritual tourism. Swami Vivekananda considers religion as the back born and bedrock of Indian culture. The Federation of Asian Bishops conference had chosen the theme 'Prayer: the life of the church of Asia' for the plenary assembly held at Calcutta in 1978. They wanted the churches to imbibe the contemplation of deep interiority and immanence, venerable sacred books and writings, traditions of asceticism and renunciation, techniques of contemplation found in the ancient eastern religions, simplified prayer-forms and other popular expressions of faith and piety easily available even to simpler folk[13]. Church will be seen as a community who are committed to a life of discipleship of Jesus. A community spiritually animated by the spirit of Christ. The credibility of such community is the deep spirituality and sharing of the 'Abba experience' of Jesus, and living a resultant life of brotherhood. It will be a spirit filled community whose focus is to discover the presence of the Spirit deep within the heart. The meaning of evangelization will be understood in a broader sense by overcoming the narrow understanding of 'snatching people out of hell' a phrase I borrow from J.B. Chettimattam.[14]

Various Levels of Ecclesiality

The Gospels attest the fact that not everyone had same kind of discipleship. There were different levels of belonging to the community of disciples. We know that there were the 12 apostles who formed a close circle, among them three had yet another significant role; there were the 72 who were also sent out; and there were the women disciples who followed Jesus wherever he went and who supported Jesus even economically and there were the 120 who came along with him from Galilee to Jerusalem and stayed in Jerusalem praying 'maranatha'. The missionary mandate given to the 12 and the 70 are the same.[15]

Similarly in the future, we should not expect everyone who accepts Jesus to belong to church in the same way. There should be various levels of ecclesial existence. Definitely there will be a minority who would want to follow Jesus radically accepting baptism. Just like religious life in the Catholic Church is not meant for everyone, similarly the baptised entry into the church will not be meant for everyone. However, there will be many who will be comfortable outside the wall of the church at the same time committed to Christ and his message and leading a life of Christian discipleship within a Hindu culture and religion.

Alongside the idea of membership in the church with begins by baptism the idea of 'belonging' needs to take central stage. People can belong to the church through definitely baptism, but by faith and devotion as well. Indian theologians in the past had limited their theological reflections to the dominant Hindu intellectual-philosophical resources. But today aware of the mosaic of Indian culture and religions, they are taking a comprehensive approach. Today in India we cannot satisfactorily witness to Christ in isolation from the context of our lives and the religiosity of the people living around us. It is a challenge for us to redefine the nature of the Christian church as *ekklesia*, a "called-out-people" and become flesh in each particular cultural and religious setting'.

An Inclusive Community of Baptized and Non-Baptized

The nature of the church in the future in India has to be inclusive. The emerging communities, have focus on the person Jesus and not on church. Anto Karokaran in the seminar in 'Church in India Tomorrow' in the year 2000 at Rajkot had called for forming fellowship of disciple-ship centred on Jesus.[16] The Indian Theological Association wants the church to radically rethink her mission and reformulate her image if she is to be faithful to Jesus Christ and relevant to her situation[17]. One of the means the Association suggests is to get out of the ghettos and be a salt in society by which they can permeate it with the values of the Gospel[18]. The whole intention of the future mission, in the understanding of the Association, should not be limited to the numerical increase of the community who seek baptism but emergence of a community of believers in Christ[19].

These kinds of fellowships or communities will lead the church to a life of communion and fellowship with the followers of other religions. The line that separates people on the basis of religion will be thinner and sometimes grey. Such communities will be the future ecclesial communities, even though their visible participation in certain aspects and sacraments of the institutional church may be a point of discussion and dispute. Such new forms of church will become customary since church is to be found where people gather in his name. However the formation of such an ideal inclusive community cannot be the result of a human plan, but the Spirit has move the church and others to come together. Nevertheless, a glimpse of such an inclusive community is visible in the emerging Christ-devotee movement in mostly north India. The Christ devotees are mostly culturally Hindus but spiritually Christians leading a life centred on Christ, but not baptized. The co-existence of the Christ devotees and the traditional Christian churches gives us a model of multiple belonging and a life of Christ centred fellowships. We shall now make a brief survey of the Christ devotee movement.

Christ-Devotees; An Inclusive Community of Baptized and Non-Baptized

Christ-devotees are now emerging in several cities and villages in North India. Practically every city now has people who are committed to both Christ and Indian culture. Although they are not united and not brought together their existence and spread is something new to both Christianity and Indian culture. Besides those living alone independently of one another, or with loos network among them, there are areas where they are united and forms a group and share their life and faith. Such a larger group is visible in and around Varanasi. In the North Indian multi-religious and multi-cultural context, on every Sunday of the week and on the second Saturday of every month thousands of people, who are not baptised as Christians, come to worship Jesus in Matridham a Catholic āśram in Banaras/Varanasi, Uttar Pradesh, North India. These people who are now called Christ-devotees (*Khrist Bhaktas*) are mainly Hindus belonging to several varṇa/caste[20] groups, who gather in the āśram in order to listen to the Word of God preached to them, to be cured of all their diseases, to sing praises to the living God in Jesus and to experience the loving touch of a loving God. They come from the neighbouring villages, cities and districts and even from neighbouring States. The total number of devotees has grown enormously to be called *Khrist Bhakta* or 'Christ-Devotee Movement'[21].

In this movement, an interesting interaction is taking place between Christianity and Hinduism. It is fascinating as it enables people from Hindu culture to remain faithful believers in Christ without discarding their loyalty to Hindu culture. However, this new assemblage brings with it fresh challenges to both Christianity and Hinduism. The Christ-devotees are reluctant to receive baptism despite maintaining a deep desire to receive the Eucharist. The Church is willing to admit them to the Eucharist only after their reception of baptism. This kind of highbred way of life opens up new frontiers in the Christian *ad gentes* mission albeit the unresolved theological issues lying herein. In this short article I am not able to take up all these issues. Hence, I limit myself to the role of Holy Spirit in this movement. However, for clarity, it is important to gather the work of the Spirit in this movement, by having an overview of this movement.

In the North Indian context, becoming a Christ-devotee or publically professing faith in Christ or even going to 'Christian āśram' invites disapproval from family as well as society at large. In this movement also mostly in the initial period many devotees were beaten up, scolded or prohibited by their family members from going to the āśram or becoming devotees of Jesus. However, since the devotees do not officially change from one religion to another, i.e., from Hinduism to Christianity, the opposition has come down. Presently around four to five thousand devotees attend the weekly Sunday *satsaṅg* (prayer-meeting) and around six thousand attend the second Saturday *satsaṅg* at Matridham, Banaras. On Sundays, many devotees go to the other small āśrams and parishes run by the diocese of Varanasi. There are a number of devotees who attend the prayer meetings at several small and big Protestant and Pentecostal Churches or assemblies. The second Saturday *satsaṅgs* at Matridham āśram is special for the Christ-Devotees and so they come to the āśram on that day. The whole number of devotees of the movement is around 60,000 (in 2006 it was 30,000 and had well outnumbered the Catholic population (19,169 in 2006) of the area). It is growing day by day. Every year at the time of the annual charismatic convention, more people join the movement as devotees. It is noted that the devotees belong to all the caste/*varṇ* groups of both rural and semi-urban areas.

The Religious Practices of the Christ-Devotees

Faith although is an internal matter, it cannot be hidden completely. The faith practices of the Christ-devotees will present us with the extent of their commitment to Christ. And when a community starts to live their faith the expressions become tangible. Christ-devotees courageously display their commitment to Christ in their prayer meetings and other occasions given below.

The Second Saturday and Sunday Satsaṅgs

The most important and visible place where one can observe the faith practices of the devotees is the Matridham āśram. They come in large number on every Sunday around four to five thousand and on second Saturdays of the month around six thousand, for the prayer-meetings. At the āśram they display a variety of faith expressions culturally relevant for them but the content of which are mostly Christian. Touching the ground and prostrating before the Eucharist, performing ārătī in the Church, sprinkling on themselves the water from the pond, prostrating or garlanding the statue of Mary, offering sweets, fruit, incense etc., at the holy places in the compound are only some of them.

In the *satsaṅg bhavan* they listen to the preaching of the Word, join the singing of *bhajans* and prayers, listen to the witnesses, raise their voice in praise and worship, participate in the adoration of the Blessed Sacrament and join in the healing prayer. While preaching the preacher makes them repeat the Word of God after him. They sing and praise loudly and shout alleluia. Most of the devotees have learned by heart the *bhajans*, prayers, quotes from Bible and hymns by repeating them in the āśram.

The devotees remain in the *satsaṅg bhavan* and attend the whole programme from 11.00 to 16.00 on Sundays and from 10.00 to 16.00 on second Saturdays. All the *satsaṅgs* begin with the invocation of the Holy Spirit. Hymns, which plead for the showering of the Holy Spirit, are sung. While singing those hymns the community joins with louder voice, with clapping of hands, and beating of symbols. It is a sight to see how the devotees long to behold the Blessed Sacrament when brought to the *satsaṅg bhavan* for public adoration. Some even try to touch the sacrament, or at least the priest who carries of the sacrament or his cloak[22]. Others express their devotion by prostrating, bowing their head to the ground and so on. Most people bring with them water and oil to be blessed and taken home. The Holy Spirit is invoked before benediction. Majority of the miracles and cures take place at the time of benediction of the Blessed Sacrament.

Some Christ-devotees from the neighbourhood attend the Catholic liturgy, participate actively in the singing of *bhajans*, and listen to the Word of God. On the last Sunday of every month, around 150 devotees attend the monthly *satsaṅg* and as part of the retreat, they join the Catholic liturgy. They listen to the preaching eagerly, sing and recite the prayers in loud voice and show more devotion during the liturgy than the baptized Christians. According to Anil Dev IMS, the father of this movement, this has improved the quality of the faith of the Catholics. Those who visit the āśram for retreat, and other purposes are impressed by the faith of the devotees. According many priests this participation of the *Khrist Bhaktas* in the liturgy rekindles the faith of the Christians.

The Family Prayer
The devotees have adopted the practice of family prayer now. Before becoming the devotees, they did not have any ritual similar to a family prayer. Many of them had a family deity placed in one room where they offered *pūjā* to the deity. The *pūjā* consisted of lighting the lamp (*diya*), incensing deity and saying personal prayers or chanting the mantra and ārătī. One member of the family either the father or mother performed it. Other members of the family did not take part in it. Once they became the Christ-devotees, they took the family deity to the āśram to be buried under the cross of Christ and now keep the picture of Jesus and other Christian symbols at home. They also wear Christian symbols such as the Cross, Rosary etc. If the members of the whole family are devotees, then they have a special place for prayer. After becoming the devotees of Christ, all the family members gather for the family prayer, which is done mostly in the evening. It includes lighting of the lamp, intercessory prayer, Rosary, sometimes reading from the Bible, *bhajans*, praise and worship. The prayer is concluded with the ārătī. The more devoted spend one or two hours in prayer. The women mostly

lead the prayer and perform the ārătī. Some devotees, normally the women pray in the morning also. The Morning Prayer is a short one where they limit it to lighting of the lamp, small personal prayers and an ārătī. They also display in a prominent place the pictures of Jesus, Mary, Bible[23], Cross, prayer book and devotional hymns book published by the āśram[24]. Before becoming devotees, it was not normal for them to have their religious symbols displayed in the prominent places, but it was limited to one room or place normally away from the prominent place, where the family deity was installed.

The Village Prayer Meetings
The Christ-devotees gather in the villages under the guidance of an *aguā* for the common prayer meeting once a week. Conducted normally in the house of *aguā* at 12.00, the prayer meetings are mostly attended by women. The gathering is generally of small size, sometimes with just 10 to 15 women, and other times, in certain villages, from 30 to 50 people. Additionally, those who wish to become devotees also join and ask for prayers. Some devotees, who are not able to go to the āśram due to either objection from families or some other reasons like sickness, also attend the village meetings. Sometimes the head catechist from the āśram joins the prayer.

The prayer meetings begin with the lighting of the lamp and singing of *bhajans*. One person leads *bhajans* while the group repeats after the leader. Sometimes the devotees sing *bhajans* composed by some of the devotees themselves in their local dialect (*bhojpurī*). Such *bhajans* are rather longer and narrate the events and incidents from the Gospel. Mostly, while singing the *bhajans*, the devotees join by ringing bells, playing tambourine (*kartāl*)[25] or clapping their hands. Intercessory prayers, praise and worship follow it. During the prayer meetings the devotees intercede for various needs of the people in the village, especially for the sick. Towards the end of the prayer meeting, the healing prayer is held if sick people are present. The devotees extend their hands towards the sick while making the healing prayer. The prayer session lasts for three hours. If a priest is present, he preaches the Word of God and mostly leads the healing prayer. It is concluded with ārătī and distribution of *prasād*. The ārătī is given to the picture of Jesus and then taken to all present for reception.

Other devotions and faith practices

There are many other daily as well as occasional faith practices of the devotees. The occasional faith practices include the monthly retreats, fasting and penance which are optional. Invariably they are also devoted to Mary the mother of Jesus. They also regularly participate in the annual programmes like Christmas, Easter, annual charismatic convention and *Gurupūrṇimā*. The Holy Week is the time for their spiritual renewal with as many as ten thousand people attending the three-day programmes with much devotion. Without giving much description about these practices let us now probe their religious experiences of the new-found faith in Christ.

New Religious Experience

After having surveyed the faith-practices of the devotees it is important that we take stack of their religious experiences as well. The intention of many people when they come to the āśram or the movement for the first time is to fulfill their curiosity, since many people speak about it. Some people come to get freedom from evil spirits, while others come to get cured of physical ailments etc. But once they come, they are captured by the atmosphere, prayers, preaching, miracles etc. There are cases of those who came only for the sake of curiosity but became a devotee at the very first time and then an *aguā* not long later. Let us explore how and what is the experience of their new found faith in Christ.

Experience of Miraculous cures

Several people, especially the rural folk suffer from various kinds of problems and illness and have either less means to go for the medical treatment in time, the treatments have not given any result, or the problems of life are such that they do not see any solutions. Mostly people turn to witchcraft or sorcerers who are called *ojhās*. *Ojhās* collect money and materials like chicken, liquor etc., and go on with their witchcraft while the suffering remains. There are also instances when medical treatment for longer periods has not given any progress. Hence, people are desperate for cures of their ailments. When they hear about the miraculous cures happening in the āśram they flock to it. People who are suffering are eager to get cured and as they take part in the prayers and healing services often they get cured miraculously. It is true that many may come to āśram just for the sake of physical cure. But once they experience the cure with the divine intervention, they become committed Christ-devotees.

Freedom from Evil Spirits

Another important aspect of their experience is the freedom they receive from the spell of evil spirits. There is widespread believe in the existence of evil spirits and the spirits of the dead roaming in the villages. They believe that the spirits of the dead people have to be appeased. People find evil spirits as the source for almost all calamities and sicknesses. In order to get rid of the spell of these spirits, or to appease them the people usually go to *ojhās*. When they realize that the *ojhās* could not keep the evil spirits away forever or another evil spirit has come to disturb them, or their enemy has set an evil spirit against them, they come to āśram to get rid of their sufferings and the attacks of evil spirits. The story of Jesus who cures the people from satanic forces is very appealing to these people. When they see the miracles and hear the witness of the people who have received miraculous freedom from the spell of evil spirits, their faith increases and eventually many of them receive freedom from the spell of evil spirits.

Experience of a Loving God

Another experience of the devotees is the experience of God as a friend and a benefactor and not as someone to be feared. When people become Christ-devotees, they take the house deity or the icon of the house-deity and bring it to the āśram. They leave the deity in āśram "to be buried under the foot of the cross" so that it can do no damage to the family. Many times the family members are afraid of taking the deity themselves and ask the staff of the āśram to take it away. The deity was seen as someone to be feared. The focus of their spirituality was on propitiating the deities. They often believed in the wrath of God and were careful not to displease the deity. They are now taught that Jesus is the saviour whom they need not fear but love. They are also taught that God is love and that God does not need to be propitiated. Thus they learn to love God and experience God as loving.

Expressive Prayer: Charismatic and Communitarian
For the Christ-devotees expressive prayer and community-prayer is something new. In Hinduism prayers are mostly offered silently by individuals. Even when there is a gathering in the temple, each person approaches the deity individually. In the āśram the *Khrist Bhaktas* are taught to pray loudly, as one family and to pray for one another. Unlike the Hindu temple where the *pūjā* is offered for each individual, there is only one liturgy, one adoration and one healing prayer etc. for all the devotees.

The charismatic form of prayers said aloud and in community are new experiences for them. It seems that the charismatic method of prayer and preaching of the Word of God leads them into a different level of spiritual freedom and inner healing. They seem to experience the power of the Spirit during the *satsaṅg*s. The people who are afflicted by poverty, social oppression and having lots of physical and psychological problems find solace in these prayer meetings. The physical and psychological healing that is happening during prayer adds to their devotion and faith. They are also freed from various superstitions and bondages, which lead to peace in their personal and family lives.

Experience of Heavenly Visions
Although not extensive, a few devotees receive visions of Jesus, Mary, etc. Some of them have frequent visions, while some have only occasionally. One medical student Meena who receives frequent visions tells that

Mary feeds her quite often and then she feels no more hunger whole day even if she does not take any physical food. Other devotees approach the visionaries with requests for prayer as the devotees think that the prayer of the visionaries have more effect.

Concluding Remarks

The Church must read the signs of the times and "recognize and understand the world in which we live, its explanations, its longings, and its often dramatic characteristics".[26] In the west mostly the church is moving towards a choice paradigm with fewer people opting to remain within its fold. However, the paradigm of humanity as reflected in the Pontificate of Pope Francis has given it a new lease of life. In the case of India, similar sparks are visible in some humble models kept alive in the peripheries.

"In achieving various goals, problems can be identified which need to be solved in order to achieve the goal. If we really understand the problem, the answer will come out of it, because the answer is not separate from the problem" said Jiddu Krishnamurti. What is the crux of the real problem that we face today? On the one hand the Christians have the divine mandate of proclaiming the Gospel and the question of the freedom of spreading one's religious faith in India while on the other hand there is the persistent opposition to this Christian right by several groups. Now why is it that in India a country known for its religiosity opposes Christianity? Why is it that the conversion to Christianity is opposed in India with all possible rules and regulations? There can be several reasons like, political, cultural, sociological, religious, or even selfish reasons and motives. However, it is a fact that the churches in India comes across to the people as a European entity.

A close scrutiny shows that Hindus oppose the social aspect of baptism, while leaving freedom on the spiritual level. Christians stress the spiritual level while allowing sufficient freedom on the social level. This distinction paves the way for some possibilities of mutuality between Hinduism and Christianity. Christians do not intend the negative social, legal, and communal consequences of baptism. They do not intend to break up the community by baptism but want the community to grow spiritually and be united in the name of Christ.

The most important significance of the Christ-devotee model is its ability to exploit the gap emerging from the Hindu understanding of religion and social community, together with the Christian understanding of faith. The Hindu understanding offers possibilities for a Christ-devotee to remain within the community and culture without legally changing the community, while accepting Jesus as the only Lord and saviour. It allows a devotee to remain faithful only to Christ and remain Christian on a spiritual level while allowing sufficient freedom on the social level. And the Christian commitment to Christ enables the Christians to preach Christ and spread faith in him.

What I have done is to draw some contours of the possible shape of the future church in India. I have argued for forming communities based on Jesus Christ not from a theoretical point of view but have given expression to what is being practiced now at the periphery. It is my firm belief that time is coming when the periphery becomes the centre.

Endnotes

[1] Cf. Richard J.Plantinga, Thomas R.Thompson & Matthew D. Lundberg, *An Introduction to Christian Theology*, Cambridge, Cambridge University Press, 2010, p. 367.

[2] Acharya Sachidananda Bharathi, *Bharatiya Dharma Rajya: Vision of Kingdom of God in India*, Delhi, Media house, 2018), p. 46.

[3] Matthias Sellmann, "Seven Characteristics of a Future-Proof Parish: The Approach of Centre for Applied Pastoral Research, in *Envisioning Futures for Catholic Church*, eds. Staf Hellemans & Peter Jonkers, Washington, The Council for Research in Values and Philosophy, 2018, p. 235.

[4] *For all the People of Asia* (hereafter shortened as FAPA) F.J. Eilers (ed.), *FAPA II*, Quezon City, Claretian Publications, 1997, p. 195-196.

[5] A. Dulles, *Models of the Church. A Critical Assessment of the Church in all its Aspects*, Dublin, Gill and Macmillan, 1976, p. 23.

[6] *Ibid.*, pp. 7-8.

[7] *Ibid.*, p. 21.

[8] E.P. Hahnenberg, 'The Mystical Body of Christ and Communion Ecclesiology. Historical Parallels' in *Irish Theological Quarterly* 70, 2005, 3, p. 4.

[9] Hahnenberg, 'The Mystical Body of Christ and Communion Ecclesiology', p. 5

[10] Dulles, *Models of the Church*, p. 24.

[11] Hahnenberg, 'The Mystical Body of Christ and Communion Ecclesiology', p. 5.

[12] Dayanand Bharti, *Living Water and Indian Bowl,*(Delhi, ISPCK, 2001)p.5.

[13] *FAPA* 1, in G. Rosales & C.G. Arevalo (eds.), Quezon City, Claretian Publications, 1997, pp. 34-35.

[14] John Chettimattam, "Post modern Post scientific Evangelism: the future of Christian" in *Mission and Evangelization*, ed. Soman Das, (Delhi: ISPCK, 1998), 67.

[15] Felix Wilfred, *Sunset in the East?*(Madras: Chair in Christianity University of Madras, 1991) 237.

[16] A. Karokaran, 'Evangelization, Identity of Diverse Peoples and Universality of Jesus of Nazareth' in *Seminar Papers, Church in India Tomorrow 2010*, unpublished.

[17] The Statement of the 19th Annual Meeting of the ITA 1996, in Kunnumpuram, D'lima & Parappally (eds.), *Church in India in Search of a New Identity*, p. 396.

[18] *Ibid.*, p. 397.

[19] *Ibid.*

[20] The term caste is the equivalent to the Sanskrit term *jāti* used in the Indian sub continent to refer to "race", "breed", or "lineage". *Jātis* are the sub divisions of the four basic *varnas*. The numbers of *varnas* are four (*Brahmins, Kshetriyas Vaiśäs* and *Śūdräs*), or five when those outside (*pañcama*) are included as a category. The number of castes which are in fact known as *jāti*, including sub-castes, is numerous and cannot be counted, as their number grows even today. Both *varna* and *jāti* are hierarchical orderings. The ranking among the four *varnas* are fixed, while *jāti* have lot of fluidity.

[21] A detailed research work on Christ-Devotee movement has been published. For more details and discussion on theological issues about the movement see C. J. KUTTIYANIKKAL, *Khrist Bhakta Movement: A Model for an Indian Church? Inculturation in the Area of Community Building*, Münster, Lit Verlag, 2014.

[22] The present writer had the experience of carrying the Sacrament. People from both sides tried to touch the Sacrament by pulling it towards them and many touched the clock, hands or feet. Some people placed their hands on the way so that while walking he may step on their hands or at least the feet might touch their hands.

[23] Some people keep the Bible covered in saffron coloured cloth (as in the Hindu custom).

[24] There are also people like Urmila Patel and Mr. Prakash, who have rooms meant only for prayer where the room is filled with holy pictures and atmosphere.

[25] *Kartāl* (literally means the rhythm of the hand) is made of wooden blocks with holes for fingers and circular copper plates.

[26] *Gaudium et Spes*, 4.

Part Four
Lived Models

Abhiṣiktānanda:

A Priesthood in the Spirit
Yann Vagneux

O n December 21ᵗʰ 1971, which marked the thirty-sixth anniversary of his ordination, Henri le Saux (1910-1973), better known in India by the name Swami Abhishiktananda, wrote in his private diary: "Consecrated for a ministry. But a ministry that extends beyond its so-called ecclesial manifestations; a ministry at the service of the *mystery*, the revelation of the Mystery. Revelation to human beings of their own personal mystery and also of the total mystery, the mystery in itself; what is called God or the Deity... The monk disappears, passes into the mystery. The priest reveals this mystery. But who can truly reveal it without being lost in it?"[1] These lines admirably summarize the priesthood of a Christian monk who, more than twenty years earlier, had forsaken his distant homeland, Brittany in France, to settle on Indian shores, where his priestly ministry was mainly lived in the midst of his Hindu brethren. For sure, Abhishiktananda's priesthood and life are unique and cannot be transposed. Yet the unique glow of his priesthood has lost none of its power to inspire any soul who, like Henri le Saux, is moved by a deep desire to meet the real heart of India and transmit to it the newness of Christ.

Quaerere Deum: the Quest of God
Like so many boys at the time, Abhishiktananda was very young when he entered the minor seminary in 1921, at the age of eleven. Five years

later, he pursued his training at the major seminary in order to become a diocesan priest. However, following the death of one of his friends who had wanted to become a monk, Henri Le Saux felt called to take up this unfinished vocation; in 1929 he entered the Benedictine abbey of Kergonan near the Atlantic Ocean. A few months before he became a postulant, he confided to his Master of novices the reason behind this new calling: "What has drawn me from the beginning, and what still leads me on, is the hope of finding there the presence of God more immediately than anywhere else. I have a very ambitious spirit – and this is permissible, is it not? when it is a matter of seeking God – and I hope I shall not be disappointed."[2]

In this confidence full of youthful enthusiasm, we can hear an echo of what St. Benedict set into the heart of his *Rule* as being the goal of monastic life: '*quaerere Deum*', 'to seek God' and '*nihil amori Christi praeponere*', 'to prefer nothing to the love of Christ'[3]. In his very beautiful lecture to the representatives from the world of culture in Paris, Pope Benedict XVI has explained what the '*quaerere Deum*' meant to the Benedictine monks: "Amid the confusion of the times, in which nothing seemed permanent, they wanted to do the essential – to make an effort to find what was perennially valid and lasting, life itself. They were searching for God. They wanted to go from the inessential to the essential, to the only truly important and reliable thing there is. [...] They were seeking the definitive behind the provisional."[4] Here we seem to be hearing Henri Le Saux's very words as he took his final monastic vows on May 30th 1935, on the feast of the Ascension. He was then ordained priest few months later, on December 21st which at that time was the day the Latin Church celebrated the feast of Saint Thomas, apostle to India.

It is important to insist on the fact that Abhishiktananda first lived out his priesthood in the Benedictine monastic atmosphere which, right up to the end of his life, left an indelible imprint in him. His priesthood was fully inscribed within the '*quaerere Deum*' about which Benedict XVI also declared: "*Quaerere Deum*: because those monks were Christian, this was not an expedition into a trackless wilderness, a search leading them into total darkness. God himself had provided signposts, indeed he had marked out a path which was theirs to find and to follow. This path was his Word, which had been disclosed to men in the books of the sacred Scriptures."[5] Indeed the life of a Christian monk is built around the Bible, with hours set apart for *lectio divina,* prayerful "rumination" of the Scriptures, which is very central to the Benedictine rhythm. It is the Bible alone which is sung in the liturgy during the seven daily offices held in the Choir. The Gregorian plainchant, performed by the whole community with moving sobriety, is itself entirely composed of verses taken from the Scriptures, particularly from the Psalms. As master of ceremonies in his monastery, Abhishiktananda took a passionate interest for plainchant and he retained a nostalgic yearning for it up to the end of his life; indeed, many years after, he wept when his friends in India hummed the '*Dominus dixit*', the introit to the Christmas Midnight Mass, which he had not heard for decades. At Kergonan, Henri Le Saux was also the librarian, which meant being in charge of one of the places most central to monastic life. While in daily contact with the books, he developed a real closeness to the thinking of the Church Fathers, the first Christian theologians, who developed a unique contemplative approach towards the Mystery revealed in Christ. But above all, Henri Le Saux lived out his '*Quaerere Deum*' in the deeply impressive silent atmosphere of his monastery. Such was his vocation as a monk; many years later he was to write: "In the Church, the solitary soul is the minister of the Silence of God."[6]

The nineteen years Abhishiktananda spent in his Benedictine abbey were fundamental in more ways than one, especially to his subsequent priestly ministry in Indian culture which is so deeply engrained with the figure of the monk – whether Hindu, Jain, Buddhist or Christian: "The monk is the man of the *eschaton*. It is he who, through whatever religious expression Providence has called him to, bears witness to the fact that God is beyond all things."[7]

The Priesthood of Melchizedek

In 1948 Henri Le Saux arrived in South India and he joined with Jules Monchanin (1895-1957), a French priest who was living there since 1939. Together in 1950 they founded the Shantivanam ashram near Tiruchirappalli, and took on new names of Christian sannyasis. Monchanin chose Paramarubyananda in honour of the Holy Spirit, and Le Saux became Abhishikteshwarananda[8] as a reference to the Christ, the Anointed of the Father (*abhishikta*). The wish of these two French priests was that their little ashram would serve the Church in India, already ready so rich with educational and medical institutions, by revealing its contemplative side, just as Mary sat at the feet of the Lord while her sister Martha was busy serving at table (see Luke 10:38-42). It seemed to them crucial that Hinduism should discover that the Church possessed a long contemplative and monastic tradition. They also thought that this ashram might become a place of sharing in which they, as Christians, would receive also the gifts which the Holy Spirit brought to the very heart of India. A few years later, when recording his pilgrimage to Gangotri in his book *The Mountain of the Lord*, Abhishiktananda placed these words in the mouth of his fellow-traveller Sanat Kumar – who was none other than Raimon Panikkar (1918-2010): "It is our role as Christians of India, to draw from these treasures which have been bequeathed to us by our rishis, prophets and sages, to examine their Scriptures, to drink at the most pure and primordial sources of their experience, in order that we may transmit to the Church their incomparable riches."[9] In the same book, he further wrote: "India and her Scriptures are a part of the immense Cosmic Covenant which preceded the covenant of Sinai, and by which, across all peoples of the earth in all places and at all times, the Spirit is preparing the coming and the glory of the Incarnate Word."[10]

In speaking of a 'Cosmic Covenant' Abhishiktananda set the Hindu quest back into the Plan for Salvation far earlier than the Christian Revelation. This wider theological perspective was necessary in order to give meaning to all his experiences in the course of his exploration of

India. In particular, he meditated on the mysterious 'Cosmic Covenant' encountered in so many meetings with sannyasis along the way or in the caves of Arunachala mountain. Again, he discovered this "Cosmic Covenant" in the Brahmin priests officiating in the great temples in Tamil Nadu, and in those who became his neighbours in Uttarkashi, where in March 1961 he bought a piece of land and set up a small hermitage. Abhishiktananda was really touched by the priestly communion which he experimented with the Hindu pandits; this is how he described the unique Masses he said in Latin next to them:

> I think I have told you of the first Masses which were celebrated in the Himalayan village of Gyansu. However early I decided to celebrate I never managed to do so before the sadhu who occupied the room below got up. He would already be chanting the words of the *Gita* or repeating his mantras and punctuating them with joyful burst of OM. I murmured softly the *Dominus vobiscum* of the liturgy. It was *namah shivaya* – glory to Shiva which ascended to me in reply. The *Hari Om* alternated with my *Kyrie* and *Bhagavan, Bhagavan* came in reply to my *Sursum corda*. Across the road in the temple of Shiva the bells beat out the rhythm of the *puja* that my brother Melchizedek, the Brahmin, was offering in deep piety. I must admit it seemed to me that our Heavenly Father must have stooped down with very special joy over this truly cosmic liturgy."[11]

In the course of his meditations on India and the Cosmic Covenant, one figure in particular stood out: Melchizedek, the mysterious Pagan priest who came to meet Abraham to give him his blessing (Genesis 14:18-20). Abhishiktananda, and Pannikar also, had no hesitation in perceiving the Hindu priests as the distant brothers of this cosmic High Priest:

> Look at those priests of the Temple of Mother Ganges, the ones of Kedarnath, Badrinath and of all the sanctuaries of the mountains and plains; are they not the very brothers of the Biblical Melchizedek? It was he who blessed Abraham and whom the priest of the Roman rite commemorates each day at the most sacred moment of the liturgy. Melchizedek is truly the type of the priest of the Cosmic Covenant, and it is according to his order, not according the order of Aaron, the priest of the special Covenant with Israel, that Christ wished to be a priest, and in him I also have my priesthood.[12]

Furthermore, the Church Fathers have always regarded Melchizedek as prefiguring Christ himself. Most particularly, the *Letter to the Hebrews* deeply demonstrated that Christ's priesthood did not come down from the cultic priesthood of Aaron and of the priests of the Temple in Jerusalem but, by its unsurpassable innovatory character, it could be linked back to Melchizedek's priesthood by reference to this verse from Psalm 110: "Jesus has become a High Priest forever, in the order of Melchizedek" (Hebrew 6:20; see Psalm 110:4).[13]

By establishing a link between the Hindu priests with the mysterious figure of Melchizedek and that of Christ Himself, and also recalling the fact the canon of the Roman Church makes mention of "the offering of the High Priest Melchizedek, a holy sacrifice, a spotless victim", Abhishiktananda was himself uncovering the cosmic dimension of his own vocation and the call to recollect in the sacrifice of the Mass that "all human prayer, all human desire, all true human devotion, the true search for God that is fulfilled at last in Christ."[14] Many writings bear witness to this double discovery. This is what he wrote to a friend from his hermitage in Uttarkashi: "In the mezzanine fitted up in my hut, I offer Mass each morning, seated like a Brahmin priest, with ceremonies of offering water, incense, fire. I read the Gospel in Sanskrit. [...] For here, as nowhere else in the Church, Christ reveals himself as a priest 'in the order of Melchizedek.'"[15]

Above all, *the Mountain of the Lord* gives us the wonderful record of the Mass which Abhishiktananda celebrated together with Raimon Panikkar in Gangotri on 6th June 1964[16]. What place could be more intense than the source of the Ganges for those wishing to experience the priesthood of Melchizedek? "In truth, there are few places in the world where there has been more expectation of the Eucharist and more mystic preparation for it by the Spirit than here, the source of the holy rivers."[17] Indeed that was the one place where the offertory of their silent Mass could attain the dimensions of Hinduism's age long quest which was here united with Jesus' own offering up of his own life: "The bread and wine which I shall offer here in my Mass will be the call to God of all those pilgrims of the sacred sources of rivers in the Himalayas, of all the priests, all ascetics, those of our time, of days gone and of the future, for the Eucharist transcends all time."[18]

The Guru

During the twenty-five years between his arrival in 1948 and his death in 1973, India wrought a profound transformation of Abhishiktananda's vision of his priestly ministry. It is clear that these new people deepened the monastic dimension of his vocation, especially in the '*quaerere Deum*', the quest of God so ardently tangible in many Hindu monks – as well as the ministry of silence which the Benedictine monk witnessed in some silent hermits (*muni*) hidden in the heart of the Himalayas. Living daily alongside the Hindu believers refined his perception of his vocation, dilating it into unexpected dimensions through new experiences, as described in his 1971 private journal: "[…] but a ministry that extends beyond its so-called ecclesial manifestations. A ministry at the service of the *mystery*, the revelation of the Mystery. Revelation to human beings of their own personal mystery and also of the total mystery, the mystery in itself; what is called God."[19] This last phrase also reveals that another figure of Hindu tradition played a defining part in Abhishiktananda's new perception of his calling: the figure of the Guru, the Spiritual Master.

A few months after his arrival in India, Henri Le Saux was blessed to meet Sri Ramana Maharshi (1879-1950), in Tiruvannamalai. The first darshan he received left an imperishable memory: "In the sage of Arunachala of our own time, I discerned the unique Sage of the eternal India, the unbroken succession of her sages, her ascetics, her seers; it was as if the very soul of India penetrated to the very depths of my own soul and held mysterious communion with it. It was a call which pierced through everything, rent it in pieces and opened a mighty abyss."[20] The meeting of the Guru, first with Ramana Maharshi and then, in December 1955, with Swami Gnanananda, revealed to Abhishiktananda that in the heart of priesthood lies not only a mystery of liturgical mediation between earth and heaven, but also a mystery of transmission of the

Spirit, of which the Guru is the charismatic figure. This crucial role of the Guru became preponderant in Abhishiktananda's meditation and life, as testified by his 1966 text: "The priest for whom India waits, for whom the world waits."

Every catholic priest – and *a fortiori* the priest living in India – should read this timeless text. In the very first lines Abhishiktananda delivers the essence of his vision: "In the Indian context, the Christian priest needs be a guru. [...] For a Hindu, a guru is not an ordinary preacher who simply repeats to willing listeners that which he himself learnt from his teachers or read in his textbooks. Here is a man who speaks from experience. The guru is the one who imparts the teaching of salvation; and is it not in the depths of the heart alone that the mystery of wisdom can be heard? Is it not from there that the experience of salvation wells up?"[21] The ever vivid deep impression left on him by his meeting with Ramana Maharshi empowered him to write that for a Christian:

> The guru or spiritual master is only the one who has encountered in the depth of his soul the 'true living God' of whom the Bible speaks on every page, and from thenceforth became forever branded with the mark of that encounter [...]. The guru is the one who, having in the depths of his heart discovered the spark of Being – not in the abstract, but the I AM which manifested on Horeb mountain – can no longer fail to recognize it everywhere, without and within each creature and each human being, in the most intimate essence of all that is, in every happening, in every movement of the Cosmos as measured by time.[22]

Be it in a Hindu context or a Christian one, such an experience is given by the grace of the Supreme Guru – the *jagadguru*: God residing in the heart. Yet the light of this one and only guru is diffracted by other lights that come to help the spiritual seeker along his way. For instance in the Indian tradition, the Sacred texts are called *gurugrantha*, about which Abhishiktananda wrote: "There is no doubt that the books will have assisted him in his quest for the Ultimate Reality, especially those books bequeathed to him by his Tradition and which communicate to him – insofar as communication is possible – the experience of those who were the first to gain access to the Inner Mystery."[23] Above all the

Supreme Guru manifests himself in the darshan of the Sages whose teaching is pursued in the depth of silence:

> The seeker will no doubt have been helped by masters, for it is only from others that one can receive the teaching of Salvation [...]. Indeed, that teaching is not merely communication, it is communion, we would say in Christian language. But herein lies the great secret. The Master's role is not to transmit notions. Above all, it is to awaken the disciple; to open the disciple's inner eye, the one which plunges inwards and recognizes the Mystery there. It is to open the disciple's consciousness to the Spirit which inhabits him, to that Spirit which fathoms and scrutinizes the depths of God. No doubt the words pronounced by the guru travel from mouth to ear on the outside, as does any human word that necessarily travels through the ambient air. But really speaking the guru's words are transmitted directly from heart to heart, through the unifying medium of the Spirit, so that everyone communes with the Eternal Word. This is why, in India, silence is considered to be the most favourable atmosphere for teaching Wisdom.[24]

It is obvious that in this 1966 text, Abhishiktananda puts forth a very high ideal of the priesthood, but for him, this ideal was tuned in to India herself, for "the priest for whom India waits, for whom the world waits" is also "the priest whom India hears from the depths, whom the world understands."[25] It is not surprising that the young bishop of Varanasi, Patrick d'Souza (1928-2014) tried to convince Abhishiktananda to join him on the banks of the Ganges to help him found a "pilot seminary" to train those Catholic priests who could be really heard by their Hindu brothers. Most importantly, this ideal of the priest as spiritual master was experienced in a very moving way by Abhishiktananda at the end of his life, in the company of his disciples: Lalit Sharma and Ramesh Srivastava, two Hindu Brahmins; Sister Thérèse, a French Carmelite from Lisieux who came to join him in India and Marc Chaduc. In 1972, he confided in a letter to a friend: "Next week I shall be at Haridwar with Thérèse; the ten days following with Ramesh, the young Hindu who reads the Gospel and made me discover in an inexplicable experience what a guru means for a disciple. That goes so very far beyond 'spiritual direction' and even natural – or even spiritual – fatherhood."[26] Abhishiktananda's most dazzling hours as a guru were spent with Marc Chaduc (1944-1977), a French seminarian who arrived in India in 1971. Marc was the disciple who, more than any other, had received his master's spiritual heritage. On June 30th 1973, during the ecumenical diksha in the Ganges at Rishikesh, Marc was introduced into the lineage of Hindu sannyasis by Swami Chidananda (Divine Life Society) and also into that of the Christian monks by Abhishiktananda. By a mysterious coincidence, that same date, June 30th 1973, was also that on which Marc should have received his priestly ordination with his fellow seminarians in France, but India had drawn him along a different path, even though Abhishiktananda never ceased to hope that one day his disciple would become a priest:

> The priesthood? I have a strong impression that it awaits you at some point in the course of time. A priesthood that is very spiritualized, very free from limitations, a priesthood in the Spirit. This diksha in the Ganges will signify your gift of yourself to that priesthood, and the Spirit will respond in his own time and his own way.[27]

Having become Swami Ajatananda, Marc Chaduc never became a priest but in his silent life as a *sannyasi*, he raised up to a the point of incandescence that which was the ground of Abhishiktananda's priesthood, that '*quaerere Deum*', 'to seek God and let oneself be found by him.'[28] Marc's mysterious disappearance in 1977, four years after his master's own departure, might be understood as a manifestation of the spiritual necessity to disappear which lies at the heart of the priesthood – and at the heart of every Christian life –, as clearly stated in the letter to the Colossians: "If then you were raised with Christ, seek those things which are above, where Christ is, sitting at the right hand of God. [...] For you died, and your life is hidden with Christ in God" (Colossians 3:1.3). Indeed, for Abhishiktananda, the priest – just as are all true spiritual souls – is a hidden being. This astonishing idea means that the mystery of his encounter with the Living God must remain hidden, far from all publicity and may only be shared with those who approach him with a veritable spiritual thirst. Herein resides the mystery of true recognition, of which the Hindu tradition says: "When the disciple is ready, the guru appears". Thus, concerning this "priest for whom India waits, for whom the world waits", Abhishiktananda went on to write:

> No doubt he is at times already here, that priest, in India just as much as in the world, but he is rarely manifested publicly, except when God seeks to shake up his Church: he is mostly hidden except to a few, to those in whom the Spirit has made its dwelling and who, as if by instinct, led by that same Spirit, come to him.[29]

The *Purusha Sukta* states that: "With three quarters the Purusha rose upwards, and one quarter of him still remains here" (*Rig Veda* X, 4). Another confirmation of the minute earthly manifestation of the Purusha can be found in icebergs, of which the great mass is hidden below the surface of the water. The same could be said of the priesthood in the Spirit, of which the essential part –contemplation of the Divine Mystery through silence and prayer, the '*quaerere Deum*' – has to remain hidden from the eyes of men so as to be the very soul of his spiritual action in the heart of the world. That was the real message of Abhishiktananda's priesthood: "The monk disappears, passes into the mystery. The priest reveals this mystery. But who can truly reveal it without being lost in it?[30]"

Translated by Caroline Malcolm

Endnotes

[1] ABHISHIKTANANDA, *Ascent to the depth of the heart. The Spiritual Diary (1948-1973) of Swami Abhishiktananda (Dom Henri Le Saux)*, Delhi: ISPCK, 1998, p. 335.

[2] Letter of Abhishiktananda to the novice master of Kergonan of 4th December 1928. Cf. J. STUART, *Swami Abhishiktananda. His life told through his letters*, Delhi: ISPCK, 1989, p. 3.

[3] *Rule of saint Benedict* IV, 21.

[4] BENEDICT XVI, Meeting with representatives from the world of culture, Collège des Bernardins, Paris, 12th September 2008.

[5] BENEDICT XVI, *Ibidem*.

[6] H. LE SAUX, « Le prêtre que l'Inde attend, que le monde attend », *Les yeux de lumière*, Paris: Centurion, 1979, p. 104.

[7] Abhishiktananda, *The Mountain of the Lord. Pilgrimage to Gangotri*, Bangalore: The Christian Institute for the Study of Religion and Society, 1966, p. 22.

[8] Later, he shortened it into Abhishiktananda.

[9] Abhishiktananda, *Ibidem*, p. 23.

[10] Abhishiktananda, *Ibidem*, p. 22.

[11] Abhishiktananda, *Ibidem*, pp. 34-35.

[12] Abhishiktananda, *Ibidem*, p. 32.

[13] Besides the mention in Psalm 110, the two biblical passages which refer the mysterious priest Melchizedek are in Genesis and in the Letter to the Hebrews: "Melchizedek, king of Salem, brought out bread and wine, and being a priest of God Most High, he blessed Abram with these words: 'Blessed be Abram by God Most High, the creator of heaven and earth; and blessed be God Most High, who delivered your foes into your hand.' Then Abram gave him a tenth of everything" (Genesis 14:18-20); "This Melchizedek, king of Salem and priest of God Most High, met Abraham as he returned from his defeat of the kings and blessed him. And Abraham apportioned to him a tenth of everything. His name first means righteous king, and he was also king of Salem, that is king of peace. Without father, mother, or ancestry, without beginning of days or end of life, thus made to resemble the Son of God he remains a priest forever" (Hebrew 7:1-3).

[14] Benedict XVI, *Lectio divina* with the parish priests of the diocese of Rome, 18th February 2010. In this text, Benedict XVI leads a very beautiful meditation on the figure of Melchizedek through which 'the pagan world enters the Old Testament'.

[15] Letter from Henri Le Saux to Father Joseph Lemarié of 29th July 1965. Cf. J. Stuart, *Swami Abhishiktananda*, p. 194.

[16] A few months later, at the beginning of January 1965, Abhishiktananda and Panikkar celebrated a Mass together on the summit of Arunachala in Tamil Nadu.

[17] Abhishiktananda, *The Mountain of the Lord*, pp. 33-34.

[18] Abhishiktananda, *Ibidem*, p. 33.

[19] Abhishiktananda, *Ascent to the depth of the heart*, p. 335.

[20] Abhishiktananda, *The Secret of Arunachala. A Christian Hermit on Shiva's Holy Mountain*, Delhi: I.S.P.C.K, 1979, pp. 8-9.

[21] H. Le Saux, « Le prêtre que l'Inde attend, que le monde attend », p. 100.

[22] H. Le Saux, *Ibidem*, p. 101.

[23] H. Le Saux, *Ibidem*, p. 101.

[24] H. Le Saux, *Ibidem*, p. 101.

[25] H. Le Saux, *Ibidem*, p. 100.

[26] Letter from Henri Le Saux to Father Joseph Lemarié of 5th January 1972. Cf. J. Stuart, *Swami Abhishiktananda*, pp. 289-290.

[27] Letter from Henri Le Saux to Marc Chaduc of 24 avril 1973. Cf. J. STUART, *Swami Abhishiktananda*, pp. 333.

[28] BENEDICT XVI, Meeting with representatives from the world of culture, Collège des Bernardins, Paris, 12th September 2008.

[29] H. LE SAUX, « Le prêtre que l'Inde attend, que le monde attend », p. 100.

[30] ABHISHIKTANANDA, *Ascent to the depth of the heart*, p. 335.

Vandana Mataji:
An Icon of the 'Indian Face' of Christian Faith

Louis Malieckal

Introduction

Samanvaya being a programme of contextualized theological formation, direct exposure to concrete life situations is considered essential to the method of formation. Three typical contexts of Indian life are identified, and every year the theological formation is programmed in such a way that the students get an experiential knowledge of these contexts both in theory and praxis. The three contexts mentioned are Tribal-Subaltern Context of Jagdalpur, Inter-Religious Context of Rishikesh and Urban Pastoral context of Bangalore-Bhopal. In the present article we are concerned only with the second context, namely.

Inter-Religious Context of Rishikesh

After having completed first year of theology in the rural-tribal context of Jagdalpur with the central theme "God and the World", the students come to Rishikkesh context in the second year with the central theological theme "Christ and the Human". Accordingly the theological search is directed to a deeper understanding of the person and mission of Jesus Christ, who as the Way-Truth-Life would answer the human dilemma. The students are guided to discover Jesus as the human face of divine compassion in their manifold encounters with the people in Rishikesh – *sadhakas* and seekers, *munis* and hermits, *sadhus* and ashramites, *sannyasis* and *sannyasins*, locals as well as globals, or *deshis and videshis*. As the late Prof. Raimon Panikkar would say, "In a multi-religious country like India, to be a religious person is to be an inter-religious person." But this is not only a question of co-existence of different religionists or tolerance towards other religions in one's own life situation; rather it is transforming and enriching oneself as a better human person through dialogue with other faith-holders.

It is here that Vandana Mataji's legacy stands out for the Post-Vatican II Church in India as well as for the students of Samanvaya Vidya Dham in Rishikesh. We shall try to unearth different aspects of this legacy in the following pages. We shall start, presenting a short biography of Mataji, the way she transformed herself first into an authentically 'Indian face' of the 'Christian Faith', and finally the manner in which she proclaimed or communicated this image to others in India.

How an Indian Face of Jesus or Christian Faith was Discovered

Sr. Vandana, rscj, very fondly called by people in India by the name Vandana Mataji, began to discover the ' face of an Indian Jesus' in the late 1970s when she founded the Christian ashram, now famous as Jeevan Dhara Ashram on the banks of the river Ganges at the foothills of the Himalayas.[1] The shades, lines and colours that went into the making of this face, she discovered through personal reading of Hindu-Christian scriptures, deep meditation as well as experience sharing of great Gurus (masters) of Hinduism and Christianity for several decades, since her conversion at 20 years old from Zoroastrianism to Catholicism. She has described this discovery in different ways, particularly in an article written in 1989[2], as she simultaneously tried to realize it in and through her life and thus to proclaim Jesus to the people of India until her death on 26Feb.2013 aged 92 years. Therefore we shall first discuss the elements that make up this 'Indian face', as discovered by Sr. Vandana, and then proceed to discuss the way she lived and realized them in her own life to become herself an Indian face of Christianity for others in India to follow Jesus himself.

From her study of the Hindu Scriptures she discovered the contours of this face consisting of some basic qualities and virtues like honesty, interiority/ inwardness, simplicity, fearlessness, compassion and so on. Let us see how she explains them.

Honesty And Truthfulness

According to her, a first quality of this face is "what the Isa Upanishad calls 'the face of truth hidden behind a circle of gold.'[3]" Though we often claim to love truth or rather truthfulness more than life, how easily we lie to ourselves and to others to 'save face', to save our reputation, through fear or human respect", she asks. And yet she thought that an Indian face of Christian faith could be revealed in India by shiningly incorrupt lives of Christians, so that "those gazing on us may be reminded that 'the immortal soul is pure like a drop of water on the lotus leaf' (Maitri Upanishad) and see in us the reflection of Him who could say: 'I am the Truth (St. John).'[4]

Inwardness and Interiority

As a second quality of an Indian face of Christ or Christian faith, she discovers "a face turned inward (*antarmukhi*) towards the Antaryamin (the Indwelling One)" rather than drawn outwards to external objects of the senses and hectic activities. Only thus would our Hindu brothers and sisters recognize in and through us 'the Atman (Spirit) who is hidden in all things as cream in milk' (Svetasvetara Upanishad). Then they would recognize the Spirit of Christ and joyfully exclaim looking on us, as though they were looking on the face of Christ: 'The Spirit far away within thee is my own inmost Spirit' (Isa.Up.).[5]

Simplicity/ Non-duality Experience of God

According to Mataji, an Indian Christian must be able to translate the Upanishadic vision of 'the same Self in all things and all things in the

Self' (Isha. Up.6) into the Biblical vision of 'loving one's neighbour as one's Self'. Then he/she will be able to understand Jesus' instruction that giving a cup of water to another person in need in His name will be giving to Jesus Himself, as in fact giving to oneself.[6] Sr. Vandana also believes that the face of Christ will then be recognized through those Christians in India who believe that God is one and the same, wherever or however he is worshiped in Spirit; 'neither in this mountain nor in Jerusalem, but in spirit and truth' (St. John)."[7]

Fearlessness through Identity Experience

Fearlessness will be part of an Indian face of Christ, because 'he who sees all things in the Self, and who sees the Self in all things is devoid of fear', says Upanishads. And how often Jesus has told his disciples, "Fear not ; it is I", "Why are you afraid, you men of little faith?" etc. Therefore the Indian face of Christ would be of one who has received, and is therefore able to give to others, *abhaya-dān* (gift of fearlessness).[8] "What has anyone to fear?", she asks, "when he or she looks on a face serene and peaceful, being sure of and secure in God's all pervading presence which is love; and this love is shown through compassion."[9]

Compassion (*Karuna*)

The fifth quality of an Indian face of Christ and Christianity is thus compassion (*Karuna*), she discovers. This is expressed through selfless services (*karma-yoga*), and consists in eradicating results of centuries of oppression, injustice, violence. First we have to practise non-violence (love), by practising non-attachment (*vairagya*), non-possession (*asteya*) and non-hoarding (*aparigraha)* so that we do not have more than we need; we do not possess comforts and conveniences, when so many are homeless and without essentials."[10]

Another aspect of this compassion is removal of ignorance (*avidya*) through works of education, primary education[11], formal and non-formal, which is needed perhaps even more than bread in India. "The compassionate face of Christ would then be the *Face of an Educator* bent over His children, for, of such is made the Kingdom of Heaven", she observes, and adds that if spirituality and theology do not get harmonized with daily life, overflowing into 'active contemplation', they may remain sterile, like knowledge that is not transformed into love, because God is knowledge-love combined.[12]

Trinity –Saccidananda Experience

Finally the Indian face of Christ is Trinitarian, she says. As the Father is Being (Sat), and as the Son is the Father's self-knowledge, His consciousness (Chit), the Love between the two is perfect Bliss (Ananda), perhaps the mother and in her strength, the Shakti-Spirit. This Trinitarian Love-Life in the interior of Christ is seen shining in the Light of His grace as Saccidananda (*sat-chit-ananda*), one of the earliest names of God which is still venerated and for many is still very meaningful.[13]

How she realized this face in her life

Sr. Vandana, through her close association with some great Hindu Gurus, like Swami Krishnananda, Swamy Chidananda and others, and also her long stay in several of the ashrams, both Hindu and Christian, in the South and North India, she learned how to realize in her life the contour lines, colours and shades that would go to the making of this Indian face of the Christian faith.[14] We shall discuss below some of the important means and methods she had made use of in order to achieve this goal.

Inter-religious Dialogue

In the spirit of Vatican II, inter-faith dialogue is a meeting of religions prompted by love –the self-gift which enables us to be open, to learn, to share, being increasingly conscious of the great phenomenon of religious pluralism, especially in our country India, where so many world religions co-exist – Hinduism, Buddhism, Jainism, Islam, Sikhism, Christianity, as well as scores of Tribal religions. For a long time before Vatican II, the Church's relationship with other religions was one of confrontation, conquest and conversion under the presumption of religious superiority and salvation-monopoly. The Council demolished this presumption and accepted the value and role of every religion for its followers. Moreover, instead of confrontation, dialogue has been accepted as the most welcoming and suitable method of relation with other religions.

Encouraged and enlightened by the Council's clarion call for 'acknowledging, preserving and promoting the spiritual and moral truths of other religions' (NA 2), Sr. Vandana sought to embark upon this voyage of dialogue of religions, for," she has the unique distinction of being born in one religious tradition (Zoroastrian), then embracing another (Christianity), and having tasted two traditions from within, entering into dialogue of a unique kind with a third religious tradition (Hinduism). She has the authority to talk as an insider of two, nay three different religious traditions."[15]

Her whole life after becoming a 'Zoroastrian-Christian', lived in the multi-religious context of India was one, committed to the Council's clarion call for inter-faith dialogue and understanding, notably between Hinduism and Christianity. She has not only written, travelled and spoken widely for the spread of this message, but produced her *magnum opus* "great work" of more than 900 pages towards the evening of her life.[16] The book is a voluminous piece, not only in the number of pages (814+lxviii pages), but very much in the collaboration of more than 100 contributors for the promotion of inter-faith dialogue from both Hinduism and Christianity, from the fields of philosophy and theology, art and literature, family life and ashram life etc.

Listening- Silence - Receptivity

Of the several pre-requisites of meaningful dialogue, first comes listening, she would say. It is an art that needs an even more difficult art of inner silence, which helps you to listen to God, and then one is better equipped to be a partner in dialogue. Jesus, who was himself the Eternal Word of God, proceeded from the Eternal Silence who is the Father. And as the Gospel of John testifies, he spoke only what he "heard from the Father" (cf. Jn 8: 26, 28; 5: 19). Jesus manifests a tremendous inner silence issuing from a deep and constant dependence on the Spirit within, the Spirit of the Father, leading him to extraordinary receptivity. Thus these three attributes -silence, listening and receptivity were present in a unique way in the Mother of the Word also; they are feminine qualities. The person wishing to enter on true dialogue must have these qualities.[17]

All this requires honesty and truthfulness. Dialogue cannot take place between persons bearing masks or false fronts, prejudices or duplicity of heart. One cannot start dialogue with a 'hidden agenda' of converting the other, but only with an open mind of mutual enrichment and conversion of hearts, and this requires true spirituality, not merely a religious spirit. Quoting the Gandhian sage Vinoba Bhave she adds, "Religions divide; spirituality unites.", for the Spirit is one and his work is "One-ing", since He is the Love (*Ananda*) between the Father (*Sat*) and the Son (*Cit*). Thus Saccidananda, one of the oldest names of God in Hinduism was to be revealed by Jesus centuries later by his inner Trinitarian life.[18]

Phases of Inter-faith Dialogue

Having understood and experienced the meaning of Jesus' incarnational pedagogy, Sr. Vandana explains that dialogue can take place only between equals; it presumes that none of the partners considers him/herself superior or inferior. However, she also discovers that there can be different phases of dialogue:

Dialogue Phase 1: It means getting to know each other and each other's faith, shedding prejudices and studying the matter more at the heart level than mind level.

Dialogue Phase 2: This involves discovery of the authentic values in the respective religious traditions; learning to respect and to respond to them with creativity.

Dialogue Phase 3: In this phase the partners would set out to explore together new areas of reality, meaning and truth of which neither had knowledge or experience before.

Dialogue Phase 4: This would be a walking together towards the Truth-Love, hand in hand in encouraging friendship; yet always respecting the other if he/she prefers to go thereby a different road, because dialogue is not system-centred but person-centred.[19]

Sr. Vandana then goes on to speak about different types of dialogue like **Discursive Dialogue** which involves listening sympathetically and respectfully on the intellectual level, **Secular Dialogue** which is a joint concern and action on a social cause irrespective of faith-differences etc. Then she comes to the most important type of dialogue **called Interior Dialogue** or dialogue "in the cave of the heart". Citing the splendid examples of Swami Abhishiktananda, Sr. Ishapriya and others, she holds that to know God in deep mystical experience in the depth of the soul is the only way where Hindus and Christians can truly meet in dialogue. She then describes her long stay in Shivananda Ashram, Rishikesh as well as her own Ashram Jaiharickal and shows how life in such Ashram context can enhance our capacity for true inter-faith dialogue, helping us to become men and women of an Indian face of Christ.

Dialogue in and through Ashrams

Let us first of all see some salient aspects of ashrams as experienced by Vandana Mataji which helped her to put on an Indian face of Christ:

Salient Features of Ashrams

Ashram is not materialization of a project, but realization of a community of *Guru-sishya* relationship. When one or more persons come and say, 'Teach me master', an ashram is born, provided the disciple is considered '*adhikari*' (ready and worthy) and accepted by the Guru. Now, a Guru is expected to be "experienced" in *Brahma Vidya*, that means not merely academic knowledge as a *pandit* or *shastri*, but a person (man/woman) well-versed in the Scriptures and rooted in God (*Srotriyam Brahmanishtam*). If the life in a Christian ashram is to flow truly from the life and thought of India, it is essential that there should be one or two persons at the ashram who has(have) had the basic experience of God in the Indian mode. The ashram needs to contain at least one Guru, from whose God-touched heart the ashram is born, who can lead people towards the True or *Sat Guru*, who for the Christian is Christ[20] Apart from being a community of God-seekers gathered around a God-experienced man or woman, ashrams will have other salient features like the following:

An Open Community

This is one of the basic characteristics of an ashram. First of all, its premises will not be "walled in on all sides" with a closed imposing gate about which Mahatma Gandhi has made a thoughtful remark.[21] Secondly Vandanaji herself notes as follows:

> It is very important that an ashram is open to all; men, women, married, single, rich, poor, and of any culture or nationality in the world; the only condition being that people come for God-seeking. To be open means a readiness to share both all one has, and all that one is. The emphasis must not be on 'enclosure', as in Western monasticism; but rather on being an open centre of communion with God to which others are naturally drawn.[22]

This however does not mean that such an open community may lead to chaos and confusion, because as Fr. Bede Griffiths notes,

> such an ashram is 'primarily a place of prayer, conceived according to the Indian tradition, as a place where people come to realize God, to experience the inner depth of their own being - a place where people can come to find that 'restful awareness'.[22]

To cater to such a "mixed community" a great amount of flexibility is required in the life-style of the ashram. At the same time visitors, if any, would also join in whatever activities the ashram community has; they would share whatever meals are prepared. The Guru or Acharya plays a great role in making and keeping such a community an ashram community. It is left to the Acharya's judgement whether somebody may be admitted to the community. The only criterion is whether the person is a genuine God-seeker. It is also the Acharya's responsibility to maintain a proper balance between ashramites and visitors, as it is also his duty to see that every visitor is somehow enabled to get in touch with God within.

Simplicity of Life

Simplicity of life-style is a hall mark of such ashrams - simplicity in food and dress, language and communications, as well as relationships. Two very important virtues that go together with it are non-stealing (*asteya*) and non-storing (*aparigraha*), and in Gandhian ashrams there are 11 vows or principles, namely Non-violence (*ahimsa*), truth (*satya*), non-stealing(*asteya*), self-discipline (*brahmacharya*), non-possession (*aparigraha*), bread-labour (*sarirashrama*), control of the palate (*asvadya*), fearlessness (*sarvatra-bhayavarjana*), equality of all religions (*sarvadharma-samanatva*), use of locally made things (*svadeshi*), removal of untouchability (*sparsha-bhavana*). A visit to one of these Gandhian ashrams, e.g. Vinobaji's ashram Brahma Vidya Mandir in Paunar, near Wardha enables us to see how the 'vow of poverty' of Christianity can be lived more realistically and radically in the Indian context.

Contemplative Experience

Prayer-life of the ashram community requires that the structure of the ashram is minimal and all geared to contemplation. Community prayer and place of worship would always have an Indian colour (chants, Scripture readings, recitals by-heart, bhajans, namjaps, bells, arati, incense, flowers etc.). The Christian "Hours" of community prayer will have to be structured around *Samdhya* (time of prayer as well as prayer of time).

Vandana Mataji goes on to suggest that ashram is the ideal setting for experimenting and exploring matters of inculturation in liturgy and worship in general as well as theological reflection. "Only so will the Church in India become truly Indian and play its rightful role in the Church universal. And this could lead to a renewal in India as earth-shaking as Vatican II was in the world."[23]

Freedom and Flexibility

These two are equally essential for ashram living. In order to create such a free and flexible community, there must be openness to the Spirit that does not bind the community to rules or regulations, written or otherwise. Ashram thus needs to be a much less rigidly structured community than a traditional Christian monastery or religious house in which there is an atmosphere of prayer, each one praying freely to let the Spirit pray in him rather than having a well-ordered, regular and disciplined life of prayer. In the ashram, liturgical prayer, while retaining an important place, will always need to be flexible, less structured and more oriented to contemplation.[24]

This flexibility also extends to the other structures of the community life. This means that in Hindu ashrams there can be different levels or degrees of membership of the inmates: There will be a tiny group of *sannyasi*s or *brahmachari*s, forming the nucleus of the community. Around this permanent nucleus would be other people, who wished for shorter or longer periods to be seekers of God.

Individual visitors can choose one or the other more experienced member of the nucleus group for his/her Guru, in case there is no singular outstanding spiritual leader.

Although this situation seems to be acceptable, says Sr. Vandana, because the bond of unity between members of the ashram would then be not attachment to a place, to a community or even Guru, but simply that of the common search for *Brahma Vidya*, "saving knowledge of God", however, she personally wonders whether true Christian ashram could develop in this way. Even if ashrams may have more God-experienced persons, helpful for others on the spiritual path, there must be one head of the ashram, whether called Guru or Acharya.[25]

Inculturation and Ashram Life

Earlier we have seen that Sr. Vandana had identified ashrams as most suitable setting for experimentation in inculturation or cultural adaptations of various types. In particular she has reflected deeply on the question in connection with the issue of inter-faith dialogue and she has tried to unearth the rationale behind the Council's call for inculturation, and thus to clear the nebulous state of Pre-Vatican II mind of some Christians as well as suspicious mind-set of a class of the Hindus who fear inculturation as a stunt for conversion.

Culture Versus Religion: An Advaitic Relationship

Often Christians ask the question: "Why should Indian Christians who for all these years were happy to follow Christ like the Westerners, suddenly bend over backwards to take on Indian names, sing *bhajans, kirtans*, do *japa*, dance Gospel stories in *Bharat Natyam* or other classical *nritya* and want to use Indian/Hindu symbols, gestures, scriptures during their liturgy ?"[26]. At the same time, while some Hindu brethren suspect inculturation attempts of the Church as a new stunt for conversion, the old wolf in a new sheepskin, perhaps a minority among them appreciate these efforts to get back to her national roots after centuries of colonization. It is against this back ground that Mataji tries to explain the rationale of inculturation.

She discovers a non-dualistic (*advaitic*) relationship between culture and religion, because "a meeting of cultures in depth is always a religious encounter. Therefore inculturation is a religious affair, not a religiously neutral act."[27] She further explains this, quoting the words of Raimon Panikkar, who holds that "when Christians borrow, for example, OM or the Gayatri mantra to chant, they are making fundamental theological statements regarding the nature of both Hinduism and Christianity, that they join the Hindu tradition in seeing OM as the recapitulation of the universe similar to what Christians see in the eschatological Christ........ that they are not pronouncing the sacred name in vain."[28] Therefore in the use of symbols and rituals of another religion there is a kind of sharing and participation. "Through the gate of OM the Christian enters, as it were, into communion with the Hindu tradition. But the

Hindu also takes part in the communion of the Body of Christ," says Mataji, adding that "sharing is not plundering"; it is mutual enrichment.

Moreover, history of world cultures shows that at the birth of any major classical culture there has always been at least one major religious component. For example, the Greek, Roman, Egyptian cultures in the West and Chinese, Indian and Japanese cultures in the East. If we take the modern western culture, Christianity can be seen as a major component at its birth, though other belief systems -- Islam, Marxism and so on, like tributaries flowing into a stream, to make a great river, have made their own contributions from time to time. In the same way we can find at the birth of modern Indian culture, Hinduism as a major component; but it cannot be denied that in the making of the present Indian culture, there have been a variety of contributions by Sikhism, Jainism, Islam, Christianity and others.

That is why, Vandana Mataji, speaking about the rationale behind inculturation, holds that "the introduction of Hindu values, customs, ritual gestures, doctrinal vocabulary into Christianity entails a **change also in the Christian self-understanding.**[29] Rightly therefore "Panikkar contends that to accept or reject inculturation, we need to develop a theology of pluralism[30]. Therefore the driving force behind the dynamism of the Spirit, which urges inculturation is neither "conversion motif", nor "number game". Panikkar detects a deeper force and explains it in terms of what he calls "inter-culturation": Namely, being seriously concerned about our imperfect common terrestrial condition, "we realize that we are not self-sufficient and able to fulfil our human calling in isolation. We need each other's religious cultures for this 'planetarian task ....the liberation of Man.'"[31]

These reflections on dialogue and inculturation lead us to the following conclusions in the thought of Sr. Vandana: Both dialogue and inculturation are gradually being acknowledged as essential, as something inherently human and religious in themselves, if at all we are to survive peacefully in the world and in the universe. They need no other justifications for their existence and operation.

More concretely, inculturation is not a means for something else, any more than dialogue is for some extrinsic reason. "It is the natural outcome of two cultures entering into symbiotic relationship." Gradually fear and mistrust will go, for, pride will give way to humility. Through inculturation we shall feel so natural and at home with each other's cultures and religions,[32] that Christians will be happy to call themselves "Hindu—Christians" and Hindus "Christian-Hindus", as in fact happened in the case of Brahmabandha Upadhyay, the famous Bengali Brahmin convert to Christianity. Dialogue will then be fulfilled, leading to respect and love for each other's religions, for our indigenous culture. Gradually there will be no more quarrel or concern for "mine" and "yours", but only for "ours". This however will not wipe away the distinction and uniqueness of either Hinduism or Christianity in any way; consequently "there will be detachment from the quasi-slavish attitude we have had in the past towards all thins Western and foreign, and a growing ability to present *Christ's message intelligibly in a culturally diverse world*."[33]

About Evangelization, Mission and Conversion

After having seen Mataji's enlightened ideas about dialogue and inculturation, we shall now listen to her similar ideas about the triad – evangelization- mission - conversion, which are subjects still very relevant for us to day.

Evangelization

She holds that our role is to present Christ's message that God loves us, since He is Love. And this must be lived and proclaimed by our lives and our very presence. "There are numerous Christians who seek only to live out their Christianity right where they are, and they make Christianity credible as Good News for all."[34]

Thus, while making her mind clear on what is meant by evangelization, she makes a distinction between this and recruitment for Church membership, asking, "Does the command of Christ to bear witness to him, to make people his disciples and to establish God's kingdom mean the same thing as recruitment of people for Church membership without inner conversion?" And she adds, "This is a critical question for Christians when they approach the issue of conversion today."[35]

Mission

Quoting great theologians like Moltmann and Legrand, she shows the correct relationship between Church and mission. Moltmann affirms: "It is not the Church that has a mission of salvation towards the world. It is the mission of the Father and of the Holy Spirit sent by the Father. This very mission has a Church, and it creates for itself a Church on its way.[36] Legrand shows quoting Mt 28:19f that mission is also an activity of Jesus, and Church constitutes the milieu in which the mission of Jesus is to be exercised.[37]

She argues that mission should not be tied uniquely to the so-called "command" of Jesus in Mt 28:19f. For, the Gospel is Good News first of all for the one who announces it and lives it. It is our mission to convey this joy in our life to others. People will see our good work done in the secret chamber of the heart, done only for love in the spirit of *nishkama karma*, seeking no result. This is the "salt" which we, Christians are asked by Jesus to be "in the world". Similarly we must also be the "light that shines in darkness and is seen."[38] Connecting the concept of evangelization and mission she continues,

> If we concentrate on becoming more truly the 'salt of the earth', evangelization and mission will automatically be done! If we think more of the Kingdom being established first in own our hearts and less of the church, then our mission of joy-bearing, light-bringing, and peace-sharing will make the earth a happier place. We must concentrate on transforming ourselves rather than worrying about 'the other'.[39]

Though the Mathean way of understanding mission as a "command of Jesus" as in Mt.28: 19-20 is not without justification, yet it seems incomplete as **it misses out on the "joy of the good news" and indeed lacks incentive to motivate the young generations, as it tends to make mission a burden rather than joy[40]**; makes it part of law rather than the gospel of love. In fact in the NT Church, mission begins as a kind of explosion of joy. The news that the rejected and crucified Jesus is alive was something that could not in any way be suppressed. This is, in particular, the perspective of John the 4th Evangelist. In fact in the 4th Gospel, the Mathean mission command text (28: 19-20) is **overshadowed by the theology of "great love of the Father" (Jn. 3:16); and so we need to take the Johannnine understanding of mission as sharing of life and joy and use it to balance the synoptic understanding of command- conversion.**

Conversion

Mataji argues that 'conversion' first and foremost means conversion or change of heart, and she holds that in the course of authentic dialogue, the partners – one or both – would experience the conversion to which the Spirit calls. They may discover that they are not living out their respective faiths in their own lives. Or they may come to new understanding, deeper or more authentic, of their faiths. Both may discover new dimensions of the mystery of God in the other, through the other. This is conversion of heart or *metanoia*. This is always needed, and it is a conversion of my heart, without which I cannot enter the kingdom of heaven, as Jesus has said.

But if I do this, other hearts also will be transformed by the Spirit, because the same Spirit or Self is also in the other. Thus in the process of converting myself to a more truthful and authentic person, I may discover, or perhaps will never know how/when/where the other saw the Light of Christ in my eyes or smile or felt the touch or His heart through my love. This would be loving my neighbour as myself. This sort of "conversion" no Hindu, even the most fundamentalist/conservative can object. It is a turning of the heart towards God.[41] What Hindus normally are against is 'manipulated conversions' by means of false promises and offers. Hindus also need to ask themselves, if conversion to other faiths may not be a symptom of unjust and exploitative structural conditions in the Indian social order. Just as Christians must revise their ways and thoughts concerning conversion, Hindus must also examine the context of the wider social order and seek to make it less exploitative and more just. Then these the so-called 'manipulated conversions' will disappear, rightly observes Mataji.[42]

Concluding Remarks

In the efforts of the students of Samanvaya Vidya Dham, Rishikesh to discern and discover the authentic face of Christ among the manifold 'faces of humans', they may encounter in and around Rishikesh, they shall not miss the model lived and personalized by Vandana Mataji for about seven decades from her conversion at 20 till death at 92 in the year 2013. As we have explained in the foregoing pages, this model has demonstrated an Indian face of the Jesus of the Gospel, and more concretely, an Indian face of the Christian faith. Although we may find other models of an Indian face of Jesus, like that of Swamy Abhishiktananda, Professor Raimon Panikkar, Swamy Sadanand and so on, that of Vandana Mataji must have special appeal to students of Samanvaya Vidya Dham, because she lived and worked for several decades in the context of Rishikesh, founding two Ashrams one on the banks of river Ganga and the other at Jaiharickal, a few kilometres up from Rishikesh on the hills of the Himalayas. Moreover, having experienced personally and exemplified in her life a truly Indian face of the Christian faith for so many years, she has left for us towards the evening of her life a legacy as follows:

> We must make the study of the Gospels a priority in this New Millennium. Unless we meet the dynamic personality of Jesus daily, unless we study how he felt, thought, reacted, challenged, and above all forgave and loved, how can we truly imitate Him? The daily lives of our religious and priests should show the Gospel in action.......It is our own loving and humble service and our lives of prayer, more than our institutions, for which we may hope to be praised, and especially **let us be leaders in**

our spirituality and mysticism. Through this may our Indian Church become respected both in the West and in the East.[43]

Her life and legacy beautifully illustrates how we can make deeper discovery of our faith in Jesus Christ, in dialogue with other faith-holders and through increasing knowledge of their Scriptures as well as through authentic inculturation of our life and prayer-forms. In particular she has challenged us to become **leaders in spirituality and mysticism**, not in holding positions of authority or in raising institutions of enormous wealth and power.

Endnotes

[1] Later she immortalized the meaning and message of this Ashram when she brought out a booklet titled *The Living Stream – Jeevan-Dhara* in the year 1998 to celebrate the Golden Jubilee of her religious profession which was in 1948. In that booklet she has made reference to the many wells and springs of the OT, associating them with the Patriarchs Abraham, Isaac, Jacob and others. In that connection she has also compared the well-side meetings and conversations in Israel as well as India (Radha and *gopis* beleaguered by Krishna). Armed with the rich figures and metaphors concerning springs and waters, she now dwells more deeply on the symbolism centred on the incident of Jesus meeting of the Samaritan woman (Jn 4).

[2] Sr. Vandana, rscj, "The Indian Face of Christ", in *Word and Worship*, NBCLC:Bangalore, 22(1989)105-107.

[3] Isha Up. 15 (*hiranmayena patrena satyasya apihitam mukham*)

[4] Sr.Vandana, art.cit. p.105.

[5] Ibid.

[6] In other words, Sr. Vandana here advocates a strictly non-dualistic (advaitic) understanding of the relation between God and creatures.

[7] Sr. Vandana, op.cit. p.106.

[8] We are here reminded of the Sadhvi Prasanna Devi who was for a long time a hermit in the interior of the Girnar hills, Gujarat, home to wild animals. If people from the surrounding villages would go to her for *darsan* and blessing, it was because they believed, she had the gift of fearlessness (*abhayadan*), shining on her face.

[9] Ibid. p.107.

[10] Sr. Vandana insists that ministry of education has to focus not on higher (university) education, but primary and secondary education. For, since the time of

the British rule, the focus was on higher (university) education so that even to day millions are illiterate, and although thousands are being 'turned out' as Graduates, they can neither think for themselves, nor earn a decent living (p.107).

[11] Ibid.

[12] Ibid.

[13] Vandana, *Gurus, Ashrams and Christians*, St. Pauls: Bandra, and ISPCK: Delhi, 1989

[14] T.K.John, SJ (Foreword) in Vandana Mataji: *Living with Hindus (Hindu-Christian Dialogues) – My Experiences and Reflections*, IJA, Bangalore and ISPCK, Delhi, 1999, p.xiii.

[15] Vandana Mataji Ed. SHABDA-SHAKTI-SANGAM, NBCLC, Bangalore, 1995

[16] Sr. Vandana,rscj, " Dialogue – In and through Ashrams", in *Word And Worship*, November 19(1986), pp. 323-336+352.

[17] Ibid. p.327.

[18] Ibid.p.328.

[19] Ibid.p.332; For a comprehensive concept of guru see Vandana, *Gurus, Ashrams and Christians, pp.23-38.*

[20] "I do not want my house to be walled in on all sides and my windows to be stuffed.........Mine is not a religion of the prison house. It has room for the least among God's creations; it is proof against insolent pride of race, religion and colour" (M.K. Gandhi, *Young India* of 1.6.1921 pp.170-71) quoted in *Gurus, Ashrams and Christians* by Vandana,p. 47.

[21] Ibid.

[22] Ibid.

[23] Ibid. 54

[24] Ibid 56

[25] Vandana, Gurus, Ashrams and Christians,p.52.

[26] Vandana Mataji Living with Hindus, pp 66-71(66).

[27] Cf. R. Panikkar: " The Perspective of Inculturation in an Indian Christian Theology of Religious Pluralism": Prologomena to Inculturation, (Paper written for ITA Meeting, December,1989), quoted by Vandana ibid. pp.67-68.

[28] Ibid.

[29] P.68 of Vandana, op.cit.

[30] Ibid.p.71

[31] Ibid.

[32] Ibid.

[33] Ibid. p.73.

[35] Ibid.

[34] Jurgan Moltmann, *L'Eglise dans la force, de'lEsprit*, French Translation, Paris,1980, quoted by Vandana, op.cit. p.72.

[35] L. Legrand, *Dieu qui vient*, Paris, 1988,p.110, see Vandana, op. cit. p.72.

[36] Vandana,op.cit. p.74.

[37] Vandana,ibid.

[38] Remember the Apostolic Letter *Evangelii Gaudium*,"Joy of the Gospel" of the Pope

[39] Vandana ibid. p.75.

[40] Ibid. p.77.

[41] Vandana Mataji, "Has Our Life-Style been Drastically Changed" ? IN CHRISTO 39/2, (2004) 84-87 (87).

Thomas Kochumuttam:
A True Sadhak

John Chakkanatt

Introduction

The attempt to write a profile on Fr. Thomas Kochumuttom CMI may be compared to measuring a colossal mountain with a small inch scale of a school boy. What Fr. Joseph Pathrapankal mentioned about Fr. Thomas Kochumuttom on the occasion of his feast at Dharmaram College in 1980 is worth mentioning here.

"Many of you may not know that Fr. Thomas has a middle name, Angel. He is Thomas Angel Kochumuttom".

It was the practice those days that a novice was given an additional name with his baptismal name to indicate that a new person is born at the beginning of the novitiate (Later on this option was given to the candidate to choose a name). Only when the reader comes to know that Fr. Thomas Kochumuttom had an additional name Angel, that all who know him would closely associate him with the angelic look and behavior. The cute angelic qualities of meekness, gentleness and affective nature of Fr. Thomas Kochumuttom CMI are the very first introduction of him to anyone. Fr. Pathrapankal also asserted that he was a lamb, meek and humble of heart, innocent and harmless by nature, and endearing. He does not lose his temper and can tackle any grave matter composed with an angelic smile and with an aura of grace around him. Consequently, no one can get offended with him. The attempt here is to describe a great personality like Fr. Thomas Kochumuttom CMI a true *sadhak* of our time, a true seeker of the Divine, and a true guide for others to find the Divine in their own way.

All who know Fr. Kochumuttom would easily associate what Kunjunni Master of recent Malayalam freelance literature said about himself, "Lift me not, who am of short stature, my greatness is in being "small". These words of Kunjunni Master are true in Fr. Thomas Kochumuttom in the worldly sense of the word. He does not want to be lifted. He is a contented *sadhak*, who has no ambition of greatness. It can also be truly said about Fr. Thomas Kochumuttom's life that what we read in the Book of Proverbs, 'a contented life is a continued feast' (Pr.15:15).

Time Line
Fr. Thomas Kochumuttom was born on 7 August 1941 at Baselehem in Kothamangalam Diocese, Kerala State. He had his high school studies at Infant Jesus High School Vazhakulam where his father (Mr. Augustine Kochumuttom) was a teacher. He joined the CMI Congregation during his high school studies in Vazhakulam as an aspirant. Later he started his religious and priestly studies at Neeleswaram and did his novitiate at Christ the King Novitiate, Karukutty and made his first religious profession on 16 May 1962. Fr. Thomas did his philosophy and theology studies for priesthood at Dharmaram College Bangalore. He was one of the four members who were sent for Sanskrit study, others were Fr. Alexander Thannipara CMI, Fr. Joseph Thondipura CMI and Fr. Augustine Thottakkara CMI from Dharmarm College.

Ordained on 3 January 1971 on the feast of the Saint Kuriakose Elias Chavara, he did his higher studies in Indian Philosophy and Comparative Religion before earning a PhD from Lancaster University, UK, in 1978. He was professor of Philosophy in Darsana Institute of

Philosophy Wardha, and Spirituality and Philosophy at Dharmaram Vidya Kshetram, Bangalore, and held very few administrative posts in the CMI Congregation other than the Provincial Superior of Muvattupuzha Province.

Alone with 'The Alone'

Fr. Mathew Valiakandathil CMI who had been in Jeevandhara ashram with Fr. Kochumuttom since 2001 in Jaiharikhal Ashram testifies that life with him was an enriching experience. Nobility, sanctity, and authenticity are at the core of his being. He further elaborates that Fr. Kochumuttom's passionately virtuous life was what kept him in the Ashram, for many years. He affirms that Fr. Thomas Kochumuttom is a mystic in the sense that his direct communication is with the divine in a state of spiritual ecstasy rather than his insights transcending ordinary human knowledge. He spends many hours exclusively with the Lord. Fr. Mathew testifies, "I experience the depth of his prayerful life when I travel with him. All the time he is in prayer and deep contemplation. His very presence is an inspiration for his fellow travelers". It would be better to say that prayer for Fr. Thomas Kochumuttom is not a time bound obsession rather a passion.

In his outfit he does not have a "conceived" Christian, religious or priestly robe but that does not betray his Christian identity. What strikes the readers hearing the name Fr. Thomas Kochumuttom is a spotlessly white clad short figure with a bald head and an angelic face in Gandhian coarse *khadi kurta-pyjama* with a white shawl.

He tells his *sadhakas*, "When you travel if others do not recognize your identity it is a sign that tragically you miss something of your faith".

His presence and conduct have a high witnessing power. Fr. Thomas rarely held any office as customary with other priests, religious or a missionary like manager, administrator, director etc. But as Fr. Mathew Valiakandathil claims, he achieves a lot with his being rather than with his performance.

Rector, Darsana Institute of Philosophy

When the CMI Congregation decided to start a mission institute of philosophy in North India and chose Wardha in central India, the centre of Gandhian works of village centered India, Fr. Kochumuttom was the undisputed choice of the superiors as rector. The pioneering struggles of starting a mission philosophy institute with very minimum facilities molded the future missionaries of the congregation in his guidance. The students had the immediate text of philosophy of life for a mission from him rather than from the text books. Fr. Thomas was with his students for prayer, work, food and studies; students also watched him praying late hours conversing with the Lord. No preaching or reprimands were needed to tell them the necessity and efficacy of prayer. His simplicity motivated the young minds to lead a simple life of a missionary, religious priest in the north. The village oriented Gandhian institutions in Wardha, as Gandhji believed "India lives in her villages" were other sources of inspiration. So the CMI congregation found Wardha the suitable place to train the future missionaries in this milieu and no wonder the best choice of the rector of the new seminary fell on the shoulder of Fr. Thomas Kochumuttom. And aptly it was christened Darsana Institute of Philosophy, imbibing the '*darsana veed*' of Saint Kuriakose Elias Chavara. The motto of the institute was also coined by him '*Pavitrataya Devadarsanam*' imbibing the Gospel message, Blessed are the pure in heart, they shall see God" (Mt. 5: 8). The Darsana Athem is also made by him in this vision. Darsana is a known institution in Wardha which every ordinary people would easily locate and remember. His student priests in CMI as well as other congregations fondly remember and appreciate him as their best rector in the formation of their priestly life.

Acharya in the Himalaya

Jaiharikhal is a small village outside Lansdowne Cantonment in the Garhwal Himalaya in Pauri District of Uttarakhand. This centre was started as a mission station of the Diocese of Bijnor in the year 1977 with a convent and a school but in a short period of time the school and convent were shifted to Lansdowne Cantonment. In the year 1983 this was taken up by Sr. Vandana (popularly known as Vandanamataji) RSCJ (Sacred Heart Congregation) as an extension of her Jeevandhara Ashram in Rishikesh. For the purpose of accommodating the *sadhakas* she built **kuttia** (huts) in and around and built a chapel too. This retreat centre functioned very well giving solace to many for twelve years. As Vandanamataji was getting old and due to shortage of personnel in her congregation this was given back to the Bijnor Diocese.

When Fr. Thomas Kochumuttom had completed his tenure as Provincial Superior of CMI Carmel Province, Moovattupuzha, he opted for prayer for one year in a *kuttia* in Rishikesh. This was a period of enlightenment and transformation in his spiritual journey, where he developed his own style of Indian Christian spiritual *sadhana*. In this context he also realized the presence of CMIs in Kerala was saturated and it was high time for the congregation to launch for an Indian-Christian-spirituality way of life as the response to the vibration of the Indian interiority and also guide people in that direction. In 1999 he joined Bijnor St. John's Province opting for a life of contemplation and carried out innovative exploration in Indian spiritual *sadhana* at the Jeevandhara Ashram at Jaiharikhal in the Himalayas, where he is presently the *acharya*, and guides *sadhakas* in personal and community spiritual guidance.

A known retreat preacher, Fr. Kochumuttom is constantly on preaching retreats for groups of religious and priests in the ashram as well as outside. Apart from guiding individuals and groups in annual retreats, he also guides the religious teams in the preparation of their congregational chapters, preparation for religious jubilee, etc. An authority in Chavara Spirituality he has preached over 35 retreats on Chavara Spirituality alone in India and abroad. Among his books two of them, namely, **Blessed Kuriakose Elias Chavara** (2014), Bombay, St. Paul's Society, and **Spirituality of Saint Kuriakose Elias Chavara** (2017), Bangalore, Dharmaram Publications, are on Saint Kuriakose Elias Chavara the founder of his congregation. People come to Jeevandhara

Ashram because of the presence of a prayerful person, a person who truly experiences the presence of God. The people in the neighbourhood and the *sadhakas* who frequent there experience the vibrations of a spiritual radiance in the atmosphere of the ashram, which in its fullness is found in the person of the *acharya*. The ashram reflects the depth and spirituality of the *acharya*. Since ashram reflects the Indian spirituality with its culture, art and architecture our Hindu brethren feel at home and easily elevate their hearts to Christian mysteries.

The ashram atmosphere is serene and silent. When people cross the ashram gate and enter in they feel they are in a different world. The neighbours acknowledge there is peace in the ashram compound. When they enter into the ashram compound they enter into a different milieu. It is an extension of the *acharya's* spirit into everything here. They meet the universe and the maker of the universe in this saintly person and in the simple atmosphere of the ashram in Jaiharikhal.

Simple Living and High Thinking

A vegetarian by choice and conviction (it has also helped him to suit to his health) Fr. Thomas Kochumuttom's life is simple as his very look and appearance suggest to any stranger, leave alone his friends and acquaintances. It has indeed made many inroads in his spiritual quest. What is noticed in Fr. Thomas Kochumuttom by all his *sadhakas*, disciples and friends is that he can explain any complicated theory in simple words that any unlettered persons can easily grasp. He never uses any pompous style or words but simple language and tone. This is reflected in his speech, class and writings as well. In General and Provincial chapters of CMI congregation as well that of other religious congregations he is sought after for guiding and presenting papers and leading discussions.

Though he has preached many retreats, takes classes on Christian, Buddhist and Bhagavat Gita doctrines and spirituality and other subtle subjects with conviction, he never claims to be an authority on any. Whatever he speaks and writes comes from his heart as the Lord himself said "the mouth speaks from the fullness of heart" (Mt. 12:34). He never exhibits the treasure of his knowledge unless asked for, and only in proper places. Fr. Saju Chakkalakkal CMI explains an incident when there was a heated discussion on a journey in a car along with him and others, when the arguments were on various aspects of Buddhism, its tenets and practices; but Fr. Kochumuttom who is an authority on Buddhism with a solid doctorate on Buddhism from Lancaster University, United Kingdom, kept silence and did not join the argument. The full vessel never spills. It is the half empty vessel that spills.

The *acharya* has tremendous faith in the providence of God. The day-today expenses of the ashram are met with the humble offerings of the *sadhakas*. There is no fixed rate for anybody that attends any programme there or stays there for ashram experience, irrespective of the time they spend there. What he looks for is the spiritual enrichment of the *sadhakas*. No *sadhaka* feels that the ashram has some monetary interest. Another instance is shortage of water supply. Ashram mainly depends on rain water harvesting. When *acharya* realizes that there is shortage of water in the ashram, he invokes divine intervention. On such occasions one can see the *acharya* before the Eucharistic Lord in the late hours: and miracles happen.

Acharya has a special charism to convert foes into friends. He has a special style to persuade any body through his meekness, sweetness, simplicity and humility. One day a group of people came to the Ashram to check the activities there. They showed a paper claiming that they had been authorized to check the ashram activities through a court order. At the first sight the *acharya* could understand their craftiness and politely dealt with them. He told them,

"But we have no information regarding this."

People who came for confrontation were mellowed by his very first approach. He continued, "This is an ashram. This is open to all. All are welcomed here. You can ask any thing regarding this ashram."

They couldn't withstand in front of his dignity and openness. In simple words the *acharya* explained the prospects of the ashram and asked the boy to show them everywhere, everything. Acharya invited them to stay overnight to know more about the ashram. This type of gentle approach was beyond their dream. They apologized for the inconvenience caused. *Acharya* again extended a standing invitation to visit the ashram any time in future.

He is a true disciple of Jesus. Acharya has a forgiving and open heart. He accommodates anybody in the ashram. When some *sadhakas* fail to cooperate with the ashram discipline and ethos *acharya* gets hurt, but with loving gentleness tries to correct the person. If the person persists on, the *acharya* prays for him with tears. He had shed tears for many. When other 'ashramites' sometimes request *acharya* to expel such non cooperative *sadhakas'* stay in the ashram, the *acharya* would respond,

"He is one of my brothers. How can I act against my brother? Let's accommodate ourselves to him, let our prayer, forgiveness, and love touch his heart and prompt him to change his ways and attitudes."

A Friend in Need is a Friend Indeed

He cares for the minutest details about the members and *sadhakas*. He is very much concerned about them. He is so empathetic and bares their pain and sorrows. All experience his caring love when someone is sick. Often he could be found at the sick person's side attending to every detail. His loving care and concern go not only to *sadhakas* but also to his students, helpers or anybody who comes across in his life. This reminds us the love of Jesus towards the multitude who were like sheep without a shepherd. Fr. Thomas Kochumuttom above all is a good friend of others, even of his students and joins them in cracking jokes and laughs too heartily. He is always engaged in work, but he can always find time to help others. He reaches out to others. He can understand the feelings of others. He shares the joy and sorrows of others. He understands the feelings of others. He lives to give joy to God and humans.

Conclusion

Indeed Fr. Thomas Kochumuttom is a rare gift to the CMI congregation and to the present generation. What Nobel Laureate Bernard Shaw for literature in his award conferring ceremony said may be remembered at this instance! He said, "Napoleon and other men of his type were makers of empires. But there is an order of men who get beyond that. They are not makers of empires, but they are makers of universe. And when they have made those universes, their hands are unstained by the blood of any human being on earth. Ptolemy made a universe which lasted 1400 years. Newton also made a universe which has lasted 300 years. Einstein has made a universe and I can't tell you how long that will last."

Fr. Thomas Kochumuttom is one of the makers of the universe in the spiritual realm as Francis Assisi, St. Theresa of Kolkata or St. John of the Cross. He is a living Saint Chavara!

Contributors

Benny Thettayil CMI is the dean of Samanvaya Theology College Bhopal. He is a scripture scholar who is currently teaching at various theological faculties. He has published several books and articles besides editing several research volumes. He is also the editor of *Herald of the East*. He has been engaged in guiding the students of Samanvaya both in Jagdalpur and Bhopal since last 12 years. Presently he is also the programme coordinator of Poornodya Training Centre, Bhopal.

Bishop Gratian Mundadan CMI is the retired bishop of the catholic diocese of Bijnore. He was the first bishop of this Himalayan diocese. He led the church in this part of the world with a clear vision of making the church contextual. The Jeevandhara Ashram at Jaiharikhal, the hermitages at Rishikesh and chamaria and the several centers for differently abled and rehabilitation centers besides the numerous education and social work centers are but only a glimpse of his theological vision. He has taken keen interest in the development of contextual theology. He has been teaching the students of Samanvaya at Rishikesh for past several years.

Cyril Kuttiyanikkal CMI is a resident staff of systematic and practical theology at Samanvaya Theology College and a visiting faculty at St. Joseph's College, Khammam. He has gained his PhD from Tilburg University, the Netherlands. His publications include *Theological Formation in Context*(Editor) *Khrist Bhakta Movement: A Model for* *an Indian Church, Fortress of Solitude: A Guide to Spiritual Seekers at Rishikesh* and *Interface of Cult and Culture* (editor). Presently he is the director of Inter-religious center at Rishikesh besides being the Master and Prefect at Samanvaya Vidya Dham Rishikesh.

Davis Varayilan CMI is a lecturer in systematic theology and former dean as well as former rector at Samanvaya Theology College Bhopal. He has vast experience in contextual theology as a staff member both at Rishikesh and Bhopal. He is a visiting staff at several theological institutes. He is also one of the editors of *Jeevadhara*. He has published several scholarly articles and books. Presently he is the vicar provincial of CMI St. John's province Najibabad, U.P.

George Kaniarakath CMI holds an L.S.D; D.Th from Rome and has been teaching the Bible in some faculties, like Samanavaya. He has written over half a dozen books and more than 50 articles. His thesis was The Person and Faith of Apostle Thomas in the Gospels. His latest book is The Centrality of the Mystery of Incarnation in the History of Salvation.

John Chathanatt SJ is professor and a former Principal of Vidyajyoti College of Theology, Delhi. He is also a visiting professor in many Theology Faculties including JDV Pune and Samanvaya Rishikesh. He has been the Vice President and Research Director at the Indian Social Institute, Delhi. He has a Ph.D from the University of Chicago. He was an International Visiting Fellow at the Woodstock Theological Centre, Georgetown University, Washington DC. Presently he is the Director of Sahyog Delhi.

John D. Chakkanatt CMI has a post graduate degree in Philosophy from Jnana Deepa Vidyapeeth (JDV), Pune, M. Phil and Ph. D degrees from Madras University. His major literary works include *Tirthyatra – Pilgrimage Unto Eternity, Of God and Mamon, Public Action and Religious Praxis* and *Religio-Cultural Plurality and Nation-state* (edited). A lecturer in Philosophy, Theology and Religion, in various institutes of learning like, Darsana, Samanvaya, and Jamia Millia Islamia, New Delhi.

He has served as editor and correspondent in journals and newsletters like SARNEWS.

Joseph Chittooparambil CMI, is a resident staff member and former dean at Samanvaya Vidya Dham, Rishikesh. He has gained his Masters in theology from Christian chair at Madras and his PhD in inter-cultural hermeneutics from Vidyajyoti Delhi. He has published several books and articles. He has been engaging in theological formation and education for a long time.

Joy Philip Kakkanttu CMI is professor of scripture at Dharmaram Vidya Kshetram Bangalore. He has been associated with Samanvaya for a long time. He was the former dean at DVK Bangalore. He is a visiting faculty at several institutes and faculties. He is also a musician and an artist. He has published several books, especially on Old Testament and published articles and edited several research volumes.

(Late) Louis Malieckal CMI was one of the pioneers in Indian theology, Indian liturgy and Indian theological education. He was the founding rector of Samanvaya Theology College. He has also served as the rector of Khristpremalaya Ashta and has served the CMI Bhopal province as it's provincial. As a thinker and writer, he has several books and around 100 theological articles in several journals. He is credited with the composing of first Indian Christian Bhajan even before the second Vatican Council. He was instrumental in making an Indian Mass for the Syro-malabar Rite.

Naiju Jose Kalambukattu CMI completed a Licentiate in Systematic Theology from DVK, Bangalore and holds a doctorate in liturgical studies from the Pontifical Oriental Institute, Rome. He is a full time teaching staff, and currently the Prefect and Master of students in Samanvaya Theology College, Jagdalpur. His publications include *Apostolic Roots of Syro-Malabar Liturgy* (2011), *Roots to the Wings: The Apostolic Christ-Experience and Its Organic Growth in the Syro-Malabar Eucharistic Liturgy* (2018), *Theologizing in Context: A Hermeneutic of*

Living Dialogue between the Word and the World (2019) and articles in various journals and edited works.

Sebastian Elavathingal CMI has been engaged in contextual theological formation for 12 years in Samanvaya Theology College, Bhopal and its regional centres at Jagdalpur and Rishikesh. He has published articles on Art, Spirituality, Missiology and Aesthetics, apart from his book on Inculturation and Christian Art. Dr. Elavathingal is the Editor of the CRI Magazine *In Christo*. He visits different theology and philosophy institutes for classes.

T. K. John SJ, a leading theologian and a Professor (emeritus), of Vidyajyoti College of Theology, was member of two Commissions on formation (Inculturation Commission and Formation Review Commission (of Jesuits), President (former) Indian Theological Association, two term Consultor (Asia Sector) Pontifical Council for Inter-Religious Dialogue, Principal (formerly) Vidyajyoti College of Theology and member of People's Union for Democratic Rights. Chairperson (former) Editorial Board, Dalit Bible Commentary of Centre for Dalit/Subaltern Studies, Delhi.

Thomas Srampickal CMI has been teaching Bible in many theological faculties like, Khristpremalaya, Ashta, Samanvaya Theology College Bhopal and Khrist Jyoti, Sambalpur. He is a trained teacher and has gained his PhD from Rome. He has long experience in guiding the students in contextual theology. Presently he is engaged in writing articles and publishing books.

Yann Vagneux MEP is a French priest of the Foreign Missions of Paris. He holds a doctorate in Dogmatic Theology from the Gregorian University with a research on the Trinitarian theology of Jules Monchanin, founder of the Shantivanam Ashram. Since 2012 he lives in Varanasi where he carries on with his studies in Sanskrit and works in the field of Interreligious Dialogue with Hindu Pandits.